Alley Kat Blues

Karen Kijewski

Alley Kat Blues

DOUBLEDAY

New York
London
Toronto
Sydney
Auckland

PUBLISHED BY DOUBLEDAY
a division of Bantam Doubleday Dell Publishing Group, Inc.
1540 Broadway, New York, New York 10036

DOUBLEDAY and the portrayal of an anchor with a dolphin are
trademarks of Doubleday, a division of Bantam Doubleday Dell
Publishing Group, Inc.

ISBN 0-385-46852-0

For Wendy
Who pointed out the light in the darkness so many times

Acknowledgments

Thanks to my friends in law enforcement, Russ Martin, Detective, Sacramento County Sheriff's Department, and John Anderson, Chief, California Highway Patrol, for their expertise and generosity in sharing it.

And to my friends and colleagues Robert Irvine, Annette Meyers and Alan Russell (Read their books!) for graciously sharing time, know-how and unfailing good humor. To Terry Baker for listening to, and encouraging, wild off-the-wall ideas.

My appreciation and gratitude to the Sacramento Writer Gang, and especially to Deborah Schneider, my agent and my friend.

Friday, May 6

Las Vegas

One

Seven Deadly Sins

Courtney was dead and I was in Las Vegas.

A guy with a chorus line of hot-pink naked girls on a jazzy purple-and-jungle-green shirt jostled past me sloshing his beer, clutching a roll of quarters, and arguing with an ugly thin ageless woman. She wore black stretch pants, silver heels and blouse accented by mauve lipstick and nails. Silver earrings in the shape of skulls with red eye sockets and a silver charm bracelet dripping with bad omens completed the look.

Omens.

The McCarran Airport in Las Vegas is like no other airport in the world. The sound of slot machines assaulted my senses. Cigarette smoke packed my nostrils, filtered into my brain, and began the process of wantonly killing off brain cells. Las Vegas, home of the Seven-Deadly-Sins-Advertised-And-Advocated-In-Neon-Twenty-Four-Hours-A-Day, greeted me. Only the headliner this month wasn't a singer, or a show, but the Strip Stalker.

A serial killer, not a long-legged dancer.

Las Vegas is not my favorite place. And if you tough out the initial ugliness, it gets worse—not better. My eyes smarted as I walked past the slot machines to the car-rental agencies. Cigarette smoke.

Sacramento, my hometown in California's Central Valley, seemed a long way from here. A long way however you measure

and span it: in miles and culture, in neon, in feathers, and sequins. And more.

I was in Vegas and Courtney was dead.

But that comes later.

Sacramento is famed for its tomatoes, camellias, and rivers, not
for a high homicide rate.

That comes later too.

I picked up the car keys at the rental-car counter, although
not, of course, without a hassle. The kids at the counter get
younger and less experienced every year. This one didn't look
old enough to drive, maybe not even to talk in complete sentences. It took me over thirty minutes to get out of there.

Outside the breeze hit me and then the sunshine. Eighty-five
degrees and I was in the desert in springtime. Wonderful. I
found the rental, a current cliché in beige, climbed in, powered
down the windows, and threw it in gear.

I was headed for Hank's. It was that or putting his picture on a
milk carton: *Has anyone seen this missing boyfriend?*

And I was a surprise. Two can play the What-The-Hell-Is-Going-
On? and the I'm-Not-Telling game. Hank wasn't returning my
phone calls or letters, so here I was. Time to find out what was
going on.

I drove down a quiet street with a lot of cottonwoods, palms,
and cactus in an older part of town where the houses were set on
good-sized lots. There I parked in the shade of a cottonwood not
far from Hank's house, a Spanish adobe with a red-tile roof. I
couldn't see his car but that didn't mean anything. He kept the
Mustang in the garage most of the time.

I got out, pocketed the keys, left my bag in the trunk. I opened
the wrought-iron gate and entered a small courtyard enclosed by
adobe walls. A fountain in the courtyard splashed and sang, the
fish swam, the greenery and flowers were lush and vibrant, the
cactus spiny and aloof. I caught my breath at the sight, as I always
do. Springtime makes it even more beautiful.

The heavy wooden door opened into a cool interior. I didn't
bother with the doorbell, just used my key. I looked around at
the simple, lovely house I know almost as well as my own: white-
washed walls, worn wood floors with Mexican and Indian rugs
scattered about, matter-of-fact furniture in earth tones, a stone

fireplace with a bleached cow skull above the mantel, a Georgia O'Keeffe print, and handmade pottery and baskets.

I sighed and tossed my purse onto the couch, glad to be here. The house felt quiet and empty. No Hank. I went through the kitchen to the back door. Mars, Hank's black Lab, was at the door, eyes alert, ears up. When he saw me, he went into ecstasy orbit. I played outside with him for a bit and then we came in. I toyed with the idea of making a snack but didn't. I wasn't hungry enough and I was too tired. I'd gone to bed late last night, gotten up early this morning to catch a seven forty-five plane. The long hours, the tension, and worry had finally caught up with me.

I called Hank's pager number, punched in his familiar home number after the beep, and headed for the bedroom. Time to curl up, to sleep and dream quiet dreams for a change, then to wake up to Hank. Mars padded along happily at my heels. I stumbled as I walked, more exhausted than I realized, impatient to tumble into bed, smell the familiar smells of soap and Hank, and slide into oblivion. He would kiss me awake when he got home. Just like Snow White.

No.

What was wrong with this picture?

The bedroom was dark with the curtains pulled and the shades down. And stuffy, almost claustrophobic, as though the windows hadn't been opened for some time. Odd. Hank likes fresh air and waking up with the first uncurtained light. It took my eyes a moment to adjust in the darkness.

It was going to take my mind—and my heart—a lot longer.

Someone was in the bed. I had my fairy tales mixed up. I wasn't Snow White after all, more like the three bears coming home and finding their beds occupied. Only this occupier wasn't Goldilocks.

The medium-sized shape curled up in the center of the big bed stirred slightly and made a sleepy noise. Mars butted his head under my hand, not for attention, I thought, but to remind me he was there. Moral support. I stood there, frozen as a popsicle.

On the rug beside the bed a pair of sling-back sandals lay at a jaunty and rakish angle. Panty hose trailed from the shoes to a chair where what looked like a skirt and blouse had been tossed. Flimsy, silky, satiny underwear was piled on top of that, the bra almost off the chair and dangling by a strap. Victoria's Secret underwear. Designed to charm, to seduce, to be taken off. Apparently it had lived up to the billing.

There was a lump in my throat. Mars pushed in closer but I was beyond comfort. Way beyond. The sleeping form stirred again and a bare arm partially flung back the covers, exposing the soft curve of a breast, the deeper flush of a nipple. "The Three Bears" was the wrong fairy tale too. It was "Sleeping Beauty." I tried to think of reasons why a naked woman would be in Hank's bed. I could only come up with one.

I turned and walked out. Mars followed me, whimpering softly. The phone rang as I was on my way to the door. I answered with a *"hello"* that didn't sound like me at all. But that made sense. I didn't feel like me at all.

"Amber?" It was Hank's voice and he sounded puzzled.

"No. It's Kat. Amber's still asleep."

I hung up. As I picked up my purse and walked out the front door the phone started ringing. After six or seven rings it stopped. I left Mars inside. I couldn't bear to walk back through the house that was no longer my home away from home. I closed the door gently behind me. The phone started ringing again almost immediately.

What's going on?

Why isn't Hank talking to me?

How come he's never around and doesn't answer the phone?

I had the answer to all those questions now.

Two

Dead in the Water

I drove straight to Maggie's, hoping she'd be there, not knowing what I'd do if she wasn't. I knocked on her door, then leaned against it, forehead and palms pressed against the cool wood. When the door swung open, I fell in on top of Maggie.

"Kat! What's the matter? What happened?"

"Do you think underwear from Victoria's Secret is important to a relationship?"

"What are you talking about?" Maggie pushed the door closed with her foot and pulled me into the kitchen, sat me down. "Tell me: What's the matter?"

"There's a naked woman in Hank's bed."

"I'm sure—" She started but stopped. There wasn't any "sure" anymore. "Have you spoken to Hank?"

"No." I didn't count our brief telephone exchange for obvious reasons. "I've been trying for days—at work and at home. Davis knows something's wrong but he won't tell me. I called him too." And then I couldn't think of anything else to say except the kind of thing that everyone always says and that often turns out to be wrong. *He would never do this to me. This can't be happening.* But I guess that he had and it was.

"I don't care what it looks like, how bad it seems, you can't make assumptions," Maggie said sensibly. "You need to talk to Hank. There's probably a perfectly logical and innocent reason for this."

I stared at Maggie. She's a calm, rational person, true, but this was taking calm and rational to an absurd extreme. Of course she hadn't seen the shoes kicked off by the bed. And the panty hose. And the sexy underthings.

"Do you want coffee, Katy?"

"No," I said. "Thank you," I added, a footnote courtesy. I looked at the clock. Ten forty-two A.M. "How about a margarita?" I headed for the cupboard and got the blender down.

Maggie frowned. "Isn't it a little early?"

"It's five o'clock somewhere," I said lightly.

"Katy, is this the best way to—"

I turned quickly, almost knocking the blender off the counter. "It's not, no, it's not even the next best, or the next next but right now I don't give a damn."

"We're out of tequila." She got down two wine glasses. "There's wine in the refrigerator. When did you last eat?"

I thought about it and couldn't remember.

Maggie shook her head. "I'm making you a sandwich."

"I'm not hungry."

"And you're eating it."

I took a bottle of white wine out of the refrigerator, rummaged around in the drawer until I found an opener, then uncorked it. My hands were surprisingly steady and I poured without spilling a drop. I handed Maggie her glass and held mine up in a toast. "Here's to . . ."

"To friendship," Maggie finished gently when I didn't continue.

I nodded and drained my wineglass, poured another. Maggie put the sandwiches on the table. I was on my third glass and she was on her third sip.

"Has Davis mentioned anything?" Davis Merkowitz is Hank's partner. He is also Maggie's husband.

She shook her head. "Eat your sandwich."

I took a bite. The chewing went fine. It was the swallowing that was tough. I put the sandwich down.

"I'll call Davis and tell him you're here," Maggie said. "Eat your sandwich."

I took another bite. When I finished the sandwich and the wine, I went to bed. No dreams. It was after three when I woke up, my head a little heavy and my heart numb. I pulled off my jeans and stuff and got into a swimsuit. I found Maggie at her computer and asked if she wanted to swim.

She smiled up at me. "No, you go on."

I did laps for forty minutes. Then my head and body felt fine but my heart was still numb. I climbed out of the pool and shook my head, whipping hair and water droplets around. Maggie sat on the deck with a pitcher of lemonade and two tall glasses on the table beside her. I filled one and drank thirstily. We sat in easy silence. In the distance I could hear odd musical notes that didn't add up to a tune. *Like my life right now,* I thought. Davis found us by the pool.

"Hey, Katy," he said affectionately.

"Hey yourself." I returned the affection.

Maggie refilled her glass and handed it to Davis as he leaned down to kiss her hello.

"I told Hank that you were here," Davis said to me.

I nodded. Hank and Davis were both detectives in the Las Vegas Police Department.

"He'll be over as soon as he can. He had a few things to do first, he said."

"Housekeeping chores, probably," I remarked. "Picking up trash."

Davis looked puzzled.

"I went to the house this morning, straight from the airport. There was a naked woman in his bed."

Davis's mouth tightened. *"Fuck* there was."

"There was. Her underwear was from Victoria's Secret and I will never buy anything there as long as I live."

Maggie snorted. "Did you ever?"

I shook my head. "No. Actually, I can't be bothered with that kind of thing."

Davis was still silent, his mouth still tight, his eyes as hard as they get. I'd only seen him like that once before and then he was staring down a felon with a rap sheet around the block and back again.

The doorbell rang twice and Maggie got up to get it. I stared at the pool. A large bug whose species was unknown to me struggled in the turquoise water sending out little concentric circles in waves. An SOS nobody saw or cared about. Except me, and I didn't care either. I had my own worries.

I heard the slap of Maggie's sandals on the deck. I stared at the bug. Then at a man's thighs as he stepped between me and the turquoise water.

"Katy," Hank said.

I thought about looking up. It seemed more dignified to stare at his face than to stare at him crotch level, to wonder where that crotch had been recently. I would have to look up pretty high. Hank's a big man—tall, with broad shoulders. And muscular.

My eyes dropped to his loafers, traveled up the dark slacks, past the belt where he still carried his gun, badge, and handcuffs, up the pin-striped button-down collar shirt. His sleeves were rolled up above the elbow and his tie was loosened, his collar open. I could see his white undershirt and a few dark hairs. His face was serious, his eyes warm and loving as they almost always are when he looks at me. His hair is dark and curly and he is tan and incredibly handsome. We've been together for over two years.

I love him with everything I've got.

"Katy, I'm so glad you're here."

"Really?" I stood up.

"Really," he said, and smiled.

I took a step toward him. His arms had been at his sides but now they reached out to touch me, hold me, love me. Another step. And then I pushed him. I gave it all I had. He wasn't expecting it and all I had was more than enough. The expression on his face as he landed on his back in the pool was wonderful—gratifying and satisfying big-time. It was a classic Photo-Op-Kodak-Moment only, dammit, no one had a camera.

The splash sent the bug shooting up on a plume of water. His little opalescent wings flapped madly and then he was gone. I was a Good Samaritan, after all. Hot damn. Drops of water sparkled like multifaceted crystals in the sunshine and then disappeared.

Hank bobbed up, started to sink again, his clothes and police hardware pulling him down. I felt bad then, about shoving him in the pool. This was not the way to handle things.

It would have been better if he had been in uniform.

Much better.

I smiled for the first time that day.

Three

Only Circumstantial Evidence

Hank made squeegee, squashy sounds as he climbed out of the pool and walked over to us.

Davis handed him a towel.

Hank took the towel but didn't say anything. He retreated in the direction of the house leaving an intricate series of tide-pool-type shapes behind him. He stripped down to his shorts, piling his clothes on an empty chair, took his gun out of the holster and dried it off. Ditto badge, handcuffs, and wallet. Then he wrapped the towel around his waist and took his shorts off, hung them out to dry too.

And walked over and sat down across from me. "That was a welcome?"

"Not as good as me finding a naked woman in your bed," I agreed, "but a start."

His face darkened. "I can explain," he said.

I laughed. Davis and Maggie started to get up. "Don't," I said. "Please." I needed friends with me. They sat down again.

"It's not what it looks like," Hank said.

It was funny in an odd, sad way. *I can explain. It's not what it looks like.* "How many times have you heard that as a cop, Hank? And how many times was it a lie?"

Hank said nothing. Davis held his hands out palms up, then dropped them. A bird called out and far away another answered it. In the street a car backfired. And somewhere babies cooed and children laughed and lovers kissed but I was a sad and cynical private detective and I didn't care. The crack in my heart widened a little. I thought about having another glass of wine, and then I reflected that if my life stayed this stressful, I was going to have to come up with some healthier coping mechanisms.

"Katy."

It was my turn to say nothing.

"Talk." That was Davis. His voice sounded harsh, ugly. Like a cop.

If Hank noticed, he didn't show it. "Amber is nothing to me." Nothing. Oh right.

He spoke to me alone, as though we were the only two people in the world. He often made me feel like that and I had always loved the feeling. I didn't now. I felt left out.

"I am not sleeping with her. We are not having an affair."

I said nothing. Again. I mean, Hank's a cop. I don't have to explain the importance of circumstantial evidence to him. Not to mention underwear from Victoria's Secret. Maybe it was Frederick's of Hollywood? Not that it mattered, of course.

"I've been helping her out."

I snorted. Not a great response but it was that or something much worse. Davis cracked his knuckles. I looked at Hank's legs, strong and muscular and brown in the sunshine, and thought of them wrapped around Amber. Then I thought about what a stupid name Amber was. Not a real name—a showgirl name, a dancer's name, a hooker's name.

Hank made an impatient gesture with his hand. I saw that hand reaching out for her breast, for her—*God* . . . would someone please amputate my imagination? I put my head in my hands. Too much pain and confusion. I was used to Hank being on my side, I was used to him being the good guy. Forget coping. Time to start drinking again.

"I'm starting at the beginning, Katy."

I stared at the pool. No hapless, luckless bug to catch my eye, to divert my attention.

"It was right after our vacation and I was at the gym. Working out."

I love the way the muscles in Hank's arms and chest are so defined, so strong. I often trace them, follow them with my fingers, make him shiver with pleasure under my touch. Of course, I also love the way I never worry about Hank when we're not together. Better make that never *used* to worry. Bitterness—like thick, ugly bile—rose in my throat. I reached for the lemonade, then stopped. The pitcher was empty.

Maggie cleared her throat and stood. "I'm getting a glass of wine. Who wants something?"

"I'll help." Davis stood beside Maggie.

"Me, too." I didn't want to be alone with Hank. Not now, not yet. Who knew when?

In the kitchen Maggie set a big tray on the table and Davis went to change. I sat down, my legs suddenly weak. Maggie is slim and tan and pretty and a very dear friend. She got out a bottle of wine and three glasses. Then a bottle of beer for Davis. "Hank? Will he want beer or wine?"

I shrugged, as in "Who cares?" Hank was on his own. No shit, Sherlock. Maggie hesitated, then put out another beer, a bowl of chips, and some cheese and crackers dumped on a wooden cutting board. Then she splashed a jar of salsa into a bowl. She stood back and surveyed the tray critically. "I don't know, Katy, I think I missed my calling. I should have been a caterer."

I shook my head. "Unh-uh. Look, almost everything—crackers, cheese, chips—is in the same color range, beige. Real caterers break it up with parsley and radishes and stuff."

We laughed. Comic relief. Davis reappeared in a swimsuit, looked at us, kissed his wife, then spoke to me. "Just listen to him, Katy. He's a good man. Okay?"

"Will he lie to me?" Nothing was certain in my universe now. I wouldn't have asked this yesterday. I would have known the answer.

"He won't lie," said Davis.

I wasn't reassured but maybe that was because I didn't think I was going to like the truth. Davis picked up the tray and carried it out to the pool.

I followed the wine.

Any port in a storm.

We'd done this a million times before, the four of us—cocktails and chips by the pool. And it was one of my favorite things, eating, drinking, and talking with friends. It was the subject under discussion that I didn't like: The Naked Woman. My life was starting to look like a lurid, trashy novel. This was not a comfort. After we settled down with drinks there was an ugly silence. Hank broke it.

"I met her at the gym a couple of weeks ago. I was working out on the weight machines. She came over and said, 'You're a cop, aren't you?' When I didn't answer, she said, 'I saw you on TV one night last week.' "

I thought I was going to look him right in the eye. I thought I was going to stare at his lips and watch for sneaking, lying words to escape but I found I couldn't do it. I looked away.

"Were you on TV?" I asked.

"Yes. It was when we found one of the Stalker's victims dumped in an alley off the Strip. Someone leaked it to the media and the place was crawling with reporters and TV cameras. This case has gotten a lot of press down here, Katy. Everyone's jumpy. The pressure is on."

"Meanwhile, back at the Naked Lady," I said, refusing to be diverted, distracted, or sympathetic. The Strip Stalker was the least of my worries.

"I told her I was a cop, yeah, but that I was off duty. The last thing I wanted to do then was talk about work. I don't have much time off now and when I do, I want to get away from it."

I got tired of looking at the pool and looked at the sky instead, big fluffy white clouds up there. I tried to find shape and meaning in them but couldn't.

"She was waiting for me outside when I came out of the gym. She asked if she could buy me a cup of coffee or something and would I please listen to her story."

"So you did," I said.

"So I did," he agreed. "It wasn't a big thing, Katy, I was just trying to be a nice guy, to give her a few minutes, maybe try to help."

I said nothing even though it sounded like a line to me. Two lines, hers and then his.

"There are hundreds of stories like hers in Vegas." His voice was tired, defeated. I snuck a look at him. His face matched his voice. "Her younger sister is missing. The girl is seventeen and she's been a runaway on and off for several years. She left home and came to Vegas. She wanted to be a showgirl, a dancer like

Amber. Amber said she could live with her but that she had to go to school and play by the rules."

Amber was pretty selective about rules, I thought. It wasn't okay to quit school but it was okay to run around with someone else's boyfriend. Rules? Hah.

I looked back up at the sky. "Could we cut to the Naked Woman in Your Bed part?"

Hank went on with his story as though I hadn't spoken. A cloud started to look like a gun, my imagination on murderous time-and-a-half overtime.

"The kid sister didn't play by the rules. They had a fight and she ran away. That was ten days ago. Amber's worried. Her sister fits our profile of the Stalker's victims; she's right to be worried."

The cloud stopped looking like a gun and started looking like a noose. "And you're worried because Amber's worried? How sweet. Is anyone worried that I'm worried because I found a woman in your bed?"

"She asked me if I could help her find her sister."

I guess that answered my question by default: No. We were still supposed to be worried about Amber. Was I supposed to take a number, stand in line? But the only number I wanted was One.

"I talked with her on the phone a few times," Hank continued.

"And met her a few times," I said.

"Yes. We went looking for her sister. I even took her to the morgue once to check out a possible. Katy, I was just trying to help."

"Does Amber take her clothes off all the time, or just now and then?" I asked in my best dispassionate reporter-of-the-vagaries-of-human-nature tone.

He ignored it. "Last night she dropped by. She—"

"Oh? And what the hell was she doing with your address?". Okay, I'd left dispassionate behind me in the dust.

"I'm in the book, Katy," Hank answered patiently and reasonably. "She looked it up, I guess."

I could feel myself starting to lose it. Nothing is more infuriating than someone acting patient and reasonable and as though *you* are the problem when really, *they* are. I gritted my teeth and watched the noose cloud change into a dagger. With drops of fluffy white blood. Beauty is not the only thing that is in the eyes of the beholder.

"So she came over and you invited her in for tea?" Yeah, right —now I was getting sarcastic too. But can you blame me?

"She came over in the middle of the night. Hysterical. I calmed her down and tried to send her home. She got hysterical again. By the time she'd calmed down, she was in no condition to drive."

"Oh, right," I said, "the old no-condition-to-drive routine. Wildly original."

"I put her to bed, fully clothed, in the guest room. Then I went to bed. I woke up when she climbed into bed with me."

"Naked," I said. We were getting to the naked part. Finally.

"Yes. I got up. I told her I wasn't interested. She knows I have a girlfriend."

"Had," I said.

He ignored me. "She cried and apologized. She's been under a lot of stress, Katy."

"Oh, yes, I can imagine. And naturally, hurling one's naked self into an almost-stranger's bed is the first thing that comes to mind as a stress reliever. Right, Maggie? Right, Davis?"

Maggie said nothing but did eat another chip. Davis laughed. A curt, hard laugh, not a happy one.

"She asked if she could sleep for a while. I agreed but told her not to come by again or call me at home. It was a work situation and she had my work number."

"Was much of her naked body in view as you were having this professional conversation?" I looked away from the clouds and at Hank.

He flushed. Anger or embarrassment? "Katy, I admit I didn't handle it as well as I could have. I'm sorry. I'm sorry you walked in on it and were upset about it, though I don't understand why you assumed the worst, why you didn't trust me—"

I stared at him, speechless.

"Oh, Hank, *really!*" Maggie exclaimed.

I recovered my voice. "Fuck you and the horse you rode in on." But not my diplomacy.

"Is that what you would have assumed," Davis asked Hank, "if the situation had been reversed, if you found a guy in Katy's bed?"

Yes. Good question, Davis. Hank flushed again. So, no, it wasn't. He would have assumed what I assumed. And that's not even counting the underwear from Victoria's Secret which would not have applied to the hypothetical guy in my bed.

"Katy, I'm sorry. It was a mistake, but it wasn't an affair. I feel bad for Amber's situation but she's nothing to me personally. Nothing. You are." He stood and reached out for me, then grabbed for his towel as it started slipping. Hank resecured the towel, red-faced again. Maggie and Davis went inside. I walked over to the pool and trailed my toe in the water.

Hank's hand brushed the small of my back and I shivered. "Let's go have dinner, Katy." He kissed the nape of my neck and I pulled away.

"You're *sorry*? Man, that's getting off *way* too easy."

"It is, yeah." He nodded somberly.

This time he saw it coming. He went into the pool, no problem —it was another damn good shove—but I went too—he was holding on to me. Tightly.

We kissed. Underwater. Above. Frantically. This kind of thing is very scary. After a while we sat in the water on the pool steps.

Then I spoke. "Hank, you're in Homicide. Send Amber to Missing Persons, okay?"

"Okay. What do you want for dinner?"

"I don't care." He kissed me again. I thought it through. "I want dessert first."

He laughed and kissed my eyes as I closed them. Then I could just feel him, feel his body hard against mine. "Wanna arm wrestle?" I whispered.

"Let's go home, sweetheart."

I shivered. "You go first. Make sure Amber's dressed and gone. Throw away the underpants she's left under the bed. Change the sheets, do a load of laundry. Okay?"

"Okay." He kissed me lightly. "Ask Davis if I can borrow a pair of shorts, will you? And another towel? I think I'll just stay here in the pool until I'm decent."

After Hank left, I stood around in the kitchen and watched Davis and Maggie make dinner. And talked—well, interrogated —Davis.

"What do you think?"

"About what, Kat?"

"About the price of tea in China, the future in hog shares, and whether the moon is made of green cheese—what the hell do you *think* I mean, Davis? Sheesh!"

He grinned. "Testy, aren't we?"

"Yes."

"I don't like it, Kat." The grin was gone. "He's not handling it right."

"Amber?"

"It's gotten personal for him, he's got a stake in it. You have to be real careful about that. Sure you care and you want to find the kid, or get the bad guy, but you can't get too personally involved. If you do, you lose your perspective, your judgment."

"Can you say something to him?"

"Damn right."

That made me feel better.

At Hank's the windows and shades in the bedroom were open, the bed freshly made. There were flowers in the kitchen and a big pot of spaghetti sauce simmering on the stove.

It was a start.

Four

The Night's Still Young

My good mood lasted until the morning. When the phone rang, I was in the kitchen making coffee and Hank was in the shower. It was Amber—she told me so in a sweet, sexy voice. Swell, huh? Nice start to a day. No kidding.

"I'm sorry," I said politely (Miss Manners, please take note), "Hank's not available. May I take a message?"

"Oh. Ummmmm. No, I guess not. Well, tell him I'll be working tonight and I'd love to see him if he wants to come by."

"What time and where?" I asked.

"Oh, well, he knows."

"I'll just make a note of it," I said, still ever-so-polite.

"After six, at Blackie's."

"Blackie's?" I asked, politeness dripping from my lips and eating away at me like acid.

"It's a club. He knows."

"I'll give him the message."

"Thank you." She was all sweetness and light and I was all hypocrisy.

I hoped, spitefully, that the elastic in her fancy underwear gave out in magnificent synchronized precision. At the *worst* possible moment.

When Hank came into the kitchen, I was holding coffee I wasn't drinking and staring at a newspaper I wasn't reading.

"What do you want for breakfast, Katy?"

"Overdose pancakes and hemlock tea."

That stopped him, that dropped him.

"I lost my appetite. And Amber called."

"Oh?" His voice was (elaborately? I couldn't tell about *any-thing* anymore) casual.

"Sweet of her to respect your request not to call here, wasn't it? Probably an emergency, although," I said thoughtfully, "she didn't mention one. She did mention that she'd love to see you. She'll be working if you want to come by."

Nothing. Okay. I picked up the conversational ball again. "She said you knew where she worked."

"She's a bartender at Blackie's, a club in town."

"You've been there before?"

"I picked her up at work a couple of times. We drove the Strip looking for her sister."

I took a deep breath. "Hank, I hate this. Davis says maybe you're fucking up and Betty called me in Sacramento to say that she hasn't seen you this bad since Liz died."

Betty and her husband, Joe, are old friends. Liz was Hank's wife. She'd been killed by guys trying to get to Hank and he'd come dangerously close to losing it then.

I kept going but it took guts. His face was hard and cold and dark. "Neither of them is given to exaggeration. I hate feeling uncertain and unhappy and wondering if we're okay. It's never been that way between us. It shouldn't be now, but . . . but it is, and it all seems to lead back to you."

Hank got down a mug and poured coffee. Slowly. Carefully. This wasn't what our morning was supposed to be like. I started to have hateful thoughts about Amber, then suddenly wondered if it wasn't a lot bigger than that. I was just starting to follow that thought when Hank spoke. I tried to hold on to the thought, to footnote it for later, but it slipped away, dust in the wind.

"You're right, Katy."

I looked at this man I love so much. He is honest, decent, loving, and that is only the beginning of a long list. It was difficult for him to say this, but he was saying it.

"The Stalker has killed six young women so far. We're standing around waiting for number seven because we can't stop him. The last two murders have been less than two weeks apart. And we're not any closer to finding him now than we were two weeks ago, or two deaths ago.''

"You have a profile?" I was referring to the intensive research the FBI has done on serial killers, the startlingly accurate profiles they can come up with, given the data in a particular case.

"Sure. We got all that but nothing that doesn't fit hundreds— hell, thousands of guys. And in a city like Vegas we're dealing with a large itinerant population. We need a break, a description of the guy, or his vehicle, a victim who gets away, a partial on a plate, anything. We've got extra patrols out, unmarked cars. We're doing everything we can. Chances are it won't be enough. *Chances are he'll kill again.*"

I got up to get more coffee, refilled our cups, then stood behind Hank where he sat at the kitchen table, my arms around him. I couldn't keep looking at the defeat in his face. I touched a hand to his cheek as he leaned his head back against me. On the front page of the newspaper on the table I saw six photographs. A row of pretty, dark-haired, smiling young women. The Stalker's victims. I looked away.

"The killings show a combination of elaborate planning and incredible viciousness. This guy selects his victims carefully. We think he watches them for a while, then somehow picks them up for a 'date.' These girls aren't pros. They were turning a trick here and there for extra money or they were runaways. Three were familiar faces on the Strip. One girl was a tourist here with her family.

"He knocks them out with a sedative in a Coke or a drink. No rape. No indication of sexual assault. He gets them in his car— drives them away from the Strip, away from the bright lights and neon—then he bludgeons them to death. He beats their faces in until there is nothing left, nothing recognizable, just a bloody, pulpy mess where the face used to be. He doesn't touch the body anyplace else, he's done. He dumps it for us, usually in an alley, usually just off the Strip.''

Hank took the hand I had rested on his chest and pulled me around, settling me onto his lap. I felt his cheek resting against my hair.

"You feel so damned helpless: the smashed bodies, the short lives of these pretty young women, the devastation in their families. And it won't stop until we get him, or until we make it too hot here and he moves on. The victims are similar in appearance. Medium height, five-three to five-six or -seven, straight brown hair, shoulder-length or longer. Slim-figured with a tendency to full-breasted.''

I saw an endless line of victims, like paper dolls, featureless and bloody. Courtney was there too, and I wanted—needed—to talk to Hank about Courtney.

"That's a general description of Amber's kid sister. Katy, when I'm cruising the streets, I'm not just looking for this girl. I'm looking for any girl like that, for a guy on the lookout for these girls.'' His arms tightened around me. "I'm trying to stop the next one, and the ones after that.''

I thought again about what Betty had said—that she hadn't seen Hank this bad since Liz had been murdered. I had never met Liz Parker, but I had seen photographs of her, of the two of them.

"It's an okay description of Liz, too, isn't it?'' I listened to the refrigerator hum and the kitchen clock tick in the silence that followed my question. I marked time with that beat until Hank answered.

"Liz was a few years older. But the resemblance is there.''

"Davis says that you're getting too involved in this, that it's getting too personal.''

"It happens. Let's eat, Katy.''

He stood and plopped me on the floor giving me a last little hug. But he didn't answer my question.

"I'll make it clear to Amber, Katy. Don't worry about it.''

"All right.'' I wasn't worried about Amber. Just about Hank. And about obsession.

We were having biscuits and sausage and eggs. I made the biscuits, Hank did everything else. I rolled out the biscuit dough and carefully cut a biscuit.

"How long are you staying?''

"I should go back today.''

"No.'' He sounded stunned. "Stay another night, Katy, at least.''

I looked at his eyes. It wasn't just the eyes. Voice, too. "All right.''

"I'm working late tonight. Nine or ten.''

"I'll call Maggie, or Joe and Betty. Maybe have dinner with them."

"Good. Katy . . . I'm glad you're staying."

The sausages sizzled, the biscuits baked, and Hank smiled. Life was almost sweet again. I felt a little guilty, but not too much. No need to bore your boyfriend with all the details of your life, is there? Not at all. He was working late. I would have dinner with my friends.

And cocktails with Amber.

Blackie's was in the phone book. I'd looked.

Blackie's was the kind of place a tourist probably wouldn't stumble into and—in the unlikely event he did—would probably stumble right out of again. No restaurant, just a bar. It had a couple of slot machines but this is Vegas. Supermarkets, drugstores, and laundromats have slot machines. Vegas.

Mostly, though, Blackie's was the kind of place regulars, not tourists, frequent. It had a heavy old wooden bar that was scarred and scraped and dented with decades of beer bottles, glasses, and dice cups. There were wooden stools and booths with red vinyl benches. Some neon, but not much by Vegas standards. It was a dimly lit establishment with a large cracked mirror behind the bar and an unusually well-stocked liquor bar.

The bartender was also well stocked. Just a candid professional observation on my part, of course. I climbed up on a bar stool.

The bartender smiled at me from the cash register. "Hi there, be with you in a sec."

"Sure." I settled right in, always at ease and comfortable in a bar. I'd been a bartender for too many years not to feel that way.

The TV was on and, automatically, I watched, captive. A guy in moussed hair and a frown was holding a microphone out to a young woman. She looked about seventeen and was pretty with dark hair and big eyes under elegant arched eyebrows. She wasn't smiling either.

"Who's next?" she queried, looking away from the man with the mike, and directly into the camera. The cameraman zoomed in on her face. "Who will it be?" she asked me and everybody in TV land. "I could be, or you could be, the next dead girl." Her calm, rational tone made the words even more chilling. "We live in fear now, trapped in our homes and afraid to go out to school,

to work, to the store, afraid to do *any*thing. They—the police—
they're not doing enough. I know they're trying, but it's not
enough. Because he's still out there, still stalking women, still
killing them.''

Caught in a freeze frame, she gazed into the TV camera, silent
and accusing. A white-chalk body outline with long hair and
short skirt was superimposed on her face. Then the face faded,
leaving only the outline, which multiplied into six.

"How many more?" a male voice demanded, and then they
cut to a commercial break. From the screen another young
woman looked out at me but she was worried about white teeth
and toothpaste, not murder.

"Hey, what can I get for you?"

I jumped, startled, and looked over at the bartender. She
walked the length of the bar, all smiles and curves and cleavage
in skintight jeans and a leotard tank top, a gold locket on a heavy
chain around her neck. I remembered why I was there and ordered a light beer, no glass and put a ten on the bar. I saw a
couple at a booth, two guys at the bar—regulars, judging by their
banter with the bartender. I assumed the bartender was Amber
but had no way of knowing since I'd only met her naked right
breast and her underwear, and both were presently out of sight.

A beefy, good-looking guy in his late twenties and a construc-
tion-worker tan sauntered in, sat down a stool away from me.
"Hey, Amber Echo, what you got for a hot and thirsty man?"

The bartender popped the top off a long-neck Budweiser and
placed it on the bar in front of him and in the center of the
cocktail napkin she had tossed there.

Amber Echo? You could choke on that one. It went really nicely
with the sexy silk underwear, though.

"Hey," the guy with the Bud said, swinging his stool around to
me, "I'm Roy. What's your name?"

"Candy," I answered promptly.

"Well, Candy," he laughed, "are you a sweet thing?"

Aw, shit. I should have thought of that. Amber Echo smiled at
me. "Don't mind Roy. He doesn't mean anything by it. Sometimes his mouth is bigger than his brain, that's all."

I smiled back. If I wasn't careful, I was going to like her in spite
of myself, and in spite of her cleavage and underwear.

"Amber Echo, that's a really pretty name. Unusual. Is there a story behind it?"

"I guess you could say that."

"Hey, Amber, can we get a drink down here?" one of the two guys at the end of the bar called out. She left to make their drinks and I stared at the crack in the mirror.

"I'll take another, too, Amber." Roy picked up a couple of quarters from his change on the bar, chugged his beer, and ambled away. I heard the clink of coins in a pay phone.

Amber came back and leaned on the bar on her elbows just down from where I sat. It was a stunning view of her cleavage.

"My name's sorta a long story," she said, picking up just where we left off.

"I'd love to hear it."

That was all the encouragement she needed.

"When I was a little girl I saw the Rockettes on TV. I'd never seen, never even imagined, anything like it in my whole life. I was frozen in my seat. I was *gone*. I was six years old and I knew what I wanted to do with my life. I made my ma enroll me in dancing class the next day and I figured I'd have to move to New York when I grew up."

She fingered the gold chain around her neck and laughed. "Course it wasn't long afore someone turned around and told me about Las Vegas. And a year or so later someone brought me back pictures of showgirls. Those costumes! Wow! I wanted to be a showgirl, a dancer, real bad. My friends, they made fun of my name, said it was just a no-account name and I'd have to fancy up."

My cue. "Oh?"

"Joanne Marie Larkin, can you *believe*? But everyone called me JoJo or JoJo Ann Marie. Can you imagine? That's a mouthful, huh? How could I dance with that ol' name weighing me down? When I was in high school I used to read romance books and dream that my life'd be like that some day."

Okay, that figured. She learned this stuff from novels.

"And the girls in them always had wonderful names like April, Alicia, and Amorata."

Amorata? Give me a break.

"But Amber and Echo were my favorites, only I couldn't decide between them. So one day I just decided I'd have them

both. And I did." She gave her head a satisfied little snap from
one side to the other.

"Good for you. Are you a dancer?"

Her face clouded over. "I hurt my knee, so I'm doing this for
now."

Subject closed. There was more to it, but I couldn't ask. Not
now. Not yet.

"Hey, Candy, buy you a beer?" someone said. "Candy?"

Ooops. I shook myself mentally. Time to wake up. I'd forgotten I was Candy.

"I'm fine, Roy, thanks."

"Aw, what the hell, bring us another, Amber. Yup," he said to
me, "our little Amber is Bakersfield's loss and Las Vegas's gain.
Ain't that right, Amber?"

"You bet."

"You're from Bakersfield?" I asked.

"Yeah. You know it?" She put the fresh beers on the bar in
front of us and scooped money off Roy's pile.

"Not know it, no. But I've been through there."

"Best way. Bakersfield ain't much more'n oil, cotton, and
ranches, country music and Kmarts. Not too damn much to stop
for lest you're into that. And hell, who is? Life's more than that,
you bet. I couldn't *wait* to shake the dust of Bakersfield off my
feet."

"Las Vegas would be an exciting place to live"—I crossed my
fingers so there'd be no cosmic confusion about this lie—"but
it'd be a tough place to raise a family, I imagine."

"Aw, hell, Candy, Amber here ain't got a family, and just as
well—she's not the world's most patient person." Roy winked at
Amber.

"That's the truth." Amber bobbed her head at me, dark roots
in blond hair. Touch-up time had come and stayed to testify. Not
that it would show from the stage if she was a dancer.

I sighed and really started lying. "I know what you mean. I had
to take care of my niece once and it like to drive me crazy. She
was seventeen and *talk* about a mind of her own."

"Yeah, that's the truth," Amber agreed.

"What you talking about, Amber? You don't know nothing
about children, or teenagers neither." Our pal Roy was more
informative than supportive.

"Everybody's got a sister, or niece, or something," I said.

"Naw, Amber's an only child. Ain't that right, Amber, honey?"

An odd look crossed her face. Before she could answer, someone punched in the door and the sidewalk belched in three vociferous patrons. This was neither their first stop nor their last and they were loud about wanting Amber's attention.

I looked at the clock: 7:42. I was out of here. I tipped well enough so Amber would remember me, not well enough to make her wonder.

Roy didn't try to hide his disappointment. Big surprise there. "Hey, Candy girl, night's still real young. Lotta fun waiting to be had. Lotta fun." He licked his lips. It's fine to lick your lips over ice cream, to smack your lips over a juicy steak, but a woman? This kind of thing makes me glad I'm not in the singles scene.

I smiled at him anyway. Just like a politician. Damn. My fun was waiting someplace else but I didn't say that either; I kept my comments to myself. Just like a politician. Candy and I were out of here.

I stood in the last of the daylight, the sun sliding fast now down the sun chute in the sky. Not that sunset would matter; neon would take over then. White stars, red arrows, gold and silver dollar signs, streams of neon cash cascading down three night-dark stories in the sky. Signs everywhere: WINNING SLOTS. CAESAR'S PALACE. PINK FLAMINGO. MIRAGE. Neon money, neon cocktail glasses, neon wishes and dreams. Most of it was mirage.

Abandon hope all ye who enter here.

I looked around for the rental car whose color I vaguely remembered as beige. There were several on the street that qualified. Vegas is full of rentals. I figured it out and headed for Maggie's.

On the way over I thought about Amber and wondered what an only child was doing with a kid sister. I smelled the cigarette smoke in my hair and on my clothes and wrinkled up my nose in distaste.

It wasn't just the cigarette smoke that smelled.

It wasn't just neon hopes and promises.

Five

Spilling Your Guts

Maggie answered the door with a smile on her face and a potato peeler in her hand.

"I'm late, I'm sorry. Am I in time for dinner?"

"You bet." She gave me a quick hug, keeping the potato-peeler at a safe distance. "Come back to the kitchen, Kat."

Forty-two seconds flat and I was peeling potatoes and listening happily to Maggie's chatter about her day. I found it indescribably soothing. The front door opened and closed and Maggie smiled again. Davis.

"Hey, Katy, what are you doing here?" Davis asked me after greeting his wife. "I thought you'd be home with Hank."

"He told me this morning he wouldn't be home until late."

"Yeah?" Davis looked at his watch. It was eight-fifteen. "We're through for the day."

I finished the potatoes and let Maggie take charge of them. Davis got a beer out of the refrigerator.

"Quit for the day?" I asked. Maggie patted my arm in a gesture of reassurance as she walked by. "Davis, did you know about Amber before last night?"

"Yeah."

"More than Hank told us last night?"

"No. You know what I know now."

"Wrong," I said. My voice sounded a little funny. "I know quite a bit more."

Davis looked at me for a long five count, then pulled out two kitchen chairs, one for me, one for him. "You want to tell me, Katy?"

I did, yes, and I started with this morning's conversation, with what Hank had said about the Strip Stalker and the girls and the bodies and how it had ahold of him. *The way Courtney had ahold of me.* Davis didn't comment. I heard Maggie running the water and washing things, salad things maybe. I wished I could wash all this away as easily as grit off lettuce. Of course, if wishes were rockets, we'd all be stars. Davis's face was expressionless.

"Does this surprise you?" I asked. "Does it happen, this—" I didn't want to say "obsession."

"It happens." Still expressionless. *It happens.* Hank had said the same thing.

"It's not good?"

"Sometimes a crime gets solved only because it gets in some cop's gut. He or she won't let it go, lives with it day and night. Lives with it until he gets it."

Or it gets him.

We neither of us said those words.

"You knew Liz, I know." Davis nodded his assent and Maggie made a peaceful murmuring sound. "And you remember what she looked like." Not a question. They did, of course. "Like a slightly older version of the Stalker's victims."

"God*damn!*"

Maggie sucked in her breath.

"Hank?" Davis asked.

"Yes. I mentioned it this morning. He didn't say anything. He knows."

Davis paced around the kitchen. "I don't like it."

Good. That made two of us. "What does Amber want, Davis?"

He twisted the top off his beer. "Katy, it's hard, I know, but could you go with the obvious? Forget her underwear for a minute" (Take *that*, Victoria!) "and give the woman the benefit of the doubt, assume she wants to find her kid sister and goddamn, in this town right now that sure as hell is understandable."

"And if she doesn't have a sister?"

The corner of his eye twitched. "Tell me," he said.

I told him—about my visit to Blackie's, the conversations I'd had, what Roy had said. "It's not enough to be sure, but . . ."

"Yeah." He sounded tired, ran his fingers back through his hair in an irritable gesture. "What are you going to do?"

"Find out more."

He picked up his beer, put it down without tasting it.

"What else could it be, Davis?" I asked.

"Go with the obvious, Kat."

"Amber wants Hank?"

"That's what a woman in my bed would suggest to me," he said dryly. "Let it go. She'll lose interest when she sees Hank doesn't want to get something on with her."

"Davis, does Hank have enemies?"

"Yeah, well, we all do, but still— You mean the woman? It seems a little far-fetched, doesn't it, Katy?"

It did, yes.

"Stick with the obvious for now."

Sensible advice, but I thought there was more to it than the obvious. Of course, there usually is.

"Hank's off and he's not here with me. Not having dinner with us. What do you want to bet he's at Blackie's?"

Davis put his beer down and ran his fingers through his hair again. "You want me to go see, Katy?"

I shook my head. I didn't, no. Later I would ask Hank why he had worked longer hours than Davis and what he'd been doing if he hadn't been working. I wanted to help, not to spy. That was what our relationship was about.

The three of us had a nice dinner and a good time, each carefully stepping around loaded conversational topics like the Strip Stalker, Amber, and Hank.

And I thought of Courtney, her head and face smashed in too, though not by a stalker. Spilled blood and brains. Nothing more would happen in that case until I went home and back to work on it. Back to my job. Hank? He didn't need me to figure out his problems. He needed me, but—I shook my head in frustration, trying to clear out the ugly jumble of thoughts.

Hank got home at eleven, smelling of bars and cigarette smoke.

"I had dinner with Maggie and Davis," I said. "We missed you. Davis said you got off at eight. You went to Blackie's?"

He nodded. I waited for more, but that was it.

And the slight gap between us widened. I didn't know what to do about it and Hank wasn't trying. One more day, I told myself. I'll give it one more day and then I'm going home. I couldn't help Hank but I could help Courtney.

I woke up with nightmares. Blood slippery on the highway. A sad sweet smile on a face that appeared and disappeared in the bloody red haze of my dream like a demented Stephen King version of the Cheshire cat. Heart-pounding, adrenaline-racing, mind-punishing nightmares.

Roadkill.

I swerved the car sharply to avoid the badly mangled body.

I couldn't tell whether it was a man or a woman.

The Bronco skidded, slid before it came almost to a stop on the shoulder of I-80. I yanked on the hand brake, flinging open the driver's-side door while the car was still in motion.

"Lindy, get me the flashlight in the glove compartment." She did as I asked. "Stay in the car."

I ran down the freeway but I knew it was too late.

She was dead.

I could see it was a she now. I flashed the light over her quickly. I knew it was a she because of the short skirt hiked up around her butt. The face, the head, the hair was about gone, drenched in blood and mush.

Guts spilled out.

Blood everywhere.

Smells.

I went back to the car, got flares, told Lindy—in my no-kidding-around-goddammit voice—to get back in the car and stay there. And ran again. Down the freeway. Past the body. Five yards. Ten. Like a football game. No. I lit four flares, placing them some distance apart in the number-four lane.

I'm a private investigator but I never see this kind of thing, deal with this kind of thing. I'm not good at it.

Almost back to my car I saw a silver low-heeled pump with a rhinestone clip lying by the roadside. It sparkled, jumped out at me in the lights of a passing car. I started toward it. The car passed me. Darkness again.

Another car. Light. I reached out for it without thinking.

There was a foot in the shoe. Blood, torn muscle and flesh, bone.

I ran, threw up before I reached the Bronco, then sat in the car with Lindy until, finally, the Highway Patrol came. Then fire and ambulance. Spinning lights, flares, talking, walking, joking. I got out of the car to talk to the officers, threw up again—dry heaves—until at last they let us go home. Lindy held my hand. She's seventeen and hasn't done that for a long time. I didn't know whether it was for her comfort or mine. I didn't care. We held onto each other tightly.

I crawled out of bed, body slick with sweat, heart pounding. I needed light. When I didn't come back, Hank got up, too, then built a fire and sat on the couch in shorts and a T-shirt. It was spring in the desert and although the days were beautiful, the nights were cold. The fire was welcome—the warmth, the comfort both.

"What's the matter, Katy?" he asked. I saw the effort it took to wrench his mind away from the Strip Stalker, from Amber and her sister, from sleep.

From his obsession to my obsession. I didn't answer him.

"I'm sorry, lately I've been too preoccupied to notice much." He frowned at himself.

About time, I thought, accurately if not generously.

Mars watched us, wary and alert. He knew we weren't supposed to be up. We should be in bed, dreaming of spring and new beginnings. Dog biscuits. Something.

Dreaming.

The red washed over me again. You think you can leave it behind but the past is like a ribbon, sometimes a bullwhip, and you never know when it will tangle snarl flick curl snap into your present, reach into your future, yank you around.

Hank tossed another log in the stove. "Come sit with me, Katy," he said as I paced about madly, wildly.

I made an effort, still pacing, to tell him—stumbling over that night three weeks ago, stumbling over remembrance. "She was young. Like Lindy." I started to choke up. Bad sign.

Hank stood, pulled the afghan off the back of the couch, wrapped it around me—net of warmth and comfort and love— picked me up and walked back to the couch, sat down holding me in his arms, holding me tightly.

I tucked my head into the space between his chin and shoulder, like a child, like my kitten.

"Her name was Courtney. She was in her early twenties and pretty. I saw the photo on her driver's license."

His hand stroked my hair. I slid off his lap so I could look at his face, at his eyes, but stayed next to him on the couch, stayed in the warm circle of his arm. My hand rested on his bare thigh, his muscles hard and alive in warm, solid flesh.

"It was a blowout. The left rear tire. The trunk was open, the jack out and assembled although not under the car. No emergency lights. No flares on the road or in the car."

He let a breath out slowly and I remembered his anger—rare in Hank, especially rare directed against me—when he discovered that I had used up the flares in the Bronco and not replaced them.

"People think of themselves as off the road, as safe because they've pulled onto the shoulder," he said, "but they're not. They get hit changing tires, attempting road repairs, just walking down the freeway going for help. We see it all the time. We lose cops that way too, which is why we try to avoid standing on the roadway side of the car."

I thought of the mangled form on the road.

"Could she have been hit more than once?"

"Yes. The impact sometimes throws the body out on the freeway. People can't see it in time and run over it."

It.

"Usually one or two drivers will call in to report running over a body."

A body.

"Usually? Cars run over people and the driver *doesn't* report it?"

"Yes. It happens all the time."

I swallowed hard. "The CHP said they'd try to find the first car, the hit-and-run. Will they?"

"Try? Yes. They probably won't find it unless they get lucky, unless someone reports it. There will be considerable damage to the vehicle, the fender maybe, the grille, a headlight. There will be physical evidence on the vehicle connecting it to this accident."

I didn't ask what the evidence was. I knew. I'd seen it. Mars was at my feet. The fire sparked and popped and I was still cold. Hank put his arm around my shoulders. And that didn't warm me either.

"Even if they wash the car—? The evidence—? Will it—?"

"Yes. You can't get rid of everything."

It. The body. The blood.

"Her name was Courtney Dillard."

"Don't, Katy."

But it was too late. Here's the deal: You don't walk away from something by naming it. Call it *It. The body. The deceased.* Naming it, naming *her,* gave the situation power, tied me in like a fish on a line. Not it. *She.* Courtney. I bowed to that power.

"Who notifies the family?" I couldn't leave it alone. Not then, not now.

"Let's go to bed, Katy." Hank could leave it alone, no problem. Could leave *this* alone.

"How do you forget, Hank? How do you get those pictures out of your mind?" I asked instead.

Something in my voice caught him.

"You dissociate, disengage. You can't think of the person as a human being. In a homicide you think of the body"—*it*—"as evidence that will help you solve the crime and get the perpetrator. Soldiers do the same thing in war. They call the enemy krauts, gooks, yanks, whatever it takes to disengage. Anything to make you forget that they are people just like you, with families and lives and with the same hopes and fears and feelings you have. It's difficult to disengage with children. It's difficult to disengage when the victim reminds you of someone you know and care about."

Like Lindy.

"You don't disengage very well, Katy."

This was not news to either of us.

"It gives you a passion, a drive, a fierceness; it also interferes with your thinking, sometimes screws up your judgment."

Disengage.

Much easier said than done. No kidding.

"There was a shoe." I wasn't disengaged yet.

Hank waited patiently for me to make sense of that.

"It was a silver alligator pump with a rhinestone clip, the kind you wear to a party, the kind you wear when you're happy and celebrating. But she didn't wear it to a party." *She wore it to her death.* "Her foot was still in it," I added. "Sort of like Cinderella in reverse."

Hank made a growly kind of sound.

"I know. I can't help it. Something about it, about the accident

. . . Courtney's mother doesn't believe it's an accident." I put my head in my hand.

"What?" Hank asked.

I'd skipped a few steps but I didn't go back. "She swears her daughter would never leave a disabled vehicle. Courtney's mother is suggesting murder. Murder with no who, no why, no evidence. Pretty thin, huh?"

"Yes, on the surface that's foolish, senseless. How do you know the mother?"

The key words here were *on the surface*.

I stared at Hank.

Just like an Easter Island statue.

And with about as much of a clue.

"She came to me three weeks ago," I said at last. "She hired me."

He nodded. "You can check it out, Katy. A blowout at high speed leaves physical evidence."

"I did check it out. I found no scrape or gouge marks on the pavement. No rim cuts, although there was a hole in the tire. People, pedestrians, who are hit are often thrown or carried a considerable distance down the freeway, aren't they?"

"Yes. One to two hundred feet. Where was the body in relationship to the vehicle? Close?"

I pulled the bloody pictures out of my memory bank. "Less than ten feet, I think."

"A body lying or dumped on the highway wouldn't be thrown, wouldn't move any distance."

Body. Dumped. Like garbage, not a person.

"What else did you see that night?"

"Not much. All I did was place the flares, throw up, take care of Lindy, and wait in the car for the Patrol."

"That was a lot, Katy." He said it with gentleness and compassion.

"How difficult would it be to make a hole in a tire look like a blowout?"

"All you need is a good knife and the knowledge."

"Could an investigator"—meaning a California Highway Patrol investigator, not me—"tell the difference between a blowout and a slash?"

"The direction of the fibers, out or in, would indicate one or the other. Easy enough to find out. In a hit-and-run there are often skid marks and evidence of impact at a high rate of speed.''

"Evidence. Like broken glass, plastic reflector lights, parts of the car grille in the roadway?''

"Exactly.''

I had looked for that and hadn't found it. I had taken pictures of what I hadn't found. They were in my mind too.

"Let's go to bed, sweetheart." Hank crossed the room to check the fire. I stumbled to the bedroom, peeled off my T-shirt and panties, and climbed into bed where I shivered in the cold sheets until he wrapped his warmth around and in and through me.

Death is an ending.

Love is a beginning.

Dreams are a clue.

Six

Sawdust and Arsenic

Hank left early the next morning. Without breakfast. Without kissing me. Mentally, he was already on the job. I am not the only one who doesn't disengage well.

"I'll call," he promised. "Let you know."

And I had nodded my head on the pillow with feelings of sadness and death and other women and discarded silk underwear welling up inside me until I felt like a stopped-up storm drain. Trash and debris seemed to clutter things up everywhere. He didn't notice and he didn't kiss me good-bye. I went back to sleep. That was no way to start the day; I figured I'd try again later.

At ten-thirty I was reading the paper and eating my breakfast. The lead article on the front page was:

CASINOS BEEF UP SECURITY

In response to public concern, management at all major casinos has added on numerous security guards and patrols. The new personnel are both in uniform and in plainclothes. They will circulate in the casinos and in the nearby sidewalk areas.

Casino managements have also announced that an escort service is available upon request. Escorts will accom-

pany women to their rooms, cars, or to
a taxicab.
There have been no known incidents in the casinos, but . . .

I was eating scrambled eggs, toast, and juice but it could have been sawdust and arsenic and I would have been hard-pressed to tell you the difference.

The phone rang. Hank.

"It's anytime now for the next one, Katy. It's been ten days."

His voice was official, detached. I was talking to a cop, not to my boyfriend. I took another bite of sawdust, chewed carefully, washed it down with arsenic.

"Everyone's jumpy," he said.

Yeah, I thought. *Me, too.*

"Extra patrols and coverage. I'll be on the Strip until midnight at least. Undercover."

"In a car?" I asked. "On foot?"

"Car."

And that was it, that was that. I considered going home as fast as I could drive my yucky beige rental to the airport. What did I have to look forward to? Another evening alone, nightmares, maybe another morning without sweetness?

Another cocktail with Amber?

"Hi, Candy. God, I'm glad you came by. It's so slow I might fall asleep on the cash register here. You wanna beer?"

"Sure. Thanks, Amber." She remembered my name *and* my drink. I was moderately impressed. "How come it's so slow?"

"Dunno." She yawned, patting her mouth delicately with long, slim vampire-red-tipped fingers. "The happy-hour crowd died early and the evening crowd never picked up. Might not now." She glanced at the clock, almost ten, picked up the remote, and clicked the TV on to the news. Another yawn. I yawned too. It's catching.

The picture came into focus first on the lights on the Strip— the garish neon, the twenty-four-hour glitz and glitter—then on the car headlights as they drove by in slow motion, rubbernecking. Then the flashing red and blue of police and emergency vehicles. The camera zoomed in on a taut yellow plastic tape that said POLICE LINE DO NOT CROSS   POLICE LINE DO NOT—

"Now what?" Amber said, but her eyes became alert, her body tense.

The camera panned slowly over patrol cars, uniformed and plainclothes cops—that's when my eyes went on alert and my body tensed—and on a mound on the pavement covered with plastic sheeting. My heart sank. Amber gasped.

The voice-over had been droning throughout the footage. *The Strip Stalker struck again tonight, claiming his seventh victim. The victim, a young woman with a slim build and dark hair, has not yet been identified. Police say they are not surprised the Stalker struck again although—*

"Oh-ma-god oh-ma-god oh-ma-god," Amber moaned in a low, toneless voice. "Oh-ma-god oh-ma-god." She came around the bar, pulled out a stool, and slumped down next to me, still clutching the remote. "Oh-ma-god."

"Are you all right?" I asked.

Across town the tragedy went unremarked at the gala opening of the—
Amber turned the TV off and put her head down on the bar.

"Amber?"

"I'm so worried." Her voice was muffled. "I hope it's nobody I know. Oh-ma-god." She started crying.

The bar door opened, and high heels clicked across the floor. "Amber? Hey, Amber, you okay?" A dark-haired woman in her fifties who had once been beautiful and now looked like she'd had too much sun, too much plastic surgery, and been rode hard and put away wet 1,002 too many times glared at me suspiciously. "Whad'd you do to her?"

"Shush, Brandi, nothing. It's the Stalker. He got another girl. *Shit!"*

Amber got up and walked behind the bar, picked up a bottle of tequila and a shot glass, poured, slugged, poured, slugged. No lime, no salt. This was medicinal, I guess, not recreational. She shuddered and wiped the back of her hand across her mouth, smearing her lipstick.

"I'm going over there. I know a cop who's working this. I'm sure he's there and maybe he'll—" She poured another shot, downed it.

"Maybe he'll what?" Brandi demanded.

"Maybe he'll let me see her. I got to know—"

"You got to know what?"

"If she's . . . if she's someone I know." Amber reached under the bar and picked up a straw bag decorated with seashells.

"Doesn't matter who you know. They're not going to let you anywheres near that poor dead girl. That's assuming you were sober and could drive, which you won't be when those shots hit you. You're not going anywhere except home. I'll close up here if you want."

"Okay," Amber said vaguely. Either the tequila or the shock was starting to kick in. She poured another shot. Insurance, I supposed.

"I'll call you a cab, or maybe your friend here can drive you." Brandi eyed me.

I shrugged. No point in looking eager when plain old agreeable would do fine. "Sure."

"We just met," Amber mumbled.

"I don't mind," I said.

"You look nice enough." Brandi said it grudgingly. "What's your name, honey?"

"Candy." That lie was tripping off my tongue easy as pie and smooth as silk now. Kind of a bad sign. I belatedly congratulated myself on the name choice, though. Brandi, Amber, Candy—shoot, I fit right in.

"I gotta go to the john."

Amber mumbled but she walked a straight line—I watched. I turned to Brandi, who was flicking rapid-fire through TV channels. "Will she be able to give me directions?"

"Her? Oh yeah, this ain't nothing to what she can drink. I don't get it with the panic over this creep's victims, though. Amber's all fired up and hot as a piston over it."

"Pistol. Hot as a pistol," I said automatically, then bit my tongue.

"Huh?" Brandi had found a basketball game. "Look at those bodies, willya? I wouldn't mind shooting a few hoops with one of those guys." Her eyes flicked over the screen greedily. Then she turned and spoke suddenly, almost fiercely. "Candy—you're going to take her home, right?"

"Right." I nodded.

"Good. Get ready, then. Here she comes and she ain't no bride."

It was almost eleven by the time I got Amber away from the

tequila and back home. Not that this was a problem. Time was something I had plenty of. Hank wouldn't be home tonight, not a chance—he'd be working through. And when he did get home . . . I didn't much want to think about that.

Brandi was right, Amber held her liquor well. Her directions were fine and she even sounded surprisingly sober. Clearly I was watching a professional at work. Her condo was in a simple two-story stucco with a red-tile roof and wrought-iron grillwork on the balconies and along the walkways in the central courtyard. Sporadic palm trees and bushes and plants that looked only moderately desperate for water clustered in banal groupings in the courtyard. Uninspired, cookie-cutter Southwest. I parked my car on the street and cut the engine.

There was a new moon. I could see it rising.

Amber stirred and sighed. "Come in, Candy, okay? For a drink or something. I'm sorry, I don't mean to bug you but I don't want to be alone right now. *Please*. I don't, really. I'm so worried about— Oh, that poor girl. It's awful to wish this on someone but I do, on anyone but— Will you come in, will you? Just for a bit, maybe? Please?"

"Okay," I told her. "For a little while." I didn't want to sound too eager, even though this was the game plan. If she hadn't asked, I would have offered.

She sighed again in relief and climbed out, dragging her purse behind her. One of the shell "flowers" caught on the seat-belt buckle and exploded in a shower of shell petals.

"*Shit!*"

"I'll get them."

"Forget it." She slammed the door. "It's nothing."

I shrugged, slammed my door, and followed her. When in Rome . . .

Home Sweet Home was not Amber Echo's motto. Furniture and style both were minimal, though not necessarily inexpensive. Most of it tended to glass, chrome, and plastic. The walls were covered with carefully matted, expensively framed posters of dancing girls—Follies Bergere to Vegas—and photographs of Amber as a dancer. A neon martini glass hung in the hall and greeted us with a blinking olive as we walked in. Other than the dancing girls, the martini, and a photograph of a young woman in a silver frame, there was very little that was distinctive or personal.

First stop: TV.

Second stop: liquor cabinet.

Amber had a lithe and beautiful dancer's body but I didn't see how she could maintain it if she drank like this all the time.

"Beer?" she called. "It's in the fridge. Help yourself." She was already in the kitchen splashing tequila into a tumbler with ice. The kitchen was clean in the way that rooms nobody uses much are. The refrigerator confirmed that supposition. Beer, wine, Bloody Mary mix, vodka, olives and onions, hot sauce, salsa, and Pepsi. People didn't eat in this house; they drank. How long had the kid sister been gone? Surely she ate?

I kept those thoughts to myself and followed Amber out to the TV where the regular programming had been preempted by a special news bulletin on the Strip Stalker and his latest victim. A police spokeswoman made an announcement saying no more than what we already knew.

Amber was *oh-my-godding* again.

The camera panned, showing police officers and the bleak back-alley scene we'd viewed earlier. A familiar-looking plainclothes officer turned so the camera caught his face briefly. Hank. Amber gasped. The phone rang. We both jumped. Talk about action.

"Yes?" she answered the phone. "Oh! Hi-i-i-i!" Her voice went high and excited. "I don't believe this. I just saw you on TV and everything."

Then Amber shut up and listened carefully.

"What? Really? Are you sure? Oh God, oh thank you. Thank you. All right, yes. All right. 'Bye."

She pirouetted on a toe, sank into a chrome-and-vinyl chair, leaning back and lifting her legs in an elaborate dancing pose, then dropping them and leaping up again. Her face was ecstatic.

"Amber?"

"It's not her, it's not, it's not! Did you see that cop on TV? That was him. Hank, the cop I know. He called so I wouldn't worry. The girl's been identified and it's *not* my sister!"

"I'm so glad for you."

"Yes." She winked at me. "And if you saw this cop, you'd be even gladder."

Highly debatable. I let it go. "You're dating this guy?"

"Not yet. He has a girlfriend but she's out of town, so big deal. He's *something*."

I counted to ten, then decided to change the subject. For Amber's health as well as mine. "You couldn't just call your sister? You know, to make sure she's okay."

"No. I don't know where Belle is right now."

Belle. Another Vegas name.

"It used to be Annabelle Mae but she changed it when she got here. Look, here's her picture." Amber danced over to an end table, picked up a black-and-white photo in a silver frame. It showed a dark-haired shyly smiling girl in what looked like the five-by-seven size from a high-school-graduation photo packet. She was pretty in an understated way, in an Annabelle, not a Belle, way.

"She's the world's absolute *sweetest* thing." Amber frowned. "Well, most of the time. God, I can't wait to get her back here and all."

"I thought Roy said you didn't have a sister."

"Roy doesn't know everything." Her tone was frosty.

I stood. "I'm glad everything's okay. I'd better get going. . . ."

"Really? Hey, well . . . yeah, it's late, isn't it?" She'd lost interest in me.

I got home to a quiet, dark house. Mars was glad to see me. I had a glass of lemonade and made a reservation for a seven-thirty flight in the morning. Hank didn't call. He hadn't wanted Amber to worry but I was on my own. Sometime around dawn he came home, showered, and crawled into bed without waking me. I kissed him good-bye when I left in the morning. He didn't wake.

Monday, April 18

Sacramento

Seven

Blood
in the Springtime

The death on a Sacramento freeway seemed like another life-time, a long-ago thing before this trip to Vegas and naked women and killers and wandering boyfriends, but it had been only three weeks ago. I thought back to that April day. The woman's voice on the phone, three days after Lindy and I had found the body, had asked for Kat Colorado, had stuttered awkwardly.

"This is Kat Colorado," I had replied when she'd given me the chance.

"My name is Medora Dillard . . . Courtney's mother."

"Courtney?" I knew who she meant but I was surprised, off base and off guard, so I hid briefly behind a question.

"The other night . . . the accident . . . You were there, the police told me. I got your name and number from the accident report. Only . . . only . . . You're a private investigator, I know that, too, and I need your help. I need to talk to you, may I? Please. *Please.*"

That had been the official start of my involvement in this case. Now, just back from Vegas, I drove to my office—a Victorian in Midtown Sacramento that was home to four offices. I got there a little after eleven, cleared off my desk, put the fresh flowers I'd brought in water, and restocked the minirefrigerator with sodas and juice. Then I picked up messages and mail, sat down to sort it out and wait.

Medora Dillard was prompt for her eleven-thirty appointment.

Eleven twenty-nine and she tapped timidly at the door. "Miss Colorado?" Her voice was tentative, timid, anxious, and she looked at me briefly, then away.

"Yes. Please come in. Call me Kat. Won't you sit down?" I came around the desk and indicated a chair for her, then perched on the edge of my desk, one foot swinging slightly.

I caught myself looking for a resemblance between this woman and Courtney, an exercise staggering in its futility as I had no basis on which to compare the live woman to the dead girl.

Mush. Brains. Guts. Blood. A broken foot. No. Nothing at all.

"How may I help you?" I asked, pulling myself away from bloody memories.

"I talked to the police. They were very nice, very kind, but they are not going to help me, I can see that. So I'm hoping you will. Please!"

"Tell me what kind of help you need," I invited Medora Dillard gently. Her eyes skittered away from mine.

"All right. Yes, of course. It's just that, just that . . . I need to know . . . *Oh.* Tell me first how you found my daughter."

I was at a loss then. I didn't want to describe the scene on the freeway. I saw no need for this bewildered, grieving woman to have a graphic picture of her daughter's violent death.

"How did you find her?" she prompted me.

"I was traveling on the freeway and I passed the accident scene." I gave her the simplest possible answer.

"And stopped?" she asked, speaking like someone who couldn't get a grip but was desperately trying.

"And stopped," I agreed.

"There was no one else there?"

"At the accident scene? No."

"No one? You're *sure? Sure?"*

"I'm sure, Mrs. Dillard." I made my voice gentle, patient. "I looked around. The officers did too. There was no one."

"You're an investigator? The police report said that."

Her voice was still tentative, unsure. Everything she said sounded like a question. Death puts a lot up to question.

"Private, yes."

"Oh."

Her voice was vague, blurred now. She was vague and blurred

too, like a picture ever so slightly out of focus, colors faded by time. Or tears and sorrow.

Mrs. Dillard was in her early sixties. Or maybe not; her skin was still young. Maybe she just dressed and carried herself like an older woman. Shapeless dress in a flowered synthetic, shortish gray hair that looked like it had been slept on wrong and combed haphazardly, no makeup except for a smear of peachy lipstick that had smudged. Her shoes were very sensible, very no-nonsense. The only jewelry she sported was a narrow gold wedding band.

"Can you help me?" Her smeary, smudged lips formed the plea carefully and then pushed it out into the air in front of us. She looked utterly helpless and lost.

"Why are you here, Mrs. Dillard? What kind of help do you need?"

She took a shaky breath; her hands clutched her purse, the knuckles whitening. "Courtney . . . my daughter . . . it wasn't an accident. I know it wasn't. It was m— mmm— mur—"

She gave it up right then, right there; *murder* is a tough word. For all of us.

"Someone hurt her." Her eyes filled up with tears. She took her eyes from mine and directed them to her hands. Slowly the hands unclenched and she pulled out an old-fashioned handkerchief. It was a fine cotton with hand-embroidered initials and a crocheted lace edging. She dabbed at her eyes. "They hurt her to death," she whispered. It was as close as she could come to the concept, to the word, *murder*.

"What makes you think that, Mrs. Dillard?"

She looked at me for a beat. Or two. Or three. Measuring and long enough for me to get restless, jumpy even. Long enough for her to decide something.

"You saw her, didn't you?"

"Yes."

"They wouldn't let me see her, although I asked. They said it was better not?"

A question again.

"They were right," I said. I didn't shudder. It was difficult.

"They said she didn't suffer?"

I didn't know who *they* was. I didn't ask. True or not, someone had offered her those words of comfort. I would do nothing to take them away.

"No," I agreed. "She didn't suffer."

"I thank God for that," she said, tears in her eyes. "She was so pretty. *Beautiful.* And a good girl. Smart."

A mother's words. Maybe true. Maybe not. And nothing in them added up to murder.

"Almost two years ago one of Courtney's friends ran out of gas. It wasn't that late, not quite dark even, so Lauren started to walk for help. A man . . . he . . ."

Raped her, I thought. I knew. I asked the question anyway. "Rape?"

She nodded dumbly. "Lauren was never the same afterwards. It was a great shock and sorrow to all of us. And it affected Courtney deeply. She swore she would never leave her car like that, that she would never run out of gas, ever, and that if she had a flat tire, she would drive on it. Because"—Mrs. Dillard's hands flew around wildly and then suddenly, abruptly, clutched the purse again—"because a tire, a wheel is *nothing* compared to a person's safety."

I looked at her evenly. "Is that all? Is there more?"

"No. That's all. No more." Her eyes ran frantically around the room, then settled on me, scared, rabbity. "Please say you'll help me, Miss Colorado. Please say you'll find whoever hurt my daughter. Please." Her hands tugged at the clasp of her purse. "I'll pay you as much as I can. I'll get more."

She dragged out a checkbook stuffed with cash. Old, worn, and faded greenbacks, as blurred now as she was.

"You think that someone tried to hurt your daughter, that someone killed her. Who would want to do that, Mrs. Dillard?"

Her eyes met mine, met the question squarely but dropped quickly. She shifted in her chair.

"I don't know. I'm not sure. That's why I need your help." Her hand clutched the checkbook still. She held it up to me as if to implore, as if praying.

"Let me think about it, get back to you," I said then, and the pain my answer caused her showed in her face. "I'll get the official reports. Let me see what I can find out. Please leave me your address and phone number."

Hope flickered in her eyes. I hated myself. I was taking the easy way out, believing I would probably say no to her on the phone later. I would read the reports but I didn't think that I would find anything more than an accidental death and a mother's anguish.

She took both my hands in hers with more strength than I had thought she had and thanked me.

"May God bless you," was her parting line. They didn't sound like idle words but like a heartfelt blessing.

I felt sad. Again. Was this a constant state now? I felt her sorrow, but I wasn't sure I could help. At least she had her God.

Not me. But I had a plan.

I would read the police and coroner's reports. I would go see Courtney's car. I would also go for a hike, a scenic hike on the freeway. And I'd talk to a few people.

Down the block kids hollered. I heard a ball bouncing in staccato rhythm on the sidewalk and a dog barking. There was a siren in the distance, high-pitched and aggressive. The front door to the building closed with a slight slam. It was all comfortingly everyday.

Of course, compared to murder almost anything was.

It had seemed real clear-cut, had looked like a hit-and-run. *Seemed. Looked like.* And—what do you guess?—nine times out of ten what it looks like is what it is? But nine out of ten leaves one.

A vehicle with a blow-out. The jack out, other tools too, the driver of the car and the registered owner the same. Clear-cut. Common. But not clear-cut enough for Medora Dillard.

I had to search for my camera, then dust it off. Luckily I had four backup rolls of film. I found the accident site easily enough. The ragged ends of the flares were still scattered around. There was a dark stain on the road where the body had been.

I took pictures of everything.

Or rather of nothing.

No scrapes or gouges in the pavement, no skid marks. No evidence of the driver abruptly losing control of the car or suddenly braking. No bits of blown tire, shards of glass, no miscellaneous car parts. No evidence of an impact at a high rate of speed. Of course, the tow-truck driver could have swept all that up. Technically, it's part of his job; in reality they hardly ever do. Or maybe it wasn't there because it never had been there. That could be checked too.

The freeway was relatively quiet; early afternoon is not a real busy time of day. I took two rolls of pictures, the sun warm on my back, the breeze gentle and sweet. I closed my eyes and tried to pretend that the rush of cars was the sound of faraway surf. It didn't work, so I opened them again. The ceanothus was in wild blue-purple bloom, the ice plant and freeway daisies coming up in yellows, whites, and pinks. The oleanders in the center divide were strong and green but not yet in flower. It was a spring day full of promise and beauty and life with no hint, no tangible reminder— The bloodstains on the pavement hit me in the face and stomach again. *Make that almost no reminder.* —of the mayhem of a few nights before.

An eighteen-wheeler rolled by. The driver blinked his lights, honked and waved. It scared the socks off me. A truck blast at close range is no fun. I gave him the one-finger wave, picked a sprig of ceanothus, and finished another roll of film. Then took a last look around and drove back to my office. In Midtown I parked and walked over to Celestine's for lunch. On the way I tried to pretend that death wasn't part of my life. The food, hot and spicy, was good, was the opposite of my mood.

While I ate, I thought about Medora Dillard. Mothers, even bereaved and distraught ones, do not automatically jump to homicide as a conclusion, not by a long shot. Courtney Dillard did not fall into a convenient murder-suspect category. She wasn't a gang member, a drug dealer, or a prostitute. On the contrary, she was a "good girl," and nothing I'd learned so far indicated murder. Nor could I understand how seeing Courtney as a murder victim would be any source of comfort to her family. I did understand the obsessive need to know the truth, no matter how horrible.

Later, back at my office after lunch, I reached for the phone, then stopped, looked instead at the address in front of me. It was an address in the River Park area, an older neighborhood, a nice neighborhood. I picked up the phone and punched in numbers, talked to a vague, disembodied voice in the coroner's office, then an authoritarian one at the Highway Patrol. I wondered if voices took on the personality of a job. Both voices told me I could pick up the respective reports anytime during business hours. I could have made another call too. But I didn't.

I had a few more questions. Before I picked up the official

paperwork, before the death became more real and vivid to me than the young woman Courtney Dillard had been alive.

It took me less than fifteen minutes to get there. It was a quiet tree-lined block with homes that had been built forty or fifty years ago. They were tract homes, but upscale, and the landscaping camouflaged and individualized the repeats. I rolled the window down and listened to the birds, to the wind rustling in the new spring leaves of the trees I was parked under. I didn't see any tricycles or toys or hear any children. Older families, as well as older homes.

The Dillard home was wood with three-foot-high brick trim at the foundation. The house was painted cream, the shutters and the trim in red to complement the brick. Camellias and azaleas marched along the front of the house in pinks, reds, and whites. It was, judging from the size, a four-bedroom two-bath. The mat at the doorstep said WELCOME FRIEND!

I pushed the bell. Thirty seconds later, as I was thinking of ringing again, the door swung open.

Medora stood there, her mouth slightly agape in a silent O, her eyes terrified. *Terrified?*

Welcome?

Eight

Sex, Drugs, and Rock 'n' Roll

"May I come in?"

She snapped her mouth shut and nodded, tried to smile—it worked pretty well with her mouth but not with her eyes—then stood back so I could enter. "Just for a bit, though. I've got things to do. Housework and . . . and . . . things. I could come to your office tomorrow. That would be *much* more convenient."

"Is housework more important than Courtney's death?" I asked gently.

"Oh," she said. "Oh no." She closed the door behind us. "Would you care for lemonade or peppermint tea? Sit down. Here?" She patted the couch and I sat, declining refreshment. "Why are you here? I don't understand. You're taking the case, then?" A note of hope.

"I need to know more about Courtney, about what kind of a person she was."

"Oh," she said. "Yes, I see." She wrung her hands. Her head dipped. Her eyes stayed away from me.

"May I see a picture of her?"

Mrs. Dillard nodded and left the room. I looked around me. It was like being in a Sears Roebuck catalog, circa 1950. Heavy overstuffed furniture, worn but well cared for, the colors faded now into dull, indeterminate stripes. Pole lamps and veneered end tables. A corner cupboard held a collection of assorted china and what looked like religious figurines. The carpeting was dull and worn too. I saw no books, magazines, or pictures, although there were a lot of silk flowers and plants. A large state-of-the-art TV dominated one wall. Everything was immaculately clean and uninteresting.

It was obviously a home that had been used and lived in and yet, oddly, it bore little trace of those users, as if the living had been done long ago or the personality of the whole was more important than the individuals.

A faint smell of baking hung in the air, teasing and tempting. Except for the rhythmic tock of a clock on the mantel, the house was silent. This was not a place where information was volunteered.

Medora Dillard reappeared with a heavy album, a leather look-alike, sat beside me on the couch and balanced it on our laps. The album was crammed with pictures, many pasted in, many stuck in loose. She paged through it purposefully. "Here's Daisy when she was a baby."

Daisy? "Daisy?" I asked.

"Oh." She met my eyes and, for a moment, there was regret and longing and other things I couldn't identify and then they went blank. "You don't know. I forgot. Her name wasn't Courtney then, it was Daisy. She changed it a year or so ago. We still call her Daisy in the family but her friends, her *new* friends"— Was there a note of disapproval there?—"knew her as Courtney."

"Legally changed?"

"Yes. It—" She thought better of that sentence and started on another one. "Yes. I . . . I tried to call her Courtney when it was just the two of us. I wanted to respect her choice even though it went against— Oh my. Well, never mind." She substituted a brisk tone for the sad one. "I *always* think of her as Daisy when she was young, though."

I liked the name Courtney better than Daisy, even though Courtney had a yuppie ring and Daisy had a nice down-home quality about it. I thought, too, that Courtney was a name a young woman might have outgrown in time just as she had Daisy. On the street outside, a car approached and slowed and Mrs. Dillard stiffened, head to one side, listening until it passed. Then she sighed and turned back to the photos.

"She was our youngest of six."

Daisy had been a cute, healthy-looking bald baby with no identifying or distinguishing characteristics. Except for drool, and that—though I know next to nothing about babies—didn't seem remarkable.

"I had Daisy late in life. I hadn't thought to be blessed again." Her voice was troubled. Blessings were greeted with more joy and enthusiasm, surely? "Here she is in the third grade." I looked at a solemn little girl in a starched cotton dress with a pinafore, two neatly plaited braids and large eyes. She looked like she belonged to another time—a Dorothy-in-the-Land-of-Oz time, perhaps.

"And junior high, and then high-school graduation. And her prom, of course." I was watching the metamorphosis of the caterpillar to the butterfly. Gone was the solemn little face framed by pigtails. I stared now into the flashing eyes of a gorgeous young woman with abundant dark curly hair, pierced ears, and a slim but full-breasted figure. A smile curved across her face with anticipated promise and the aura of knowledge she should have been too young for but—these days—probably wasn't.

She fits the profile of the Strip Stalker's victims. The thought flashed through my mind before I could stop it. Then I wondered at the note in Medora Dillard's voice: foreboding? The young man next to Daisy in the prom photo had a blond crew cut, a tux, and a goofy smile. He looked like he was both pleasant and clueless. He was, no question, out of his league with Daisy and seemed aware of it.

"I don't have too many more pictures after that, not good ones." Mrs. Dillard flipped through quickly. "Christmas, my son's wedding."

They were group shots that didn't tell me a lot about either Daisy or Courtney. I was about to ask about Courtney's brothers and sisters when Medora flipped past a family shot with a vast white-marble edifice in the background.

"The Mormon Temple in Oakland?" I asked.

"Yes. We're Mormon. That was one of the things that Daisy— well, Courtney by then—rebelled against, the Church. There were many things, but that was what broke our hearts. I hoped it was just a rebellious thing, a thing of youth, you know, and that

she would come back, be reconciled, but there was no time."
Her voice cracked.

We sat without speaking for a moment and listened to the
ticktock of the clock.

"Well," she said briskly, "I mustn't keep you. You have many
things to do, I know. So busy, so busy." She shut the album and
stood, as did I.

"May I see Courtney's room, her things?" I asked.

"Now?" she asked with a frown. When I nodded, she said,
"Oh. Oh, well, yes, all right." Again I heard her reluctance. I
followed her into a small bedroom with two twin beds. The
shades were pulled and the colors in the curtains and bedspread
faded but still recognizably pink.

"This was the girls' room."

It was a room that had personal touches. Mementos. Medora
wandered about, picking up things, holding them, handing them
to me. It was both a pathetic and heart-warming display: a sixth-
grade penmanship award; a pen-and-ink drawing and a water-
color, both signed by Daisy Dillard in big, round, childish letters
and placed in dime-store frames; a cheerleading costume, slightly
faded and grass stained; a well-loved teddy bear with one and a
half eyes and a wobbly head; a charm bracelet with religious
tokens, a cable car (*I Lost my* ♡ *in SF*), little animals, and a heart;
a school yearbook—*Roses are red / violets are blue / friends are special
/ just like you!!!;* pressed flowers in a battered copy of *Little Women.*
Mrs. Dillard was teary-eyed by the time we finished.

I knew a great deal more about Daisy. Something about Courtney. Nothing about her death.

"You mentioned that Courtney was rebellious?" I trudged on
through business as Courtney's mother valiantly blotted at her
tears. "Her name change was part of that?"

"Oh, yes. She didn't want to sound Mormon." Her eyes were
sad and incredulous both. *Imagine!* they said. "She thought
Courtney Dillard had a fine ring to it.

"But nothing is as fine as being in your church and with your
family. *Nothing!*"

It was a fierce statement, one that admitted no deviance,
brooked no discussion. I backed up.

"How else did Courtney rebel?"

Her mother sighed. "She wore fancy clothes that were too old for her, high-heeled shoes, even makeup, and then she started staying out late and going to parties." Her voice was harsh and condemning, vengeful and unforgiving.

I took a deep breath before speaking. One of the things that I detest about many churches and much religious fervor is the intolerance. "Your daughter was a teenager, Mrs. Dillard. Isn't that pretty typical?"

She ignored my question. "And she went about with people not of our Kind or Faith. Why, she once dated a Negro boy."

Another thing I detest is the bigotry.

"Her father put his foot down, of course."

And the righteousness.

"He condemned to her the sins of alcohol and tobacco, said that she must not violate the Word of Wisdom. We called in our bishop, of course. He, too, spoke to her, spoke over and over— not just of the evils of alcohol and tobacco, but of following the Word of Wisdom."

"And did it work?" I asked but I knew the answer already. I had seen Cinderella's shoe, not a glass slipper but a silver pump with a rhinestone clip. This Mormon Cinderella with the flashing, almost bold, eyes had gone to the ball.

"No." Her angry eyes met mine. "She quit going to school, got a job as a receptionist in an office, and moved in with one of her new girlfriends. She wouldn't come home when her father was there, only during the day sometimes to see me."

"Drugs?"

"I don't think so, but I don't know." She took a shuddery breath. "There was a man, too, I think." She said it in the same tone of voice that I would say "raw sewage" or "gutter slime."

"She went too far with that. She was not good. And she died."

"She died because she wasn't good?"

"Yes."

I thought, then, of all the people who really weren't good: Charles Keating, the Lincoln Savings and Loan three-piece-suited executive thug who bilked and defrauded thousands, many of them elderly and on a pension and last chance; Richard Ramirez, the Night Stalker, who had raped and terrorized numerous women and their families; Saddam Hussein; brain-dead skinheads who thought Hitler was a swell guy and whose sole ambition was to be just like him. All these people were lousy human beings and they were still alive.

"Had Daisy stayed in the family, in the Church, none of this would have happened," her mother said firmly.

Oh, well, that was quite possibly true, although if we all played it out by playing it safe we would die in our beds—not ever having dared, not ever having lived.

"How was she not good?" I couldn't say bad—it didn't seem right—and I asked the question, though I suspected I knew the answer: sex, drugs, and rock 'n' roll.

"She drank coffee and Cokes. Alcohol, too, I am sure."

Drugs.

"And there was this man she was seeing . . . maybe . . . maybe sleeping with."

Sex.

"And . . . and I think she did wild things."

Rock 'n' roll.

"Wild things? Like what?" I pushed, getting desperate for facts, for specifics.

"I don't know exactly, but things, things a good Mormon girl wouldn't do."

Which probably covered a lot of territory. "Who do you think killed your daughter, Mrs. Dillard?"

She looked at me steadily. "Won't you call me Medora?" she requested. "Please." The eyes dropped. "I don't know that either. I know—knew—so little about her life, the one she lived now. She wouldn't tell me because I couldn't understand and wouldn't approve. She was my daughter and I loved her, but I didn't, wouldn't, approve. You understand, don't you?"

She didn't want or wait for an answer and I didn't give one.

"But her feelings about cars, about what happened to Lauren, hadn't changed. We talked about it. She had spent the morning with me while two of her brothers worked on her car. Her brothers were very protective of her, of their little sister. They always made sure that her car was in good shape, that it was safe. That very morning she asked about Lauren. She never recovered, you know."

Into the silence birds sang and then a car without a muffler blasted down the street drowning out the birds. I followed Medora back to the living room.

"Lauren?" I asked. I was lost in vague and confusing pronouns.

She started nervously and picked at an invisible piece of lint on her dress before answering. "Yes. Before it happened, before she was hurt, she was engaged to be married. He is a very nice boy, to be sure, but afterwards . . . afterwards something changed and then he married someone else. Their first child is due anytime now. Before, Lauren was going to be a schoolteacher, a kindergarten teacher.

"And now?" I asked, still sorting through ambiguous pronouns.

"Now, well, now it's so sad. Courtney asked the same thing, you know. Lauren dropped out of school and never went back. Now she lives at home and makes the most beautiful quilts. Each one is intricate and perfect, a work of art. She has gotten very thin now and is not so pretty. And she is afraid. She rarely leaves the house except to go to church with her family.

"So you see," she continued, as though she were a prosecutor summing up the evidence, "Daisy would *never* have done what Lauren did. She would *never* have risked that. *Never*. And so I must know the truth."

I didn't have everything I needed yet. "May I have the names of her friends?"

"I can give you the names of the ones she grew up with, surely, but not her new ones. Her closest friend was Julie Williams. After Lauren, of course, Lauren Davidson."

"The name of her boyfriend?"

"No." She shuddered. Medora must have had a hard time with a lot of the things in the nineties. Or stayed home a lot. Or both.

"Where did she work?"

"I don't know. She just spoke of it as 'the office.' I didn't ask for any other information. Not about him either." *We didn't approve,* her tone said.

"You do know where she lived?"

"The address, yes. I have never been there." She copied an address from a small book lying by the phone on the table next to the couch.

"May I have a few photographs?"

Medora let me choose whatever I wanted. She told me nothing

more of importance but did give me addresses and phone numbers.

"Is there *anything* else you can tell me that might help?"

"No. Just that it wasn't an accident. I know that. I *know.*"

Not a lot to go on.

"I know someone hurt her and I want you to find out who. I want—I want Justice."

She said it firmly and with a capital letter for the *J.* This time she wasn't leaving it up to her God, she was putting it to me.

"I need to meet and talk to your husband and Courtney's brothers and sisters as soon as possible."

Her hand flew to her heart. Outside, a car door slammed. Medora froze, a deer-caught-in-the-headlights look in her eyes. I heard a key in the lock. Medora was unmoving—a trapped animal waiting for the end, not fighting it, not questioning it.

Nine

Caught in the Light?

He was a small man, shorter than my five seven, and skinny with a protruding potbelly. He wore brown polyester slacks, a white shirt, and a tie in ugly shades of green. Thin, hairless white arms poked from the sleeves of his short-sleeved shirt. His pale, almost bald head poked out of a collar that was loose on his scrawny neck and his ears were red. He looked like a country cousin of Willy Loman as he stood there, keys in one hand, a cheap plastic briefcase in the other.

"Who is this?" he asked Medora.

No *Hello*, no *Hi honey, I'm home*. Apparently manners were not high on his list of priorities. There was an odd look on his face, a surprised note in his voice, as though he were amazed that he should have to ask, that anything should be out of the ordinary.

Medora started stuttering. After five or six agonizing attempts at speech, I spoke up.

"I—" But that was as far as I got.

"I am speaking to my wife," Dillard interrupted, informing me coldly.

Okay, I was wrong. Manners weren't on his list at all. He looked at his wife sternly. I guess obedience was, though.

"I—she—" Medora took a deep breath, her eyes wide with apprehension. "Orson, I invited her by to talk about the teachings in our Church. She is interested in knowing more, perhaps joining. We—we were looking at pictures too." She gestured at the photo album. "And—" Her voice trailed off weakly into silence.

Dillard's face softened. Medora began to relax. The deer-caught-in-the-headlights look disappeared and a faint smile struggled on her thin lips.

Almost home free. Almost, not quite.

"My name is Kat Colorado. I am a private investigator. I am here to look into your daughter's death, not your Church." I did not care to be a part of Medora's lie, although I gave Orson Dillard one of my own—the implication that I was here by my design, not involved because of Medora's request.

An involuntary sigh that sounded like air escaping from a sad balloon came from Medora's direction.

"And you let this person into *my* home!" Dillard thundered at his wife.

She hung her head, looking deflated, worn, and much older. And she said nothing. Dillard turned his thunder on me. I was surprised at the powerful, deep, and resonant voice coming out of his squeaky little body. He put his briefcase down and his keys in his pocket, brushed his hands together. He had taken care of his wife; now he would take care of me.

"Young woman, you are not welcome in my home. Neither is any discussion of Daisy permissible in this house. She defied my orders, threw aside her family's wishes, left our Church.

"Did she believe she could defy her father—though we are told by the prophets that the patriarchal order and authority is of divine origin and will continue through all time and eternity?" he thundered.

"Did she believe that she could leave her Church—though the Prophet Smith has said there is but one Church and all other creeds but an abomination in God's eyes?

"Did she believe she could defy her family's wishes, her father's orders and the teachings of her Church and not be damned in God's eyes? No!" He thundered the answer to his own questions.

"She did wrong. She committed evil. She walked along Satan's path and in his footsteps. What began as a young person's foolishness and defiance ended in the embrace of Satan and his evil ways.

"When God created us, He saw, in His infinite wisdom, that

some of His beloved children would be faithful and follow in the path of righteousness and that others would be false and tread the path to destruction. He saw that His commandments would be disobeyed and His law violated. For man is a free agent, free to choose a life of sin or a life of righteousness.''

Like Medora, I listened mutely—not just in the expectation of learning more about Daisy's background (which I certainly was), but in the absolute conviction that it would be impossible to interrupt this thunderous preaching.

"Is it any wonder that one who chooses not to walk God's path and in the protection of His almighty righteousness and power should meet with an accident and come to an unfortunate end? No!" he thundered.

Human thunder must have oxygen. Orson Dillard paused for a deep breath.

I spoke up. "Suppose, Mr. Dillard, that it was not an accident, but murder?"

He blinked but didn't answer me. Dillard liked his own questions better than mine, I guess.

"For the purposes of God are infinitely superior to the designs of men and of devils and he that puts himself in Satan's hands does so to his infinite peril.

"Has not Brigham Young told us: 'There is not a man or woman who violates covenants with their God that will not be required to pay the debt. The blood of Christ will never wipe that out. Your own blood must atone for it.' And he wrote that if 'it is necessary to spill a sinner's blood on the earth in order that he may be saved, spill it.' *Spill it!*" He poked a finger savagely at me.

"My daughter sinned. Her blood was spilled on the earth."

"There are laws of man as well as God, Mr. Dillard, and if Daisy met her death at the hands of—"

"It is forbidden to speak that name in this house, to speak of her. I do not permit it. My daughter wrote to the bishop and asked that her name be removed from the Church membership rolls. And it was. She was excommunicated. Therefore, in life we shunned her and in death she is condemned to hell."

There was a mewling sound in the background.

Belatedly, Dillard remembered Medora. "Go to the kitchen, wife. Tend to your duties." He turned to me. "Young woman, you are but a wrongheaded tool of Satan sent to do his evil work and thwart the work of the Lord. You are not welcome here. *Satan is not welcome here.*" He waved his skinny little arm in my direction, pointing a finger first at me, then at the door.

I left. The door slammed behind me.

In the investigation of a homicide, talking with family members is one of the first things cops do. Seventy-five percent of violent deaths are at the hands of someone known to the victim. "Friendly murders," the cops call them.

Sin.

Spilled blood.

Salvation.

I didn't like this trinity. I didn't like Orson Dillard. I didn't like the setup. The sensible thing to do here was walk. In my mind I saw the spinning lights of the police and emergency vehicles, saw a shattered body in a flickering, constantly changing pool of light, in a pool of blood. Cinderella's dream dead. The rhinestones mocked me.

If I dropped this case, the investigation was over, I was certain of it. Medora would not start again with another investigator and further defy her husband.

I didn't like that either.

Ten

All Victims Are Equal

I got to my office the next morning about seven, fuzzy-headed and tottering along sleepily still, clutching a lethal cup of coffee. I'd stopped at Java City. By seven forty-five I was wide awake and wired and it was (almost) a reasonable time to start making phone calls.

A woman answered my first call on the second ring. She sounded awake, alert, and cheerful. "Hullo!"

"Is this Courtney Dillard's roommate?"

"Yes." Still alert, but hesitant now, wary.

"My name is Kat Colorado. I'm an investigator Courtney's family has retained to look into her death."

"Oh! You *know*? Know about her death, I mean?"

"Yes."

"I thought you didn't and that I was going to have to explain and that's so hard. Oh. I'm so glad. That you know, I mean, not that she's dead. *Of course* not that!"

I couldn't disentangle this. Dispassionately, I asked, "May I come see you?"

"To talk about Courtney?"

"Yes."

"Okay. Sure. Do you want to come today? I have most of the morning off. Come about ten. Do you know where we"—her voice snagged—"where I live?"

"Natomas. I have the address. I don't have your name."

"Janie. Janie Saracen."

I found it easily enough. Like so much of Natomas, it was a blah condo in the middle of a blah condo farm in the middle of a blah condo settlement. Some were beige, some were washed-out tan, some were a pinky beige, and so on, you get the picture. Shutters and trim razzle-dazzled in dead tones of brick-red, mud-brown, and last-to-be-chosen green. There were trees though, trees and iris and pink-and-white azaleas in full bloom and lawns greening up nicely after winter.

I parked in front and walked up to the one-story ranch-style residence. Someone made a quick peephole in the miniblinds, then let them snap back. I rang the bell. The door opened immediately.

"Janie?"

"You're an investigator?"

I laughed. "What did you expect?"

"I don't know. Not *this.*"

She looked at me: curly brown shoulder-length hair, green eyes, dimples; jeans, a silk shirt that almost matched my eyes, and flats that matched the shirt; an oversize brown leather purse.

"I left my fedora and trench coat at the office."

She grinned. "And your gun?"

"I don't even own a three fifty-seven Magnum," which didn't answer the question, but she either didn't notice or chose not to pursue it.

She did laugh at it, laugh and wave me in. It was a neat and tidy home, prettily furnished with overstuffed stuff and decorated with lots of dried flowers and things that are supposed to look like antique artifacts but aren't and mostly just look out of place and as though the buyer got what she paid for, expensive fakes. It was homey, though, and welcoming.

"Would you like a diet Pepsi?"

"All right, thanks." Cold caffeine sounded terrific.

We took our drinks out to a patio hung with the first spring geraniums in lush bloom and riotous color. The patio faced a small yard boringly landscaped in lawn and bushes of the Califor-nia-sturdy-guaranteed-low-water-low-maintenance-minimal-attrac-tion variety. Janie sat across from me in a plastic lawn chair, her tan, long, lean legs stretched out in front of her. Her white tank was tucked into khaki shorts. She wore a white shell anklet, white sandals, and had painted her toenails bright red. Her hair was very blond and very short. She was strikingly pretty in that unmistakably wholesome California girl way. In my mind I could hear the Beach Boys singing about California girls.

"Tell me about Courtney."

Janie looked at me hopelessly, then frowned and shrugged. "I don't know where to start."

"What did you notice first about her?"

"Oh." She laughed. "That's easy. I should have thought of it myself. Her attractiveness, her almost-but-not-quite sexiness."

I stared at her. It was the *last* thing I expected to hear.

She laughed again. "You're surprised, I can see that, but you wouldn't have been if you'd known Courtney. It wasn't something she worked at. It was just there. Like Marilyn Monroe. Of course, Marilyn Monroe worked at it, but even if she hadn't, it still would have been there. Do you know what I mean?"

I knew. I thought.

"It wasn't like she flirted or came on or anything like that. She didn't at all. It was just something she had. She didn't even seem really aware of it, of the power she had. Guys knew, though. Guys noticed. And it wasn't anything obvious like sexy clothes or makeup. Usually she dressed, well, nothing special." She shrugged. "Nothing special at all. Some makeup, sure, but nothing much, nothing provocative." She leaned forward. "Here's what a guy told me once. He said Courtney looked like a girl who would be great in bed but hadn't figured it out yet about sex."

Sleeping Beauty. And everyone wanted to be the Prince, the one to kiss her awake, the first to put desire in her mind, longing in her heart, and fire between her legs.

"Did it make women jealous?"

"No. Odd, huh? She was so unconscious of it and she always treated everyone—guys and girls—the same, very polite and easygoing. She came from a big family and she knew how to get along with people. She really liked people and most people really liked her right back."

"Was she an easy person to share a house with?"

"Oh, yes. She was quiet and considerate and always did her share or more of things. She seemed like a private person in a lot of ways but she was always ready to go out and do something, have fun, especially if it didn't cost much. She didn't have much extra, she was saving to go back to school." Janie shrugged and drained her Pepsi, the ice clicking against her teeth. "Course, these days, who does?"

"How long had you been roommates?"

"About a year." She sucked on a piece of ice, then crunched it. "Look, why are you asking questions, investigating this? It was an accident, wasn't it? What's going on?"

I was prepared for this question, had a lie all thought up and ready to roll. "Her mother wanted to know more about Courtney. I gathered that Courtney had been close to her family most of her life but wasn't particularly at the time of her death."

Janie crunched another piece of ice, then stood. "Hang on, I'm getting the Pepsi." She returned with a two-liter plastic bottle and refilled our glasses. She spilled some on my jeans but didn't notice. Her hand was shaking.

"In some ways," Janie said, "she was dead to them already." She put her glass down on the table with a click. A trailing geranium vine dragged through her hair and she swatted blindly, angrily at it. A shower of hot-pink petals rained down on her.

"I thought religions were supposed to be about love." Her voice was tough and angry.

I shrugged sympathetically. I didn't get the connection but I disagreed with her. To my mind organized religion was about love in roughly the same way that the Mafia was about family. Not.

"But religions are really about power and money and making people do things, things that maybe aren't even the best choice for them. My mother was Catholic. I hated—" She let the hatred or the memory go on a long breath. "I'm sorry. You didn't come here to hear *this.*"

But maybe I had. "This has to do with Courtney, doesn't it?"

She nodded and brushed a petal off her knee. "We met because we were in the same history class at Sac City. We'd been reading about all those women who were burned as witches in the Middle Ages. As we were leaving class one day Courtney said, 'They still do that, you know. Oh, maybe not actually burn witches but a twentieth-century equivalent.'

"So that was the start. We went out for coffee or something and she started telling me all this stuff—she'd obviously been thinking about it for a long time—probably too long, but I don't think she'd ever had anyone to talk to before. Anyway, she told me about a Mormon woman named Sonia Johnson. Courtney is, well, was, a Mormon, you know. Anyway, Sonia Johnson was this Mormon who came out and supported the ERA. The Equal Rights Amendment, for godsake—you'd think *everyone* would be for *that.*"

The naïveté and optimism of youth. I said nothing.

"So when Sonia Johnson wouldn't back down, they excommunicated her. Do you know what that means?"

I thought of Courtney and nodded.

"That means nobody in the Church could have anything to do with her. They couldn't even talk to her. *Nobody.* Not her friends, not her mom and dad, not her husband and children. Nobody! She was dead to them."

"And Courtney?" I asked, nudging her gently back toward the subject at hand.

"Courtney didn't like it. And she didn't like the way her dad treated her mom. She didn't like the way women got treated in her Church." Janie's eyes glittered with a kind of horrified fascination. "Guess what? A good Mormon man automatically goes to heaven where he becomes like a god in his own kingdom or universe or something. And a good Mormon woman? Does she?"

I thought I could see it coming. She didn't wait for an answer.

"A good Mormon woman doesn't automatically go to heaven, or not to the best part of heaven—only if her husband says so. Anyway," she took a big breath, "this kind of thing made her crazy, made her wild. She tried to talk about it at home and even with her bishop, but everyone just told her that that was the way it was, that was God's will, and she had to do it that way."

"And she didn't?"

"No. She thought all people should be equal. She left the Mormon Church and they excommunicated her. That took a lot of courage, you know."

I nodded.

"So her family wouldn't have anything to do with her, or they weren't supposed to—everyone in the Church was supposed to shun her. I think she saw her mom sometimes, maybe her brothers and sister occasionally. She had to drop out of college, which she hated. She planned to go back as soon as she could afford it.

"Anyway"—another deep breath—"we started talking and I

really liked her and I told her I needed a roommate, so she moved in.''

"Her job?''

"She got a job as a receptionist at a stockbroker's office—Brimmer, Something, and Something, I can never remember. The pay wasn't great but it was a start and the people were okay. She was glad to have it, but she really missed school.''

"Her mother seemed to think that Courtney was living a wild life?''

Janie snorted. "I think Courtney's mom thought if you walked and talked and chewed gum at the same time that was *wild*. And of course Courtney didn't mind her father or go to church, so there you go: wild.''

I thought of Medora. Mutter frog in that woman's ear and she'd probably hop.

"Courtney wasn't wild. She was nice, a real good kid.'' There were tears in Janie's eyes. She got up abruptly and walked around smacking the trailing vines of the geraniums and raining petals down on us. A red petal stuck to her cheek like a drop of blood.

"She was my friend and I loved her.''

Smack. Smash. More petals.

"She drank Cokes and coffee. If you're Mormon that's bad, you know.''

Yes. Caffeine is forbidden as well as alcohol and tobacco.

"And sometimes, not often, a glass of wine or a beer or a strawberry daiquiri or something. Wild? Ha. Puhleeeze!'' She laughed an empty laugh.

What was wild? I thought about gang-bangers and drive-by shootings and drug parties and wildings and gang rapes for kicks and hijackings and carjackings. Wild.

"Was Courtney seeing someone? Did she have a boyfriend?''

Janie frowned, looked around. Very few petals left on the geraniums. She clenched and unclenched her hands as she thought over her reply.

"Yes.''

It was a short, clipped answer for all that thought. Disapproval was written in capital letters on her face.

"You didn't like him?''

She laughed. "That obvious?''

"He wasn't a bad guy at all, he wasn't." Damned with faint praise. "He just wasn't the right guy for Courtney."

"Why?"

"She was twenty-two but really young and inexperienced for her age, because of her background, you know. He's twenty-eight and pretty slick. Smooth. He's one of the brokers where she worked and thinks he's God's gift to the brokerage, to the exchange, and to women."

"And Courtney?"

"She thought so too, I guess. He asked her to marry him and she accepted." Medora Dillard hadn't known that. Or hadn't mentioned it to me.

"What's his name?"

"Chad Wharton."

"Can you find out the name of the brokerage?"

"Yes. I've got it written down somewhere."

"Do you know where she was the evening she was killed?"

Janie looked at me quickly. Was killed. Bad choice of words. *Died. Was in the accident.* Either would have been better.

"She was with him. Chad. He was taking her to meet his parents and they were going to announce their engagement. She was excited and nervous about it. She asked me to help pick out an outfit, to help her decide what to wear."

My mind flashed back. I couldn't remember her clothing. Just the shoe. The shoe and the torn, mangled body.

"What did she wear?"

"A black dress with silver shoes and accessories. She looked wonderful—simple, elegant, and sparkly. I had never seen her happier." Her voice was soft, her look brooding. She picked a sliver of ice out of her glass and bit down savagely on it.

"She was so happy, Kat. Why did she have to die? Why not—why not a *fucking* drug dealer?" Standing there in the geraniums with petals all around her, Janie started crying. Tears ran unchecked down her cheeks. "It's not fair."

I wanted to reach out to her. She was old enough to know that life wasn't fair, young enough not to accept it.

"I'm sorry," I said at last into the silence punctuated by ragged gasps that followed the tears. "I'm sorry you lost your friend." I sat her down and poured Pepsi onto the dregs of her ice.

"Do you know anyone who might have wanted to hurt Courtney, anyone who would have been glad if she'd been hurt in some way?"

Teary young eyes stared at me in silence. Horrified. Dumbfounded. "Oh my god, no, no." The tears started again.

Eleven

Money, Licorice, and Murder

I stood in front of a new concrete-and-glass office building in Sacramento. The address matched the one on the paper in my hand. I was looking for the offices of Barton, Brimmer, & Johnston, specifically for Chad Wharton, broker. Janie and I had looked up the address. She had also given me the name of their history professor at Sacramento City College.

I didn't have an appointment with Chad Wharton but I did have a small fortune to invest (I'd made it up on the way over), and I figured that would get me in the door just fine. If greed is the issue, money is the answer. I'd bequeathed myself $250,000, a nice round quarter mil.

The offices of Barton, Brimmer, & Johnston were modern and spacious, elegant and monied. Every note harmoniously, sedately, and subtly assured me that I could leave my money here and that it would grow and prosper, as would I. If profit by association worked, Barton, Brimmer, & Johnston were onto something.

The receptionist was young and harried. She greeted me politely and had started to inquire as to my business when the phone tweeted. She snatched it up, stumbled over the company name, and then began to take a message as another line chimed softly at her. Her voice sped up. As she wrote, she unconsciously chewed a nail. Her nails were all bitten to the quick, raw, ragged.

I sank into a plush chair the size of Cleveland under an overbearing silk fern to wait my turn.

There was a hall to the left of the receptionist's desk. I could hear the sound of male laughter, hearty, full, alive. It made me want to smile in response, to know the joke. A good-looking man of five-ten or -eleven with black curly hair, brown, almost black eyes and the ruddy tanned complexion of an outdoorsman—no, I revised that, of a tennis player—strode in. The laughter, the smile, was still in his eyes. Those eyes took in the situation immediately.

He smiled at me.

"Our temp seems overwhelmed. May I help you? Our regular staff is, uh—"

He stopped there, naturally hesitant to say *dead*. I rescued him. "I'd like to see Chad Wharton, please."

"I'm Wharton, how may I help you?" The smile in his eyes traveled to his mouth and then to me, as tangible as a gesture. The lightness of laughter was in his voice still.

Courtney's been dead five days, I thought.

I stood and introduced myself and we shook hands. "I've come into money. Do you have time to talk investments?"

The smile deepened. "Of course."

Smashed and puddled onto the freeway. Blood and guts and bone—his Cinderella had not come home from the ball. Yet he smiled and laughed with me?

"Come on back to my office, Ms. Colorado, and tell me what you have in mind."

I followed him across luxurious carpet and then sank into yet another voluptuous office chair in yet another well-appointed room. "Who would have thought," I said conversationally, "when Great-aunt Sophie kicked the bucket" (too callous, I wondered?) "it turned out she had two hundred and fifty thousand dollars and she left it all to me?"

"Lucky you." Chad Wharton grinned. Nope, not too callous. "And good for old Sophie." Familiar, too, with nary a word of regret for my dear departed Sophie or of commiseration for me. "Where is it now?"

"It's all in CDs."

A sobering thought for any broker. Wharton's expression took on a grim/glum effect. He steepled his hands and intoned, "The elderly investor is often very conservative. The war, the depression left—'' He searched around for a word, couldn't find it, abandoned the search, and returned to smiles and me. "We can do better than that. Do you have anything particular in mind?'' The eyes were speculative now.

"Yes." I nodded vigorously. "Tax-free municipal bonds." They were one step up from CDs, virtually risk free and relatively low yield. Not the kind of investment you turned over according to market conditions, either. Tax-free munis were long-haul dependable and very short on commission potential. I watched closely. He didn't even blink. It was admirable.

He nodded in apparent approval. "Always a good choice," he agreed. "May I suggest some other investment possibilities?"

"Please!" I said, just a shade too eagerly. He smiled and talked. I ummmed and ahhhed and took notes. We did this for an hour, an extremely profitable hour. My profit real, his fantasy. Then, suddenly, I was bored, sated with high finance and glib smiles.

And ready for blood. Maybe stockbroker blood.

"I hope I'm not being too personal . . ." I let the sentence drift off into implied-question land.

"Not at all." The smile again. It was starting to grate on my nerves just a wee bit.

"Please accept my condolences on your loss."

The eyes narrowed, hooded over instantly. An eyebrow went up in question.

"I know Janie, Courtney's roommate. And of course I heard of her horrible accident."

"Thank you." His voice sounded choked and sad; his brown eyes were unreadable.

"I found her, you know. Odd how life works. I had heard of her but never met her. Not that I knew who she was that night."

"I don't understand." He didn't. His eyes were full of questions. "You found Courtney?"

"A friend of mine and I were coming home. We were the first to see and stop at the accident scene."

He came out of his chair like a bottle rocket. "You saw her? Courtney? Was she alive? Did she say anything? God, *tell* me she didn't suffer." He started to reach out and grab me, then regained control and yanked violently at his silk tie instead. "Courtney? *Tell* me!"

"She was dead. I'm so sorry."

Strong emotion, emotion I couldn't read, contorted his handsome features. He wiped his hand across his eyes.

"It was so sudden. One day everything was great. We were at the beginning of our lives together, our future. She was planning our wedding. And then—" He rubbed his eyes again. "It's hard for me. I try to be the same in here, to keep going, keep up my work, even to laugh and joke around. I don't want people to feel bad being around me but— We were supposed to go shopping the next day. She had a wedding dress she wanted me to look at." He stared out the window. "She was so young and pretty and happy. It was all just beginning." He looked back at me. "It's hard."

And I was about to make it harder. "I spoke with an off-duty police officer I know. From evidence at the scene he felt there was some chance that it wasn't an accident, that her death was deliberate."

"Deliberate? You mean murder?" His voice was incredulous.

That was the word. That was what I meant. We were a long way from Great-aunt Sophie's quarter mil now.

And he had noticed. Wharton retraced his steps, sat down in the chair behind his desk. "Who are you really?" His voice was cold.

"Kat Colorado."

"But you're not an investor. There is no Aunt Sophie, is there." His voice was flat.

I skated over that one. "I am also a private investigator. Courtney's mother has asked me to look into her daughter's death. She believes Courtney was murdered."

He looked suddenly older. His complexion was still tan but with no healthy glow, no ruddiness in it.

"Murder? My God." He put his head in his hands, looking down, shielding his face.

"Do you know anyone who would want to kill her, who had a reason, a grudge, a—"

"No." He spoke with absolute conviction. "No one. She was sweet, kind, loving, good as the day is long. She never intentionally hurt anybody or anything in her whole life. Never. No. There was no reason for anyone to harm her."

"A rejected boyfriend? A jealous girlfriend?"

He shook his head. "She was a wonderful person. I can't think of anyone who would have any reason to harm her. Everyone loved her." He put his head in his hands again.

"Especially you," I said gently. "I'm very sorry."

"Especially me," he agreed bleakly. "Why didn't you just ask me? Why the song and dance?"

"I wanted to meet you, to talk to you on more neutral ground first." It was an answer but not the answer to his question.

"I see." He stared at me. "And Aunt Sophie?"

"As it turned out, she cashed in her CDs before she died and bought licorice drops."

"Two hundred and fifty thousand dollars' worth?"

"She was an addict. The family, me included, was shocked. Stunned."

A faint smile twitched at his lips. "My sympathy."

"Thank you. May I have your help as well?"

"In your investigation?"

I nodded, then waited while he straightened his desk and considered the question.

"Yes." The word was more positive than the tone of voice. "I think you're crazy, though. I think it was a terrible accident and all we can do now is miss her, and mourn her, and go on." He cleared his throat. "But I'll help any way I can, do anything I can. My love for her didn't end with her death." He got up, signaling the end of our conversation, and walked out with me to the front office. The phones had fallen silent, the receptionist had abandoned her desk.

"Have you gotten over Aunt Sophie's death yet?" he inquired.

"Not yet. Of course, I hate licorice, so I'm pretty bitter about it."

He smiled. "Come back and talk when you have money, Ms. Colorado. That would be more to the point than this investigation."

I was starting to agree with him.

"The cop who's a friend of yours," he said casually. "What'd he find?"

"I dunno exactly." I played ignorant. "Enough to convince

him, though.'' I exaggerated. "I'm following up on this end until he has a chance to look into it.'' And there I outright lied, but there's no question that a cop's opinion on murder carries more weight than a PI's. I felt a twinge of guilt, the lying came so easily. Too easily. It's the sort of thing that worries me. I got over it pretty fast, though, which is also worrisome.

"Is he city or county?'' Meaning Sacramento City Police or Sacramento County Sheriff's Department.

"Neither. He's a Vegas cop. Hank Parker.''

"I'll be glad to help, Ms. Colorado. I'll do anything.''

The phone chirped.

The harried receptionist scampered back in.

I scampered on out.

Twelve

Philosophic Melancholy

One-thirty. My stomach growled. I'd been doing fine until then, until I realized it was lunchtime and then some. Now I was starving. I riffled through my purse and found an opened pack of stale gum, unwrapped two sticks, and chomped away. Stop gap.

I was due back at Janie's at five-thirty, after she'd finished her afternoon classes at Sac City. She'd said that nobody from Courtney's family had called or come by and sure it was all right if I went through Courtney's things if I did it later, after her class. Then she had started crying again.

"Look, Kat, could you maybe help me pack away her things? I'm not looking forward to it, all the memories and stuff. If I got some boxes, could you—?"

I could. I would. I promised. Still, I didn't really want to see Courtney's belongings disturbed, packed away just yet, not until the cops had a shot at it. Assuming I could get them interested. Maybe Hank—*Hank*. I swallowed hard.

One thing at a time. My stomach growled again. I chewed my gum harder. On impulse I decided to head on out to Sac City. Lunch could wait.

I took Interstate 5 to 99 South and exited at Sutterville. I love going out to this part of town. It's one of the older and more beautiful parts of Sacramento. I passed the Sacramento Children's Home on Sutterville, then the college athletic fields, and turned right on Freeport Boulevard. Freeport will eventually take you all the way out to the town of the same name in the Delta, another tempting possibility. Sac City is across from Land Park. Fairy Tale Town is there, and the zoo, and all around is the Land Park area of old and gracious homes with lush plantings and greenery. The streets here, as in so much of Sacramento, are lined with grand and stately generations-old trees.

I found a parking spot easily enough on a residential street bordering the park and across from the college, then walked back. Azaleas and camellias were everywhere in abundant, soul-stunning bloom. The college is laid out around a quadrangle area with grass, trees, and flowers, crossed by pathways and dotted with benches and seating areas. It is lovely and peaceful, and presumably conducive to learning.

It took me three tries before I found someone who knew where the history department was. The young man in the department office directed me absently to Mr. Stumford's office, the professor who had taught the class where Janie and Courtney had met. I found his office, then stared at the closed door, moved my eyes to the right, and read the index card posted on the bulletin board there. Office hours: Tu-Th 3–5.

I looked at the institutional clock stationed severely on the wall. Two-fifteen. It was Tuesday. My stomach growled. Perfect timing. I went off in search of food. I was back at 2:57, my stomach appeased but not happy with a stock-issue tuna salad with mayo and mustard (mustard? on tuna? and I hate mustard anyway) on soggy white bread. The mushy apple hadn't helped but the double-double-chocolate-chocolate-chip cookie was great. No wonder people eat junk food.

Mr. Stumford was there, door open, term papers spread out across the desk in front of him. I tapped on the open door and he looked up at me through the top half of his bifocals.

"Come in," he invited. "How may I help you?"

It was said with a gentlemanly graciousness, manners I attributed to another age. Stumford looked to be in his middle sixties. He had a lean, bony build, hair well past thinning and into balding, long, slim fingers that rested on the term papers, and sharp eyes that rested on me. He wore a striped shirt and tie, a corduroy jacket, and an inquisitive look. I took to him immediately.

"I'm looking for information," I said as I entered. There were books everywhere, on shelves, on the desk and floor, and covering all but one chair.

"I've got plenty of that. Limited as to time periods, though." He chuckled. It was a rich sound and surprised me at first. It seemed incongruent with his lean, slight frame.

I introduced myself and he stood to shake my hand, sat again, and waved at the one open chair. "Please have a seat."

I cut right to the chase. "I'm here about Courtney Dillard, a student who was in one of your classes."

He nodded. "In European history, yes," he said impassively.

"Have you heard of her death?"

His face registered an immediate shock, then crumpled, making him look older and very tired. "I hadn't, no, and I am saddened to hear it. Courtney was a very bright and promising young person. She was ill?"

I shook my head.

"No. I thought not. An automobile accident, then? So many young people . . . excessive speed . . . drinking, daredeviling."

"It was an automobile. Her mother believes that it could not have been an accident."

"No?" He looked puzzled. "What, then?"

Movies, TV, and books notwithstanding, murder is not the kind of thing that flies to mind. Not with people you know, not sitting in the sunshine in an academic office, not thinking about a pretty college coed. I didn't answer the question, just let it sit and stew and then fester.

"She was *murdered?*"

"Her mother believes that. She has hired me to look into it. I am a private investigator." I handed him a business card.

He took it without looking, then placed it carefully on his desk, got up, walked to the door, and shut it.

"You believe she was killed by another student?"

"I don't know. That's why I'm here. I'm hoping you can help."

He wagged his head back and forth like a top-heavy skinny-necked bird. "I don't see how, but I'll do whatever I can."

"How well did you know Courtney?"

"She was my student in European history. Her work was careful and thoughtful, well researched and polished without being original or especially insightful in any way. I had a feeling she was brought up in a very traditional family, one in which she was not encouraged to question or to think independently, although those are qualities that might well have come through in a different environment.''

And with more teachers like him.

"It was my observation—" He broke off and scowled. "You *are* asking me for this kind of information, are you not? That is why you are here?"

"That's why I am here," I agreed. "And I appreciate anything you can tell me."

He put his hands together, palms apart, fingertips touching, and rested his chin lightly on his fingertips. It reminded me suddenly of a child's finger game. *Here's the church and here's the steeple, open the door and . . .*

"I think that the questioning process for her had just begun." He tipped his head back. Tap, tap, tap went the fingers. "She seemed in particular very upset about something she had learned in my class. She even came to speak with me about it."

"The burning of witches and heretics?"

He smiled gently, dryly. "I am not, I see, the first person to whom you have spoken. The burning of witches and heretics, yes, but really that became symbolic of the much larger issue of intolerance and, carried to the extreme, of intolerance that accepts only an extremely narrow view of the world as truth."

Briefly his fingers danced and tapped about, then settled. "It has been my experience that young people brought up in, ah, let us say, for the sake of discussion, a fundamental religious home, often think of things in highly simple and simplistic terms: good versus evil; right versus wrong; black versus white. The good, the right, of course, are the tenets, strictures, and beliefs of their particular system, cult, religion, whatever. This often works quite well for the years when the child is kept in a rigid environment of home, church, school, often religious school.

"You understand when I say 'well' "—he smiled sadly—"I mean from the parental point of view of effective control of a child's mind and outlook and not, say, from an educator's standpoint?"

"Yes." Silence after my agreement. I broke into his ruminations. "And then the student goes off to college, or work, or the military and sees a far different world, hears very different ideas, is exposed to new values and standards. Questions start. The system begins to break down."

"Yes," he agreed. "Interestingly, such a person frequently does not move from a position of a rigidly controlled world picture to a position of tolerance and openness but rather from one narrow world view to another. What was once white and correct becomes black and wrong, and vice versa."

"Different positions but the same philosophical approach?"

Tap, tap. "Exactly."

I waited patiently. I had a sense of where he was going and I felt sure he would eventually come back to Courtney. A minute or so passed, Stumford lost in reflection and me revising my earlier estimation of my patience. "And Courtney?" I prompted.

He started. "Courtney, yes. We can, I think, say with a considerable degree of certainty that Courtney was engaged in this process." More bemused reverie on his part, more barely controlled impatience on mine. Again I cracked first.

"Could this have any connection with her death, Mr. Stumford?"

His eyes met mine and held. "Well, my dear, I think that we may postulate with equal certainty that such people are often not very easy to be around. And the young, especially, are frequently very vocal about it." He shrugged.

"You see, with extremes there is, quite naturally, no middle ground, no gray area. There is only black and white. Such positions can become extremely, umm, abrasive, even volatile, and quite rapidly at that. Moderation and rational discourse and procedure generally do not prevail."

No. I thought of the wars all over our world in the name of "truth"—religious truth, political truth, economic truth. I said, "This could certainly lead to murder."

"Time and time again, it has. Whether it applies in this case I leave entirely up to you. She was a very sweet young person, Courtney was. She was also highly principled and, in her newfound views, very definite, *very* definite, particularly in her view of what constituted right and wrong. Nor did she appear to be at all afraid to speak up. She had just begun to question things and was quite excited, quite passionately involved in that process."

Tap, tap, tap went the fingers. "And now, my dear, if you will excuse me?'' He waved in an explanatory way at the stacks of term papers.

I stood at once, thanked him for his help.

"Anytime, anytime at all. Please come back. Let me know what you discover. Poor child, poor dear child. So promising."

There was a sadness in the eyes behind the thick bifocals. Not the immediate heart-wrenching pain I had seen in Janie and Chad but the quiet, dispassionate, philosophic melancholy of the historian. As I left, he returned placidly to his papers. I heard his fingers tap one last time.

Thirteen

Overrated Clues

It was the first faint glimmer I'd had of a reason why someone might want to hurt Courtney. I unwrapped the rest of the pack of gum and popped it in. Took me a while to get it going—we're talking stale, *really* stale here. Her mother felt certain someone had killed her but didn't know who or why because, except for the defection from home and Church, Daisy/Courtney had been a good girl. Her friend and her fiancé said the same thing: Courtney had been a good person, lovable, kind, responsible. She had had no enemies, no one with even a grudge against her. Not even a mild dislike.

No one. Nothing. No way. Just a torn body and a nagging question mark, and then Stumford and his quiet suggestion that was a supposition and the only clue—if I could dignify it with that label—that I had.

Of course, clues are overrated in my business. The way it works is not by following a neat linear line of clues down a marked road until *Bingo!* you add everything up, deduce, and come up with The Answer.

No.

The way it works is that you slog along up and down numerous roads, many (most) of them dead ends, and you accumulate a minimum of 10,000 bits of largely unrelated, pedestrian information of which 9,686 bits, however occasionally interesting and diverting, are of no use to you whatsoever in your investigation—although you do not, of course, figure this out for some time.

Another 300 or so bits are related but irrelevant, or relevant but too small or inconsequential to help. So then, if you're lucky, you have 14 useful informational bits after hours and hours of slogging. You can't skip the first steps, the 9,000-plus bits and the slogging, though, because that's the only way you recognize the other pieces as important. Finally, after many more hours, you might be able to shove them around, fit them in, add them up so they tell you something.

This is what investigative work is all about. Fun, huh? It's more glamorous, exciting, and entertaining on TV, I can tell you that. A lot more.

Black and white and gray: a glimmer, that was all. I sighed. I pushed at it as hard as I could but it didn't make sense to me. I didn't think, couldn't imagine, that anyone would kill Courtney Dillard just because she was questioning various belief systems. This, after all, is not big news. Young people do it all the time. They're the designated hitters in the Philosophical Question Game of Life. And for most of them, as for most of us, it goes away in time. They get older, marry, buy a house, have babies, and settle down, making way for a new crop of kids—designated hitters all—with the same kind of dogged questions.

The glimmer dimmed. If this was an idea on a rheostat, it had just gone from dim to off. I sighed again. Chewed my gum harder.

Bummer.

I needed more to go on. I contemplated the notion of information and facts with wistful yearning. Glimmer and supposition were not going to cut it.

I was back at the house Courtney had shared with Janie a little after five-thirty. I beat her there, so I sat in my car with the windows rolled down listening to the birds and the distant roar of traffic. The birds were outnumbered and outgunned.

A bright-yellow Geo beeped at me, then pulled into the driveway. Janie hopped out, calling hello to me as I got out of the Bronco. We crossed the lawn and Janie fit her key into the lock. "C'mon in."

I watched as she dashed around pulling up the miniblinds and opening the windows.

"I *love* spring, don't you? It's so wonderful. All the new beginnings, the fresh starts." Her shoulders slumped. "Courtney's room is this way. I know that's why you're here but—hey, you want an iced tea or something?"

"No, thank you."

She looked disappointed. She wants to talk, I realized. "Would you like to come with me, to help?" I suggested.

"I don't think I'll be much of a help." Her voice was doubtful.

"To talk, then?"

"Sure. Oops, I forgot the boxes. Maybe I better run out and—" She was suddenly nervous and jumpy, spooky and sparky as fireflies on a summer night.

I caught her by the elbow, trying to slow her, calm her. "Not yet, Janie. Come on."

She led the way down a short hall to Courtney's bedroom, then quickly retraced her steps, returning with a kitchen chair which she plopped down in the hall outside the bedroom door.

She flashed me a smile, one that faded instantly. "You'll have more room this way," she explained. "And—and, well, it's too hard. Do you believe you can *feel* a person by being in their place, their space? I don't mean like a ghost or anything but, well, do you?"

I nodded. I do.

"Sometimes I think I hear her footsteps or the click of the bathroom door or the way she always used to hum under her breath. That's memory and imagination, I know, but sometimes I have a feeling that she's close by. It's not anything bad or scary at all, it's like she misses me and she's sad we didn't get to say good-bye." A tear spilled out and started down her cheek. Janie swiped angrily at it as she had at the geraniums that morning, then glared at me, daring me to notice.

"I think that's one of the hardest things," I said gently, "not being able to say good-bye. I think you were very fortunate to have such a dear friend, even if for just a short time. I'm sure you're right and that she is trying to say good-bye."

The tears were now running down Janie's face. She made no attempt to hide them or brush them away.

"I didn't forget the boxes, I lied about that. It's just . . . just that it doesn't seem right to pack up her stuff when she's here. I mean, I know she's not *really*, but—"

I smiled at her. "I'm glad you feel that way. I would like her things to stay here for a while. May I pay two weeks' rent and we'll just leave everything as is?"

"Oh *yes*, that's great." She smiled at me, then breathed out in relief and rubbed the palms of her hands across her face just as a five-year-old would, wiping and smearing the tears away. "I guess that's silly, huh, imagining she's still here?"

I laughed.

Janie's smile instantly metamorphosed into a hostile ugliness. She scowled at me.

"I'm sorry," I said quickly, contritely. "I was remembering a conversation I had with a real-estate broker." Janie's frown deepened. "She said that some houses were ridiculously easy to sell because the minute you walked in you sensed that it was a home where people had been happy. And others were just the opposite. There was a heaviness, a darkness about them. She said that, and I thought she was just being fanciful."

Janie had stopped glaring at me, was now staring at me in fascination.

"So we bet on it. She took me to five different houses one morning."

"And?" She was curious in spite of herself.

"I paid up, bought lunch without protest. She even had two desserts and I didn't say a thing. Because she was right. You can tell almost the instant you walk in."

Janie sighed and a smile flirted about her mouth. "And?"

I glanced around. "This is a nice room. Peaceful. Kind. Decent. Like Courtney?"

"Yes."

"Did her boyfriend ever come here?"

"He came to the house to pick her up, or visit, or stay for dinner but not for the night. Is that what you mean?" I nodded. That's what I meant. "They always stayed at his place. He owns a condo down by the river, off Garden Highway."

I looked around the room again. Courtney had been dead for five days. The air was stale and there was already a slight layer of dust on the furniture. A vague fragrance lingered.

"Is this how she left it?"

"Have I changed it, you mean?"

"Anyone. Not just you."

"No." She said it without hesitation. "It's just like it was."

I looked at the earrings tossed on the bureau, the scuffed black flats tucked under a chair, the neatly made bed. Then I crossed to the window, opened the curtains, and let the late-afternoon sunshine flood in.

It was a medium-sized room painted in pale yellow. The curtains I had pulled back were white and yellow stripes dotted with blue flowers. The flower pattern was repeated in the comforter on the white wrought-iron day bed in a chaste single size. Lace-trimmed pillows in white and yellow were tossed on the bed. An oval braided rug in faded blues and greens graced the carpeted floor. There was a medium-sized desk, a banged-up bureau with mirror, and a bookcase crammed with books. The style of the furniture was vintage yard sale.

The secondhand effect was easily overshadowed by the softness of color, the vases of dried flowers, the carefully framed photographs and obviously treasured knickknacks. Love had lived here before death came.

"What are you going to do? Are you looking for clues? Clues for what?" Janie's voice was soft but insistent.

The phone rang. There was a phone in the room but either it was a different line or the ringer was turned off. Janie left to answer the telephone and I moved into action. There is a time to question and a time to toss. I could hear Janie's voice, animated and laughing, in the background.

I started with the walk-in closet. Easy enough to walk in—there wasn't much there. Half-a-dozen work outfits: mostly skirts, jackets, and blouses in basic hues. A jacket, raincoat, and umbrella. Several pairs of jeans, sweaters, and a sweatshirt folded on the shelf above. Half-a-dozen pairs of shoes—pumps, flats, sandals, and sneakers—neatly arrayed on the floor below.

There was a ring box on top of the bureau. Empty. Earrings and a gold chain. A comb. A small silver hand mirror. Two dried bud roses had been laid on the doily that tried to cover the gouges and water stains on the bureau top. Underwear, nighties, panty hose, exercise clothes: The drawers contained the usual, all folded and arranged first by category, then by color.

The bottom drawer wasn't clothes. It could be news. I heard Janie walk down the hall, then the scrape of her chair. I shut the drawer.

"Sorry about the interruption. Sure you won't have an iced tea? Or diet Pepsi? Did you find anything? You know, I've been thinking over what you said this morning, what you asked me: Would anyone want to hurt Courtney? Does that mean you think it wasn't an accident? What was it, then? Kat—" Her voice demanded, then pulled at me when I didn't answer in the two-second pause she allotted me.

"You just asked me twenty-two questions in a row," I said laughingly.

"Well, okay, but pick one."

"Diet Pepsi."

We both laughed at that.

"Sure. But you're not off the hook, you know."

I knew. I answered her as we drank Pepsi, me sitting on Courtney's bed, Janie on the chair in the hall, leaning forward now, elbows on her knees, concentrating on me.

There was no way to ease into this. "There is some physical evidence suggesting that Courtney's death *may* not have been an accident. It is not definitive or—"

"Or it wouldn't be you, it would be the cops, huh?" She hummed the theme from *Dragnet*. I thought—probably for the three billionth time—how Americans watched too damn much TV.

"What is it? The evidence?" she demanded.

Why wasn't she more shocked, surprised, stunned? I wondered. "I am not at liberty to disclose that," I said stiffly, formally. It was a TV answer but, since Janie had been raised on TV, she accepted it. Convenient in the small picture, worrisome in the large.

"So if the accident wasn't the reason, there's got to be another one?"

"Yes." We were out in the open now.

"Look, you're . . . you're talking about murder, aren't you?"

"About that possibility, yes."

"No. It's impossible. I don't care what you say. Nobody could have wanted to kill her. *Nobody.*"

She crunched down on the ice cubes that were all that was left of her drink. There were gold crowns in this kid's future, no kidding. Janie swept off her chair and down the hall.

I started through the desk: notebooks for college classes, term papers and final exams; supplies of varying kinds—paper, pencils, paper clips, and the like; one drawer with personal records, canceled checks, and income-tax files.

I took my time. Everything was in order. No surprises. I set aside several term papers, the income-tax records, and canceled checks and statements. Not because there was anything there, but because I was desperate, because I was clutching at straws. Then I pulled open the bottom bureau drawer again. Inside was a large manila envelope stuffed with letters and photos. I added that to my pile, pushed aside the kitchen chair in the hall, and walked toward the front of the house, my arms full.

"Janie, I'm borrowing some stuff. I'll bring it back."

"Okay." She walked in from the patio, her face cold and closed up. "See ya." Icy.

Murder does that.

Fourteen

The Cleavage
and the Bulge

It was looking like an evening of paperwork. I headed back to my office trying to remember if I'd left a window open. I didn't think so, which meant, I thought glumly, that my office could be hot enough to bake cookies in. I unlocked the door, shoved it open with my foot. Not as bad as I thought. I dumped my pile on the desk and opened the windows, sighed as a breeze hit me.

"Hey, Kat!"

Uh-oh. Surprise. I turned quickly. "Hi, kid. What's up?" I'd been worried about her since the night we'd found Courtney's body, but of course with a teenager it wouldn't do to say that.

"I'm not really a kid, Kat." Lindy straightened her shoulders and tossed her hair back. "I'm more of a grown-up. Well, a young grown-up." The way she threw her head and shoulders back made her breasts stand out. She was right, she wasn't a kid anymore.

"Hi, young grown-up. What's happening?"

"I'm going shopping. For a prom dress."

"Who are you going to the prom with?"

"With whom am I going?" she asked primly, mimicking me with a straight face.

Teenagers. Yuck. "With whom are you going?"

"Jeff."

"Ah." At least I'd heard of Jeff, though I hadn't yet met him.

"He asked me last week. I was afraid that— I thought

maybe—'' She stammered to a stop and tried to look cool. Pretty much failed. "Can I have something to drink, Kat?"

"Sure. Help yourself." I didn't even correct her and say "May I," I just hugged her as she passed me on the way to the minifridge. "Honey, that's great. I'm so glad." I laughed in pleasure at the smile on her face, at the way she glanced at me shyly through long lashes. I remembered clearly the day Lindy had first walked into my office two years ago, a fifteen-year-old young/old, hard/hurting, impudent streetwise hooker. Now she was a B—sometimes even an A—student at McClatchy High, and Alma, my grandmother, was her permanent legal guardian.

"Can I have a candy bar too, Kat?"

I glanced at the clock in an automatic response—six forty-five. "Have you eaten? No? Better not. It'll ruin your appetite for dinner."

I caught myself then, caught Lindy's eye and we started laughing. Lindy could consume a medium-sized brontosaurus and still have room for dessert.

She popped open a 7UP, grabbed the largest chocolate bar—a Hershey's with almonds that would feed a family of boat people for a week and a half—and plopped down in one of the visitor's chairs, one leg slung over a chair arm. She took a long slug of soda, put the can down, shifted her weight, and pulled a paperback out of the hip pocket of her jeans, tossed it on my desk.

It was the cleavage that caught your eyes first, the cleavage and the heaving bosom. Then the flashing eyes, the tossing hair, the scanty clothing. That was the female. The male bulged everywhere: pecs, quads, biceps, and, of course, crotch. We were in pheromone country, no question. *Passion's Sweet Revenge,* the title screamed at us in lurid pink.

"My English teacher, Mrs. Miller, won't let me do a book report on this."

"Gee," I said, eyes wide and innocent, "I wonder why?"

That started us laughing again, Lindy choking and hacking over her drink and me with tears in my eyes. It seemed like I hadn't laughed for a long time, too long. Or cried. Some of the tears would be for Courtney; some for Lindy, who is a great kid and could, I know, be dead if she were still on the streets; some for the dead girls in Vegas and . . . Mentally I shook myself.

"Is the book as good as the cover?"

Lindy snorted. "Well, it's not big on plot or characterization or—" She shrugged. "Or anything. Even the sex scenes are pretty bad. What should I read, Kat?"

"Trollope. I read in the paper the other day that every educated person should read Trollope. So there you go. Easy."

"Have you read Trollope?"

"Next on my list, I swear."

She giggled. "*Seriously,* Kat."

"What do you like to read?"

"Science fiction."

"*Handmaid's Tale.*"

"Seriously?"

"Seriously."

"Hi, guys."

Charity waltzed in, hugged Lindy, waved at me, then frowned as her eyes were caught by the lurid and lustful debauchery on my desk: *The Cleavage and the Bulge* in raging pink, cool green, and blazing blue. Charity is a nationally syndicated advice columnist, my best friend, and Lindy's "aunt." She is not known for biting her tongue and keeping her opinions to herself.

"*Really,* Katy. I can't imagine why *you're* reading this disgusting kind of trash, but whatever the reason—if you can call it reason —Lindy *certainly* shouldn't be exposed to it."

Lindy and I lost it again. Charity helped herself to Lindy's chocolate bar and first frowned, then stared at us. "Would somebody care to tell me what is going on?" She spoke with a somber, humorless dignity that made us laugh even harder.

"Help. Help. It's the Thought Police." Lindy was gasping for air.

"The Moral Minority." I collapsed on my desk.

Charity tapped her toe slowly and with restraint to indicate the limits of her patience. I started to get the hiccups from laughing so hard.

"It's my book," Lindy said at last. "I have to do a book report and—"

I hicced. That set us off again.

Charity wrinkled her nose in disapproval, swooped down on the book, swept it up and dumped it in the trash can. "*Really,* you two." She popped a piece of chocolate into her mouth and chewed. "Are we ready?"

"We?" I went on ALERT. "Ready for what?" I know Lindy and Charity well, remember.

"To go shopping for Lindy's prom dress."

"No," I said with utter conviction and to no one's surprise. Shopping is one of my least favorite activities. I shop only in dire need or under duress, and neither state currently applied.

Lindy bounced up. "Yes!"

I started humming "I Could Have Danced All Night," and Charity broke off another piece of chocolate.

"Lindy," I asked, "if your car had a flat on the freeway at night—"

"What car?" she asked eagerly. "Am I getting a car?"

"Hypothetical car," I elaborated patiently. "What would you do?"

"Is this a quiz, Kat?"

"No," I said.

"Yes," said Charity at the same time.

Lindy looked at me, then at Charity. "I'd lock the car and wait for help. For a *cop,*" she added quickly. Charity beamed at her.

"No, *really.*" My voice sounded as dubious as I felt.

"Really," she said firmly. "Anyway, I don't know how to change a tire and it's dangerous to walk on the freeway. The safest thing is to stay in your car and wait for the police or a tow truck. That's what they taught us in driver's ed." Her voice had a singsong teacher quality to it.

Charity beamed some more, patted Lindy's shoulder, then broke off another large hunk of chocolate. She's a chocoholic beyond help.

"Do I get a car now?" Lindy sounded hopeful but not overly optimistic.

"No, you get a prom dress." I winked. Charity finished her chocolate and jingled her keys. Lindy danced in place. I saw them to the door with hugs and waves and they started down the hall giggling and amping themselves up for shopping.

"Lindy?" I called.

"Hmmmm?" She swung around.

"Suppose you were brought up in a very religious family but—as a young adult—you couldn't go along with the teachings and beliefs of your Church and family, what would you do?"

"Is this a quiz?"

"No," I said.

"Yes." That was Charity.

Lindy studied my face for a moment. "It's a case, isn't it, Kat?"

"Yes."

"The one the other night?"

I said nothing.

"How old am I?"

"Twenty or twenty-one."

"Do they—my family—try to force me?"

"Probably not force, not physically, but they never stop, never let up on it."

"Mental abuse," Lindy said firmly. I didn't comment. We both knew that Lindy could define mental, psychological, and physical abuse from personal experience. "If I could get a job and move away from home, I'd leave. I'd leave as soon as I could."

"Even if it meant quitting school?"

She thought about it. "Yes. Because you can't work or live right with people at you like that. And you can work and still go to school."

I nodded. "Thanks."

"Did she?"

"Yes."

"Kat, is everything going to be okay?"

"To*day*, you guys," Charity said impatiently. *"Today."* Her foot tapped. Her keys jingled. "Lindy, we only have a couple of hours before the mall closes."

Lindy looked at me, knew the answer from my hesitation. I gave her a quick wave. "Good luck, honey. Find the best prom dress in the world!"

She nodded, memories and thankfulness in her eyes. The phone rang as they walked down the hall. My heart jumped. Probably not business at this hour. Hank, I hoped, and crossed my fingers like a little kid.

A child's voice politely asked to speak to Amy. I told Amy's friend she had the wrong number.

"Amy moved?"

"You dialed wrong. Ask your mommy for help."

"Okay," she agreed happily.

I thought about all the children whose mommies didn't/ wouldn't/couldn't help. Then I called Hank. While I waited for him to answer I pulled *The Cleavage and the Bulge* out of the waste-basket. It was full of pirates and kidnappers, lords and ladies and maids, desecraters and despoilers and put-her-on-a-pedestalers. There were rape and lust scenes to the point of boredom but there didn't seem to be any love. And no one in its pages seemed to have a clue about life and the way things really work.

Hank wasn't home. I knew this after six rings, never mind the double-digit numbers I was into now. I hung up the phone and tossed the book back into the trash.

I was not in a good mood.

I turned reluctantly to the manila folder on my desk. I'd been ignoring it, shoving it around, piling stuff on top of it all day. A slim, innocent folder—full of death and destruction. The CHP report on Courtney's accident and the autopsy report. I opened the folder with serious reluctance and made myself read. *State of California/Traffic Collision Report.* It was a standard form with lines and boxes, some of which had been filled in and all of which reduced a human life and death to lines and *X*'s and scientific and technical terminology. No emotion. No blood.

I read:

CITY: unincorporated
COUNTY: Sacramento
NUMBER INJURED: 0
NUMBER KILLED: 1
HIT AND RUN MISDEMEANOR:
HIT AND RUN FELONY: X
Courtney Dillard
Wh Fem/brn hair/brn eyes/ht 5′5″/wght 123/DOB 5-12-72
DATE/DAY OF WEEK/TIME
Officers R. Torres, J. Rampart
TOW AWAY: Dwight's Towing

I moved on to the second page. More lines and boxes:

VEHICLE CODE SECTION VIOLATED: 20001 (a) . . .
WEATHER/LIGHTING/ROADWAY CONDITIONS . . .
Third page: WITNESSES/PASSENGERS. Hank and I were listed there.

A typewritten report followed. I skipped over the weather, lighting, roadway conditions etc., hesitated, then made myself read the excerpts taken from the coroner's report:

Ms. Dillard received fatal injuries as a result of this collision. She was pronounced dead at the scene by CHP officers.

That wasn't so bad, not too graphic.

Then it got worse, much worse:

External

1. Deep lacerations on the left and right cheek and throat area with the entire cranial vault crushed and open and the brain absent with brain tissue present on the body.

2. Multiple abrasions of . . .

I started skipping and skimming.

3. A deep laceration . . . 4. A large laceration . . . 5. Fractures . . . 6. More fractures . . . 7. Left foot severed and . . .

I closed my eyes and tried to remember the laughing, happy, alive young woman of the pictures Medora had given me. It was difficult. I opened my eyes, looked again at the report.

Internal

1. Lacerations of the heart nearly transecting it between the left atrium and left ventricle.

Courtney's heart had nearly been cut in two. I stopped there, closed the file. It helped to know that Courtney was dead before this happened. Helped, but not that much. It was a long time—I don't know how long, I lost track—before I opened the report again.

Conclusions and Recommendations: Suitable follow up to attempt to locate the hit-and-run vehicle.

Nothing in the CHP report suggested murder.

A heart had almost been cut in two.

What was suitable?

Quickly I leafed through the coroner's report. Most of it was medical terminology largely unintelligible to me. Death by physical trauma. Many, maybe most, injuries inflicted after death. Nothing in the coroner's report suggested murder.

I flipped back through the collision report to check on the towing company. Then I buried the folder on my desk again.

I felt weighted down by the death. The reports, neat black lines and words on white paper, were clean, clear, and cold, and nothing like the spilled life on the freeway. I saw again the glitter of a rhinestone buckle on a silver pump winking at me in the flash of oncoming headlights.

I was tired and drained. It was long past dinnertime but I had no desire to eat. I grabbed a cold diet Dr Pepper. *Caffeine.* And broke off a chunk of the chocolate bar Lindy and Charity had been working on. *Sugar rush.*

I pulled the packets of material I'd gathered in my search of Courtney's room across the desk toward me and stared at them, hoping insight and inspiration would kick in. Or caffeine and sugar. Something. Anything.

Fifteen

Rhinestone
Warning

Thirty minutes later I had a bunch of neat piles: canceled checks
and statements; copies of Courtney's tax records for the year—
filed early—I hoped she'd gotten her return and spent it on
something fun. School papers, notes, and records. That, on a
cursory glance, was it. Humdrum and ho-hum. On a closer in-
spection it would probably be the same. Humdrum and ho-hum.
There was a pile of personal letters, a bunch of photographs, a
few trinkets and mementos.

I was still waiting for insight and inspiration.

I started with the letters.

More ho-hum and humdrum. I saved the best for last and read
it slowly.

Dear Daisy,

I am writing one more time. Though you have left me, I
must try to save your soul. How can you question this in me?
How can you question your father, the bishop, the teachings
of the Church? We are here to help you and direct you.
There is no greater glory for a woman than wife and
motherhood. It is fulfillment for a woman. Education is not
necessary, is not God's way for a woman. Be careful that
Satan has not deceived you and led you toward your
destruction. You will lose not only your own goodness but

your family and all you hold dear. As you have lost me. Remember the Blood of Atonement.

Yours in Love and Faith,
Robert

I read the letter through several times. Robert didn't know a thing about paragraphing but his meaning was abundantly clear. I was not surprised that Daisy would leave him. His views of marriage, of life, and of education sounded very different from hers.

He started with the statement that Daisy had left him, ended with her having lost him. Interesting. The blood of atonement. That again. I tried to remember, thought it was a ritual widely practiced by early Mormons, reportedly still practiced by splinter groups and factions. If a Mormon sinned, he or she could be saved/redeemed only with bloodshed. His, of course. Or hers. The sinner was—in theory—slashed and disemboweled with the entrails strewn about. In practice the atonement was more widely made by merely (merely!) slashing the throat from ear to ear. In largely Mormon Utah a condemned person still has the option of death by firing squad so that blood atonement will be realized. Nice stuff, this.

Unbidden, unwanted pictures of Courtney's body came to mind: spilled blood, the heart nearly cut in two. Atonement? Surely that was far-fetched?

I looked at the date on the letter: February. Over three years ago. In the time we'd had, Medora hadn't spoken of Robert. He seemed memorable, to say the least. But, perhaps, ancient history. I made a note to look him up as soon as possible. How far would self-righteousness take a man? Murder? *Remember The Blood of Atonement.* Threats, at least.

I took a deep breath. There were two more letters from Robert. Letters from Medora, a mother's letters, full of chattiness, family affairs, and love. Filled, too, with guilt and reproach, reminder and reprimand. *I miss you every day. Did I do wrong that you would leave us and the Church? This makes your father so sad. Please come home to us.* There were birthday and Christmas cards, a Valentine's Day card from Chad Wharton—sentimental, almost mushy, not flippant or sexy.

There was a theater program, a concert program, the announcement of a gallery showing. Several notes from girlfriends that were brief and unexciting, sweet but uninteresting. Also three small cards of the kind that come on professional flower arrangements. All bore messages from Chad, first warm, then affectionate, then loving. Half-a-dozen matchbooks and souvenir napkins from restaurants in Sausalito, San Francisco, Mendocino, and Tahoe, as well as Sacramento.

The cards, letters, and mementos were in no way remarkable except in their indication that there were many people in Daisy/Courtney's life who had cared for her, even loved her deeply.

The photographs were of Daisy and her family, of Chad, of Chad and Courtney, and a few of Courtney and girlfriends in wide smiles and scanty swimsuits somewhere on the river.

The canceled checks and statements confirmed what I had already surmised. The monthly checking activity was minimal: a rent check; a second check to Janie for what I assumed was Courtney's half of utilities and shared expenses; three or four checks made out to the neighborhood supermarket in amounts just large enough to provide her with groceries and incidental cash; an occasional check to a clothing or other retail establishment. Her tax records confirmed this simple lifestyle: $13,492.36. I hadn't realized receptionists made so little.

The school papers and notes substantiated Stumford's observations that Courtney was an intelligent young woman who was just beginning to wake up, to open her mind and ask questions. The most interesting was a paper she'd written on women and witchcraft in the Middle Ages. It was scholarly in a pedestrian and pedantic way with an occasional spark of horror, dismay, or outrage. "*Nine million* women were burned alive at the stake as witches by the *churchmen* of their time." The emphasis was hers.

I sighed and pushed the papers aside. I knew a great deal more about both Courtney and Daisy than I had before, but if there was an ominous pattern in all this, I didn't see it. I didn't see murder.

The pounding at the front door startled me. The outside door to our building is locked around five unless someone has a late appointment. I had locked up at seven after Lindy and Charity had left. Generally I won't answer the door unless I'm expecting someone. Tonight I did. Whoever it was, it was better than what I was contemplating. Blood atonement. Spilled life. The hollering started. I recognized the voice.

I opened the door to a triumphant Lindy and a gratified Charity. Lindy was jumping up and down, waving boxes, swinging a garment bag, and whooping. Charity was more subdued, but smiling broadly.

"Wait'll you see, Kat! It's *gorjus!*" Lindy raced back to my office. We followed more sedately, arrived as she whipped out her dress and held up a slinky *way*-above-the-knee black number with spaghetti straps, off-the-shoulder sleeve stuff, black sequins everywhere, décolletage, and a plunging back.

I gasped.

"Cool, huh?" Lindy strutted around with the dress clutched to her. It wasn't as daring as the one featured on the front of *The Cleavage and the Bulge,* but it came close.

"It's what they're all wearing, Katy," Charity said, correctly interpreting my gasp.

I felt like a mom looking at her little girl growing up. I know it's not realistic to expect Lindy to wear pink and white, ruffles and bows, but *still*—Jeez.

"And—" Lindy triumphantly yanked open a shoe box and pulled out black patent-leather high-heeled pumps with rhinestone clips. For a moment my heart stopped. I couldn't help it.

"Kat?" Lindy's voice was worried. "You don't like it?" My opinion means a lot to her, I know.

I smiled reassuringly. "I do, Lindy. It's gorgeous and you are too." I gave her a little hug. "You're going to knock Jeff's socks off."

"Yeah!" she agreed with a quick, shy smile. "I am." She giggled.

I wanted to grab Lindy's youth, to stop time and hold on. But I couldn't; I didn't even try. I understood more about Medora's feelings for her daughter.

"Kat, have you eaten?" Charity, not Lindy. Lindy was packing up her sexy, skimpy dress and sparkly shoes. I shook my head. "Oh good. We called ahead and ordered a pizza at Zelda's. Come with us?"

"Lindy, don't wear the rhinestone clips on your shoes." I blurted it out.

"Why? They're not right? You don't like them?" Her voice was anxious again.

"They're perfect and I like them." My eyes filled with tears.

"It's a . . . a superstition, I guess. Please." There's detached professional poise for you.

Lindy gazed at me for a long moment. Charity said nothing. I willed my tears to evaporate but they didn't. Lindy took the top off the shoe box and pulled off the clips. "Here. You keep them for me, okay?" She pressed them into my hand.

"Lindy . . ." I wanted to explain but I couldn't.

She flashed a radiant smile at me. "It doesn't matter, Kat. It doesn't." Then she pressed her cheek against mine and whispered something that might have been "I love you." "Charity's going to let me borrow her diamond earrings and necklace," she added proudly. "How about that!"

How about that, indeed. Through my tears I smiled at them both. My family. And family is everything. Lindy punched me in the arm. Ouch. I used to get big hugs and kisses. Now it's punches, thumps, and friendly insults. Adolescence. Fun, huh?

"What kind of pizza?" I asked as I turned on the phone machine, turned off the lights. Zelda's is a Sacramento institution with great pizza and comparable ambience. Knowledgeable hungry patrons, like Charity, phone in ahead; on arrival, your pizza and table are waiting. I never do, but, then, I'm an ex-bartender, and I like to sit at the bar, order my pizza, and have a drink. Good bar, too.

"Are you kidding? One with everything!"

"Anchovies?" I queried worriedly.

"C'*mon,* Kat. Like we don't *know* you." Lindy punched me in the shoulder again and I winced. "Of *course* not."

Zelda's was packed but our table was waiting and our pizza arrived within minutes. I ate pizza and contentedly listened to Charity and Lindy yak about makeup, perfume, and prom-dress accessories.

"No perfume," Lindy declared. "It's gaggy."

"Not *expensive* perfume," Charity stated firmly.

"I don't have any expensive perfume," Lindy objected.

"I do. We'll try it beforehand, okay? Just a little, just try it?"

"Okay." Lindy used her fork to maneuver a massive slice of pizza onto her plate. Charity poured white wine from the bottle we had ordered and Lindy waved frantically at the harried waitress and could she pleeeze, pleeeze, pleeeze have another Coke?

"Lindy, if a boy you were going with asked you to do something for him out of love, would you do it?"

"Is this a quiz, Kat?" Lindy stopped eating and looked at me suspiciously.

"No."

"What kind of thing? Big thing or little thing? I mean, if he asked me to pick him up a cheeseburger and a shake, well, sure."

"If he asked you to believe what he believed. Maybe he would even threaten to break up if you didn't."

Lindy stared at her pizza carefully, then rearranged a slice of pepperoni. The waitress bumped my chair as she edged past with a heavy tray, dropping off Lindy's Coke as she went.

Lindy looked at me with big serious eyes. "No way, Kat. You're the one who taught me that people who love you don't ask you to do things that hurt you. Or are bad for you or wrong for you. People who love you respect who you are and what you want to do. And they let you decide what's best for you, once you're mature enough."

Charity started clapping.

"It *was* a quiz," Lindy said, and grinned. "I passed, huh? Do I get a prize? I want a car."

It wasn't a quiz but, yes, she had passed. I remembered the tears and anger, the times Lindy had lashed out at all of us who loved her, had tried and tested and slowly built a new sense of herself to replace the one that a grossly negligent mother and a sexually abusive stepfather had stolen from her.

"That means I get dessert, huh?"

"You *always* have dessert," I pointed out reasonably.

"True. Two?"

"As many as you can eat." I shoved a pizza crust around on my plate. "Do many girls get pressured by their boyfriends?"

"Sex?"

"Not necessarily. To do things the guy's way."

Lindy wrinkled her nose. "I dunno. Guys with anything together wouldn't do that, they'd just bring it up to talk about. Course," she reflected, "then again, how many guys have it *that* together?"

"And girls?" Lindy's the only teenager I know, my hot line to The Teen Scene.

"Depends."

"On?"

"If a girl has a good sense of herself and what she's doing, she's going to tell him to lighten up or get lost. Right?"

I nodded. "Right."

"And sometimes you have to say that to your family too, right?"

"Right," I agreed. "Except for me, of course." We laughed.

Lindy frowned over the menu. "You know, Charity, the desserts here are *really* not that great—sort of blah."

The dessert connoisseurs looked at each other and nodded in instant consensus. "Somewhere else," Charity said.

"Ice cream?" Lindy asked. "Yum. Hot fudge? Yum."

They dropped me off at my office on the way to a million calories. Ten-thirty. On an impulse I called Hank. No answer. It makes me crazy that he won't get an answering machine. He has a pager for work but I wasn't in range.

I headed home and fed Ranger, my dog, and Kitten, who has outgrown his name and become a huge, clumsy adolescent cat with an endearing personality despite the devilish black ring around one eye and the lurch in his gait. I poured a half glass of wine and we three sat out in the cool darkness and stars of the patio. Then we came inside and I read a little. The last thing I did before going to bed was call Hank again. One-thirty. No answer?

That night I dreamed of witches wearing rhinestones. I saw Hank close to me and I called out and waved but he couldn't see or hear me.

Great dream.

Tuesday, May 10

Sacramento

Sixteen

Junkyard Jerk

Kitten jumped on the bed, skidded off the pillow, and landed on my face. This is typical of him. It is also why I was awake, if not exactly alert, at six-thirty A.M. Kitten draped himself across my chest and started kneading my hair into the pillow and purring. Then he yawned, showing me a perfect pink tongue, and stuck a paw on my chin. I rolled out of bed, Ranger and Kitten in excited attendance. Like it's special. Like we don't do this every morning.

The shower started to wake me up. Then the juice and coffee and the cool morning air that smacked me in the face with spring. Birds sang and glad-handed it up all around us. I took my coffee outside to the patio, tripping over Kitten who managed to squeeze himself between my legs as I walked. That and sticking his head under the cat biscuits as I pour them into his bowl are his favorite tricks. We're not talking cat rocket-scientist material here.

I read the morning paper and drank coffee. The Las Vegas Strip Stalker had made the front page. His killing spree was national news now. In a back section of the paper I saw several ads for "Vegas Getaways!" The prices were ridiculously low. Come-on prices. Murder is not good for the tourist business.

At seven-thirty it was too early to call Courtney's friends but not too early to check out Dwight's Towing. Not too early to call

Hank again, either. No answer. I was starting to worry big-time. What was Hank stalking: a killer or a stripper?

I was on the road and headed for Dwight's Towing *(You Blow It, We Tow It!* the yellow page ad informed me cheerfully) in Citrus Heights a little after eight. Even with the traffic it was an easy fifteen minutes.

The address was on Auburn Boulevard somewhere on the scenic *(sic)* stretch between Sylvan Corners and I-80. I drove west on Old Auburn, made a right, and picked up Auburn Boulevard. The first stretch isn't too bad. There's a school, a well-tended cemetery with a lot of plastic flowers, and an old-fashioned drive-in in a startling shade of turquoise. It's pretty much downhill from there.

A handful of small businesses are tucked between biker bars, convenience stores, and gas stations. A dazed, dispirited, and disoriented man in yesterday's clothes sat on the sidewalk in front of a sleazy bar called the Hideaway. The bar looked better than he did, and that was saying something.

I passed a doughnut shop (open) and a Thai take-out (closed). Then, in rapid succession, a tire store, pizza place, auto parts, and tattoo parlor. Huh? Tattoo parlor? I did a double take on that one, sure that it was a new addition. That Cher, she's been a bad influence. Citrus Heights is a happening place, for sure.

No Macy's or Nordstrom's or I. Magnin's hereabouts, but we've got a Kmart and a Thrifty drugstore down by the freeway. And before that there's the Satin Lady, a topless bar whose parking lot starts to fill up around noon with guys who presumably don't have a life, an imagination, or a clue, but do have time and money to throw away. Not to mention a tanning salon, a Radio Shack, and a rental-car agency. You get the picture.

Dwight's was closer to the freeway than to Sylvan Corners. I pulled into the parking area out front—space for eight, seven now—and looked around before I got out of the car. The front of the yard took up half a real short block on Auburn Boulevard but extended out back quite a ways—a lot of wrecked or semiwrecked cars' worth—down the block in the other direction.

Left to right: On the corner was the beginning of the storage lot, which stretched out back, then an office, a driveway going to the back with a cast-iron gate that now stood open, then a garage. The lot was surrounded with fencing inhospitably topped with barbed wire in two versions, stretched and rolled. The buildings were old stucco and dirty glass with heavy wire cages covering them. I slung my bag on my shoulder and walked down the drive past the gates and looked around.

No one. Out of the corner of my eye I thought I saw a large dog. Or a small gorilla. Something that belonged either in a junkyard or on a PBS special. I don't hang out a lot in storage yards or auto-dismantling shops but I could tell going in that this was a kissing cousin to every one of them.

Dumpsters. Fifty-five-gallon drums, one of which (EPA: please take note) leaked black sludge at a slow but steady rate, a pile of beat-up wooden pallets, and a forklift whose paint job was mere memory. That, not counting cars, took care of the scenic overview. Most of the vehicles were in one of two states—totaled or wrecked. A few looked like stored or impounded cars.

Neat rows of wrecked cars stretched back along the fence, the far row headed by a forlorn VW bug with a yellow body, white hood, blue front fenders, and a smashed-up rear. It was almost a metaphor. I tried not to think about it.

I worked my way back, past cars that were once someone's pride and joy—*Look, Ma, there she is!*—now without wheels and up on blocks, past cars in various stages of dismantling, past a stack of fenders, bumpers, and miscellaneous auto parts—some looking like new but most rusted or busted out. Nimble as a ballerina, I threaded my way through the metal chaos and stepped over hubcaps full of rusted-out lug nuts.

Without warning a large, mean-looking dog (not a gorilla—I was wrong) emerged from behind the shell of a pickup (no wheels, no hood, no engine), stared at me, then soundlessly lifted a lip exposing yellowed teeth. Yup, this place had everything.

I backed up a little. You're not supposed to, I know, but I couldn't help it. The expression "mean as a junkyard dog" doesn't just come out of nowhere. Then I struggled to look nonchalant as I backed up and hollered *Hullo!!* at the top of my lungs. I tried to catch sight of a greasy dismantler or yard operator. It was only eight in the morning but there had to be one, and his clothes would be dirty, his hands and face greasy, and he'd have a three-day growth (nothing like Don Johnson). Hey, right now I wasn't picky.

The dog lifted his lip again. Uh-oh. I took a deep breath and got ready to holler again.

"Yeah," a disinterested voice said behind me.

Oh, and a surly, snarly, unfriendly attitude—I forgot that part. Silly me.

"You lookin' for somethin'?"

He had on greasy overalls, a T-shirt that couldn't remember when it had last known white, plastic booties covered with new grease over boots probably covered with old. Three-day beard growth, grease, with comb marks, in his hair, grease—no comb marks—on his face.

What did I tell you? Days like this I should forget investigation and head for Reno, play blackjack.

"You Dwight?" I couldn't resist.

"Naw. Ain't no Dwight. I'm Harry. What you want?"

"I'm looking for a white Ford Escort, eighty-nine, a CHP storage. I've got authorization from the family to look it over." I pulled out an authorization that I had typed and signed in Medora's name with her verbal phone okay.

Harry gave it a distant once over, your basic I-could-give-a-shit look, didn't read it. Shoot, didn't even unfold it. Maybe he couldn't read.

"Lemme get the keys. What's'a plate?"

I gave him the license-plate number and then Junkyard and I just stood around taking in the scenery and ambience until Harry got back. A mangy one-eyed bobtail cat drifted by, hissed at me, hissed at the dog. We both pretended we didn't notice and weren't scared. It didn't fool the cat, who was one tough cookie. After the cat left, Junkyard snarled at me to show me who was boss. Right.

"Here you go." Harry flipped me the keys from ten feet away, tossing them short so I had to step over yet another rusting hub-cap and lean into the catch. Harry's face told me he was disappointed I caught it. The day a mechanic, auto dismantler, or tow-truck driver treats a woman with courtesy and respect is the day I drop dead in shock. No kidding.

"Know where it is?"

Harry shrugged. Read: *I know, but I ain't talking.*

I looked around, picked out the most accessible area, figuring the most recently towed cars were probably there, picked up on a couple of possibles, and ambled on over through the grease undergrowth. Two steps out I "accidentally" punted a hubcap filled with lug nuts up against a rusted-out fender. The noise exploded like gunshots in the early-morning quiet. Harry and Junkyard jumped as though I'd hit a vital organ. I wish.

"Sorry," I murmured. Read: *Two can play this game.*

The mangy cat smiled at me, I swear.

I stared at Courtney's car for a while before I approached it. Something seemed wrong, but I couldn't figure it. Then I got it —nothing. Correction: It was me, it was expectation. It didn't seem right that, except for its left rear tire, the car was fine, was perfect. Somewhere inside me I had expected the car to be destroyed. Like Courtney.

The windows were closed and the car was locked. I walked around it. Nothing that I could see was out of the ordinary. I unlocked the driver's-side door and climbed in. The seat was pushed all the way back, too far for someone of my height, and Courtney was shorter than I.

I went through the inside and the glove compartment and found the expected: maps, a flashlight, a can of instant tire inflator—not much help there in a blowout—a small pink plastic container with spare tampons, a notebook with a ballpoint pen clipped to it, scraps of paper with directions to people's houses (which I pocketed), a couple of spare keys, and a bottle opener. Nothing in the ashtray but gum wrappers. The rearview mirror was cocked at a crazy angle. No telling when that had happened.

I crawled into the backseat. A small teddy bear lay facedown on the floor in back, shoved most of the way under the driver's seat. I picked it up and sat it down, looked at its solemn little face.

Something winked at me. Not the teddy bear. It looked like a scrap of foil from a gum wrapper at the edge of the floor mat. It looked like that, but it wasn't. When I pulled up the rug, I saw a thick gold band with a diamond the size of a pea. It didn't take a crackerjack investigator to figure this was an engagement ring.

I dropped it into my purse. Harry would be sick if he knew he'd missed this. I crawled through the rest of the car but found nothing. The inside was clean, as though it had been vacuumed recently. I popped the trunk. The jack and tools had been thrown in haphazardly. Otherwise, nothing.

Outside? Just white metal. Nothing remarkable except for the left rear tire, the blowout, which is where it had all started. I kicked away a metal scrap on the dirt and squatted down. The junkyard cat—who seemed to have revised his opinion of me—ambled up, peered at me through his one good eye, and sat down to wash his face. *Good luck, buddy,* I thought. It was looking to be a long job, what with the grease and all.

Okay. *Raise your right hand. Do you swear to tell . . .* I ran my hand over the tire. *Are you an expert on tires, Ms. Colorado?* It was worn, but—I fished a penny out of my purse and stuck it in each tire tread—it had a safe, reasonable quarter inch, easy. *What, exactly, is your experience with tire blowouts?* I rocked back on my heels. Just TV, your Honor, although I would like to emphasize that I do know the difference between TV and real life.

Your exact expertise, Ms. Colorado? Ah. Zip. Nada. None. The cat strolled out by my feet and made a noise deep in his throat, lifting his mangy head into the sunshine. I touched the fibers of the steel-belt radial in front of me. *Are you familiar with different sorts of tire damage, Ms. Colorado?* Do pigs have wings? There were fibers going in both directions. I thought *(Thought, Ms. Colorado, or* imagined?) that there were more going in, as though the cut had been made from the outside and then an attempt made to pull fibers outward to be consistent with a blowout. I ran my hand over the tire again. Dust. Dirt. A smear of grease. No rim cuts that I could discern, and I thought *(Thought, Ms. Colorado, not* knew?) they would be very discernible.

I took photographs of the car from every angle. And of the tires, each with a scrap of paper next to it identifying position. LF, RF, RR, LR. I took a whole roll of close-up shots of LR. And finally one of the teddy bear in the backseat with the ring in his lap and shots of the teddy bear and the ring where I had first found them.

You are a photographic expert as well, Ms. Colorado? Well, heck yes. I am hardly ever without my trusty Brownie, Your Honor.

All right, so maybe I'm not the perfect expert witness.

The cat rolled over on his back, exposing his tummy so I could scratch it. I started to, then took a closer look and reconsidered. The matts and grease blobs were the first things I noted. Then there were cuts and scrapes, only slightly festering, and under-the-fur-motion. I shuddered. But he was alive. He was purring. Courtney wasn't. The cat followed at a dignified distance as I walked toward Harry who was, if possible, greasier and dirtier now than he had been a half hour ago.

"Hey," I called. He turned and lifted a lip just like the dog. I wondered who was the teacher, who the pupil. "Thanks." I tossed him the keys. Short toss. He reached out. Missed.

I allowed myself a smile.

The cat did too.

Back at the office I called the Highway Patrol and asked for either Officer R. Torres or J. Rampart, the officers whose names were on the CHP report. Torres and Rampart were on patrol or otherwise unavailable, I was told. Could someone else help me? I was asked. I requested the sergeant on duty and was put on hold.

"Sergeant Haverson," a deep male voice said after four and a half mind-numbing minutes of Muzak. "May I help you?"

I identified myself. I referred to the CHP report by number. I carefully explained the situation and indicated my concern about the possibility of homicide. Then I waited in a beat or two of heavy silence.

"I am not familiar with the accident in question," Haverson said. "Let me review that and get back to you. May I have a number where you can be reached?"

I gave it to him. We disconnected and I called Medora. Maybe I was a little curt, but there you go, I'd been running with some tough customers at the junkyard. And talking to cops. Both of these are things that can make you edgy.

"You didn't tell me about Robert." I heard the accusation in my voice and tried to stomp down on it. It wasn't her fault we were interrupted. "Will you tell me now, please?"

"Oh dear," Medora fussed. "I didn't, did I? But it just seemed so long ago. It's not as though I forgot but—"

"Will you tell me now, please?"

She skidded to a verbal halt and took a breath. "They were high-school sweethearts and then, after high school, Daisy decided she didn't want to see him anymore. She never told me why. I *asked,*" she added plaintively. "Daisy told her sister that she thought Bob was very full of himself. What ever *that* means—she never told me. Anyway, Bob left for his mission shortly after that, so of course we didn't see him for two years." Young Mormon men frequently leave home for a year or two on a mission. Their goal is to educate and make as many converts as possible.

"Bob didn't come home at all?"

"I don't think so. I don't remember it. Missionaries rarely do. No, wait, he did come back when his father became ill and he stayed for the funeral after his death. I remember now."

"Did Daisy and Bob— Is it Bob or Robert?"

"It was always Bob until he came back from his mission. Then he changed it."

"Did they see each other when he came home?"

"Well, yes, I'm sure they did, but at the stake house or at his father's funeral. Not dating or anything. He was a *missionary.*"

"Missionaries don't date?"

"Oh, my, no! For that period they are God's ministers and committed to God's work only."

"What is a stake house?"

"Our meeting place—like a church."

"Is Robert in town now?"

"Yes. After his mission he returned to go into his father's insurance business."

"May I have his last name, his number if you have it?"

"I can't *imagine* that—"

"Please."

"Corwin. It's Corwin Independent Insurance. I don't have the number but—"

"I need to speak with Courtney's brothers and sisters."

"Oh my," she said softly. "Oh, I have to go." A soft good-bye and she hung up.

I stared at the receiver for a moment in frustration and then I hung up too. The phone rang almost immediately. A voice I recognized as the charming baritone of Sergeant Haverson asked for me. Uh-oh. This was much too fast for anything but a polite brush-off.

"I have had a chance to review the accident in question, ma'am. We do not find anything to indicate homicide. I suggest that you address any concerns you might have"—his tone was politely bland—"to the Sacramento Sheriff's Department. Perhaps they can be of assistance."

Because you won't, I thought. "It was a felony hit-and-run?"

"Yes, ma'am."

"Have you found the other vehicle involved?"

"No, ma'am. We're still looking, of course."

Of course. I thanked Haverson and hung up. Of course? Ha. Dollars to doughnuts here's what happened: The next morning at watch briefing the sergeant on duty briefly covered the hit-and-run and asked officers to be on the lookout for an unspecified vehicle with front end damage. The officers dutifully took notes and stuck their memos in the visors of their cars. At the end of the shift someone cleaned out the patrol cars and threw out the memos.

And maybe a blurb had gone into the newspaper with the time, place, and description of Courtney's car and the incident, asking any witnesses to please call the Highway Patrol with information. Then everyone forgot it.

Everyone but Medora.

And now me.

Seventeen

Arm Wrestling

I called Bill. Call it courtesy. No, that's a lie. Call it Covering My Butt. Call it Just In Case.

"Henley, Homicide," he snarled into the phone. That Bill, such a sweet-talker. Maybe he figured an intimidating voice tone would discourage murder. It worked for me.

"Yo, Bill. Kat Colorado."

"Hey, Kat. What's happening? Every time you call me, it's bad news. It's something I don't want to hear."

"Are you unfair or what? At least half the time I ask you out to lunch or bring you doughnuts."

He grunted, let go with—not a laugh; that would be too expansive—more like a chuckle.

"And you never buy me lunch unless you want something," he said.

Well, rats, there you go. Course, you can fool cops for only so long, then, whammo, they're onto you. So why pretend? "Bill, can I buy you lunch?"

He sighed. "See what I mean?"

"Don't hold yourself back, either," I said generously. "Steak and potatoes. Dessert. The works."

He laughed. "Can't. The wife put me on another friggin' diet."

"Chef salad and low-cal Jell-O?" Quick on my feet, huh?

"I got that sitting on my desk." He sounded glum. "C'mon by the office, Kat. See what you can talk me into."

"I'm there," I said, and hung up.

Henley had left my name downstairs, so after I showed ID, the counter person behind bullet-proof glass shooed me right through the locked metal doors and on upstairs. As I punched a button on the elevator, I reflected glumly that knowing your way around the homicide office in the Sheriff's Department was not, on the whole, an encouraging life sign. I found his office right away, another not so encouraging sign.

"Hey, Kat." Henley almost smiled, for him a warm welcome. "You look good, what's up?" Cop eyes swept over me in appreciation.

I flexed my right arm and bulged a bicep. "Been working out. Wanna arm wrestle?" I leaned forward and growled into his ear. "For money."

I got a laugh. So there.

"*Hot damn*, Bill! I haven't heard you laugh since the spring of aught six."

"Aw, Kat." He looked a little sheepish. "It's not *that* bad."

I socked him affectionately on the shoulder. *See.* That's hanging out with Lindy for you. "It's not, no. How's the little one?"

He beamed. First grandchild. "She's crawling already. Cutest little thing you ever saw and, hell, I'm not even prejudiced." He winked. "What can I do for you, Kat?"

"I've got a long shot."

He tipped his chair back with a loud screech and focused his attention on me. Nothing like a cop to give you full attention. I ran the whole thing past him. He listened without interruption.

"You took it to the CHP. What'd they say?"

"They were real polite and cared less. Suggested—still real polite—that I come to you guys. Probably figured I was full of shit. You?"

"Full of shit?" He shook his head. "No. Course, I know you, they don't. And face it, Kat, a lot of PIs are—" He broke off politely.

"Opportunistic scumballs," I said glumly.

"Yeah. And that's on their good days. But—like I said—I know you, Kat. You say something, I listen. You don't have anything yet.

You get it, though, I'm interested, real interested. You get some of it, enough to move on, I'll move.''

His chair creaked and he snapped his red and blue and green suspenders on a belly that bulged out the buttons of his pale-blue shirt. I looked at this middle-aged, balding (with dandruff! talk about the worst of two worlds), decent cop and smiled. I was glad the wife had him on a diet.

"Thanks, Bill. Rain check, okay?"

"Huh?"

"On that lunch."

"Yeah. That'd be good. Be careful, Kat. Watch your butt and don't play Superwoman."

"Right." I flexed my bicep again. "I'll give you a rain check arm wrestling, too, if you're man enough." I punched his arm and scooted out of there, could hear his laugh all the way down the hall. On the way I passed a bunch of cops, all in their shirt-sleeves and wearing guns. They looked a little snarly. And *they're* the good guys. Murder makes you feel snarly. Come to think of it, I was a little snarly myself.

I grinned as I walked out into the sunshine. A little snarly might be just the right mood to chat with Robert Corwin. I'd called Corwin Independent Insurance just before toddling over to the Sheriff's Department. His secretary had told me that Robert—well, *Mr.* Corwin to me—would be in all day and happy to see me. I'd said I would drop in. I'd allowed her to assume it was about insurance. Tsk. Naughty me.

The Corwin Insurance Agency was in a relatively high-rent strip mall in North Natomas. Strip malls—my kind of place. I walked in and was greeted with a perky smile by a perky gal in a perky outfit.

"Hi!" she enthused.

Oh, good, her attitude was perky too. I gave her my name and stated I was here to see Robert Corwin.

"Oh, you!" she said in perky recognition and I wondered briefly how Corwin could take this much constant upbeat shit. "Of course. I'll let him know you're here." She bounced up and practically skipped into the back.

I was trying, and failing, to read the stuff on her desk when she returned. I really wish I could read upside down. I give it all I've got, too. It's just that all I've got is not nearly enough. Write it off to a lack of aptitude, I guess. Darn it. Reading upside down can be very useful in my profession.

"He'll be right out," she burbled as she perked her way back to her seat.

I nodded solemnly. All this perkiness was kind of getting me down.

"Do you ever have bad days?" I asked. I couldn't resist.

"Oh, yes," she chirped. "Yesterday I forgot to put mayonnaise on my sandwich."

"Really?" I was dumbfounded.

She nodded.

"Bummer," I managed.

"Yeah. It was *so* dry, you wouldn't believe."

"Miss Colorado?" a man's voice said.

"Ms." I said politely. I'd like to say I said that just to set the record straight, but really it was to be obnoxious. I don't think that Mormons recognize a state—socially or physically—for a woman between Miss and Mrs. Except maybe dead.

"Will you come this way, please?" Corwin said it blandly and preceded me down the hall and into an equally bland office.

I did a quick take on him: IBM. Mormon. Same difference. Dark suit, white shirt, plain dark tie, short haircut, no facial hair, humorless expression. Well, okay, it could be FBI, too, I'll give you that.

Robert Corwin was an attractive man in his midtwenties but you had to look twice to see it, to see beyond the regimentation and notice the wide-spaced eyes, high cheekbones, and lips that could have been sensual. They weren't, though. I can't stand it when people don't smile. He probably only went for it a few times a year and didn't want to use all those smiles up before Christmas. Especially on a stranger.

He indicated a seat for me and seated himself, then picked up a fountain pen and rolled it between his fingers. He wore a wide gold wedding band.

"How may I help you? What kind of insurance do you need?"

"I don't."

He stared at me, puzzled. It's ridiculously easy to throw people off track. Not even a challenge, really.

"I don't understand."

"You knew Daisy Dillard." Not a question.

"Yes." He agreed to it. "Knew?" Good. He was picking up speed.

"Will you answer a few questions for me, please? Her mother has asked me to look into her death."

His face went white and he started to double up as though someone had punched him in the gut. He caught himself on his elbows on the desk, then slowly pushed, heaved himself up. It cost him. His face—cheeks and lips—had gone flaccid and flabby, IBM gone to seed. The emotion was real, though. Or he was really something as an actor.

"Dead? Daisy's dead?"

"Yes."

"How? What— You're looking into it? I don't understand." He put his hand on his plain silk tie and loosened it. I guess he did, anyway. I couldn't see much difference.

"May I ask you a few questions, Mr. Corwin?" He was taking it pretty hard, I thought, for someone who hadn't seen his old girlfriend in about three years. He stared blankly at me. I took this for assent.

"When did you know Daisy, Mr. Corwin?"

"I—we—we always knew each other. We were in Sunday school together, school, youth groups, stake meetings. It seems like I've always known her. *Dead*? Daisy? No."

"You went together, I understand."

"In high school, yes. For almost two years."

"And then?"

"After high school I went away on a mission to Germany. For a while we wrote. I always thought that she'd be there when I got back, that we'd get married." He rubbed his right eye with his fist, like a little kid who was tired and confused, a little kid who wanted a happy-ever-after ending and suddenly realized he wasn't going to get one. "But things change. Tell me what happened to Daisy."

"She died in an automobile accident." He took the cap off his fountain pen, then snapped it back on. "Did your relationship end with a quarrel, a disagreement?"

I wondered if he would tell me to mind my own business, to buzz off, but he answered. His guard was down, or he had nothing to hide. Or he did and was pretending not to. Good, huh? That's how detectives work. We're proficient at narrowing things

down like that. That's why they pay us the big bucks. Robert and
I waded through the long pause.

"Mr. Corwin?"

"What? Oh no, no. Nothing like that. We just grew apart, that's
all. Nothing major, nothing dramatic. We just grew apart. It's sad
when that happens, though," he said wistfully.

I glanced at the gold band on his left hand. "You're married?"
Like I had no clue from the photos on his desk: wife and one and
a half kids; in one of the photos she was pregnant. He nodded.

"I'm surprised that you hadn't heard about Daisy's death if
you're in the same church."

"We're in different wards now. Golly," he said, and then the
fist-rubbing gesture again. "I must call the Dillards. Daisy dead."
He said it as though by repeating something often enough, he
might finally get it.

"She'd stopped going to church, you know?"

"Yes. I was saddened to hear that. I wanted to talk to her about
it but, after we broke up, I didn't have much influence with her.
Perhaps she'd started moving away from the Church even then."
He said it sadly.

"When was the last time you saw her?"

"At a wedding, I think, a year or so ago. But to talk to? Not for
a long time. After we broke up there wasn't much to say."

"Who broke it off?"

"It was her idea at first, and when she wouldn't go for counseling and pray over it, why, I agreed. There wasn't much else I
could do."

"Can you think of anything that might help me?"

"No. Nothing. But, as I say, we haven't been close in years."

"Thank you for your help, Mr. Corwin." I stood, nodded,
walked out. Counted *one-thousand-and-one one-thousand-and-two
one-thousand-and-three* and stuck my head back in. Was there a
look of relief on his face? It was a strong emotion and it wasn't
grief. "Mr. Corwin—sorry about your loss."

He looked over, startled, recomposed his face. "Yes, uh, thank
you."

Then I left for real.

Eighteen

Suffering
Fools Badly

I went back to my office to check for messages. And to read Courtney's letters again. On the surface Robert Corwin seemed a nice enough young man, a hardworking, responsible family man. He had no sense of humor, true, and couldn't smile, but maybe that wasn't a problem for him. He seemed nice, on the surface, but he was a liar.

The man I'd just met didn't match the one that I'd met in Courtney's letters. The writer of those letters had been impassioned, almost wild. *How can you think of breaking up? You are The One for me and me for you. I prayed. I asked God and He told me it was right. How can you think to go against Divine Revelation? Do not follow Satan's way or you will be sorry!* That kind of thing.

And the stories didn't line up either. *Nothing major, nothing dramatic, we just grew apart.* No, the story Corwin told me today didn't sync with the story the letters told. Not even close. Nor did I like the threats, even though they were three years old and veiled.

One phone message. From Hank. Finally. *Kat. Sorry to miss you. Call you later.* I stared at the answering phone machine in disbelief, then pounded it. That was it, that was all? *Kat,* not Katy, to add insult to injury. The machine whirred busily at me, rewinding the tape. *Damn.* This is exactly the kind of thing that makes me want to drop everything and dash off to Vegas. *Goddamn.*

I pulled out one of Robert's letters again. Hello, I'd forgotten a threat. *If you do this, you'll be sorry, I promise you.* This one was signed Bob. He hadn't gotten back from his mission yet. He hadn't become Robert yet. I didn't like Bob all that much, or Robert either. And it wasn't just the lack of humor, or the boundless arrogance, or the chauvinism, or the lack of warmth and charity and love and compassion, or the mental, emotional, and spiritual straitjacket. Not that those things helped—they didn't. Of course, they didn't make him a murderer either.

Shit. I needed some *facts.* Let's be realistic here: Nobody ever got convicted and went to the slammer on attitude alone.

I picked up the phone and punched out Hank's work number. A little too hard, a little too fast. I *was* snarly, no getting around it.

"Detectives," a sugar-and-cream butter-wouldn't-melt-in-my-mouth voice cooed into my ear. I gritted my teeth, but not audibly—I wouldn't give her the satisfaction.

"Hank Parker, please."

"Oooooh, let me see if I can find the *sergeant.* . . . Your name please, ma'am?" She drew out the ma'am like I was 102 years old, speaking as one does to the doddering, the mentally impaired or the hard of hearing. Naturally she knew who I was. I've only been calling for two years.

1–0. Her favor.

Someday Jewel—that, believe it or not, is her name—is going to stop hating me just because Hank has never once looked at her and loves me (I hope), and is going to act like a reasonably polite secretary. Actually, she doesn't even have to be polite, just give Hank my messages. Which, of course, she doesn't. I am looking forward to that day.

I should live so long.

"Name, ma'am?" she repeated.

Ooops. By her voice I was now pushing 115.

"Katherine Karly Katrinka Kate Kristin Kelly Kristina Colorado," I said cheerfully.

"Huh?"

"Kat for short." 1–1.

"Steve—" Jewel's voice trilled musically in my ear. "Have you seen Hankie?" She said "Hankie" in a silky, bedroom voice. I gagged at that. She would never call him Hankie to his face. No one would. Give me a break.

2–1. She pulled ahead again.

"I'm *sorry,*" she trilled oh so musically, "but the sergeant's out in the field. May I take a message?"

She says this May-I-take-a-message? stuff on the off possibility there's a supervisor around and not because there's a snowball's chance in hell of a message from me getting to Hank. I left one anyway, just for the record. "Tell him I called. Katherine Karly Kristin Katrinka"—ooops, I think I had the order wrong—"Kate Kasablanca—"

She interrupted crossly. "I'll just put Kat."

I smiled. 2–2. "Thank you."

She hrummmphed.

"Look," I said, in a cordial tone of voice that should have been an immediate tip-off but—let's face it, Jewel's not brain surgeon material—"I bet you don't get paid much there, not *nearly* what you're worth."

"Oh?"

"I know the perfect job for you. *Pur*fect."

"Really?"

Talk about gullible. Talk about hook, line, and sinker.

"Yes. You have the ideal nine-hundred-number answering voice for sexual fantasies." I cradled the receiver gently. 3–2. Winners can afford to be gracious.

I stared at the phone. Now what? Lauren Davidson or Julie Williams? They were the names Medora had mentioned when I'd asked about Courtney's closest friends. It was a toss-up: I went with Lauren. A soft-spoken feminine voice answered on the fourth ring. I asked for Lauren.

"Speaking."

"This is Kat Colorado."

"Oh. Oh, yes. Medora said you might call."

"May I speak with you, meet with you?"

"Oh." Tentative. "All right."

"Would now be convenient?"

"Oh. Yes, I imagine so."

With a little more gentle encouragement I managed to coax an address out of her. Near I and 30th. I forced myself to speak slowly and quietly. The last thing I wanted was to frighten or intimidate her.

I was there in less than ten minutes. The woman who answered the door of the modest, freshly painted wooden single-family home looked like she had gotten caught in a time warp and was forever fixed in the fifties. Maybe the forties. I'm too young to remember either.

Her hair was long, plaited in two braids that were pulled across the top of her head and pinned in place. There were blond streaks in the brown hair and golden flecks in beautiful brown eyes. No makeup or jewelry. A simple cotton frock with a long apron over it. She was very thin, almost anorexic. Lauren greeted me shyly and pleasantly, hands behind her back. I didn't offer to shake hands. It would not have been welcome.

"Please come in," she invited, in that odd, soft voice. "Won't you sit down?"

The furniture matched her style in time period and looked overstuffed and underused. I sat. Lauren followed suit, feet crossed at the ankles and hands folded in her lap. She looked at me, neither curious nor eager, apparently content to wait until I spoke.

"My condolences on the loss of your friend."

"Thank you."

"You were close friends?"

"Yes, we were friends. Once we were closer. After she left the Church I saw very little of her, though I prayed for her every day and hoped she would come back to us, back to the Church." She reached to brush a nonexistent strand of hair away from her face.

"You know how Courtney—" I broke off.

"I knew her as Courtney as well as Daisy. I respected her choice."

"You know how she died?" I asked, and Lauren nodded.

"Medora says Courtney would never have left her car on the freeway that night. She says that it was because of something that had happened to you and that you might be willing to explain."

"Why?" Her eyes were clear, her hands held on to each other tightly, as if desperate for comfort.

"Why does it matter?" I asked gently, and she nodded. "Medora believes that it wasn't an accident, that it couldn't have been because Courtney would never have left the safety of her car."

"Not an accident?" The gold flecks in her eyes were illusive and tantalizing. "That means— Oh!" Hands covered her cheeks, then fell limply again into her lap.

I said nothing. There was nothing to say.

"Four years ago—" She met my gaze, head held high. "We were eighteen then, we were the same age. I was coming home from work early one evening. The car started acting funny, as though it had no gas and I knew it did, I had just filled it. It was still light so I got my purse and keys and started walking to the next freeway exit. It wasn't very far, less than a mile, and I was used to walking.

"A man stopped ahead of me on the freeway about thirty yards or so and walked back toward me. He seemed pleasant and he offered to help. I thanked him but said no and kept walking. He walked with me and asked again, still pleasant. When we came to his car, he said that I must get in, that he would hurt me badly if I didn't. I tried to get away—I fought him—but he was too strong. He made me get in the back of his car. He took me to an empty field and raped me. Then he let me go." Her eyes dropped to her hands. Somewhere in the house a kamikaze fly threw itself desperately against an impenetrable, implacable screen.

"I'm so sorry."

"Yes," she said, and looked at me again. "It was just the beginning. God helped me or I would not be here today. Sometimes . . . I know this is wrong but I can't help it. Sometimes I wish he had killed me. The police caught him. You see, I could see his car clearly when he raped me in that field. I looked at the license plate and I memorized it. I said the letters and numbers over and over again to myself as though I could make the other stop or go away. I can still remember it. I will never be able to forget."

"They found him?"

"Oh, yes."

"And it went to trial?"

"Yes. No one wanted me to do that, to testify. My family, my friends, my fiancé, my Church—they said it was making public the shame."

"You were very brave."

"No," she said. "I was very afraid." She looked away and when she looked back, she said, "There is no pity in your eyes and voice. Thank you. Everyone looks at me with pity. Even now."

"Understanding? Love?"

"Not always. Not often," she said. Her eyes filled with tears.

"You are very brave."

"The police detective told me— I do not think I could have gone through it without her. She was very nice, very kind. She didn't pity me, either. She was sad and angry and understanding, but she didn't pity me. And she never deserted me. Or looked down on me."

Tears smarted in my eyes. "People can be hateful sometimes. Often it is because they don't understand, though that is no excuse."

"That's what the detective, Sara, said too. She told me that I didn't have to testify and that testifying would be very difficult. She said that I must be the one to make the decision and that there was no right or wrong decision, only what I was strong enough to do. She said she would help me."

But Sara had known, as I knew, as Lauren, too, had known, that she would be alone in the witness stand, that she would have to face her rapist alone, fight back the panic and terror, the revulsion and shame. Alone.

"I admire you very much."

"Sara said that rapists will rape over and over again. I couldn't bear the thought of that happening to another woman and my not trying to stop it, to stop him."

The fly buzzed, rested, buzzed again.

"I was a virgin. That was the only time I—" She held her hands in a tight knot against her breast. A car passed outside and I heard the squeal of a fan belt that needed adjustment. Inside, the refrigerator hummed.

"God helped me, as did Sara and Courtney. Courtney was the only friend who stood by me. She came to court every day and stayed with me at night if I needed her. My family didn't. It was too difficult for them. My fiancé . . . Joseph broke it off. I understood. Why would a man want *me* when . . ." Her proud, soft voice broke.

"Lauren, you were the innocent victim of a crime. That does not make you less of a person, less loving, less worthy of love."

"You sound like Courtney. That's the kind of thing she would have said. She was angry with all of them for my sake. She didn't understand. But I did. I understood that they couldn't help it."

"They could try." I was with Courtney. All the way.

"You sound so much like her. She was my dearest friend. I still can't quite believe she's gone; on a vacation, maybe, but not . . ." She broke off. "Medora is right. Courtney would never have left her car. Sara told us it was better to drive on a flat tire or wait in the car with the doors locked and the windows up until help came. After what I— No, Courtney would never have done that, left her car, especially at night."

"You were close friends until her death?"

"Oh, yes, very, though we didn't see each other often. She was angry with me." There was an apology in her marvelous golden-brown eyes. "Not in a bad way, you understand, but because she cared. After the trial I stopped going out. Except for church, of course. It became very hard for me to— Courtney said that I should not stay with people who would not understand and support and love me. And she was very angry that I did."

I kept my face blank. I agreed with Courtney.

"Courtney was strong enough to leave, to be on her own. I wasn't. I'm not. And they do love me in their way." She spoke softly and with, I thought, a reproving note in her voice. "But I was very grateful for her love and her friendship. I always loved her and I know she loved me. I think my experience was one of the things that drove Courtney away from the Church. That saddened me."

Outside, I heard a car engine cut off and then the slam of car doors.

"That's my mother and aunt. You must go. I can't speak in front of them. But I will help you in any way I can. For Courtney—"

I gave her a business card, which she slipped quickly into her apron pocket.

"If I can help you—" I began, and then didn't know what to say.

She nodded and held out her hands, holding my hand between hers. "Thank you. Please don't worry. God still loves me."

The door opened.

Sunlight fell across the hall.

I started toward it.

Nineteen

Big Guys and Dogs

I've always hated jigsaw puzzles. Most of the pieces don't seem to fit anywhere and yet somehow it will all work out in the end, if you can only get there before you go nuts. I had a job that was one jigsaw puzzle after another. It was enough to make my head swim.

I had planned to talk to Julie, Courtney's other childhood friend, but it would have to wait. My conversation with Lauren had left me exhausted. I went back to my office to focus on something I could realistically handle right now, sharpening pencils, say, or sitting on the front stoop watching the world go by and reading the paper.

Four phone messages. After listening to the first one I didn't bother with the rest, just hit the save button. It was Janie, Courtney's roommate. Hysterical. Screaming. Sobbing. Not my favorite thing at all, especially when I'm already emotionally wiped out.

I called her.

"Kat, someone broke into my house—they've trashed the place! There's glass everywhere—" She broke down into an unappealing combination of gasps, babbling, and blubbering.

"Did you call the police?"

"Yes." The *S* was drawn out on a sob. "I came home and saw it, then ran to the neighbors to call. They—the cops—came pretty fast. The guy was gone and—"

"Are the cops still there?"

"They're gone too."

"What was taken?"

"I don't know. It's not like I have a lot of stuff that's worth taking. Mostly it's just a huge mess. I think they broke every single window in the whole house!"

"I'm coming over."

I think she thanked me, but the words were swallowed by a sob.

I know—I said I was taking a break from emotional scenes, but I lied. I grabbed a cold diet Dr Pepper and slammed out of there. Snarly again. Rats.

The door to Janie's place was wide-open. She sat on her front stoop with her legs drawn up and her arms wrapped around them, her head resting on her knees. She lifted a puffy, tear-streaked face to look at me, then struggled to her feet like a still-clumsy-on-new-legs fawn.

"I don't get it. Why would someone do something like this?" She shuddered.

"Let's go see." I spoke gently.

We didn't have to go far. The house looked okay from the front, but it was a false front. Every window in the house that didn't face the street and the possible curious eyes of neighbors and passersby had been smashed. The screens were bent and twisted over broken window glass—it had taken considerable force to accomplish that.

"Why, Kat? Why would anyone *do* this?" Janie whimpered as she padded behind me, sticking close like a puppy desperate for reassurance. I stopped. She bumped into me.

"These windows were broken from the outside, Janie. Maybe it was just a prank, kids who—"

"A prank!" she shrieked. "A *prank!*"

"I'm sorry." I put my hand on her arm. "It doesn't seem that way to you. Or to me. But it might to a bunch of thirteen- or fourteen-year-old kids. It might have been a dare, something stupid like that."

She sucked in her breath in outrage. Then: "Broken from the outside? How do you know?"

"Hmmm?" I answered absently. I was preoccupied.

"That they were broken from the outside. How do you know?"

"The way the glass fell." I pointed. "Most of it is on the inside."

"Did they come in, Kat?"

"I don't know." That was what I was trying to figure out—one of the things, anyway. The glass wasn't broken out evenly, cleanly, as you would before climbing through. The sliding glass doors to the patio were smashed but still locked. No one had climbed through there, either, although it would have been easy enough to reach in, unlock the door, even relock it on leaving. But why bother?

"What did the cops say?" I asked.

"That it was probably kids. I dunno, they—the cops—were nice, but they didn't seem real concerned, like they had a *lot* more important stuff to think about." She sniffed, aggrieved.

I sympathized with Janie but had to go with the cops on this one. Homicides, gang-bangers, gun-toting crazed cranksters, drive-by shootings, and minimart holdups were more important.

"Did the cops mention any similar incidents in the neighborhood?"

"Not broken windows. They said there were a bunch of bent-over car aerials, some stolen bicycles, stuff like that."

Kids.

"They said not to worry 'cause it was probably just kids and probably wouldn't happen again. They said it would be a good idea to get the landlord to install a burglar alarm—the kind that goes off if someone breaks a window. They said— Hey, Kat, are you listening?"

"Yes. That's all terrific advice. Janie, is anything missing?"

"I don't know." She sighed helplessly.

The TV and stereo were still there, I'd checked. "Computer, other electronic items, CDs, cameras, jewelry, leathers, or furs?"

We found the computer, a cheap one from Radio Shack worth its weight in macaroni and Cheez Whiz. Maybe. Tracked down the CDs, an inexpensive camera, some small items of jewelry. Everything of any value that she could remember we accounted for. Janie had stopped crying and was now merely whimpering. A welcome change of pace.

"Did you call your landlord about getting the glass replaced?" She nodded.

"Good. Let's get started."

"Huh?"

"Cleaning up."

"I *can't,*" she wailed. "I can't bear it."

"Chop-chop." I pushed her into the front room and thrust a broom and dustpan I'd found in the kitchen at her. She grabbed at them automatically. It was a start. It took us—read: mostly me —an hour and fifteen minutes. Broken glass is a bitch. After ten minutes Janie stopped making wounded animal noises, which was a boost to my morale.

"I don't get it, Kat. If they didn't take anything, what was the point?"

"Dumb-shit kids doing dumb-shit things don't need a point, Janie."

"Yeah. I guess you're right. It's just so stupid!"

Hard to argue with that.

In Courtney's room I looked around carefully. Nothing missing, nothing out of place. Everything looked exactly the same. I picked up the ornate, slightly tarnished silver-backed antique hand mirror that lay on Courtney's bureau and turned it over. The mirror was cracked.

Nothing?

The mirror had probably been passed down through two or three generations—had been used and loved, inevitably dropped. I hadn't bothered to turn it over, to look before—that was all. I did today because my mind was on glass.

Nothing. A coincidence.

"Kat, what are you doing?" Janie called.

I put the mirror down, silver side up. "Not much. I'm through." I walked out to meet her. "I should go, Janie. Are you okay now?"

"I suppose. Thanks, Kat. I really appreciate all your help."

"It'd be better if you weren't alone. Can you get a friend to come over?"

"I guess. I need a big guy, huh?"

I thought about Hank. "Get a dog. They're less trouble."

She laughed at that. I didn't, though. "Maybe you could have someone stay with you for a bit. Just for now," I suggested.

She nodded. "That's a good idea. I've got a friend coming over, I'll ask him. Kat, remember how you asked if someone had a reason to dislike Courtney?"

"Did you think of someone?"

"No. But this is all so—so weird—"

I took her by the shoulders and shook her slightly. "It is, yes, but it has nothing to do with Courtney." Which reminded me: "Did Courtney ever mention an old boyfriend by the name of Bob?"

Janie frowned.

"Or Robert?"

She laughed, a lighthearted, joyful sound, the first one in this apartment for a while. "Oh, *him.* Courtney called him Bobert. She said he'd always been Bob, but then he got too big for his britches and his nickname and became Robert."

"Did they ever fight?"

Janie's face squinched in concentration. "Courtney didn't say a whole lot about him. Just that her parents thought he was the best, and her friends thought she was lucky because he was real good-looking and because he was considered to be somebody who would move up fast in their Church, and that was very important to them. She made it sound like everybody thought he was a golden boy."

Almost everybody. Not Courtney.

"Courtney didn't like that he was so taken with himself, so self-important. She said he was like a forty-five-year-old man in a twenty-five-year-old body."

I thought about Chad. Courtney must have been very attracted to his lightness, his humor, his sense of play and fun.

"And she hated it that he just wouldn't give up."

"Give up?"

"Give her up. He was sure they should be married, not only in this life, but for eternity. Mormons do that, you know."

I nodded. I knew.

"He wanted to get married and he bugged and bugged her about it, saying that God had shown him this in a revelation. Mormons are pretty big on revelations too."

"Are they?"

"Yes. Men believe they have a direct pipeline to God, and God had said they should get married, so Bobert was determined to stick around until Courtney saw the light. He was determined to have her."

"How did she get rid of him?"

"He made a mistake, she said. One day—he was on his mission then but had come home for the funeral of his dad—he came over to talk to Courtney. Only he always called her Daisy, of course."

Of course.

"He was upset because she hadn't come to the funeral. Courtney told me she didn't want to let him in because she was all alone but he pushed his way in. They had a big fight. She said she wouldn't marry him ever. Then he slapped her. He said she had no right to deny the word of God through him that they should marry. He grabbed at her and tried to force her to kiss him, to touch him, but she managed to push him away and leave the house."

I sucked in my breath involuntarily.

"Yeah," said Janie. "Exactly. I asked her was she mad, and she smiled and said no, she was very happy. In doing that, he'd given her something to use, power over him, and now she was free."

"The slap? The force?" I asked, but I didn't think that was it. The Church of Jesus Christ of Latter-day Saints, also known as the Mormon Church, or LDS, believes in male authority. Something else was nagging at me.

"I dunno. She didn't say. I think she told *him*, though. I think she threatened him with it, told him that if he ever bothered her again, she was telling."

"And he never did?"

"No, I don't think so. And after his mission he married someone else. Does he have something to do with this?"

I didn't answer her. "Janie, why didn't you tell me this before?"

"I didn't think of it then and, if I had, I wouldn't have thought it was important. It was so long ago. It was over. Is it important?"

I didn't know. Not yet. I needed to find out what Courtney had threatened Robert Corwin with. Whatever it was, was powerful enough to make him go against what he saw as a revelation from God.

I thought about Mormon revelations. Many of them seemed to have God rubber-stamping something a man, or a community of men, wanted. Polygamy, for instance. Or each man being a god on his own planet after death, and women subservient to men in this lifetime as well as eternally.

Was it any wonder Courtney rebelled?

The doorbell rang. Janie scampered off to answer it. It was a six-foot-two guy with a build like an overgrown linebacker, a goofy smile, a pizza and a six-pack. Janie was in smiles and good hands.

I left without a qualm.

Back at my office I listened to the rest of the messages. The one from Hank really tripped my trigger: *Katy, how come you left without saying good-bye?* Well, I thought—after I'd calmed down— at least he noticed two days after the fact. And the one from Wharton was a surprise: *Kat Colorado, Chad Wharton. Please call ASAP.* Chad left me two numbers, home and work. The last message was a disconnect.

Twenty

Stick to Murder

Chad Wharton grabbed the phone on the third ring, sounded pleased that it was me.

"Listen, I found someone who wants to invest in licorice futures. What are the shares going for now?"

"Uh-oh," I said, in my pseudo-glum tone. "Bad news. We've been digging heavily into principal and it's about eaten up."

He laughed. I'm a card, all right. Then he got serious. "Coincidentally, I've got a situation that calls for a private investigator. Thought I'd like to throw a little work your way."

"Thanks. I appreciate it. I'm not sure I can take it on immediately but tell me what you have in mind."

"I need background checks on two people I'm considering doing business with."

"Are they in this area?"

"Yes."

"And you want to know what?"

"Uh . . . anything relevant."

"Other partnerships, litigation they have been in or are currently involved in, property ownership and/or liens, credit history—" I was rattling stuff off. Standard stuff.

"Yes." He sounded relieved that I knew the drill. "Exactly. Will it take long?"

"No. That kind of information is largely public record. Much of it is available by phone or at the courthouse."

"Oh," he said. "Oh, well, great."

Was that a note of disappointment?

"There is one other thing. . . . A woman I know is in dispute with her ex-husband over child custody. The child is only six. The father snatched her and—"

"I don't do child-custody cases. That's a very specialized field. And I don't do child snatches, which is all too often a very illegal field. And if not illegal, dangerous. And/or emotionally fraught and traumatic." *Right, Kat,* I thought wryly: *Play it safe, stick to murder.*

"No, no, nothing like that. I just want you to locate the child. The mother will take it from there. We had a report that they were seen in the Mexican resort town of Cancún. A lot of American families do go there. He might have changed the child's hair style and hair color, that sort of thing, but I'm sure—"

"I don't do that kind of work. And I don't speak Spanish."

"You don't have to. The father doesn't either. Look, it's one, two, three weeks, whatever it takes. . . . Hey, Kat, it's practically an all-expenses-paid vacation."

"No."

"Please. I really want a woman on it and I think you'd be perfect."

Here was a guy who did *not* want to take no for an answer. His determination probably sold a lot of stock but it didn't do a thing for me. I tried another approach.

"Chad, I won't be available for an extended out-of-town job for at least a month. In a time-sensitive case like this, you'll want someone on it right away. I can give you a referral."

"Oh," he said. "Well, no, I wanted you. I wish you'd at least consider—"

"No." I was a little impatient but I kept the edge out of my voice. This was ego on his part, not practicality. Or rather, his was the ego and mine was the practicality. "You want the child; the rest is only a means to an end."

"Well, sure, but—"

I wondered then about the advisability of working for Chad. I'm not wild about background checks and don't particularly need the work. Still, I did think that it might be useful to get to know him. And indirect was often easier and more helpful than in-your-face stuff. Against my better judgment I asked, "Would you like to give me the names for the background checks?"

"I've got it all written down, names, addresses, and all other information. Are you at your office?"

"No. I'm through for the day."

"I'll drop it in the mail, then. Or fax it?"

I gave him the number. "Let me know on the referral."

He was unenthusiastic. We left it at that. He was starting to bore me. I moved on and called Julie Williams, Courtney's other close childhood friend.

"Who?" a breathy voice which had identified itself as Julie Williams asked me in an incredulous note.

I explained who I was. Again. And what I did. Again.

"And you want to know *what?*"

I explained that again too. "I'd like to see you, Julie, to talk about Daisy." It felt like a betrayal of the dead Courtney to call her by the name she had discarded, but Julie had started to freeze me out when I had referred to her friend as Courtney, so I stopped. Not finding out what I needed to know was more of a betrayal.

"No. I mean, I can't. I don't want to. Daisy left our Church. She left us and so she's not my friend anymore. Wasn't." She drew a deep breath, floundering around in past and present verb tenses.

"Daisy was my friend but Courtney wasn't. Courtney made Daisy leave the Church. Courtney killed Daisy. Daisy was dead before this, before— No. I can't help you. My Church— No, I'm sorry," Julie said, and hung up, not sounding sorry at all.

I put the phone down and wondered if Julie Williams had been as dead to Courtney as Daisy was to Julie. I liked Courtney's new friends, Janie, Chad, a great deal more than I cared for Julie and Bobert—which wasn't, I realized as I considered Julie and Bobert, saying a lot.

I called Medora.

"I'll call you back," she whispered. "Tomorrow." She hung up on me too.

I went to bed.

Three strikes and you're out.

□   □   □   □

I was standing in my office the next morning, stunned, when the phone rang. My ground-floor office is on one side of the old Victorian that is now home to four offices, two on the bottom floor, two on the top. The outside wall of my office is practically all windows.

All broken windows now.

I picked the phone up on the third ring. Reflex action.

"Yes." My voice sounded harsh.

Medora was hesitant and afraid. Big surprise. "Kat?"

"Yes." I tried to make my tone more normal. I think I failed.

"You called me?"

I took a deep breath and stretched the phone cord so I could walk into the hall. I couldn't look at the mess without feeling the adrenaline run through me and the rage take over. In the hall I squatted on an ancient Oriental runner and looked at a six-foot ficus. It was real but someone had stuck several little silk birds and a batch of hot-pepper-red papier-mâché apples in the branches. The apples were huge and dwarfed the birds. I took another deep breath.

"I need your help, Medora. You said Courtney was the youngest of your five children. I need to talk to them."

"No."

No? I'll be damned. I hadn't realized that word was in her vocabulary. I was temporarily speechless but, as always, recovered quickly. "No?"

"Why?" she asked in a whisper.

"I'm investigating what you believe to be a"—I just caught the word, *homicide* in time—"wrongful death. Talking to family members is pretty standard. It gives me a better sense of Courtney and her life." Medora made an inarticulate sound and I paused on the off chance that it would turn into words. It didn't. I continued. "If you want me to figure out what happened"—I danced away from the word *murder*—"I need access to as much information as possible."

"It's not possible. My husband . . ."

Yes.

A pause long enough for me to count the fake apples and silk birds. Three birds, nineteen apples, in case you were wondering.

"He does not know you are working for me or he would forbid it."

"And if he did?"

"I would do as he said." She answered without hesitation, as if blind obedience were a simple thing.

Yes. Daisy had been born into a family and religion that valued the concept of family dearly. But the individual? Very little, it seemed.

"Kat?"

"Yes. I understand about your husband but Courtney's brothers and sisters?" All of them silent and obedient? I wondered.

"I cannot put them in the position of doing something their father would not approve of and—"

"They are adults, are they not?"

"Please, Kat."

I sighed. "Tell me about them, Medora."

"Ezra, Eben, and William are the oldest. Then Alice and Daisy. Daisy was born later and was the baby of the family."

"How old are they? What do they do?" Jeez, this was like pulling teeth.

"Ezra is thirty-two and is, uh, a farmer. Eben is thirty-one. He works for a shipping company. William is twenty-nine and is an automobile mechanic. Alice is married and stays at home. She and her husband, Tom, have three children."

"Do they all live around here?"

"Yes, within a half-hour drive."

"Was Courtney close to her brothers and sisters?"

"Not close growing up. There was such an age difference. Later, yes. We are a very close family, Kat. The boys are married and have children. Daisy especially loved her little nieces—Tom and Alice's girls, Mindy, Patsy, and Jill. Daisy used to baby-sit for them all the time and—"

"Were there ever any fights or disagreements, Medora?"

"Oh *no!* We are a very close and loving family, Kat."

I took that with a grain—make that a lump—of salt. I had met Orson, remember.

"Tell me more."

"Oh, Kat, I don't know what to say. Really. We are just a normal, average family. Have you found out anything?"

"It's too soon." I thought of the broken windows at Janie's house. I stared at the broken windows, the glass in my office.

"All right." It was her turn to accept an incomplete answer.

"Don't call me, please, unless you have to. I'll call you. And Kat?"

"Hmmmm."

"Thank you. I couldn't bear it if no one listened." The concession seemed to require a lot of courage from her.

"You're welcome."

"Bless you," she said, and hung up.

Because I had found Courtney's body, it had never been just a job. It was less so now. Angry, I picked up a piece of glass, cut myself. *Goddamn.* It was personal, you bet, and for more than one reason. Just for the record I walked over to the phone, punched buttons, and reported the break-in to the police. Then I took pictures. These days I was going through film like a Girl Scout on vacation. I went outside and walked around the building. All the windows were okay, except for mine.

Nothing? Just kids?

As I cleared the glass off my chair, the phone rang. Just like the movies, I thought, but no clue as to how it would end. No musical score to indicate the building of suspense and terror or impending doom. No sweet, lulling sounds to lead us into calm resolution. There was silence on the other end of the line. I said hello twice, then disconnected. Pick *a, b, c,* or *d:* a kid, a wrong number, a crank call, or someone checking to see if I had found the mess yet.

The pace was picking up.

Just like the movies.

I have a small bathroom just off my office and I headed there to wash my hands and put a bandage on the cut on my finger. The medicine cabinet was now shattered glass. My reflection—slivered and chopped up, pale, tight-lipped, and distorted—stared back at me. The eyes were dark, jumpy, and more anxious than I cared to admit.

A broken mirror is seven years' bad luck.

Nothing? Kids? A coincidence?

No.

Whose bad luck was it, I wondered?

By four-thirty the police had come, been polite and uninterested, taken a report and left. I had swept up the glass, ordered new windows, and failed to discover anything. Nothing missing that I could see. I hate it when that happens. Bad guys watch TV; they should know they're supposed to leave clues. When the phone rang, I let the machine pick it up. I was in that kind of a mood.

"Kat, it's Davis. Call me as soon as you can. I'll be at the office until six, then—"

"Davis."

"Katy, I'm glad you're there." My stomach was knotting up. Davis sounded like a cop and he wasn't calling with hi-how-are-you talk.

"Is Hank okay?" My voice was shaking. I put the danger of his job out of my mind most of the time but—

"Yes and no."

I took a deep breath. He was in one piece with no holes in him at least.

"I'm worried about him, Katy."

Bad.

"We're all putting in long hours but he's really logging it in. Not enough sleep, food, you name it."

Real bad. Davis wouldn't call me otherwise, wouldn't call until he'd already tried to talk to Hank, to do something. And failed. And he probably wouldn't call me unless it could/would get worse, maybe a lot worse. My stomach unknotted, did loop-de-loops, reknotted, then stabilized in raw pain.

"What shall I do?" I couldn't ever remember asking someone else this question about Hank. Ever. If we had a problem, we talked it out. Simple. Only now I couldn't even get him on the phone. Complicated. Scary.

"Can you fly in?"

This was last resort. Davis would go through everything else before he got to that.

"Yes." Last resort is no choice. It would be my second trip to Vegas in less than a week.

"Call me back when you have a flight. I'll pick you up. Don't rent a car. The pickup's yours if you want it."

"Thanks, Davis."

"Hurry, Katy."

I wasn't the only one who cared about Hank. Davis was worried and that made two of us. No. If he was that worried, I was scared.

I was on the 6:42 P.M. plane.

Wednesday, May 11

Las Vegas

Twenty-one

On the Prowl

Davis was waiting for me in a loading zone in front of the terminal talking to a uniform. He saw me, waved, walked over to meet me, traded my carry-on bag for a quick hug, and tucked me into his car.

"Does Hank know I'm here?"

He nodded, his face expressionless.

"It would have been nice if he'd met me."

"It would have, yeah. The last one looked a *lot* like Liz, Katy. She was a college girl from Kansas come down here to look for a summer job."

"Kansas girls. Why can't they just stay put?" I asked plaintively.

He laughed. Not because death was funny but because life was hard and laughing was a break.

"Hank said he'd be late and not to wait up."

"What's 'late'?"

"He didn't say."

"The Strip Stalker?"

"They're both out there on the prowl: the Stalker looking for girls; Hank for the Stalker. Mainly."

"Mainly?" I asked.

Davis shrugged and didn't meet my look. "The woman's dug into him pretty good. Jewel tells me Amber calls a lot."

"Jewel *talks* to you? She *tells* you things?" I smarted off to cover up the pain. *Dug into him. Calls a lot.*

Davis laughed and braked behind a rental car with two mom-and-pop couples—the "guys" in front, the "girls" in back. All were gawking unabashedly at a woman with a plunging neckline and breasts that were a minor miracle of modern medical and plastic technology.

"Are they from Kansas, too?" I asked idly.

"Oklahoma." He answered automatically.

There are parts of Las Vegas that are probably pretty much like Kansas and Oklahoma. In the older sections of town and time you can find residential areas with shopping centers, schools, and churches. There is a university. There are quiet streets with trees and kids and dogs and cats and everyday dreams that families work hard to make happen. We weren't in one of those parts of town.

I guess if you come to Las Vegas from Kansas or Oklahoma you don't want to see something that looks like home. You want to see The City That Never Sleeps. The City That Sins and Smiles and Lives On the Edge. The city where vices become virtues, become what everyone is here to do. The city where reality and fantasy slide into each other until you can't tell them apart. That's what you want to see.

We weren't right on the Strip but only a street or so away. I leaned back in the car and closed my eyes, tired of the flashing lights, the arrows and brilliant neon explosions, the billboards with empty and obscene promises.

Las Vegas is a city where people lose—no, throw away—not just their money but their hopes and dreams and decency. Here the usual evils are approved and actively encouraged: gambling, drinking, smoking, whoring, gluttony of the body and spirit. Usually the people who come here go home to die. Not the girls with broken bodies discarded in alleys off the Strip. I opened my eyes.

A swarm of people was crossing the street in front of us. A potbellied guy in a yellow Beavis and Butt-Head T-shirt and lime-green shorts thumped the hood of our car and waved happily. I hate this part of Vegas. Hank and I never come here. I gave up trying to act cool and detached.

"Is Hank involved just because of the kid sister?"

The light turned green and we accelerated. "I don't know, Katy." I could hear reluctance or sadness or something else I didn't want to know about in his voice.

"Would he tell you?"

"No. He knows how Maggie and I feel about you. He knows how I would feel about that, about him fucking up that way."

We drove the rest of the way in silence. Davis pulled into the driveway next to the pickup.

"I won't come in. Explain to Maggie, okay?"

"Sure." He fished the truck keys out of his pocket. "You got my pager number, Katy?"

I shook my head.

He scribbled it on the back of a business card and handed it to me. "Stay in touch, okay?"

We climbed out. He headed for his front door.

I was headed for Blackie's.

Blackie's was the same, but busier. The bartender was different. He was florid-faced, paunchy, and wore a cheap red toupee. It seemed implausible, even in Vegas. I sat down at the bar.

Two men sitting next to me were drinking beer and good-naturedly arguing. On the bar in front of them was a piece of paper marked off in dated squares. Most of the squares had a name in the center.

The guy farthest from me slugged his beer down and put the empty bottle in the bar gutter. He grinned at me. "Hey, you want to get in on this?"

"What is it?"

"A pool."

A pool? It wasn't football season. "What kind of pool?" I asked.

"We're taking bets on when the Stalker smashes up the next girl."

"Not smashes her up, Jimmie." His buddy winked at me and corrected him. "How the hell we gonna know that, huh? When they find her, that's what it is. Two bucks, you're in," he told me.

"I don't want in."

"Yeah. Mostly the girls don't." The one called Jimmie thumped his beer bottle on the bar and laughed. The bartender gave him another beer.

"Get you something?" the bartender asked me flatly.

I shook my head as he reached for his cigarettes and lit up. No filter. A *real* man. If real men wear ghastly red toupees. I wasn't

sure they did. I was sure that decent people didn't make bets on
soon-to-be-dead girls, even in Vegas, where betting is everyone's
angle, is the name of every game.

"I'm looking for Amber," I said as he threw away his match
and exhaled smoke on me.

"She ain't working tonight. You a friend?"

I nodded, stretching the truth out to a thin black line that
threatened to snap, but so what? I was into expediency now, not
truth.

"Try her at home. Or else at the club. Maybe she's dancing
tonight."

"What club?"

But he had gone back to work, cigarette dangling from his lips
and spilling ashes into the ice, and I hesitated to ask questions
that, as Amber's friend, I should know the answer to. I reminded
myself never to have a drink with ice in it in this bar.

As I walked out Fats Domino was singing about how he found
his thrill on Blueberry Hill and I was muttering: "What club?"

On my way over to Amber's I stopped at a minimart and
picked up a soda and a package of (stale) chocolate-chip cookies.
Only two food groups—caffeine and empty carbos—were repre-
sented so my snack wasn't nutritionally sound but it would have
to do. Once again I hadn't had dinner. That wasn't the only
reason I was cranky though.

I drove the length of Amber's street—all was serene on the
condo front—parked at the end of the block and got out. My
plan was to walk back, look around—you know, case the joint.
Halfway down the block a car pulled up in front of the condos
and parked. The lights cut immediately. A tall man got out and
walked toward the building.

Just like that I scrapped my original strategy.

And started running as soon as he entered the courtyard and
was out of sight. Reaching the courtyard, I slid around the corner
in the quiet, stealthy way so favored by the professional investigator. That was Plan A. Plan B was to hit a spot of gooey gunk and
smash to my knees onto cracked concrete. That wasn't even the
worst part; the worst part was that I couldn't holler and swear.
Muttering under your breath just doesn't ease the pain the way
screaming obscenities does.

I staggered to my feet and dusted off the raw palms of my

hands—swearing inside, you bet—then counted doors and windows. Amber's was the second one in, I was almost positive. I tottered along—my best speed at that point—in Amber Echo's direction, private eye on the job.

Each condo had a sheltered front door opening out to the courtyard and a kind of balconied terrace with a wrought-iron railing to the left of the door. The condo next to Amber's was dark and I headed in that direction.

As I passed Amber's place I heard her patio door slide open. I tottered more quickly and slunk into the sheltered front-door area of her neighbor. The vine-covered latticed archway was perfect for peering through, the answer to an investigator's prayers. And I, I hoped, couldn't be seen. I reached up and twisted the bulb on the porch light until it went out. I burned my fingers even after spitting on them twice. Bashed-up knees, raw palms, and burned fingers. So far not so good.

First shapes, then voices on Amber's terrace. Sounds carried well in the evening stillness.

"Do you want a drink?"

Amber.

"No."

That was—I couldn't tell. It wasn't enough to go on. Yet.

"C'mon," she wheedled.

"I'm still working, Amber."

"A Coke, then."

"All right."

It was Hank, just like I'd thought and hoped I was wrong. He leaned over, his forearms resting on the terrace railing and hands clasped. Hank stood staring out at the courtyard as I stood staring at him. Amber danced out and sashayed around in a sexy fashion for Hank's benefit. She was wearing her best silk underwear, I could tell. Hank didn't notice, so, as it turned out, she just sashayed around for me and I wasn't a very appreciative audience. Then Amber came up next to him, put her arm around his waist, snuggled her head down on his shoulder, and tucked the Coke can seductively into his hands.

I guess it's true that eavesdroppers neither hear good of themselves nor see what pleases them. Also it's a good thing I didn't have a gun on me.

Hank straightened, pulling away from Amber, popped the tab

on the soda. "You said that you wanted to talk to me, that it was important."

"I did. I do. Can't we just talk, though? Visit—you *know?* Her voice was low-pitched and seductive, her hands on him. She knew. He knew. I knew. A box of rocks would know.

"I'm working, Amber. This is not a social call."

The pain in my heart eased a little.

"Okay, *fine.*" Amber sounded sulky. "Belle called."

"When? Where is she?" There was real interest in Hank's voice.

"I don't know. She hung up before she could say anything. Before I could get anything out of her, I mean."

"What did she say?"

" 'Hi, it's me. I'm okay.' Then she hung up."

"How do you know it was Belle?"

"It was her. Of course it was. I know my own sister."

"That's it?"

"Yes."

He put the soda can down on the railing. "I've got to get back."

"No! Wait! That's *not* all."

Hank waited. Amber flung her arms around his neck. "I just wanted to see you. I just wanted to—"

She murmured the rest into his ear so I missed it. The silhouette of two figures joined, dark against the light. Dark against my heart. Hank pulled away, but not immediately. I sucked in a breath. Well, that was Plan A, but once again, unknowingly, I was in Plan B. I had sucked in a breath and a bug. I started gagging.

They went inside. Reprieve. They were at the front door and outside. Trouble. My body made silent retching motions though I willed it to stop.

"Come back, won't you?"

"I'm working late."

"I'm dancing. Come after."

I *really* didn't like the way she said "come." I swallowed hard, wondering if the lump in my throat was the bug. Then I sneezed. Hank looked around. I held my breath.

"Good night, Amber."

Hank walked. I sneezed. Amber shut the door with a decided

snap. I lurked on the neighbor's porch wanting to give Hank time to clear out. And heard the footsteps. Uh-oh.

I stood up smartly, faced the front door, and made a cheery little *rat-a-tat* sound on the wood just as the footsteps closed in on me. I twirled around merrily, looking jaunty and expectant. I hoped. It's tough with a bug in your throat.

"Jeanette?" I chirped, through the bug.

"No." Amber's neighbor didn't have to explain. He didn't sound anything like a Jeanette. "There's no Jeanette here." And he didn't look like a Jeanette, either. He did look annoyed that the porch light was "burned" out. Now was not the time to remedy that.

"Oh. Gosh. Well, I'm real sorry to bother you."

"No problem." He peered at me. "You okay?"

I nodded and slipped past him into the courtyard. The lump in my throat seemed to be moving. The bug *couldn't* still be alive —scrambling its little legs and flapping its little wings—in my throat, *could* it? I made it all the way to the street before I threw up in a bush.

I seemed to be doing that a lot lately.

After I rinsed my mouth out with the rest of the soda, I sat, all scrunched down behind the wheel, waiting for Amber. Surveillance time is slower than anything on earth. It seemed like a decade, but it was only fifty-two minutes. Only. Taking a chance, I followed the first car that pulled out of the parking lot. I didn't know what Amber drove and I couldn't see her getting into the car from where I was parked. I followed the vehicle, a late-model Camaro, for three blocks before I snapped on my lights, and for two more before I was sure the driver was Amber.

Kat Colorado—back on the prowl.

I don't know Vegas all that well but I knew we weren't anywhere near the Strip. This was a much seedier part of town. That was clear even before I saw the signs screaming GIRLS! NAKED GIRLS! in lurid orange neon. Amber pulled into a parking area. I drove around on streets lined with concrete, not trees, killed about fifteen minutes, then pulled in after her. The clock on the dash said 10:59. Amber probably came on at eleven.

I pulled a couple of sheets of paper out of my notebook and folded them up. Then I combed my hair, slapped on lipstick— the only time I wear it is undercover—dusted off my knees, and climbed into an attitude. Okay. I was ready. I heard a noise behind me as I got out of the car and whirled around, my hands up like weapons, ready. The cops thought the Stalker worked close to the Strip but nobody really knew. I saw nothing. A scrawny alley cat strolled out, arched his back against my fender, rubbed, and meowed. A cat, not a killer. I turned my back on him.

There was a bouncer/doorman outside the club. I headed that way in starts and stops and "scared" little jumps. When I finally reached him I made my eyes wide and my voice nervous.

"I'm looking for the Amber that works here," I said quaveringly, twisting the "note" in my fingers.

"I reckon you're in the wrong place, little lady. We ain't got no Amber here. There's Sunshine, Ecstasy, Kitten—"

"Oh! Stage names? I don't know her stage name. Oh, please, mister, I've got to find her. Can I just go in and see and get someone to give her this note? It's important, *real* important."

"Well," he drawled, his eyes mocking me, "I reckon we could let you do that."

"Oh, thank you!" I started to move toward the door, then stopped and quavered. "The men won't think . . . they won't . . . ummm . . . b-bother me, will they?"

He shook his head. "They want willing, not—"

I widened my eyes and he stopped.

"You'll be all right," he said kindly. "Ask for Barry, the bartender. Give him your note." He opened the door. A blast of music, stale air, alcohol, tobacco, and raunchy, sweaty, raw sexual desire slammed into me.

I shivered.

It wasn't part of the act.

Twenty-two

Dancers
and Gargoyles

The door closed behind me and I stood in darkness. Almost all light in the club was spotted onto the stage. Lights, music, anticipation—everything drew your eyes there.

None of the dancers in the photos at Amber's house had looked like this. Exotic dancers. The woman onstage wore a G-string, five-inch heels, makeup, and a smile. That was it. She strutted across the stage, kicked, squatted, posed to flaunt the parts of our bodies we are usually discreet about. The spotlight followed her as she pranced off the stage and writhed through the crowd. Most of the tables were jammed. Guys were hollering and clapping, stamping their feet and whistling, their eyes hot and glazed, faces flushed in the light that spilled over the showcased dancer and onto the crowd.

The testosterone level was high everywhere. All in all it was a pretty discouraging view of the male population.

The dancer shimmied through the crowd, teasing and thrusting breasts and pelvis until she focused in on a heavyset beefy-lipped guy with a farmer's tan and popped-out eyes. This was table dancing, or lap dancing, depending on how far the girls took it. The music pounded and the dancer was insinuating, thrusting, shimmying, seeming to offer what she wasn't going to put out. There was a lot of lip and tongue action and hair tossing. The men were not allowed to touch the dancers except to tuck money under the silken cord I could now see around her waist. They were tucking.

I hoped Amber would be on soon and wondered how much longer I could stand it—the show, the stench of sweat and lust, the smoke and noise. A waitress walked past and stared at me curiously. Second pass, she said something. I missed the words but the tone was neutral. I shook my head to indicate I didn't want a drink and she nodded. We were into live-and-let-live country.

The dancer wrapped it up. The room went dark and silent for a long beat, then the spot lit up the stage again. Amber. A heavy rap song pounded into me. Amber had on a striking black patent-leather outfit accented with chains. Definitive fashion statement. Stiletto heels. Tons of makeup. No smile.

The music was like a weapon. Someone bumped into me, fumbled at me. I whirled. A goggle-eyed, very drunk college-age kid staggered heavily by clutching at people for support, staring at Amber (whose stage name turned out to be Ecstasy), and opening and closing his mouth like a dying fish.

I turned back to Amber, who was sliding out of clothes like a snake. She was also doing some very unusual stuff with a pole which was popular with the guys. One clown shook up a beer bottle and sprayed it on the stage. Judging by the look on a bouncer's face, this would be the clown's exit scene.

Okay, I'd caught the act. I'd had enough. I pushed my way out of the hot club and into the neon night and cold desert air. I sucked in a greedy breath of fresh air.

"You find your friend?" the bouncer asked.

I nodded, still dazed.

He threw his head back and laughed at me. "It ain't like Peoria."

It wasn't, no. Or like Sacramento either. I headed home to wait for Hank, who wasn't like Hank.

I went to bed at one A.M. No Hank. It was after three when he came in, showered quietly, climbed into bed. I sat up.

"Hi. I'm glad you're home. Let's talk."

"I can't, Katy, I'm beat. Maybe in the morning."

Since I had no choice, I gave up graciously. I tried to snuggle up but it was like cuddling with a log. I finally got Hank to put his arms around me.

I woke up alone, only the covers keeping me warm. I could hear the shower running. Habit, I guess. It was seven-thirty and he'd had a shower four hours ago. Or maybe it was murder. It takes a lot to wash off death.

I got up to start the coffee but it was already going. So I walked to the refrigerator to get some breakfast stuff, Mars at my heels. Hmmmm. Not a big choice. This refrigerator looked worse than mine and Hank's the cook, so that was bad. Orange juice, beer, and pickles, that was the size of it.

Hank walked in as I was staring into the refrigerator. Unshaven. With a towel around his waist. I didn't even try to start anything, although ordinarily I would have. Ordinarily he would love it. But nothing was ordinary and I didn't feel like facing the rejection. Mars sized up the situation and padded out of the room.

"Not much to choose from here." Understatement. But I could improvise and cope, no problem. "How would you like your pickles, sunny-side up or easy over?"

Hank poured a cup of coffee. I poured two glasses of juice.

"No time to eat, Katy." He took a sip of coffee, grimaced, drained his juice in three swallows—savoring every gulp, no doubt—then picked up his coffee mug and walked back to the bathroom.

Okay—I gave myself a little pep talk—no point in being overly sensitive and taking everything personally. If somebody offered me pickles for breakfast, I'd probably walk away too. I picked up my juice and followed him to the bathroom. He had already nicked himself shaving twice, and at the rate he was going, I was betting on three or four. I put the toilet seat down and sat sipping my juice and watching him shave.

"I want to talk," I announced.

"Okay."

"I'm here because—"

"Now's not a good time. I've got to be somewhere at eight and I'm running late." He finished shaving and stuck little pieces of tissue on the bloody spots. Only three—good low score for him this morning.

"When?" I asked politely.

He shrugged, unwrapped the towel, and tossed it on the edge of the tub. It slid to the floor. I followed his naked gorgeous body to the bedroom where I sat on the bed and watched him dress. For the record, I'm not into spectator sports.

"How about I take you out to dinner?" I asked. "Six o'clock? Meet you here or at a restaurant?"

"How come you're driving Davis's truck?"

I declined to be distracted by a non sequitur. "Or seven? Would that be better?"

I couldn't see his face. He was looking in the mirror and tying his tie. I was still trying to be reasonable; it was taking more and more of an effort.

"Davis offered me the truck to save the expense of renting a car. I came down to see you. We need to spend some time together, Hank, so let's plan dinner."

He gave his tie a final tug and turned to face me. "Your timing's bad, Katy. This is the way my job is sometimes. You know that."

"It's not just the job. You and Davis are partners but he's coming home nights. He even makes it fairly often for dinner."

"I'm not Davis." His voice was tired.

"Hank—"

"Look, Katy, you came down without consulting me, without asking if I had the time to spend with you. You're always welcome, you know that." He said that with a scowl, which made me feel welcome, you bet. Made me feel like a national treasure. Sure. I waited for the "but." It was coming; it was inevitable.

"But I'm not going to walk away from my job just because you're here." He started to walk away from me.

"That's why I'm here," I said.

"Huh?"

"Because you've always kept your perspective before, seen where the job ended and life began. Drawn the line. You're not doing that now. You're way across the line. You're looking for a missing girl. That's not your job. That's Missing Persons; you're in Homicide. You're too involved with the Stalker. Every time there's a new victim, images of the missing girl, images of your dead wife haunt you, drive you out into the street. You've lost your detachment, your professionalism. Maybe you'll catch the Stalker that way, but I doubt it. Good, solid, unemotional police work is a lot more reliable, delivers a lot better than obsession. I'm worried. Davis is worried. I'm here because of that. And because I love you.''

Have you ever seen a gargoyle? His face was a gargoyle of fury. I kept talking. ''Because I love you I'm telling you that you're fucking up. That's what people who love you do. That's what you do for me.''

I looked at my gargoyle. Everything that I'd said was true, no question. But the truth is not always—rarely, actually—greeted with happy little cries of joy. It is often received with rejection and anger. Anger? Make that stony-faced fury in this case.

''I'm going to work.''

Hank turned on his heel and left. Mars and I looked at each other. He came over and put his head on my knee, his soft eyes offering me love. The front door slammed. Mars and I both jumped. I thought wistfully of the good old days when Hank used to kiss me good-bye, holding me closely and tightly; when he used to come home to me, smiling and eager. I sighed. Mars did too.

This is the kind of thing that makes me want to jump ship and to hell with through-thick-and-thin and until-death-do-you-part, which we hadn't said anyway.

I picked up the phone and called Alma—for comfort, though that was hard to admit. Lindy answered.

''Why the hell haven't you left for school?'' I asked crossly.

''I'm just leaving,'' she replied calmly. ''What's the matter, Kat? Why are you so mad?''

''Hank's being a jerk. No, an asshole,'' I amended scrupulously.

''Why?''

''He's flipped out over a case. He's obsessed with it.''

''Like you get sometimes?''

Well *goddamn*, I thought. ''Yes.'' Reluctant yes. But we both remembered that getting Lindy off the streets had been an obsession with me.

''Where are you?''

''In Vegas. But I'm leaving. This is bullshit.''

Silence. Lindy was politely ignoring my language. Since I nail her every time she swears, this focus on the real issue showed insight as well as tact. More silence. God*damn*.

"Major bullshit." I was seriously cross and cranky. Seriously.

"You can't, Kat."

"Hah! Just watch me." I didn't even notice we'd traded roles and ages until later, that's how bad it was.

"Where would I be now if you'd gotten mad and walked off when I was messing up? Messing up over and over. Where?" Lindy asked, then answered her own question. "In jail, on the streets hooking, or dead, that's where. You can't give up on people you love."

I made an angry, growly sound.

"You taught me that, Kat. I have to leave now or I'll be late for school. Tell Hank I said hi and I've learned a bunch of new chess moves and can beat him any day. Easy. I love you, Kat. Hank does too."

I stared at the receiver until it started making whiny phone sounds at me. Then I had a shower and got dressed.

Lindy was right.

You can't give up on the people you love.

Twenty-three

G-String Dues

Bingo. Amber Larkin was listed in the phone book. Technically, Amber was Hank's problem. Realistically, she was also mine.

Today I resolved to be very realistic.

I couldn't call her yet. If she'd worked until three or four, it was much too early. I went to the store and got some food for Hank's refrigerator. Then I killed time until noon.

The phone didn't ring fifteen times but it was close. Amber sounded half-asleep when she answered. "Amber? Hi, it's Candy."

Long silence. The kind that says *I haven't a clue, not one. Who the hell are you?*

"You know, I drove you home the night the Stalker got his last victim, the night you were so upset."

"Oh! Yeah, Candy. Hey, yeah. Look, I'm sorry—I'm still half-asleep. I couldn't put two and two together and come up with"— she paused—"four to save my life." She laughed breathily and I joined in. "How you doing? Hey, thanks. That was real nice of you. Real . . . real neighborly."

I heard a little Bakersfield and down-home country girl in her. It didn't make me less mad about the scene on the terrace the night before, though. Never mind. That was Kat and right now I was Candy. "I'm fine. I've been out of town or I would have called sooner. How are *you*? I was a little worried about you." Okay, I lied.

"Doing okay." She yawned. "Hey, c'mon over. I'll make us breakfast. Want to?"

"Sure. That sounds great." Yeah, you're right. I lied again.

"You remember how to get here?"

"No problem."

Understatement.

Amber answered the door in denim shorts, the short-shorts variety, a white halter, and a tan. The tan was real. The halter could barely take the stress and rein her in. She was very pretty. A little too much makeup, true, but pretty with a clean-cut, wholesome prettiness that was the opposite of her appearance onstage. She grinned when she saw me, ran her fingers through her hair.

"C'mon in, Candy. I'm making waffles and stuff. Hope you like 'em."

"Sure." I followed her into the kitchen. A bag sat on the counter and next to it a carton of OJ, a dozen eggs, a package of frozen waffles, and a package of bacon.

"Here." She picked up a glass of iced tomato juice and handed it to me.

I pushed the lime out of the way and took a healthy slug. *Whoops!* Tomato juice with lime, seasonings, *and* vodka. Quite a lot of vodka. Oh well, when in Rome . . . Amber drained hers and mixed another. I sipped.

Amber ripped open the plastic bacon packaging with a vicious knife thrust, peeled off a half pound or so, and tossed it into a cast-iron frying pan that had what looked like little bits of hamburger and onion congealed in heavy grease. Yum. Good thing the reason I was here had nothing to do with food. I dragged my eyes away from culinary ugliness and focused on Amber Echo.

She was now breaking eggs—not all that much shell—into a bowl that looked pretty clean. Salt, pepper, and milk got dumped in and then she started whisking the stuffing out of the eggs, stopping occasionally to push the bacon around.

And to slug down more Bloody Mary.

"Have you heard from your sister?" I asked.

Whisk whisk whisk-whisk-whisk. The whisking slowed down, then sped up. She glanced at me sideways, then shook her head.

"Check the bacon, wouldya?"

I poked it around a bit, a la Amber.

"Not a card or a call or anything?"

She hesitated. "No. I sure wish she'd call, though. Sure do."
Whisk whisk.

The eggs were about whisked into another dimension. I
sighed. "I guess they don't realize how much we worry."

"Guess not." She tossed the whisk in the sink. "Hungry?"

"Starved." I looked at the bacon and then away. Okay, I had
lied *again*. "Your cop come up with anything?"

"Naw. Wanna stick those waffles in the toaster?"

Bacon grease popped and spat at me as I walked by. I hoped,
as I jumped back from the pan, that she wasn't planning on
pouring the eggs in there. Amber dragged the bacon out,
dumped it on an unread newspaper on the counter—lead-free
ink, with luck—poured most of the grease down the sink (hoped
management had gotten a sizable security deposit from her),
poured the eggs into the rest of the grease. I sighed. She was into
grease. Her Bakersfield heritage, maybe.

"Even if he doesn't find your sister, he's a good-looking guy."
I couldn't leave it alone.

"How would you know?" Her eyes narrowed and the eggs sizzled.

"I just caught a glimpse of him on TV that night but—"

"Oh, *yeah*. Right. Yeah, he is, huh? Real good-looking. Good
body."

The eggs sizzled, grease spattered, and my heart toughened. I
took a deep breath. This was what I had come to do so there was
no point in being a wimp about it. *No point*, I thought harshly.
The eggs were a solid slab of yellow fringed with grease and
dotted here and there with eggshell. Amber was better behind a
bar than a stove.

"I saw him last night." She glanced at me, a woman-to-woman
look. It was hard to ignore the coyness in her smile. Amber
turned off the burner and with a spatula cut through the egg
mass and served it up on white plates that looked like they'd
come from an all-night diner. The bacon went next to that, then
the waffle on top with syrup drenching the whole mess. A fork
was tucked in cozily on the side.

I now knew one of the reasons Belle—if there was a Belle—had
run away. Knew and sympathized with her. Amber glanced at my
full drink, then made another for herself. We carried our plates

out onto the terrace where she and Hank had stood last night. Amber stretched her long legs in the sunshine and started forking in her food. Well, not food exactly: grub, chow, eats, something like that. This was the perfect example of a time when I could really have used Mars or Ranger under my chair. I cut up my food, pushed it around a lot, ate most of my waffle, and tossed—with silent apologies—a strip of bacon and a small slab of egg at a dusty bougainvillea when Amber got up to "freshen" her drink.

"And?" I asked when she sat down again.

"Huh?"

"You saw this guy last night and what?" Glimpses of her flashed by in the fast-forward of my mind: major cleavage behind the bar; bills tucked into her G-string; her tongue licking her lips and then provocatively, suggestively, pushing out her cheek; her silhouetted form pressed up against Hank's in the shadows; her hands—

"You know, Candy, sometimes I just don't get guys." She sighed, reached out for a strip of bacon on my discarded plate, fed it into her mouth, licked her lips and then her fingers. "I wanted him, wanted him to stay, but he wouldn't."

"Why?"

"He said he was working." She shrugged a *so what?* shrug.

"I thought he had a girlfriend?"

She shrugged again, a *so what?* and *who cares?* shrug combined.

"It would be pretty hard for him to fool around on work time, now, don't you think?"

"Oh—I don't know." She grinned and bounced her tits around. "Maybe a *little* break."

"Would you want him to? Really? He's trying to find the Strip Stalker before the Stalker gets more girls. Like your sister."

The coy, excited look slid off Amber's face. She stuck her tongue out at me. "Jeez, Candy, don't be such a wet blanket, huh?"

I reminded myself that I was here as an investigator and that I shouldn't take things personally, even though watching a woman disregard work ethics and human life *and* go after your boyfriend is somewhat personal.

"Sorry," I said, a moment too late.

"Okay," she replied, dubiously. "He's a real nice guy, solid, steady, the marrying kind. That's something, huh?" But she didn't wait for my answer. "I know a lot of guys. They know what they want, all right, and it ain't marriage." She laughed. "Least-ways no one's ever asked me. Well, asked me and meant it. It's like saying 'I love you.' They say it when they're drunk and want to get laid, that's all. Know what I mean?"

I don't get involved with men like that so I could only imagine. I didn't say that, though; it seemed rude.

"You wanna get married, Candy?"

"I don't know, I'm not sure. Do you? I thought that you wanted to be a dancer and that your career was the most important thing. For now at least."

"Yeah." Her face cleared. "Guys. Use 'em and lose 'em. That's the ticket. Hank—my cop—I'm just using him, that's all. He's not important. He's nothing. He's cute."

I took a deep breath and reminded myself, again, not to take this personally. "But your dance career? That's something, that's important?"

"Yeah." She tossed her head back. "Yeah, for sure. Aw shit, Candy, things could be going better, they sure could. I ain't no Rockette or Vegas showgirl, that's for sure. I'm just another strip-per, a table dancer playing to guys' lonely imaginations and stiff dicks. It's not the big stage. It's a living, that's all."

She sighed, drained her drink.

"Just a fucking living, that's all."

"Everybody has to pay dues, work their way up. Maybe this is your way, your dues." I said it but I didn't believe it. I thought being a stripper at a cheap club was what you did on your way down, not on your way up. But it was just a guess; I didn't know the business.

"Yeah. Paying my fucking dues. Right."

The sun and breeze were on my face. Springtime. An eighteen-wheeler rolled by belching and coughing. Somewhere two kids started hollering obscenities at each other. It broke up my spring-is-swell mood.

"Can you quit that dance job, just hang in and wait for the one you really want?"

"No. Not a fucking chance." She rubbed the tips of her fingers against her thumb in a universal gesture. "Money. It calls the tune, doesn't it?"

I didn't say anything. I don't like to flat-out lie if I can help it, and money doesn't call any tune of mine. I'd work a job to get somewhere—I'd been a bartender for years going to school—but I wouldn't stay in a job that was demeaning or that I hated.

"The root of all evil."

I looked at her speculatively. "Money calls the tune" and is "the root of all evil": It wasn't a philosophic position that said much for her character. And that wasn't even counting "Guys, use 'em and lose 'em."

"Can I do anything to help you find your sister?" I offered. Out of the goodness of my heart, of course.

"I dunno. Like what?"

"Go talk to her friends and teachers, maybe. Go to the places where she hung out, just look around, I don't know exactly." Something, anything. "I'm sure you'd feel better doing something, and I'd be glad to help."

She shrugged. One of her halter straps slipped down revealing brown skin. No tan line, no bra. Not that she needed a bra to support her Made-in-America breasts. I sighed. I was snippy and cynical in the same thought. Bad.

"I don't think so. I think I've pretty much done what I can."

"Maybe—"

"Thanks anyway, Candy." Her tone was hard.

Okay, I got it. Dismissal. "Let me know if I can."

"Sure." She yawned and slipped the strap back on her shoulder. "Gotta run, do some errands and stuff. I'm working Blackie's the next couple of nights, c'mon down. Lemme buy you a beer."

"I'll try." I sighed inside. Pretending to be this woman's friend and not looking like an investigator sure slowed the pace of an investigation down.

"Maybe you'll even get a chance to meet my big good-looking cop." She winked.

There was a temptation all right. I stood and she followed.

"Thanks for breakfast."

"Sure. You bet. We'll do it again."

"My treat next time."

"Great."

I saw myself out. She was already putting on jewelry, more makeup, and a style. Putting on whatever she could, whatever would work.

I went home and did the same.

Twenty-four

Only the Lonely

My jeans were so tight I couldn't breathe deeply or bend over fast. I had on gold flats and earrings, a T-shirt even tighter than my jeans, and I was moussed and made up in the if-you've-got-it-flaunt-it mode.

I wasn't Kat, I wasn't Candy. I was Lily, a dancer looking for a job.

The neon was off at GIRLS! NUDE GIRLS! LIVE GIRLS! Inside, the morning smells were worse than the night smells. The liquor, beer, cigarette smoke, and lust were stale. The pulsing of music, the thrust of buttock and nipple, the throb of hot blood and excitement was memory—or promise, depending on whether you looked forward or back. The place was dimly lit, enough to see but not enough to discriminate. A shadowy figure was stocking beer and liquor behind the bar. A slightly more visible someone was pushing what looked like a filthy mop around a floor that cried out for gallons of ammonia and wild Lysol enthusiasm.

"Is the manager here?" I asked.

The mopper barely looked up, merely hooked a thumb toward the back. I followed it, threading my way through tables stacked with chairs, occasionally jerking my foot off sticky spots whose origin I didn't care to contemplate. The door that said OFFICE was closed and ringed with light. I knocked.

"Yeah."

Permission? Close enough. I opened the door.

"What do you want?"

"My name is Lily. I'm looking for a job."

He looked me up and down, not as a person, even a woman person, but as merchandise. "You cocktail or dance?"

"I'm a dancer," I said. "You have any openings?"

"I might." That look again. "Experience?"

I nodded.

"How much?"

"Couple of summers."

"Summers," he said, drawing out the *s* and making it a sneer. "How many nights do your dancers work?"

"Some girls work two, some five. It depends. Depends on a lot of things." He stroked his chin.

"And the money?"

"Most girls average between two-fifty and four hundred a night. That depends, just like how many nights they work. Lots of things depend." He chewed on a pencil. He had once been a good-looking man but the ravages of alcohol, smoke, and ugly low-life living had long ago eroded the good looks. As did the hard, leering eyes and the sneer. The wages of sin?

"Depends?" I asked.

"On a girl's personality, how she works the guys, struts her stuff, on how much she puts it out." He pinched his chin. His eyes told me he was mentally pinching female flesh. Mine? It crawled at the thought. "Depends on that sort of thing." He stroked his chin, fondling whatever was handy, I guess.

"The girls tip out to management?" That was a euphemism for pay to work here.

"Yeah."

I opened my mouth to ask how much, then closed it. Why bother? I already knew the answer: *Depends.*

"You ready to go to work anytime?"

I nodded. "I got a reference too. Friend of mine knows Ecstasy."

He laughed and adjusted his crotch. His face was nothing like Michael Jackson's, though. "That ain't much of a recommendation. Ecstasy can dance but she's one crazy girl, puts too much shit up her nose, maybe. Thinks she's too damn good for this kind of dancing too. Howsabout you? You think you're too damn good?"

"No." The flat-out lies were adding up.

"Well, then, let's see what we got here." He read the answer on my face. "I ain't seen the merchandise and you expect me to buy? Naw." He crooked a finger at me. "C'mon, girlie girl."

I didn't move.

"You ain't from around here. What are you—a college girl, a housewife, a gal whose husband run off and left you with a coupla kids?" The finger crooked again. "Down to the underwear, girlie. Let's see you flaunt it, strut it a little, push it up here."

"No."

"No job then." He scratched his crotch and leered at me one more time. "I got work to do. Come back you change your mind." He licked his lips.

I spat on the floor. And slammed the office door behind me. The mopper was gone. The stocker too. On my way out I passed a display case with photos of the dancers. I unlatched the case and helped myself to Amber's, aka Ecstasy's, photo. Silence followed me through the building. I knew more about Amber and her life and nothing I had found out yet was pretty.

The sunshine was welcome.

Hank called at five.

"I'll be home by seven-thirty or eight." His voice was tired. "I know you said you wanted to go out, sweetheart, but I'm beat. Could we stay home? Order pizza? Whatever."

My heart lifted. He was coming home for dinner. He was trying.

"I don't care about going out," I said, and it was true. I just wanted to be with him. "I'll cook."

There was a short silence and then we both laughed. Hank's the cook, not me. I do the baking. And breakfast stuff, I'm getting good at that, too. "Chicken?" I suggested. "I can do that."

"That sounds good, Katy. Real good. Thanks, sweetheart."

He wasn't just talking about chicken. There was a lump in my throat as I hung up. Then I went into action. Warp speed. I wanted the perfect romantic dinner and this is not like falling off a log for me. Only for Hank. Off to the supermarket again, this time for dinner stuff. Simple food, good wine. Even I couldn't screw that up. I made a cheesecake too. It wasn't silky lingerie but it was Hank's favorite dessert.

Then I had another shower—it felt like the stripper joint had sunk into my pores. I thought about all the things that I wanted to talk to Hank about and couldn't. And all of the things he couldn't talk to me about.

No good. No shit.

This is not the way it is with us. Thinking this stuff was the way I almost blew the cheesecake. Very close call. Just got it out of the oven in time. Mars and I prepared the hors d'oeuvre tray with just a taste here and there. We didn't eat more than a quarter of it, honest—okay, a third—but I had a lot to begin with. And no pickles. The day had started out badly with pickles.

Hank kissed me when he got home, whistled as he looked around. I was pretty proud of the effect—flowers, candles, the works. The place looked like something out of a women's magazine. I had knocked myself out, for sure.

Hank headed for the shower. I got out the appetizers and shoved the rest of our dinner into the oven. Except for the salad, of course. Hank returned wearing jeans, a T-shirt, Reeboks, and a smile. My Hank, not the stranger who had been making me jumpy and unhappy, scaring me.

We didn't talk about work. Not through dinner, which, by the way, was *perfect*—you hardly noticed at all that the chicken was a smidge dry. Or dessert. We were into the second bottle of wine before we started talking. And cuddling on the couch. (*Mañana* is my feeling about dishes and cleaning up the kitchen.) We'd brought the candles into the living room with us. And yeah, you're right, next time I'll get the dripless kind. Hank had a second piece of cheesecake. I was smug, remembering Amber's greasy, syrupy breakfast.

"Lindy said to tell you she's learned a bunch of new chess moves and can beat you now. Easy."

He laughed. "I wouldn't be surprised."

"And Alma says hi and when are you coming over for dinner and I say—"

He put his arms around me. "Tell me, Katy. Tell me about the case you're working on." That wasn't what I was going to say and he knew it. I answered anyway because I did want to talk about it and because love is about compromise and accommodation. And sometimes, I was learning, it's also about avoidance.

"What started out as Medora Dillard's supposition is starting to look like a possibility."

"Murder?"

I shrugged. "Not accidental death. Not the standard stalled-car-on-the-freeway-and-hit-pedestrian that the Patrol wrote up. No one who knew her believes that Courtney would have left her vehicle, alone and late at night, to go for help. The 'blowout' looks like it could have been faked, although I haven't been able to interest the cops, Patrol or Sheriff's Department, enough to take a look at it.

"On the surface Courtney's life was uneventful. She was a good student who quit school temporarily to get her finances under control. She'd had a falling out with her family because she wanted to make her own decisions about her immediate plans as well as about her religious views. But what young person doesn't, in the course of growing up?"

"Yes."

There was something in Hank's voice and I looked at him. Suddenly we weren't talking about Courtney but about Belle, about the seven young women who had become the Stalker's victims.

"And?"

"And she had friends and family who cared about her. No enemies that anyone knew of and a boyfriend who was too good to be true."

I stopped there because I had one of those too, and I remembered the silhouette of Hank and Amber last night, her arms around his waist, her head against his shoulder. It wasn't what it looked like, but it wasn't good either. You know what they say? *If it seems too good to be true, it probably is.*

I sighed. Life is an emotional minefield.

"Katy?"

I went back to Courtney. "But of course, that's just the surface—" I didn't have to tell a cop that things often weren't what they looked like. "There's an ex-boyfriend who threatened her in the past and over whom she had some kind of emotional hold. Her family is furious that she left the Mormon Church—"

"Mormons," said Hank in the manner of one who had tangled with Mormons before.

"They seem to feel she was following Satan's path and that those who do deserve whatever they get."

Hank let his breath out slowly. He has the same friendly feelings toward narrow-minded religious intolerance that I do.

"Ditto her Mormon friends. Some are understanding, some condemning. And her fiancé was laughing and telling jokes just days after her death.

"Courtney wasn't wearing her engagement ring. And someone came by her apartment and"—I almost said "my office," but I caught myself in time—"and trashed the place. Nothing seemed to be stolen. I think they were looking for something."

"And. And. And I have a way to go." I sighed.

"But you're making progress."

I thought it over. "Yes."

That brought us back to the Strip Stalker, where they weren't making progress. Or back to Belle.

"Hank?"

He shook his head. "Let it be, Katy."

Strike one. But I didn't. I couldn't. This is the man I love. "You've got to pull back, pull away."

"Don't tell me how to handle my job, Katy." Dangerous tone. Definite back-off-*now* tone.

"Somebody has to, you're not doing it." Definite looking-for-trouble remark. "Your job is homicide investigation. It's working on the Strip Stalker case with Davis. It is not Missing Persons or baby-sitting adult women or doing homicide investigation without your partner.

"Losing perspective does not make you a good or effective cop, Hank." *And it might get you into trouble.*

My helpful, thoughtful comments were greeted with silence. "Hank?" I prompted after a week or two.

"Katy, we're not going to agree on this. Nothing you say is going to change what I'm doing or how I'm doing it."

Strike two. "At least stay in touch."

"I'll try but I won't make a promise I'm not sure I can keep."

Strike three.

□ □ □ □

The candles had burned down. The fire had almost burned out, only sparking occasionally. I had simmered down. Hank had put Roy Orbison on the CD player.

We danced in moonlight that spilled in through patio doors and puddled on the floor. "Only the Lonely." "Running Scared." "I'm Hurtin'." Roy Orbison tears me up, rips out my heart. Hank pulled the sweater over my head, rubbed his hands on my bare back, unhooked my bra and tossed it. I pulled his T-shirt off. Clothes, like the moonlight, puddled around us as we danced.

I shivered. There is something so cold about moonlight.

Hank held me closer.

Roy sang "It's Over."

Twenty-five

Liars and Slime Mold

I woke up warm and content in the circle of Hank's body. I kissed him. First I had his attention, then I lost it and he was gone. Still swinging and missing. I heard the shower running and got up. When I climbed in the shower with him, he barely noticed—I just got my hair wet for nothing. Then we got dressed and drank coffee. In silence. His body was there, his mind was stalking the Stalker.

I couldn't compete. At least he remembered to kiss me goodbye. He took the news that I was going home well. Too well, I felt.

A perfect romantic evening and now this. Here is my big gripe with fairy tales: You fall in love—they tell you—and then you live happily ever after. Do you know anyone that that has happened to for more than ten minutes? No? Me either.

I decided to go see Amber on my way out of town. I was already in a crummy mood, so why not? I wanted to see if I could push some of her buttons, make her say or do something so I could unhook Hank from this whole mess.

I was in the perfect mood for trying.

Amber answered the door on my second ring, peering out at me through the four-inch gap the chain lock allowed. Perfect timing, I congratulated myself. She was up and dressed but not yet ready to go out. I smiled my sweetest don't-worry-about-me-I'm-not-a-private-investigator-I'm-your-friend smile. She bought it. I love it when that happens.

"Hi, Candy. Hey, I was just thinking about you." The door closed. I heard the rattle of the chain and then the door opened and she danced out, grabbed my arm.

"Good news!" She looked bubbly. No gobs of makeup that the happiness had to try to shine through—just a freshly scrubbed, pretty face.

"News of your sister?" I asked, but what else could it be? And it was news that made me almost as happy as it made her. *Enter sister. Exit Hank.* Yes!

"I've got an audition! It's not for anything real important or big but it could be a start. It *could* be. I'll knock 'em dead, I know I will."

Exit sister. Reenter Hank. Bummer. This would never happen in a fairy tale, but, then, fairy tales are a whole lot tidier than real life. I tried to smile at Amber, to be happy for her. "That's great. Congratulations."

Amber did a slow bump and grind. Getting in audition mode, I guess.

I walked over to the end table and picked up the photograph in the silver frame. "Is this a good picture of your sister?"

Amber bumped and wiggled a few more times, then sauntered over to me. "Well, yeah, pretty good. Why?"

"This would reproduce well. We should make up flyers and post them everywhere. Or have you already done that?"

"No-o-o." She didn't sound excited. Excited? She didn't even sound interested. "Hey, look at that!" Now she sounded excited. She was pointing out the window.

I looked out. Uh-oh. "What?" I asked as I slid behind her and away from the window, ostensibly to put the picture back.

"It's my cop! Cool."

Her cop? I queried darkly and silently. Also quickly. If I didn't move fast, I was going to be in deep shit. I moved. The doorbell rang.

"Don't answer it!" I hissed, trying to sound panicked and hysterical. Not too difficult, actually.

"Why?" She was puzzled and who could blame her?

"Amber?" Hank's voice.

"Just a minute," she called, eyes on me, still puzzled.

"I've got to get out of here. I hate cops. A cop killed my cousin." Talk about wild improvisation. "Where's your back door? I'll come back later." I sounded convincingly desperate, even to me.

Amber's face got all soft and sympathetic. God, I'm smooth. "Where's your back door?" Safe. Home free. That was me.

"I don't have one."

In deep shit. That was me.

Living/dining area, kitchen, bedroom. I headed for the bedroom. Clothes everywhere. Closets jammed to overflowing. No room to scootch under the bed.

"Candy?" That was Amber.

"Amber?" That was Hank.

"Please!" That was me. I headed for the bathroom, hopped into the tub, and yanked the shower curtain almost closed. Not exactly an original move, but I'd run out of those. *"Please* understand."

"Okay." Accommodating but deeply puzzled.

I twitched the shower curtain shut. I heard the front door open and close.

"Hi, handsome."

My blood started boiling. I always thought this was hyperbole but it's not, take it from me.

"I got your message. You said it was important."

Amber hadn't closed the bathroom door. Once the stage gets in your blood you can't help it, I guess. You can't resist playing to an audience.

"It is, it's *wonderful* news!"

"Belle?"

"No, not *that* wonderful. Oh, I wish. That would make it *perfect.*"

"What, Amber?" It was Hank's I'm-being-patient-but-you're-pushing-it voice. I know it well.

"I've got an audition. Things are really starting to happen."

He didn't respond right away. He was frosted, I bet. "That's not an emergency. I asked you not to call in work hours except in an emergency. I assumed you had news about your sister."

"Hank, *please* be happy for me. I just wanted to share it with you. You're the special guy in my life. I want to share *a lot* with you."

You didn't have to be a United Nations translator to figure out what "a lot" meant. She was probably bumping and grinding around Hank's body right now. I gritted my teeth.

"Amber, I'm working."

I wanted Hank to put her in her place, straighten her out, but instead he just gave her a typical guy answer—a statement of fact that ignored the emotional issues at hand and didn't settle anything.

"You're always working," she complained, a typical girl response. "Well, never mind. Come back later?"

Her voice was seductive, tempting. I gritted my teeth harder (don't tell my dentist) and leaned against the shower wall. Wet. I straightened up quickly and almost slipped. Ooops. I did a little shower-soft-shoe-shuffle and caught myself. Barely.

"Come back later. Let's celebrate. Let's have fun, know what I mean?"

Well, duh. Who could miss it? Hank knew. I knew. For godsakes, the slime mold on the bathroom tile—I wrinkled my nose in distaste—knew.

"Amber, I've got a busy work schedule and I've got a girlfriend."

I was second, I noticed, but at least he mentioned me. About time. How about something more direct? I've always liked *no* or *never* or *in your dreams*. Gritting my teeth, my blood at a boil, rampant nastiness: eavesdropping was bad for my health.

"Oooh." Pouty, feminine disappointment. "Can we look for Belle later? Together?" She was improvising too.

"No."

"Oh. Well, could you come over? After work. Please. I just get so lonely and scared and I need someone to . . . to . . ."

. . . *to fuck*. I finished her sentence under my breath.

There was a long silence broken by little clothes-rustling sounds and then Amber made a happy little murmur sound. What was going on out there? Hugging? Kissing? Serious body contact? I was getting pretty steamed so I took a couple of deep breaths to calm down. It didn't work.

"Puhleeze!" Cute and coy. I started to gag. Let's face it: Snooping by eavesdropping is not my forte.

"No, Amber. I appreciate what you're saying and you're a very attractive lady, but no. I've got a girlfriend."

I steamed some more. Phooey, talk about lukewarm!

"But this is *so* special."

Amber was no quitter, I'll give her that.

"Do you mind if I use your bathroom?"

Uh-oh. I scrunched down and to hell with the wet tile and slime mold, then took a deep breath just in case I didn't get to breathe again for five minutes. Or whatever.

"Oh . . . well, okay."

Like me, Amber was less than enthusiastic about the plan. Hard to say no, of course. Having offered him her body, it was difficult to refuse him the use of her bathroom. I heard steps, then the click of the bathroom door as it closed inches away from where I crouched. This never happened to Sam Spade or Lew Archer. Where was I going wrong? I decided not to do this kind of thing again. Ever. *Really*. And this time I meant it. You can hold me to it.

I heard metal sounds—hardware kinds of sounds that I couldn't quite figure, then paper rustling, a rip and a crumple. Silence. The flush of the toilet. A token on/off of the water faucet.

Well, well. We were all playing games.

Then doors opening and closing and happy little good-byes on Amber's part and silent gagging in the bathtub on my part. Moments later Amber burst into the bathroom and slashed the curtain open. I wiped the snarly off my face and stepped out with grace and aplomb. Or a reasonable facsimile thereof.

"I'm real sorry about that, Candy. Are you all right?"

I nodded. Except for the psychic damage. I also registered the fact that she didn't look a bit sorry. She looked excited and sexy, her face flushed, her eyes sparkly.

"Isn't he *neat?*"

She bounced around like a five-year-old, except a five-year-old isn't built like a brick shithouse and supercharged with excess hormones in overdrive.

"Can you see why I like him? I'll get him too, I will, just you wait and see."

Usually I admire perseverance and git-up-and-go but there's an exception to everything. "Give it a rest, Amber. He said no. He said he had a girlfriend."

"He'll change his mind." She giggled. "Wanna bet on it?"

I didn't, no.

"As for the girlfriend—hey, who cares? If she can't keep him, she doesn't deserve him."

"How would you feel if some other woman tried to grab on to your boyfriend?"

She shrugged, tossing hair, tits, and attitude around. "I don't know. No one's tried."

It made me long to drive a silver stake through her heart. Just in time I recalled that I had come to push Amber's buttons, not vice versa. I love the way I never become emotionally involved in an investigation.

"Why won't you put out a flyer?"

"Huh?"

"With your sister's picture, a phone number, maybe even a reward for information."

"Oh, well . . ."

"It's almost as though you didn't want to find her." After all, that could—God forbid—end the meetings with Hank.

"Oh, how *can* you *say* that?"

Easy. Especially after listening to you put the moves on my boyfriend. "If you wanted to find her, you'd be doing more to make it happen. Seducing a good-looking cop is not Step One in finding a missing juvenile." Duh.

She laughed.

I hated her. And I don't care if she had a lousy and deprived childhood.

"Don't be such a silly moralist, Candy."

And I hated the name Candy.

"Hey, wanna go shopping?"

"You didn't answer my question."

"Well, I'm not gonna, so there. Wanna go shopping?"

I didn't want to go shopping. I was sick of Amber and sick of Las Vegas. I wanted to leave. So I did.

At the airport I called Hank and Davis on their pagers, punched in the number of the airport phone booth I had staked out. Then I lounged around "my" phone in a territorial manner and waited for it to ring. Sort of like a drug dealer. This was the kind of upbeat thought mode I was in.

When the phone rang, I jumped a foot, then lunged for the receiver. Hank.

"I'm at the airport," I said.

"Have a safe flight, Katy. Call me when—"

"Have you seen Amber lately?"

Here's how I had it worked out: If he was honest and forth-coming, I had nothing to worry about. If he lied, then there was either more than I knew about, or there would be soon. It was taking Hank a long time to answer. I watched a woman laden with baggage chase a gleeful toddler with a red balloon. My money was on the kid.

"Katy, why—"

"It doesn't matter why and you don't have to understand, just answer, okay?"

"Yes. I saw her this morning."

The pressure in my heart eased. "Business?"

There was an almost imperceptible pause. "Yes."

My heart tightened again.

"Katy, we've been through this. Don't worry."

Right. Easy to say. Of course I knew about the giggles and the boasting. He didn't. I hoped he wouldn't. I felt sick and tired all of a sudden.

"Hank, I've got to go."

"Okay, sweetheart. I—"

" 'Bye," I said, and hung up before he could say words I wasn't positive he meant anymore. I sat there for five minutes—limp rag, not drug-dealer alert and cool—before the phone rang again.

"Merkovitz."

He could tell by the unfamiliar phone number that I wasn't a known factor and I could tell by his voice that he thought he was calling an informant.

"Davis, it's me."

"Katy." His voice became kind. "What's up?"

"I'm at the airport. I'm going home. I talked to Hank a lot but I couldn't get through to him."

"Katy?"

"I don't know what else to do, Davis. I've got to go now. They're calling my plane. Thanks for the truck, the keys are un-der the mat. Love to Maggie." I hung up. It was a lie about my plane. I had fifteen minutes.

A guy with black baggy pants, a black T-shirt, black slicked-back hair, and mean little sapphire-blue eyes walked over and stood in front of me, legs apart, hands in fists at his sides—your basic macho aggressive posture. *He* looked like a drug dealer.

"I need to use the phone." He sneered it out of the corner of his mouth.

I looked around. There were empty phones no more than an airline terminal block away. "Fuck you." I sounded evil too. It made me sad.

Mr. Macho folded and walked.

I sat in the phone booth for a minute or two before setting out for the departure gate. We think it's a tragedy that Romeo and Juliet died young, but maybe it's not.

They knew love and they never knew betrayal.

Friday, May 13

Sacramento

Twenty-six

Soap Opera, Sex, and the Voice of God

I went to Alma's house, a Victorian in Midtown, on the way home from the Sacramento airport. Alma's full of common sense and good advice—though not very grandmotherly in tone—and I was in desperate need of both.

"Katy, dear, how are you?" She gave me a big hug and hauled me in the house. "Have you eaten lunch?"

"Not even breakfast."

"No? Well, let's have that, then. I like breakfast better than lunch, anyway. I'm sure I've got some cinnamon rolls. Sit down, dear."

I obeyed and watched as she tossed stuff around in the freezer. Alma's eighty-two and a cannonball. Today she had pulled her thick white hair back into a French braid that hung halfway down her back and was wearing baggy jeans, a flannel shirt, and hiking boots with that L.L. Bean feel.

"You look like a lumberjack," I told her affectionately.

"Hmmmm? Oh, I'm a zoo volunteer later this afternoon. Eggs, dear?"

"Sure. How's Lindy?"

"Fine. Isn't her prom dress something? Oh, lordy, but I wish we'd had party frocks like that in my day! I had the figure, too." Still a size seven, she smiled complacently.

"Can I help?" Alma doesn't like anyone fussing in her kitchen, especially me, as I'm all thumbs.

"No. What's wrong, dear?" She always could read me like over-size print with illuminated technicolor diagrams.

"Hank's screwing up."

She thought that one through. "How?"

"He's too involved with a case." I had to explain the Strip Stalker to her because she won't read the papers or watch the news. Alma claims she's only interested in what she can change and that she's too old to worry about anything on a big scale. Which explains why she volunteers at the zoo and mans the Granny Hot Line for troubled kids. And why she takes in strays: me, years ago, and Lindy. "The dead women look sort of like Liz."

"Oh dear." Alma put plates piled with eggs and cinnamon rolls on the table and scrunched up her chair. "That happened to Sasha once."

"Sasha?"

"Yes. Two years after her husband died—he drowned in a train wreck"—I didn't ask, tempting though it was; with Alma it's better not to—"anyway, two years later Sasha finally started dating again. He was a real nice guy too. And all of a sudden she began having terrible dreams and flashbacks. She saw his face—the husband, that is, not the new boyfriend—in the lily pond, on the television screen, in the butter and jam on her toast, even in—"

Lily pond? TV screen? Butter and jam? "Alma, is Sasha a real person or a character in a soap opera?"

"Yes."

That narrowed it down. I frowned.

"Yesterday, Today, and Tomorrow. It got so that poor Sasha could hardly—"

This could, I knew, go on for a while. "There's more," I said.

"Oh?"

I told her about Amber Echo, not leaving anything out.

"Hmmmm," she said. Alma's a big Hank fan—they correspond and trade recipes even—and she did not like this one bit. Still, I thought she was being much too calm about it.

"Well, dear, I don't think you should worry. Hank's a sensible person. Sooner or later he will remember to act like it."

I hoped later wouldn't be too late.

"And *he* is looking at this thing with the missing sister in a professional manner even if *she* is not," Alma added.

"But that's not his job."

"No." She looked at me pointedly to remind me of all the times I'd stepped out of my job description. "It's just that he's trying to be nice—he *is* nice, Katy—and to be helpful."

"It could get him into trouble." *It could get him killed.*

"It could, but there's nothing you can do about it, so I'd just assume the best, not the worst."

Oh right. I said nothing.

"I know it's not easy, dear, especially for someone like you, because you fuss about things so and take it all so seriously. But why worry until you have to? The worst will probably never happen. Oh my, Katy, don't blame him for his concern—all those poor girls being killed. *When* will we learn to be kind to women? And so often it is the young ones, the youngest and the best. Like Courtney."

Yes. Like Courtney. Or Lauren. And, Alma was right, like Belle.

"We have to save them if we can."

Like Lindy once.

"And if the worst does happen?"

"If it does, you help pick up the pieces." She scooped up our empty plates. "Because that's what love is all about. Everybody gets to make his own mistakes. You can't change that. Nobody's perfect, Katy."

Another reminder, I thought glumly.

I glowered at her. "Victoria's Secret, for godsakes."

"Well, no one is asking you to buy stock in the company," she replied sensibly.

I hate it when she's this solid and sensible. It was what I had come for, true, but it's still irritating.

"Oh hell's bells," Alma exclaimed crossly. "If I don't step on the gas, I'm going to be late."

"Shall I do the dishes?"

"Phooey. Never mind. Come for dinner soon, dear. Lindy wants to see you too." She had to stand on her tiptoes to kiss me. "Don't worry," she declared. "It'll all be all right."

"What happened to Sasha?"

"Hmmmm?"

"Sasha?"

"Oh. The poor girl had a nervous breakdown and went to an insane asylum but then she escaped and was in a plane crash where *she* almost drowned, only at the last moment a child crippled by polio saved her. That snapped her out of it and then she adopted the child, who was an orphan, only then the child's father showed up and she almost lost her mind again but instead—"

Alma is such a comfort.

"Instead she didn't and they got married. It'll be all right, you'll see, dear," she concluded cheerfully.

Would it? I wondered as I drove away. If this was a fairy tale, we would all live happily ever after. But it wasn't. And life doesn't come with a guarantee or a money-back offer.

I had names; it was time to start kicking ass. I called Lauren, Courtney's childhood friend. She said I could come over if I did so right away and didn't stay too long. I hoped this time we could finish our conversation. Uninterrupted.

She looked the same as last time—simple cotton dress on a too-slim body, apron, hair pulled back, no makeup. She invited me in as though she were doing something daring.

"You want me to help you?" she asked after our greetings and in an incredulous voice that told me how unusual it was that anyone asked her for help, or at least for help that didn't require an apron and housekeeping skills.

"Please tell me about Robert Corwin, Courtney's ex-boyfriend."

She sucked in a breath. I waited in silence.

"Tell you what?" she asked softly.

I didn't answer that. We both knew what.

"About him now or then?"

"Both."

"He was a good student and he played football. He was well liked and popular. Everyone thought Daisy was so lucky to have him, tall and good-looking and all. And he was very involved in the Church. We all knew that Robert was one who would rise in the Church, that he would be very important someday."

"And has he? Is he?"

"Oh, yes, and I think that it is just the beginning for him."

"Was all this important to Courtney?"

"Yes and no. Robert's older, two years ahead of us, and Daisy was flattered, maybe a little awed with his attention. He asked her out and she went, of course."

"Of course?"

"Any girl would have. Daisy was lucky—Robert seemed to be one of God's favored and chosen, and she was his."

"Did Daisy recognize her good luck?" I tried to keep the sarcasm out of my voice.

Lauren didn't notice. "Yes and no."

"That again."

She looked at me and smiled faintly. "Daisy was always something of a 'freethinker.'" She said "freethinker" in the same tone of voice that I would say "pederast" or "poleax murderer."

"Is that bad?" I queried innocently.

She drew her eyebrows together, furrowing her brow, but when she spoke, it was gently. "It is not good to question authority."

"Authority?" I asked, still innocently.

"The scripture, or the Church's position, or an official of the Church. The First President is as the voice of God. When he speaks, it is as scripture. We must follow the word as it is written or spoken to us. And a woman, of course, must abide by the direction and authority of her bishop, her father and older brothers, then her husband, and later her sons."

Of course?

"Such is a woman's divinely appointed role in life. This is her gift and blessing and also her sacrifice, that she should place her role as wife and mother above all else, and most particularly place her husband first. It is her duty to sacrifice for her husband and family and for the Church."

"And Courtney?"

"She questioned this." Lauren hung her head sadly and I silently cheered. "Some of our young women do question. They think"—her voice was chagrined and mildly reproving—"that woman is equal to man." Here her voice dropped to a whisper, as though she were afraid of offending someone.

"But men are God's chosen and voice. Men are His priesthood. Women are weak and fragile vessels put on earth to serve God and men, to take man's direction and authority in all things. Man is the power, the doer, the active principal; woman the receiver, the facilitator, the passive principle. Woman was created for man's use."

Benignly, Lauren smiled at me. She would never question this, never do what Courtney had done.

"This is God's law as written in the scriptures. Daisy found some of this . . . difficult to accept." Lauren was sorrowful. "Robert strove mightily—his duty as a member of the priesthood, as well as her fiancé—to help her keep her faith, to believe and to accept.

"He was not successful in that. None of us was." She raised her eyes. There were tears in them. "Many is the time I have prayed for her. Many, *many* are the times."

She spoke as though it was present as well as past, as though Courtney was still in her thoughts and prayers.

"This unwillingness to accept Robert's direction caused a great rift in their relationship."

"Who broke it off?"

"Officially they were still engaged when Robert left to do his ministry. But soon after he left, Daisy wrote to end the engagement."

"How did Robert take that?"

"He implored her not to act so. He had prayed, you see, and received God's will in a revelation that they be married. A revelation," she repeated in a hushed tone. "And they had the blessings of their families."

"Nevertheless, Courtney broke it off?"

"Yes."

"She followed her own counsel, not God's—as revealed through Robert, that is?"

Lauren looked at me sideways through her lashes, considered before she spoke. "Yes," she answered.

"And that was the end of it?"

"Yes." This time the hesitation was longer.

"I know that Robert saw her when he returned to his father's funeral. I know that they fought."

She sighed. "What use is it now to drag up that, Miss Colorado? She is dead. There is no need to smudge a good man's reputation."

"There would be no need if we knew absolutely that they were not connected."

Her eyes were wide and startled. "That cannot be."

I said nothing, less given to black-and-white pronouncements and unquestioning acceptance than she.

My silence stung her. "It cannot be!"

"If it cannot be, then there is no harm in telling me."

She thought it over, trapped. Then, reluctantly: "They did argue. Robert is a man of strong passion, though now he channels that strength into family, business, and, of course, the Church." Piously she folded her hands.

"You knew him well?"

"We often did things together, Robert and Daisy, Joseph and I." Her eyes dropped. "Before," she whispered.

"Before?"

Her face flushed deeply, painfully. Her fingers twisted white-knuckled in her lap. "Before my . . . my trouble."

"I'm sorry." I spoke gently. "I wasn't thinking, I didn't mean to hurt you." I kicked myself mentally but not as hard, not nearly as hard as I kicked Joseph, who had walked away from his raped fiancée. "Please go on, Lauren. At the time Daisy broke off their engagement, Robert's passion was not so well channeled?"

"No. He was . . . He was so in love with Daisy. Once, when they quarreled and she didn't speak to him for a week, he lost weight. It literally ate away at him."

"Was he as angry as he was passionate and obsessed?" I forced myself to go slowly, to draw this out of her bit by reluctant bit.

I had used some of her words but she looked a little worried at the sound of them. "He was angry," she agreed. "He came to Daisy's because she had not been at his father's funeral. He said that was the reason."

The barest emphasis on said. I followed it. "And the real reason?"

"He felt that . . . that Daisy was wrong for not marrying him. For not fulfilling his revelation and doing the will of God."

"As revealed to him?"

She looked puzzled at the question. "Yes."

"And?"

"And then he left, I guess." She shifted in her seat.

"Lauren, you're a terrible liar."

She sighed. "I *hate* bringing all this up."

"Was Robert a loyal and loving friend after your 'trouble'?" I honored her choice of euphemism. Again she flushed deeply.

"Courtney was," I reminded her gently. I wished, fervently if briefly, that Lauren would pray for spunk, not forgiveness.

"Robert, Daisy told me, was hot-blooded, not just in anger but—" Silence.

"Sexually," I finished for her. Sex, like rape, was clearly a word that went unspoken.

"That day he—" She looked at me helplessly. This was difficult for her. "He—he slapped her. He said she was evil, a temptress of Satan, a Jezebel, and that she had aroused impure thoughts in him. Then he slapped her again and forced her to her knees. He made her pray to God for forgiveness for the sins that she, Daisy, had made him, Robert, long to commit."

The convoluted reasoning here took my breath away.

"Had Courtney been flirting with him, coming on in any way?"

"Oh no! She had done nothing but try to bar the door to him and ask him to leave once he forced his way in. And then—" Tears filled her eyes. "He said that because she had defiled his mind with impure thoughts, it was only fitting that she should be defiled as well and that he would take her body, for then, in her impure state, she would beg him to marry her, as who else would wish to?"

Lauren's face was hidden in her hands now; she was sobbing. For herself, I knew, as well as for her dead friend. I went looking for the bathroom and a box of tissue. So this was what Courtney had against Bobert/Robert. I found the tissue and took it to Lauren, patted her shoulder.

"What happened?" I asked as her sobs subsided into sniffles.

"She fought him and then he suddenly seemed to come to his senses. He ran off."

"They were alone at the time? There was no one at home with her?"

"No. And he was wrong in that, too. He was a missionary. Missionaries are forbidden any sexual contact during their mission; they are forbidden even to be alone with a woman."

"And if they are?"

"It could mean excommunication."

"Would it have?"

"I cannot think so if he had merely come to the door to say

that he had not seen her at the funeral. And left, then, upon
realizing that she was home alone. But—"

Yes. *But.*

"But it was so much more. So much—"

"Way across the line," I supplied.

"And after that he left Daisy alone. He returned to his mission.
He did not write or call."

"And if anyone had learned about what he had done?"

"It would have been very bad. I think, though, that he would
perhaps not have told it all, that he would have made it seem as
though Daisy had tempted him and that he had resisted and
fled."

"Would that have been believed?"

"Everyone knew that Daisy had rejected him over and over.
Still, his word would probably have been taken against hers, although his action in going there would have been held against
him. Very much so."

"And now?"

"If it came out, you mean?"

I nodded.

"He would deny it, I am sure, but it would be damaging to his
rise in the Church. He would not want that to happen."

"Would he face excommunication?"

"I don't know, I don't think so, but he is so ambitious. To be
merely Brother Corwin and not, some day, Bishop Corwin, or
stake president or elder—No. That would not do for Robert."

"Who knows about this?"

"Now that Daisy is dead, I am the only one. And now you."

And Robert, too.

"Why did you call him a good man? Why do you wish to protect his reputation? He tried to rape your friend."

"Oh no, it wasn't that, it was— But he—" Her mind struggled
with dogma, male authority, and reality, then surrendered.
"Please," she begged me, so I gave it up too.

"Lauren—would you like to go out to lunch?" I asked impetu-
ously.

Her eyes were startled, afraid. "Oh, *no.* Thank you," she
added.

"Just lunch." I smiled. "We'll have fun. We could go to the
river or a museum or something, too, if you wished."

"I can't," she said, and her eyes had a trapped look in them. Hunted, haunted. "Truly. I can't. I don't go anywhere except church."

She was a Mormon woman in a cage.

Or is that redundant?

Twenty-seven

This Business
of Revelation

I called Robert at the Corwin Insurance Agency. The secretary was as pert and perky as before. She cheerfully took my request, then plunked me into Muzakland, was back in a flash.

"Oh, I'm so-o-o-o sorry. Mr. Corwin doesn't have time to speak with you just now. He also asked me to tell you that he could be of no further help to you." Her voice made it clear that that would be the end of the discussion. Apparently Corwin was used to getting his way. "Have a nice day," she perked.

"I'll leave a message," I persisted.

"Oh?" Puzzled. Since Mr. Corwin had spoken, what else was there to say? "Tell him I have information on Bobert. I will be at this number"—I recited my office number and looked at the clock, four fifty-seven—"until five o'clock."

"Bobert?"

"Yes."

"But—"

"Thank you." I hung up.

One minute and seventeen seconds later my phone rang. Didn't have to hit that boy between the eyes with a two-by-four, no sir. I answered it in my no-kidding-around business voice.

"Robert Corwin."

"A number of intriguing pieces of information have come to my attention in the course of this investigation, Mr. Corwin."

"Miss Colorado, I have no intention of talking further with you on this. I am deeply grieved by Daisy's death and the pain her family is experiencing because of her accident. With prayer and God's help, however, we will all move on. I have no intention of pursuing this any further and I insist that you do the same, that you drop this immediately.''

I laughed.

He sputtered. I imagine he found women who talked back irritating in the extreme.

"This can certainly be the end of our discussion but it will not be the end of my investigation, Mr. Corwin. Or, should I say, Bobert?''

"Miss Colorado, I will absolutely not allow—''

"I'll be in my office for the next hour, Corwin.'' I dropped the "Mr." out of orneriness. I gave him the address. "The fact that I know about your nickname is small potatoes compared to what else I know.''

No sputtering. No anger. Ugly silence, though.

"I have Daisy's diary,'' I continued conversationally. "Names, dates, full accounts of all the important events in her life.''

"Diary?'' He spoke as though it were a foreign word that required translation.

"Diary,'' I agreed, and dropped the receiver gently into its cradle.

All right. Forget about what I said earlier about trying not to flat-out lie. It's an occupational hazard. If Corwin knew what I had—nothing—and what I could prove—nothing—would he spill his guts? No way. Slim and none would be too optimistic an evaluation of my chances of getting anything out of him. Blue moons could come and go and he would merely puff out his chest and inform me that our discussion was over. And he would be right.

Having a woman threaten him was probably an almost unknown experience. I shrugged. Corwin was a big boy. He could get over it, or adjust. Then I considered the kind of man who blustered and ordered and automatically expected to be obeyed by women. This kind of action and reasoning *(sic)* does not realistically evaluate a situation or the options; it merely makes assumptions, often inaccurate ones. This works, of course, if you're in total control. But he wasn't. I am a tough one to control.

Not being in control was the sort of thing I thought would

really flip Robert Corwin's switch. How far would he go? Would he say something stupid? Do something stupid? Get violent? He had with Courtney. One could only hope. And needle. I would leave the prayer to him.

I looked at the clock. Five-twenty. It was fair to say that I was waiting this one out with considerable interest. I didn't have much longer to wait.

He entered my office without knocking and then took up a large amount of space. His threatening-guy attitude said: *Don't try to fuck with me. Don't even think about it.* (Not that he would say fuck, of course.) *Do, and you will regret it.* "I am not amused by this, Miss Colorado," he snarled.

Snarled? Yo! How's that for Christian? "Won't you be seated, Mr. Corwin?" I inquired.

"I won't, no. I won't be here long." He clenched a fist, allowing me to see. More guy stuff. Then he strode around muscularly a bit. I held up pretty well, managed not to collapse in fright.

"Do sit," I said firmly. "I decline to have a conversation with someone who is storming around my office like an underfed pit bull at dinnertime."

He snarled. I rest my case. He sat. Good, at least a well-trained pit bull.

"Your visit to Daisy at the time of your father's death, and when you were a missionary, does not exactly put you in the best possible light," I began cheerfully.

"You can't know about that. I refuse to speak of it."

"But I do. And you are."

"What do you want?" He leaned forward, elbows on his knees. His posture was aggressive, the expression on his face murderous. Hmmm. I thought insurance salesmen were a lot meeker and more mild-mannered than this, especially religious ones.

"As I've told you—" I spoke patiently and patronizingly and watched him clench his jaw. He was really up on tough-guy mannerisms. "I am looking into Courtney Dillard's death. Although you told me"—an exaggeration, but not an outright lie—"that there was no reason for anyone to wish her harm, I found that to be incorrect."

"I do not, *did* not, wish her harm."

I was pleased to see that he was jumping right in, speaking

without thinking it through. There is a reason why people take the fifth and lawyers tell their clients to pipe down.

"No? *If* that is true, it has not always been so."

"Nonsense. Daisy and I were childhood friends. We participated in many youth and young-adult activities in our church. We were engaged briefly. Our engagement was terminated when it became apparent our interests were very different."

Terminated. Interesting word. I used it. "Who terminated it?"

"It was a mutual decision. And a friendly one," he added. Defensively?

I nodded in approval. "It's simple. It has the ring of truth about it. Very believable."

He relaxed visibly.

"Too bad it's a pack of lies."

It took a while for that to filter through his brain cells. I continued. "You had a revelation from God and persuaded Daisy to marry you. Then she ended your engagement; it was far from mutual. When you interrupted your mission because of your father's death, you also spoke with Daisy. You went to her house. You forced your way in even though you knew she was alone. It was not a calm discussion. In the course of it you slapped Daisy several times, forced her to her knees to pray for forgiveness, of you and God, for—you claimed—making you have impure thoughts. Then you threatened to defile her sexually—'rape' is the term in common legal parlance," I added helpfully, "so she would be impure, would beg you to marry her."

I looked at Robert and smiled. Might as well add insult to injury. He sat there, white-faced and silent.

"And all this from a young man who was a missionary at the time and—" I paused but needn't have bothered. I had his complete attention. "And who wished to rise, to become an official in his church. My *my!* I wonder if everyone would agree with your previous evaluation of the situation." I spoke politely, as bland as custard pie.

Dark eyes in a white face. Outside I could hear the whine and thunk of a garbage truck. I love it when life is metaphorical like that.

He spoke finally. "You're making a mistake."

"Am I?"

"You can't prove any of that."

"Can't I?"

"I admit I haven't always been perfect but—"

I waited and then I prompted. "But?"

"I never would have harmed Daisy. Never."

"You find attempted rape harmless?"

He flushed. "It is her brother who threatened to kill her. Many times. They fought often. Ask about Ezra. He said that she had sinned and would not be saved until her blood was spilled in atonement. Ask about *him!*"

I was glad to have the information but it didn't raise Robert in my esteem. I don't particularly respect the It-wasn't-me-it-was-him defense.

"Why did Ezra threaten Daisy?"

"I have said all I intend to." He said this with a pretty fair—if belated—amount of dignity.

So, naturally, I couldn't resist. "Care for a Coke?" I asked. "As long as you're breaking rules, why, what the heck?"

He stood in silence, stared in silence, slammed out noisily.

" 'Bye, Bobert. See you," I murmured.

He was angry enough to do something rash and stupid, I would have put money on it. The phone rang while I was still gloating. Rats. I love to savor victory.

"Kat Colorado," I said, just a bit crossly.

"Have you finished your licorice yet?"

"Howdy, Chad." Ooops, I sounded like a character in a bad western. Could have been worse, though—I could have said "pardner."

"Have I got a deal for you."

Great. I sound like a western character, he sounds like a game-show host. When life starts sounding like TV, it's almost always a bad sign.

"What?"

"White beaches, blue water, icy margaritas, and tan bodies. Not to mention"—he continued hurriedly as I started to make an annoyed sound—"the indescribable satisfaction of helping a child in distress."

Westerns to game shows to soap opera. Real bad sign.

"All this fun and you get paid too. Such a deal."

"It's tough, Chad, but I'm holding myself back, restraining my enthusiasm." Not my sarcasm, though. "I turned it down once, I'm turning it down again."

"You *sure*, Kat?"

"I'm sure."

"Okay." He sounded disappointed but not exactly surprised. "How are you coming along with those background checks?"

"Almost done. Want me to mail them to you or fax them?"

"Fax. Mark it confidential."

"You got it."

"How's your other investigation coming along?"

I played dumb. "Which investigation?"

"Courtney." His voice softened. "I wasn't thinking, but sure, you must have a lot of investigations going. Have you found anything?"

"Yes. Much of it is background, things that her family and friends already know." Nice, huh? A classic example of an answer that isn't an answer but *sounds* like one.

"And the rest?"

"The rest fits in here and there. Hard to tell exactly until I've added it all up."

"Have you found anything that leads you to believe it's murder?"

Whoa. A direct question. He was onto me.

"Ask me later, Chad. It's early on for me to be outlining, never mind filling in the details."

"But something?"

"Yes."

"And what does it tell you about—"

"Gotta run, Chad. I'm pretty tied up. I'll fax this to you the next day or so."

"All right." No humor. Somewhere in the course of this conversation it had taken a hike. Good.

"Chad?"

"Yes?"

"Forget licorice. Stick with hog shares, electronics, that sort of thing."

He laughed, but it was forced.

You know what they say about laughing: *He who laughs last laughs best.*

Or she.

Twenty-eight

Snoop du Jour

I called Medora. Since I couldn't speak with Courtney's siblings, it was on to Plan B. We exchanged polite hellos.

"Kat, I'm sorry that our meeting was interrupted, that my husband—I should have said this before, I know. It's just that it's so difficult—"

"It's all right," I said. And it was. There's something less than ideal about every investigation. What I was having an increasingly hard time with was the fact that I had to keep coming back to Medora to pry things out, to plead for bits of information she should have handed me a long time ago. Like her husband Orson's hostility to his daughter. Like Robert. Like Courtney's brothers and sisters. Like God knows what else.

Why won't people listen when an investigator says: Tell me everything. Let me decide what's important. Instead I had to dig.

"Thank you for not telling Orson—may God forgive me—that I hired you."

"You're welcome. Medora, I have some questions."

"Anything," she said.

I hoped, this time, that it was true.

"How long have you lived in your neighborhood?"

"Over twenty years. I was expecting when we moved here. We definitely needed more room."

"Is it a stable neighborhood?"

"What?"

"Do people stay for a long time or is there a lot of moving in and out?"

"Oh. Mostly for a long time. Recently several older couples—retired, you know—moved out because they didn't need the space, the children gone and all. Otherwise—"

"I want to talk to a neighbor."

"What?"

"You won't let me talk to your family. I want to talk to a neighbor, someone who has known your family over the years."

"What?"

This was today's question, I guess. "I could knock on doors and snoop around the neighborhood but why bother?"

"Oh, I don't know if—"

"Since we're working on this together."

"Oh, well . . ."

"For Courtney's sake." I coaxed her along. In the silence I could almost hear Medora thinking, wheels grinding, gears shifting. Slowly, as always.

"Oh, well . . . I guess, maybe . . ."

I doodled on a notepad—mentally remodeled my kitchen, analyzed the problems of Western civilization and then solved them —as I waited.

"Perhaps Edna Michaels?" she suggested.

"Okay." I snapped up Edna like a starving gator. "What's her address? And her phone number too, please."

"She's in a retirement home now. Sunset Dreams. I go visit her as often as I can. Edna lived in the neighborhood long before we moved in."

"Would she mind if I visited?"

"I think she'd love it. She's a wonderful person, though a little lonely now. It's so sad when you outlive your family and friends, so sad."

Yes. Though probably not as sad as dying a violent death at twenty-two.

"Medora, did Courtney ever speak of getting married?"

"To Robert, you mean? Well, yes, of course. They were engaged, you know. We were quite saddened when she broke the engagement. He is such a fine young man. Her father was angry at that. With her, I mean."

"Robert hit her. Did you know that?"

She gasped. "Oh my goodness me. What did she do to provoke him so? She could be *so* headstrong and naughty."

That silenced me. "You think it was okay that he hit her?" I asked at last.

"Well, no, but still . . . She must have done something to deserve it, mustn't she? Robert is such a fine young man. He wouldn't hit her for no reason."

I was tempted to point out that fine young men don't slap women for *any* reason, but why bother? Might as well save my breath to cool my porridge, as Alma would say.

Medora continued: "And Daisy could be so provoking, you know?"

I counted to ten. "Did Courtney speak of marriage in any other context?"

"She said she thought that young women should finish their education before marriage and that was what she wished to do."

Did I detect a slight note of disapproval there?

"Her current boyfriend—was she serious about him?"

"I don't know. She spoke of him sometimes and he sounded like a nice young man. I never really asked much about him. I didn't want to encourage it at all, you see. He wasn't LDS. It was just one more thing pulling Daisy away from her family and our Church."

"Thank you, Medora," I said, suddenly weary of young Mormon men who were "fine" even though they slapped women, and young men who were unacceptable merely because they weren't Latter-day Saints.

Edna Michaels was a treat. She was dressed in white leggings, red sneakers, and an extra-large red-and-white T-shirt that hung on her tiny frame. The T-shirt said OLDSTERS DO IT BETTER! Looking at Edna's face, lined with character and age, I not only believed it, I would have put money on it. Five minutes into our conversation I decided that she and Alma had to meet. Ten minutes in, I wondered if the world was ready for them.

"Why are you here?" she demanded immediately.

"I'm snooping around," I replied cheerfully.

"Is that your job?"

"Yes."

"You get paid for that?"

"Yes."

"Well, my stars, I am impressed! I snooped all my life and I never made a red cent. Not a red cent nor a wooden nickel, either." She looked me up and down. "Not doing too badly, are you?"

"No."

"Are you on an expense account?"

"Yes."

"So we could go out to lunch?"

"We could and we should."

She sighed happily. "The food here is quite good but blah-blah-blah and bland-bland-bland. Why do people insist on giving seniors bland food? Just because the spice has gone out of most of our other pleasures doesn't mean—"

She looked at me and I laughed. She had dimples and crow's-feet and the lines and wrinkles that come from laughing and loving and living life fully. She was beautiful.

"Mexican, Italian, Chinese, anything you want."

"Mexican." She sighed happily.

We went to her favorite restaurant. The decor was cheap Tijuana with painted pottery, velvet paintings, polyester serapes—stuff even a B-grade movie wouldn't stoop to.

Edna ordered a Pacifico. "I'm feeling wild," she exclaimed as she drank it right out of the bottle. Then she ordered a chicken taco, cheese enchilada, and beef tamale, extra extra jalapeños. "*Really* wild," she explained.

"Were you always wild?"

"Oh my goodness no. Hardly at all, and mostly I hid it. Now I figure it's one of the prerogatives of old age. I plan to go out with a bang." She winked. "But that's not what you came to talk about, is it? What is today's snoop?"

Snoop of the day, I liked that. *Snoop du jour.*

"The Dillard family."

"Ah." She piled a jalapeño on a bite of chicken taco. "Long story, I'd better fuel up."

"You know the family well?"

"Oh yes, no one better. None outside their church, that is."

She picked up her beer bottle, noted it was empty, and sighed. I waved at the waitress and ordered another. Edna nodded happily at me.

"The Dillards were determined to convert me. Ha ha. Fat chance of that happening."

I nodded. It was difficult for me to picture Edna Michaels in the Mormon Church. No beers, for openers.

"Mrs. Michaels—"

"Call me Edna." She waved her fork at me. "Where shall I start?"

"Anywhere." I didn't want to finger Courtney. I wanted an overall picture.

"They're good people, a good family and good neighbors. The Dillards helped me a lot over the years. After my husband died, especially. If there was ever something I couldn't handle or do, why, they were more than willing. Many's the time one of the boys would mow my lawn or trim back my shrubbery because they just 'happened' to have their tools out. And always with a smile on their faces too, like it was just the biggest treat to help an old lady." She nodded.

"Course, we were good neighbors to them too. It's a two-way street, that's for sure. I watched after those kids often enough, and once I even went to the hospital with Medora. I was the one who held her hand. It was her fourth or fifth, I forget now, and she was popping it out pretty fast. I was lucky to get her there in time. Time they found her husband and got Orson to the hospital, he was already a daddy again."

She smiled at the memory, then burped delicately.

"In many ways I loved them just like family. Just like. Only I never could get used to that dang religion of theirs." She sighed.

The restaurant was emptying out but no one seemed to mind that we were lingering. We had pushed our plates over to one side. Edna chewed thoughtfully on a chip now and then. Loaded with salsa and hot sauce, of course.

"Mormons are a God-fearing community of people. They take care of their own, don't smoke, drink, or cuss. I admire that about them."

I nodded. Me too.

"Not that I want to be like that."

I nodded. Me either.

"But holy mackerel, if you're LDS and aren't born a man, don't plan on having much freedom or independence. Or fun, for that matter. And everyone, man, woman, and child, does exactly what the elders in the Church tell 'em to. They even vote according to what they get told. That's too much for me, by gum.''

"The family?" I gave her a gentle push.

"Well, Orson pretty much just worked. He's in sales. He worked for others and he went into business for himself once. He is the kind who is always changing jobs, the kind who works hard but never gets ahead. You know?"

I knew.

"He took good care of his family and paid his tithes but I think that was about it. I don't think Medora had such an easy time of it, either, trying to stretch those dollars around that big family and a husband who took out his dissatisfactions with his job, his life, and himself on her. She always put a good front on it, though. All those years I never saw it slip or heard her complain."

"The kids?" Another little push.

"Good kids all. Never a problem with them when they were young. Not one."

"And when they were older?"

She giggled. "I wondered if you'd get that one."

I smiled and hoped the beers weren't sneaking up on her.

"They had two rebels in that family. Two. And that's something for a Mormon family. They generally keep those kids with their toes on the line. Why, I've known—"

"Two?" I prompted. "Which two?"

"Daisy, their youngest, and Ezra." She picked up her beer, saw it was empty, put it down again.

"Would you like another?"

"Don't mind if I do. Thank you, my dear. This is some kind of a treat, I can tell you!"

I signaled the waitress and asked for another Pacifico and a diet Pepsi. Today I was leaving the wildness to Edna. "Tell me about Daisy."

"Daisy watched her dad push her mother around her whole life. Not to mention she had plenty of brothers to push her around. She didn't want that, by golly. She wanted an education. She wanted to make up her own mind about things and she didn't want to get married at twenty. She was a sweet girl, smart and sharp, ambitious and pretty. I liked her the best of the bunch.''

''Wild?''

''Oh my no. No, no. Though the way her family talked sometimes, you'd've thought so. That was because the child asked questions and said things that didn't go down so well with them. Like that the Church shouldn't put down women and tell people how to vote. And by golly, they shouldn't. She questioned authority sometimes but she didn't challenge it. She minded her parents and went to church. When she was twenty or thereabouts, she moved out. Had enough, I guess. Wild? Pooh. If everyone was wild like Daisy Dillard, we'd have a mighty peaceful, good-hearted world.''

''And the boy? Ezra?''

''Ezra.'' Her face said that was another story. ''He wasn't so much wild as scary, the way he took things to heart. He believed in the Principle—that's how they refer to polygamy, you know. A Polyg—that's what they say. Several wives and a passel of children, I hear. Sees himself as a prophet and his word as God's word, his thought as God's command. And those in opposition, why, they should be hewn down like weeds.''

Fire and brimstone. Death and destruction.

''It happens like this, you know. It happens more frequently than the Mormons want to admit. Some you read about in the paper, the armed camps with wives and kids, guns and supplies and the word of God, they say, hot and bloody in their mouth. The Church won't have anything to do with such as them, but it gives birth to them, yes it does.''

''Ezra?'' I prompted.

''Scary, like I said. Long hair, a beard, two wives when I last heard and him always screaming hate and bloodshed. His family wouldn't have anything much to do with him when he took to polygamy and all, and then, of course, he was excommunicated. I heard there was bad blood between him and Daisy.''

''Why?''

''I never heard and she never told me.''

''Where is Ezra now?''

''Land's sakes, I haven't a clue. He went to Utah once. I have no idea whether he stayed there.''

"Can you guess what the bad blood between Daisy and Ezra was about?"

She hesitated. "Everything I told you was just general, the things a friend and neighbor would know. I don't like to be talking more personally. About Daisy, that is—I don't give a hoot about Ezra. Maybe you better tell me a little more about this snooping and all."

"Daisy died recently in an automobile accident."

"Oh my!"

"Medora doesn't think it's an accident. She hired me to look into it. Her husband, Orson, doesn't approve, so she is doing this behind his back. Medora doesn't wish me to talk to Daisy's brothers and sisters. When I asked to speak to a family friend, she gave me your name."

"Dead?" Her face had crumpled and she suddenly looked her age. "Dead?"

I hate being the bearer of bad news and death is the worst. I waited until a little color crept back into her cheeks.

"Edna?"

"Hmmm? Oh. Well, yes, of course I'll help you. For Daisy? Of course I will. I wouldn't have thought Medora would have had the gumption to go against her Orson. I'm proud of her, I am."

"Was there anyone in her family that didn't wish Daisy well?" Euphemisms again.

"No, not mostly. They all got along fine. They were a close, loving family. No one liked it that Daisy stopped going to church, but they all loved her. Love the sinner, hate the sin, you know. And there's not one in that family who'd swat a fly if it flew in his face. Not one." She sniffed. "Except for Ezra, of course. That boy was filled up with hate. He always did relish the sight of spilled blood and relish the thought of spilling it." She sighed heavily and I reached out to pat her hand.

"Daisy's dead. Take me home, dear. The wild's plumb gone out of me now and I'm just a sad, tired old lady."

So I did. We drove in silence most of the way. Then impulse triumphed over better judgment. Again. "I think you'd like my grandmother," I said just before I reached the old folks home.

"Oh?" Wary. "Does she crochet, drink tea, and read large-print *Reader's Digests*?"

"No. She's on the Granny Hot Line for Kids, shoots pool, plays bunko, and drinks manhattans."

"I think I might like her, too," Edna said, a little sparkle back in her eyes and voice.

"Bunko's every Tuesday. Are you busy?"

"I am now."

"Pick you up at seven?"

"I'll be ready," Edna promised me. "And maybe I'll think of something that could help. I'll try." There were tears in her eyes. I could tell without looking.

Why is it that those we love most are the ones we lose? I wonder about this kind of thing a lot but I rarely come up with answers. After dropping Edna off I dropped the philosophical reflections and made a more practical list instead.

Numero Uno was the brother, Ezra. I was getting pretty interested in Ezra; thought it might be time for a little heart-to-heart chat with the boy. And *goddamn* if this wasn't one more important thing Medora had neglected to tell me. Hard to believe we were on the same team sometimes.

Two was Belle. She was a runaway but not nonexistent. There's a paper trail on everyone. Time to follow it.

Three? Chad. I called Charity on that.

"Want to play cops and robbers?" I asked.

"Is it dangerous?" she asked hopefully.

"No."

"Bummer. Interesting?"

"Yes."

"What?"

I told her.

She laughed. "That sounds like fun. Tomorrow?"

"Good."

"I can take it as far as I want to?" She was humming in delight.

"Yes." That was my second rash statement of the day.

When will I learn?

Twenty-nine

Wanted:
Dead or Alive

I called Robert Corwin. Perky was not pleased to hear from me but she put me through. Corwin was less pleased.

"Yes?" Frosty. No. Glacial.

"Tell me what you know about Ezra Dillard." No please. It wasn't because I forgot.

"I knew Ezra as a child. I know nothing of him now."

"Where is he?"

"I don't know."

I laughed my this-isn't-funny-but-I'll-pretend-you're-just-kidding-around laugh. "Don't make me play hardball, Corwin. Where?" I waited out the silence while he made up his mind.

"Rocklin."

"Where in Rocklin?"

"I don't know. I'm not even sure about Rocklin but that's what I heard."

"What did he have against Daisy?"

"She was always talking that woman stuff—equal rights—to Ezra's wife. He didn't like it." Corwin's tone said he agreed with Ezra.

"And?"

"That was enough."

"Enough maybe, but not all."

"All," he said.

There are times when my boredom threshold is real low; this was one of them.

"You're forgetting the wrong things, Corwin. You're forgetting how much I have on you. You're forgetting I'm a born trouble-maker with a big mouth."

We sat in silence while he remembered. I started whistling "Somewhere Over the Rainbow." Nothing. I started a count-down. Ten . . . nine . . . eight . . . He didn't crack until I got to two.

"Rumor has it Daisy had an abortion. That's what Ezra said, anyway. I know nothing of it and all this happened some time ago. Anyway, Ezra held it a sin." Again Corwin's voice told me he agreed with Ezra. "He held it against her. It came at a bad time too, at a time when he and his first wife couldn't have children."

"And?"

"He spoke of saving her. Of atonement. I've got to go." He hung up.

I shivered. Atonement? Daisy had died with her blood spilled on the ground. Was her death an accident? Or could it have been blood atonement under what many still believed to be Mormon law?

I wondered how much of the story on Ezra was exaggeration. I thought Corwin would exaggerate in a heartbeat, lie in a minute to shift the focus away from himself and onto another. Ezra—bad-boy Dillard, bad-boy Mormon, survivalist, polygamist, and advocate of blood atonement—seemed the perfect scapegoat.

Ezra Dillard wasn't in the phone book. Surprise. I flipped through to the yellow pages and looked for a gun or sports shop in the Rocklin area, noted two addresses, and headed out.

Rocklin, like everything else within commuting distance of Sacramento, is changing. New developments, new businesses, some upscale housing. But there's an old part of town too, away from the malls and supermarkets. There you find a feed store, hardware, a grill, bars, and a drugstore. And it's small town. Folks know each other. The gun shop wasn't hard to find; the sign in the window was a big one. **Guns Ammo Hunting Liscences.** They could print big here even if they couldn't spell. I walked in.

Dust and stale cigarette smoke. More signs * *Insured by Smith and Wesson* * *When Guns Are Outlawed Only Outlaws Will Have Guns* * *Guns Don't Kill, People Do* * *Take My Wife, Take My Dog, But Keep*

*Your @# %$&@ Hands Off My Gun * NRA Spoken Here * A Gun Is a Man's Best Friend * Don't Pick On Me, I'm Packing * My Gun Is My Right.*

Who says the Wild West is dead?

On the wall behind a counter filled with handguns and topped by an old cash register a target had been tacked up. Hillary Clinton's picture, head shot, was in the center of the target—peppered with bullet holes.

The comforting thing about a place like this is the absence of ambiguity. You know right where you are and where you stand. A bunch of WANTED: DEAD OR ALIVE posters caught my eye but I didn't bother reading them.

An old codger looking like—I flicked my eyes over one of the WANTED posters—a certifiable bad guy slumped on a stool behind the counter oiling a gun, caressing the steel as if it were human flesh. An unlit cigarette dangled from his lips; a two-day growth of gray stubble gave his face dimension. He was at least sixty, scowling, and butt ugly.

"Help you." It wasn't a question. We both knew he didn't want to help.

"I'm looking for a man by the name of Ezra Dillard. He lives around here. He buys a lot in here." I stated it as fact to move the conversation along.

His flat eyes flicked over me. "Never heard of him." He yawned. I'd seen better-looking teeth on *Wild Kingdom*. The cigarette wobbled but stuck to his lip.

I pulled my wallet out of my purse and flipped it open to my investigator's license. "He's the beneficiary in a will and I've been hired to find him." Nothing. "There's money in it for information leading to his whereabouts." Oh criminey, I was sounding like a bad western again.

His eyes flickered now with interest. "How much?"

"What do you care? You don't know him." I put my wallet away.

"I might not and then again, I might."

They say certain foods and vitamins improve your memory but I've never seen it. In my business it's greenbacks—and the bigger the bucks, the better the improvement. I looked around the hole-in-the-wall store while Mr. Might or Might Not considered the angles. Dust and spiderwebs were everywhere except on the guns. Those were oiled, spit-polished, and shined up like a last hope.

Odd, I thought, that instruments of death were the only beautiful thing in here.

"What's it worth to you?" He pulled the cigarette off his lower lip and laid it down carefully on the cash register. A bit of paper on his lip marked where the cigarette had been.

"His address, twenty. I pay after I verify it. More information—his comings and goings, talk about him and his family, general information so I know I've got the right guy"—I shrugged—"up to fifty, maybe. It's got to be good."

"Twenty now, the rest later." His eyelid twitched. He dropped one gun part on another. It clunked, then the chamois embraced it, black against tan.

"No."

"No money, no info."

"I look like I just fell off the turnip truck?" I turned and started out past shelves filled with boxes of ammo.

"Hey."

I kept going.

"Hey! All right. Have it your way."

I came back.

He launched off into directions that involved a highway and surface streets and then moved into local landmarks.

"Draw me a map," I said. So he did. "Anything else?"

"Naw. Not until I see something for it."

"Suit yourself," I said cheerfully. "You're not the only one in town." I turned to walk again.

"How'm I to know I can trust you?"

"You aren't, no more than I know about you." I glanced around the shop. "Whatever I said or did wouldn't make a difference. Someone with upwards of three hundred guns, at least one of which is under the counter and loaded, doesn't have a lot of trust in him." I stared at him and he stared me back. "You talking or not? I don't have the time to waste."

"Ezra's a piece of work, all right. Not many like him and I say it's a damn good thing too, although he's a good customer, I'll say that for him. He buys steady and he's always interested in anything new and available. Looks like a mountain man from a hunerd years ago. Always pays in cash, don't believe in checks or credit cards.''

"He buy enough so you give him a discount?''

"I take care of my customers.'' He looked past me to the door. I could barely see that far what with the dust and smoke level. If this were L.A., there would be posted hazard warnings. A couple of old-timers slouched outside in the sunshine telling stories. The gun guy stared at them. I stared at him.

"Dillard popular with his neighbors?''

He refocused on me. "Ask 'em.''

"You forgetting you want to make some money on this?''

It was a struggle, I could tell. Would he rather make a few bucks or be a rude asshole? Tough call. He went for filthy lucre— this time, anyway.

"They think about this like I do—he's a piece of work. You seen 'm?''

I shook my head.

"Long hair. Long beard. He wears overalls and some kind of homemade shirt. The women and the kids the same, handmade stuff, the women in long dresses and aprons. They all look to have stepped out of some history book, pioneer section.''

Plural again. "Women?''

"Yeah. He's got two living there with him. One's his wife, the other's a sister-in-law or cousin or some damn thing.''

"How many children?''

He shrugged. He wasn't interested in children. "There's at least one at school age 'cause I know Ezra got into it with the authorities. He wouldn't put 'em into school, said it was a godless environment. Hell, he wouldn't even take 'em to the doctor to get 'em their shots. Said God was the only protector or doctor they'd ever need.''

See what I mean about small towns? You just have to get people going—that's the tough part.

"He's a real feisty bastard, ready to get in your face the least little thing hits him wrong. Him and I gets along. Course, we never talk about nuthin' much and I'm here to make a sale, not criticize his lifestyle.''

"So the kids aren't in school?''

"Naw. Home schooling. They worked something out. They keep to themselves, do for themselves.''

"Do they have any friends in town?"

"Like I said, they keep to themselves." He snorted. "I think they think they're too damn good for the likes of us. God's chosen, or some damn thing."

"Anyone else in town they do business with who might know something about them?"

He shook his head. "There is, I don't know about it. Closest you'd come to that'd be the librarian. They go in there a fair amount."

A bell jingled as the door opened. A blast of sunshine fell into the room but got discouraged and gave up before it reached me. A small breeze stirred and died. The codgers had finished chatting and one of them ambled through the store.

"Hey, Manny," the codger wheezed.

Time to go. "Thanks, Manny," I called as I sucked in my breath and squeezed past the codger who was short and round and took up most of the aisle.

"Hey!"

"See you."

"Hey, what about my money?"

"I'll check it out, then I'll be back."

The door closed on his third "hey." Amazing how money gets people wound up. I walked across the street into a gas station and asked where the library was. A mechanic who looked like he'd never read a book and didn't want to start now directed me. Two blocks, he said. Turn right. I walked that too, the sun in my face, breeze in my hair, spring all around. Hard to beat that.

It would, I thought, be a small miracle if I found the library open. Libraries everywhere have taken a heavy hit. In the good old days they operated on a shoestring. Now they were down to a paper clip.

The Rocklin Public Library was a small wooden building badly in need of paint. Not too many years left on the roof, either. There was a car out front, a promising sign. I walked up the walkway, cracked concrete with grass sprouting in the cracks. The grass there was healthier looking than the grass in the lawn. I can never figure stuff like that. I was still thinking about it as I ambled up the steps. The building was locked but someone was working inside. A woman politely came to the door, opening it a crack to speak to me. This is small town too, the courtesy, the personal effort.

"I'm sorry, we're closed today. I'm just shelving books, making some repairs, and trying to catch up."

"May I come in and talk to you while you work?"

"Oh?"

I showed her my license. "I'm doing an investigation. I think perhaps you can help."

"Ohhh." She breathed it out on a sigh. "Just like on TV."

"Yes." Okay, it was shameless opportunism, I admit it. It worked, though.

She flung the door open. "Come in, please."

She waved me to a seat at the library table where she had been repairing books. She was about my age but dressed and acted much older, a fifty-year-old woman in a thirty-two-year-old body. Small-town women sometimes seem to become instantly middle-aged. It happens right after marriage and the first child.

"I'm Lisa Kittredge, the head librarian." She laughed. "The only librarian, really, but 'head' sounds better, don't you think?" She didn't wait for an answer. "How may I help you?" Absently she pushed a book aside, her repair project on hold.

"I'm doing a background investigation. Ezra Dillard is part of it."

"Oh?" Alert and interested, no doubt about it.

"I understand that Mr. Dillard has very little to do with anyone in town but that he does frequent the library."

"Yes, that's true. I don't know him, however. As you pointed out, he's not very social. *Anti*social would be more like it."

"You know more than you think you do."

"I do?"

"Sure. Think of how much you could learn about someone just from knowing the videos he watched, the groceries he bought, the magazines he subscribed to, the—"

"Books he took out of the library," she finished triumphantly, bouncing a little in her chair, her voice excited. She'd been a Nancy Drew fan when she was younger, I'd put money on it.

"Oh, this *is* fun. I loved Nancy Drew when I was a girl."

See? I'd pat myself on the back but, really, it was way too easy.

"Do you have records of the books an individual checks out?"

"No. Only if they haven't been returned in time. But it doesn't matter, I can tell you what you need to know."

She beamed at me and I beamed back. Lisa Kittredge was a lovely change of pace from Manny. And books beat guns any day.

"*Never* any fiction. Well, occasionally children's books but they are usually Bible stories or stories from history. I tried once to get them to give the children some storybooks but they wouldn't." She sighed. "It was sad to see the excitement in the little ones' eyes as they looked at the books and started to reach for them. He, Ezra, slapped one child's hand. Their eyes went out like lights. Those children just stood there, their hands at their sides and their eyes down, until he led them out. Sad, isn't it?"

I looked at my clenched hands and opened them slowly. Sad? Slapping a child and shutting down eager young minds? No, I didn't think sad really covered it.

"The books?" I reminded her gently.

"Yes. As I said, they were all nonfiction and most of them were how-to books on basic skills."

"Like construction?"

"Yes. And organic farming, and sewing. Baking, canning, or drying foodstuffs, all that sort of thing. He, Ezra, once said something about being totally self-sufficient."

"They drive here?"

"Yes. He always drives. It's a new truck. Beige. Maybe a Ford." Self-sufficient except for guns and vehicles.

"One day I told them that the government publishes pamphlets on just this kind of thing, that all he had to do was send away for them. They're either free or very inexpensive. I don't have the pamphlets but I showed him a listing of subjects and where to write. Ezra got all excited, wrote it down carefully, made a list of what he wanted to send away for."

"And that was it?"

"Yes. We-ell, once Ezra saw a book about that mountain man in Idaho. You know, the one who killed several men and eluded a massive manhunt for ages? Ezra took that out and one of the women—there are two living out there, you know?"

I knew.

"One of then took out a beautiful book we have on Amish quilts. I wish I could tell you more," Lisa said wistfully, "but they are really very private and unfriendly people."

"Do both women wear wedding rings?"

"Yes, plain gold bands."

"The women and children, how do they act?"

"Do you remember the slogan—Victorian era, I believe—that children should speak only when spoken to?"

I nodded.

"That's how they acted. And the women too. It was very odd. The day the one woman wanted to take out the Amish-quilt book, she picked it up, walked over to Ezra, touched him timidly on the arm, and pointed. He looked at the book, then nodded. The women occasionally spoke in a low voice to the children but I could never hear what they said. They never spoke to me. Once I tried to offer a child a book and the mother stepped between me and the child and shook her head. She never spoke a word."

I wondered how long it took to destroy children and childhood. Not very long, probably.

"Never a word, never a smile or laugh."

Gone already, probably.

"Did they look cared for?"

"The children? Oh, yes. They looked clean and strong and healthy. You know the oddest thing, though?"

"What?"

"They didn't look or dress or act like children but like little bitty silent adults."

My heart closed in pain. I stood. "Thank you for your time and help."

"Did I help?" Lisa Kittredge asked.

"Very much."

"If I remember anything, I'll call you, shall I?"

"Please." I smiled and handed her a business card.

She watched me walk out, turning my card over and over, eyes wide with excitement still. My visit had been the high point of her day. But not, I thought, of mine.

Ezra and the Ezrettes would probably take that honor.

Thirty

Ezra and the Ezrettes

It was a good thing I had a map; I wouldn't have found it otherwise. Even with a map it wasn't a piece of cake. I passed some luxury homes, then a bunch of older places, working ranches and farms. Ezra Dillard lived in a remote area with old places, run-down and shacky places for neighbors. I drove by it once, almost twice. No name, no number. Barbed-wire fencing, a metal gate with a chain lock. NO TRESPASSING signs. No welcome mat.

I parked the Bronco down the road where it was sheltered from view by a stand of trees. The strip all along the road was fairly densely planted in layers of bushes and trees, all of it untrimmed. I walked back to the gate. There was barbed wire strung on the top so I climbed through the barbed-wire fencing. The lesser of two evils.

I walked down the dirt road. I wasn't exactly sneaky but I didn't advertise either. I wouldn't be here long and I wouldn't be invited back. Might as well take in as much as possible this go-around. Ahead of me the road curved. I rounded it slowly, staying in the shelter of several trees. The area before me was open, clear, and sunny.

There were two houses in the clearing, a barn and a number of outbuildings. A generator was running. I saw a propane tank, a gasoline pump, and farm equipment. All the equipment looked new and top of the line. Everything was spotlessly clean and in good repair. I could see a large truck garden and a small orchard. Smoke came out of the chimney.

I didn't hear him coming.

I heard him pump the shotgun, though, heard it just fine.

"Put your hands out. Turn around."

I did. Real slow, real easy. Hands empty and out slightly to the side.

"You can't read? It's posted: No trespassing."

I said nothing, sized him up. He looked like an Old Testament prophet in twentieth-century overalls and sturdy boots. Beard to the middle of his chest, hair below his shoulders.

He looked scary.

The shotgun was cradled in his arms. Lovingly, as a woman would hold a baby. A large dog, maybe a shepherd-rottweiler mix, stood at his heel, mouth open, a long string of drool stretching almost to the ground. One word and he'd rip my throat out.

"Who are you?"

I wanted to say *Ding dong, Avon calling* but I couldn't. I was too scared. There's a limit to my smarting off, though I hadn't known it for sure before this. I said nothing. The dog growled. The shotgun gleamed.

"You from the city, the county, the schools? What?"

I shook my head. I was still searching for my voice. It was in there somewhere, in the middle of all that fear. It wasn't just the shotgun—I don't scare that easily, though a gun would make me wary—it was the shotgun, the dog, and the eyes.

Especially the eyes.

They were the eyes of a crazy person. Someone who heard voices inside and listened carefully to them. And believed them. Charles Manson has eyes like that.

"What?" Ezra asked again, and then added: "They don't call me a patient man."

I had no trouble believing that. The dog growled, an ominous, faraway rumble like the beginning of thunder.

"Did anyone tell you that your sister died?"

"My sister?"

"Daisy."

For a moment the madness in his eyes cleared and there was a softness, almost a sweetness there. It was gone so quickly I doubted my perception.

"I have no sister. I have no family but what the Lord has bestowed upon me. For thus sayeth the Lord unto me, His servant, His Prophet, that I shall forsake all Worldly Ties and Authority and it shall be as He commands that I shall receive wives and beget children and join only with other True Servants of God that His work may go forward. All obstacles shall be removed and that is His will, thus sayeth the Lord, and I the instrument, the servant of the Lord my God and such is His work and way. Even so, Amen."

I would have thought that the Lord had a stronger command of logic, not to mention knowing a run-on sentence, or two, when He saw one. Still, I've been wrong before. I thought this but I didn't say it. The Manson eyes kept me silent.

"Murdered," I said.

"Thus sayeth the Lord: There shall be Blood Atonement for Sin, in particular for the spilling of life's blood from a woman's womb. It is the word of God and I, His Prophet, so be it. In her death was His will accomplished. Even so, Amen."

I didn't like Ezra's god any more than I liked Ezra. Vengeful, bloodthirsty, full of hate and poor grammar. I wondered if Ezra spoke like this all the time, spitting out *Thus sayeth the Lord, So be it,* and *Even so, Amen* like watermelon seeds at a barbecue.

Ezra shifted his eyes, and I turned slightly to follow his gaze. Two young women, a teenage girl, and four small children stood in a single mute line in front of the larger house, staring at me. Ezra and the Ezrettes. They weren't smiling. One of the women and the teenager were noticeably pregnant.

That I shall receive wives and beget children . . .

Lisa, the librarian, had been right. The children looked like little old people. I shivered. Polygamy—the Principle, it is called —is still widely practiced by Fundamentalist Mormons, though no longer condoned by the Church. Except historically and in heaven. In heaven each man may become a god on his own planet and gather multiple wives around him. Good old Ezra was jumping the gun, though, was a Polyg in the here and now, not the hereafter. I looked back at him. One more try.

"Your sister, Daisy, was murdered."

"Be careful, Woman, that you do not become an Obstacle in the Path of the Prophet of the Lord." He swung the shotgun in my direction. "You will leave now."

I left.

I couldn't hear footsteps behind me, neither his nor the dog's, but I could feel their presence, their insane-eyed escort. I exited the way I entered, then looked back. Ezra stood, shotgun cradled and dog at his feet, some fifty feet down the road in heavy shadow.

This was not a place I wanted to visit again. I climbed in the Bronco and locked the door behind me—as though a locked door was protection from a shotgun blast or homicidal craziness. I pulled away, driving fast.

I was thinking pretty fast too: a profitable farm; two houses; two, maybe three wives; numerous children and more on the way; new vehicles and farm equipment. This was not a shoestring operation. A corral and fenced-in fields—so they had livestock— and I had heard chickens. Not too shabby, considering Ezra had no visible means of support. Add to that the trained and vicious (yes, indeed) dog, the guns, the fencing that was a barricade, the cash-only transactions at the ammo store. You didn't have to be a math major to add it up.

I wasn't and I did. Piece of cake.

Drugs.

I wondered if he was foolish enough to be growing marijuana on his land here, or if it was in the back country somewhere. The latter probably. Or maybe a methamphetamine lab. I smiled in satisfaction. I would have to play some more with this one, see what I could come up with. Trouble, I was sure of it.

Even so, Amen.

I flipped on the radio, drummed my fingers on the steering wheel in time to the music. The song was "I Fought the Law and the Law Won." Listen up, Ezra.

Okay, the hot bets here were not on Ezra. No. I was betting that he hadn't been sending his 1040's in. Or paying his self-employment tax like a good boy and an upstanding American citizen. *Tsk-tsk.* I was also betting the IRS would be interested.

Even so, Amen.

I was feeling pretty smug by the time I got back to the office. And hungry. The pizzas started arriving about twenty-five minutes after I did. Domino's, Straw Hat, Pizza Hut, Round Table, and Steve's. They were all extra large with anchovies. Gag. Nothing I hate more than anchovies. Except maybe arguing. All the delivery guys wanted to be paid and they didn't care a bit who had ordered the pizzas or who hadn't. They wanted to be tipped, too.

By the time the fifth pizza arrived we were all clear on the concept. I was pissed. They were pissed. I'd gone from hungry to starving but it was all or nothing, and I didn't want five extra-large anchovy pizzas. The delivery guys and I agreed that they wouldn't make any deliveries to this address unless payment was guaranteed with a credit card. I tipped them three bucks each and they left.

The incident dispelled a bunch of my good humor and took me down a peg or two, no question. This is not the kind of thing that is intended as a thoughtful gesture.

Even so, Amen.

Thirty-one

Haunting Melody

First stop next morning was the Rocklin gun shop. Manny looked surprised to see me. I'd come not just to pay for my information, but to lay the groundwork for more.

"Hey, figured you to be long gone. Figured you'd copped a freebie and taken me."

"Yeah? That's because you think everyone's as unprincipled as you are."

He thought that one over. Maybe "unprincipled" was too big a word? I pulled out a couple of twenties and tossed them on the dirty glass counter. Manny stroked the money the way Ezra had stroked his gun. What is it with these guys? I put a business card in the smeared dust.

"In case you hear anything else."

He looked at it without expression, placed it on the cash register.

I had hoped it was my imagination but it wasn't. The beige Thunderbird pulled in behind me in lock step. As on the trip out, there was no attempt at subtlety. The driver was a white male with dark hair and sunglasses. He looked like a career Marine who not only had taken orders for years but had also avoided original thought. And humor.

He was polite, though. No tailgating or speeding or ugly personal stuff. And he was onto the old slow-down-for-the-yellow-light-and-then-zip-through-at-the-last-possible-moment trick, so I didn't lose him on that one. Or on the sudden three-lane-cross-over-and-abrupt-freeway-exit one. When I parked, he kept going. As I walked down the block and up the steps to my office, he cruised past. I gave him a cheery little wave but he didn't respond. I didn't let it get me down.

There was a large floral arrangement wrapped in clear plastic leaning against my office door.

Say it with flowers.

It was a funeral wreath.

I didn't let that get me down, either. I called Charity.

"Yum! Do I have stuff to tell you."

"Good. Lunch?"

"Sure."

We settled on Scott's Seafood at eleven forty-five. Then I called Chad Wharton. "Do you have some free time this morning?"

"What's up?"

"There are a few things I'd like to talk to you about."

"What?"

I waited it out.

"All right. Go ahead. Talk."

"It would be better in person."

You don't necessarily get more information in person. Sometimes it works the other way around—people talk more freely on the phone—but that way you miss the gestures and facial expressions. I wanted to see him on my turf too, not his. Idly I pulled flowers out of the wreath, trying to salvage as much of each stem as possible, and then stuck the blossoms into a water glass. Much better.

"All right." Chad didn't bother to hide his reluctance. "I'll be at your office in half an hour to forty-five minutes."

We hung up and I filled another water glass with flowers, added water, and walked them over to two of the offices in my building. Then I snipped off the remaining blooms to float in a glass bowl on my desk.

The flowers weren't sympathy so that narrowed the possibilities down: a mistake or a warning. I called the florist.

"Was there something wrong?" She sounded upset.

"Not at all. The wreath is beautiful. There was no card, though."

"The gentleman was adamant about that. He said he wished it to be an anonymous expression."

"Those were his words?"

"Yes."

"Did he place the order in person?"

"No. It was a telephone order. I spoke with him myself. He asked for one of our more expensive arrangements and left the choice to me."

"He paid by credit card?" I crossed my fingers and hoped.

"No. He asked for the total and said he would send a messenger over with the money."

"Cash?"

"Yes. Will there be anything else? I really need to get back to work."

She was tired of the third degree. I could understand. It happens to me regularly. I thanked her and hung up. For some odd reason the haunting zither melody from *The Third Man* played in my mind.

It took Wharton forty minutes and he arrived a little out of breath, a little flustered. He declined coffee, settled into his seat, and looked at me. I smiled, wondering if he'd jump in and break the silence. He did.

"Good job on the background checks, Kat. Thorough. Thanks."

"You're welcome."

"And the other . . . Courtney?" I heard just the trace of a stammer and his voice dropped, changed. Losing someone you love is bad enough; murder makes it unspeakable. "Anything there?" He'd made his voice level out and sound professional again but there was still something in his eyes.

"That's what I want to talk to you about." Not true and I dodged his question. "Tell me about your last evening together, could you?"

"The night Courtney died?"

"Yes."

He shifted in his chair, his eyes focusing on a wall where two watercolors of unlikely but lovely landscapes hung. "You think it'll help? It's . . ." His eyes, pain hanging out there, met mine.

"It could help," I said gently.

He cracked a knuckle. "It was a big evening for us. Courtney hadn't met my parents yet and we were planning to have dinner with them and formally announce our engagement. I was pleased and Courtney was excited and a little nervous, although I told her that she had no reason to feel that way, that they would love her as much as I did. Who wouldn't?" His eyes were bleak.

I stayed with the concrete stuff, the facts. "Dinner at a restaurant?"

He shook his head. "At my folks' home in Folsom. It's a beautiful home in a secluded area. I wanted her to see it, to see where I grew up."

"And you went together?"

"No. That was the original plan. Then I had to stay to finish up something unforeseen that had come in. I was running late so I called her to ask if she would meet me out there."

"Which she did?"

"Yes."

"And the evening?"

"It was wonderful. My parents loved her and the whole thing was a big success. We broke up early, about ten-thirty as I remember. I walked her to the car—"

"Had she mentioned any problem with her tire?"

"No. No, of course not. Had there been any question of that, I would have taken her home. But there wasn't."

"You left at the same time?"

"No. I kissed her good-bye, watched her drive off, and then I went for a walk like I used to as a kid. Bringing Courtney home really made me feel the importance of the commitment I was making. I was happy about it and I didn't have any misgivings, but I didn't take it lightly, either. I wanted to think things through, think about the future."

"How long did you walk?"

"I don't know. An hour, an hour and a half maybe."

"When did you hear?"

"Of the accident?"

"Yes."

"Early the next morning. The police called Janie. Janie called me."

In the background, in another office in the building, I could hear a printer running and voices, though I couldn't make out the words.

"Was Courtney upset about anything that evening? Did she have anything particular on her mind?"

"No. She was a little nervous, as I said, but that wore off when she saw how pleased my folks were to meet her."

"May I speak with your parents?"

He looked puzzled. "I'll be glad to give you their number and tell them to expect your call, but why?"

"Just routine," I said, giving him a TV answer. And I got away with it.

"Thanks for your time, Chad."

"Sure."

I stood and we shook hands, spoke the usual pleasantries. He left me with his parents' number.

Charity had called to cancel lunch sounding mad as a cross-eyed skunk and refusing to talk about it. No telling with her so I just filed it under later. Then Lauren called. Anyone else I would have put off, but Lauren was very distressed, nearly hysterical. I listened to her information carefully, soothed her as best I could, and planned to act on what she told me as soon as possible. Then I called Chad's mother.

Mrs. Wharton answered right away and knew who I was; Chad had already called. It took her about ten minutes to get through "so sad" and "what a tragedy" and "she was so young and beautiful and her whole life before her" and "what's this world coming to, a young beautiful woman like that dying alone on the freeway?"

First pause I found, I jumped in. "This was your only meeting?"

"Yes."

"And it was a pleasant evening?"

"Oh yes, absolutely, totally, without question."

At least one too many definitives in there, I thought. "Oh?"

"Well, just one little thing. I'm sure it was nothing. But . . ."

"But?"

"It hurt my feelings a little."

"Can you tell me?"

"Courtney was helping me in the kitchen. I carried the roast into the dining room just as Chad came in for another drink. She was tossing the salad. I was only gone for a minute but when I came back Courtney was saying something about being insiders.

She stopped, of course, the minute I came back in, but still—''
She hesitated, then seemed to reach a decision. "You see, I just
don't understand. We did everything we could to make her feel
at home. It wasn't insiders and outsiders at all. She was going to
be family. We tried to make her feel that and to feel welcome.''

"I'm sure it was nothing." I winced as I listened to myself
uttering this bland and stupid generality.

"I don't know. I guess we never will.''

As I thought about my next move, the Fed Ex gal knocked on my
open door. I signed for the envelope. My name was spelled Cat
and the sender was Atone Now! with a Sacramento address I
didn't recognize. I punched out 4–1–1 and asked the information operator for Atone Now! No listing and wasn't that a surprise?

I opened the envelope and pulled out a CD still shrink-
wrapped in its plastic case. Rap music. Hate music. I recognized
the group as one that had particularly violent lyrics about
women. Not that they called women women, of course. Bitches
and witches, sluts and slits, that kind of thing. I dropped it into
the trash.

Broken windows, five anchovy pizzas, the Thunderbird, a funeral wreath, and now the CD. I wasn't *really* rattled yet, but I was
rattled. What to come: poisoned chocolates and hemlock tea?

The hell with it.

I decided to go over to Robert Corwin's. Lauren's phone call
had made that imperative. He'd been violent with Courtney; he
had threatened to rape her. Was that violence part of him still?
Sometimes people change; sometimes they don't. Corwin was
threatening Lauren now. I needed to see how far I could push
him.

The Thunderbird was on my tail as I drove away.

Okay, not that much had changed.

Thirty-two

Monkeys and Sonnets

I didn't call Corwin. I didn't make an appointment. Shoot, I didn't even smile when I stomped into the office and nodded curtly to Ms. Perky. I wasn't into being sensitive and thoughtful today. Not even polite, actually.

Perky looked a little nervous. "Y-yes?" And sounded it.

"Tell Corwin I want to see him. Now."

"I'm-m-m sorry, but Mr. Corwin is out of the office right now."

I'd seen his car parked out front so I headed right on back to his office.

"No, no wait. *Please.*" Poor kid sounded desperate. I wondered if Corwin terrorized her when no one was around. Probably.

I stopped. "Now. You can tell him or I will."

"I will."

She headed back, fast. When Corwin appeared, he was alone. He didn't say hello. "I should call the police," he said.

"Be my guest."

It's always amusing to call a bully's bluff. He scowled. It's tough on them, I know. The big ex-football-player bullies aren't used to having their bluff called.

"We don't have anything to talk about."

"Okay. Want to talk about it here or in private?"

He hesitated, probably wondering how long it would take to get rid of me, then remembered that I'd called his bluff twice already and led the way back to his office. Perky scuttled past without meeting our eyes. Corwin closed his office door and walked around his desk but remained standing.

I sat down, crossed my legs, leaned back, and made myself right at home. "I'll admit that I'm prejudiced from the git go," I said with sincerity and candor. "Insurance agents, ambulance-chasing lawyers"—I remembered Alma's recent bathroom "remodel"—"contractors: We are not talking highly evolved life forms on my evolutionary scale—intelligence, ethical development, human compassion"—I remembered the contractor again —"the ability to arrive on time and complete a job."

"Get to the point, Miss Colorado."

"Ms." I said sweetly.

He ignored that but did sit down. I guess tough-guy stances are tiring.

"Just as it would be unfair for me to expect a monkey to write a sonnet, I realize that it would be unreasonable to think that you would be honest, forthright, or decent." Okay, so I was pouring it on pretty thick.

Boom. He was out of his chair again. Just like that, just like a bottle rocket and red-hot. I love it when that happens. Was it the monkey reference that got him?

"How *dare* you?"

I took it as a rhetorical question. Anyway, the answer would have taken too long, involved too much life history. "What did you threaten Lauren with?"

"Lauren?" He drew his eyebrows together and looked perplexed. Looked innocent. Good job, though not good enough. "Lauren?"

That, too, I took as a rhetorical question. Lauren's call for help had been frightened, almost desperate: "Kat, what are you doing? What have you said? The Church is *all* I have. Robert called me. I can't bear it if they take the Church away from me, if they say I'm apostate. He threatened that. Oh, *please*— They say it's wrong to talk to outsiders, only the Saints, and I . . . I shouldn't have— Kat, *please!*"

My heart had tightened. She had so little and the bastards were threatening to take that from her. This is what was on my mind as I spoke to Corwin.

"It sounds like we could play this game for a while—me asking questions and you playing dumb shit—but I'm bored with it. I want to play Let's Suppose.

"Let's suppose that I go to the top officials in your church with this 'ancient history,' as you once referred to your attempted rape of Daisy, and that I mention that you recently threatened another young woman—"

"Damn you!" He slammed a fist down on his desk. "This is the devil's work and I—"

Oh good, he did want to play, after all.

"Shut up." I said it in a low, level voice. "We're still defining the term 'devil' here. Nor have I finished my supposition. If I can see the possibilities, the possible connection between this 'ancient history' and Courtney's murder, so can the police. You should have stayed cool, Corwin. You shouldn't have threatened Lauren. That connects up the past and the present, you see, and gives you a stake in it. Big-time."

He was muttering under his breath. His face was red and his hands were clenched as though he might throttle me if he didn't hold on to them. He looked like a cartoon caricature, a bad one at that. Though not one, I reflected, that it would be wise to underestimate. I could pick out certain words in the mutterings: My eternal damnation and Satan's evil figured pretty strongly. I heard *bitch* too.

He went from red to white, just like that. This is a perfect example of how talent is wasted. What belonged onstage or on-screen had been thrown away in a two-bit insurance office. Tragic, huh?

"I am aware how often the Mormon Church has closed ranks to protect one of its own, to characterize error—however gross, derelict or illegal it might seem to some of us—as mere misjudgment or misunderstanding. So perhaps your church officials would overlook or excuse your behavior. It is past, after all."

Corwin folded his arms across his chest.

"I doubt that they will take quite such a lenient attitude toward an ongoing homicide investigation."

Corwin doubted that too, I could tell by his eyes.

"A Saint is an alleged rapist, possibly an alleged murderer? Hardly bishop material, is it?"

"She had no right to turn me down. Nothing would have happened if—"

"If?"

"She went against God's word and mine. She chose Satan. It was right that—"

"That?"

"You have no right to work against me, either. It is not a wise thing to do."

Oh, for godsakes. Was he a slow learner or what? "Don't threaten me, Corwin." He blinked. "And don't *ever* fuck with Lauren again. Don't even consider it."

It was a good exit line and I walked on it. I hadn't provoked Corwin to violence but I thought—okay, I was sure—that he was capable of it. Impulse to action is still a big jump. Action to murder is an even bigger one.

Fanatics are very frightening to me.

I was certain he was a fanatic.

No Thunderbird on my tail.

No messages at the office. No more broken windows, either.

I called Hank, who was out. Ditto Davis. Then Medora, who was home. Nice change of pace.

When she answered, I could barely hear her soft voice over the TV.

"It's Kat. Can you talk?"

"All right."

"For crying out loud, Medora, why didn't you tell me about Ezra?" I was exasperated. The list of things that Medora hadn't bothered to tell me was constantly growing. Whose side was she on, anyway?

"Oh."

In the background a soothing male voice extolled the virtues of an antiacid tablet. I decided I could use some of those, preferably right now.

"Ezra?" she bleated.

"How many Ezras do you know, Medora?" My impatience temporarily got the best of me. No problem, she didn't notice.

"I pray for him every day. And for his family. For the wife and the grandchildren I've never seen."

"Wives," I corrected. "There seem to be three, and one of them does not look like she is of legal age."

"I pray for him, we all do. That he may give up his misguided—"

This kind of reasoning slays me, it really does. Bigamy with a minor "misguided?" Wrong, it's a felony. "The fact that he's taken a child for a wife doesn't bother you, Medora?"

It was as though I hadn't spoken. "I pray for him, that he may see the right way. Still, he is my son and I love him. Even excommunication cannot change that."

"Did he and Daisy ever fight?" Always the practical one.

She sucked in her breath sharply. "Ezra has nothing to do with this."

"He spoke of his sister as having sinned in a way that demanded blood atonement."

"No, no, *no.*" She ended on a sob and hung up on me.

If you'd taken a poll of my fan club at that moment, there would have been hardly any members in good standing. Hardly any? Try none.

When the phone rang, it startled me. Hank? *Hope springs eternal.*

"You're there? Good. I'll be in your office in five minutes."

It was only three and a half. And it wasn't Hank.

"Katy, you won't believe what happened!" She stalked around the room like a half-feral cat, snarly and silky in turns. "Al and I just had this *huge* fight."

I had no trouble believing that. Not only is Charity volatile, she is clueless about her love life. She and Al, who is a swell guy, have been together for a year now.

"Charity, what about your meeting with Chad?" I asked, pragmatism, impatience, and investigator callousness surfacing at the same instant.

"Who?"

"Chad Wharton, the stockbroker who—"

"Oh *him,*" she said in her Who-cares?-Not-me voice. "Al's sister just had a baby—it's her third—and Al wants to go visit her."

"What's wrong with that?"

"Nothing. I want him to. But he wants me to go. *Me.* A baby," she added glumly.

"So? Go."

"His mother's in the hospital, his brother-in-law is out of town on business and Al thinks we should go down and help out. *Yuck.*

I hate babies, you know that. They're always leaking on you from one end or the other. Or both. And they don't sleep through the night or mind you or anything. And little kids are just as bad. They do all that stuff, plus they run around faster than you can keep your eye on them. Oh God," she moaned in despair.

"Then you stay here and let him go. No one in his right mind could possibly think you'd be a help around small children, anyway."

"I know, I *know,*" she wailed, "but Al thinks I should, and that it's a character—no, a *soul!*—flaw if I don't."

"It's your looks, Charity."

"I know, I know," she wailed again.

And that was a tough one. Charity has the serene appearance of an adoring Madonna. You expect to see an infant nestled in her arms. Small children and puppies are drawn to her, which is one out of two, as Charity adores dogs. Children she likes when they become Lindy's age—i.e., almost grown up. As an advice columnist Charity has earned a reputation for wisdom. And it's true but, like most of us, she's only good on other people's problems. She was still wailing.

"Just explain it to him," I said firmly. "Al's a very reasonable guy."

"I did. He got mad."

"Hmmm. Were you tactful?" Charity has many wonderful qualities. Tact is not one of them.

"Well . . ."

"Charity?"

She sighed. "I said I'd rather eat shit and die."

I rest my case. "Did things go as well with Chad?"

"Kat!"

"All right. Sorry. Did they?"

"We had an interesting conversation," she said in her *very* huffy tone of voice.

"Please tell me," I asked in my *very* placating tone.

She exhaled. "I told him I had a bunch of money and didn't know a thing about investments."

"You inherited it?" That story might be wearing a little thin by now, I reflected.

"No. Better. I said I just did a major book deal and they paid me three hundred thousand in advance. I also said Senator Bill

Hornby spoke extremely highly of him. Nice, eh? I must remember to tell Bill I said that,'' she commented vaguely.

"Yes?''

"And I said when I finished my book I'd get another three hundred thousand, all of which I wanted to invest.'' She giggled. He didn't drool on his tie, but it was touch and go for a minute there.''

"And?''

"Well, he asked me a bunch of questions. Like: Did I want income from it? Conservative and low yield versus aggressive and high yield, mutual funds or specific stocks, that sort of thing.''

"What did you say?'' I was getting impatient.

"I said I wanted to make money, a lot of money, and fast. Since he was the expert, I'd leave it up to him as to the best way to accomplish that.''

"He bought it?''

"He bought it.'' She laughed. Charity is a whiz with money matters.

"And? C'mon, Charity, spit it out.''

"And he suggested that I sign papers giving him the right to act for me.''

"To enter into financial transactions in your name without your knowledge of the specific transaction?''

"Yes. He threw around a lot of stuff like 'optimal purchase point,' 'maximizing investment potential,' 'market acuity and awareness.' He even threw in a couple of chestnuts like 'strike while the iron is hot' and 'make hay while the sun shines.' '' She grimaced. "It was all just words, words to make it sound good and solid and professional and minimize the fact that I would be giving him absolute control of three hundred thousand of my dollars.

"Intelligent investors don't, by and large, do that. Granted, probably relatively few brokers are actually dishonest, but relatively few are immune to the temptation of churning accounts to generate profits and accumulate commissions. And sometimes more of the latter than the former.''

"Relatively few are dishonest?'' I asked, thinking about Michael Milken, Ivan Boesky, and Charles Keating, not to mention a couple of local pyramid-investment scamers.

Charity shrugged. "People shouldn't be stupid.''

"And if they are?"

She shrugged again. "Tough luck." Tolerance, like tact, is not one of Charity's commendable qualities.

"What was your impression of Wharton?"

"Very aggressive—a shark—probably very good at what he does, though I couldn't hit him with the kind of questions that would tell me that without revealing that I was a lot more knowledgeable than I purported to be."

"Is he honest?"

"Oh, I'm sure. I mean, clearly he's intelligent and successful. He can make good money, very good money, using his intelligence in the market. Given that, why risk being dishonest?"

Offhand, I could think of several reasons. Greed. Power. Ego. Need I go on?

"Were you able to get onto anything personal?"

"No."

"If you had three hundred thousand dollars, would you give it to him to invest?"

"I might. I was impressed."

"To invest without your signature?"

She dimpled.

That was when the plumber arrived. He tipped a baseball cap that said Ace Plumbing. "Where to, ma'am?"

"What?"

"The bathroom stoppage." He studied the work order in his hand. "Just got the call, but they put it in as a priority because it was a toilet backup and overflow."

"Let me check." I knew the answer but I went through the motions anyway. The toilets on both floors were fine. No one in the other offices had called a plumber.

"Who called in the order?"

The plumber was starting to look a little confused. "Richard I. Prowell." He handed me the work order. That's what it said, all right.

"There's no Dick Prowell here?"

"No."

"No plumbing problem either, right?"

"Right."

"Can I call my office?"

"Sure."

He spoke for a moment, verifying the information on his sheet. "I dunno," he said to the phone. "Miss," he said to me, "you figure this was some kind of prank?"

"Looks like it. Sorry."

He shook his head and went back to the phone.

"Did you notice anything about the name on the work order?" I asked Charity as the door closed on our Ace plumber.

"I had a boyfriend named Dick once. He was a nerd, a *humorless* nerd, a *pimply* humorless nerd."

"The initials were RIP."

"Oh, Kat, really," she snorted. "You're taking this too far."

I might have agreed with her except for the broken windows, the beige Thunderbird, the pizzas, the wreath, and the CD. Whatever it was, it wasn't just a prank.

Nobody followed me home that night. Of course, nobody had to. When I got there, a Thunderbird was already parked down the block. Empty. I checked. It was moved once during the evening, then left unoccupied again. After dark it drove up and down the block, accelerating, then braking sharply—cruising the block in jagged bursts of energy. Once it had no lights. Fifteen minutes of nothing and it started again.

That's when I called the Highway Patrol. Description, tag, and rundown. Their response time was good, but not good enough. The Thunderbird was gone. The cops, who knew me, said they'd swing by again when they could.

I slept badly, even with Ranger on the rug at my feet and the .380 on my nightstand.

Shortly after two I heard tires squealing, a vehicle accelerating, then braking. Gone by the time I got to the window.

Nothing more that night. I know because I was awake for most of it.

Monday, May 16

On the Road

Thirty-three

Silver Linings and Tumbleweed

The next morning I was eating cold cereal and searching for silver linings. This is always tough—silver linings are big demand / short supply items—but today was a real challenge. The cereal was stale, the milk on the edge of going sour, and the banana mushy. Also, I'm not wild for cold cereal.

That's the way it goes. It's always easier to see the clouds than the silver linings. But they were there, several of them. Someone had a major stake in discouraging or distracting me. Did this have anything to do with my investigation? Tough question, huh?

I was rattling someone's cage and they were rattling back. What fun. I love interactive games. I thought about the Thunderbird's antics the night before. And about the .380 on my nightstand. The stakes were climbing. Which was good. Theoretically. I put the half-eaten cereal on the floor for Ranger.

And Vegas? Any silver linings there? I yawned and stretched and ambled over to take a peek in the refrigerator. Nothing. That's why I was eating stale cereal in the first place. Vegas. I remembered our last evening and dancing to Roy Orbison in the moonlight.

I didn't see a silver lining.

Maybe no news was good news? Maybe they'd catch the serial killer in Vegas and life would settle back into its usual patterns. Hank would be Hank again, a man involved in his job but not obsessed with it. Amber Echo would be history or at least making waves somewhere else. Belle a memory and a hope and . . .

And everyone would live happily ever after. Sure. Except that this was life and that was a romance-novel scenario. I bet cereal doesn't get stale and milk doesn't sour in romance novels. Zippers never get stuck, the grass never needs mowing, checks never bounce, and traffic lights are always green. Hmmm. Appealing, no question. Of course, in the long run anything that predictable is boring, and boredom was something I rarely had to worry about. I threw out the rest of the box of cereal, poured out the milk. The phone rang.

My no-news-is-good-news theory was about to be shot out of the water, I could feel it. Investigator intuition, you know.

"Katy."

"Hi, Davis." I mopped up a splash of milk on the counter. "What's up?"

"The shit's hit the fan."

"Oh?"

"The woman, Amber—"

"Yes."

We could go on like this for a while, I could tell, little bitty short sentences that didn't say anything or get us anywhere fast because neither one of us wanted to say it or get there.

"Tell me, Davis."

"Yeah."

"I can take it."

"Yeah."

I hoped.

"She's claiming Hank's harassing her, that he's constantly calling and coming by, both at work and home, leaning on her to go out with him, using his badge."

I felt like someone had socked me, knocked all the wind out of me. I could barely hold on to the phone. Maybe I was wrong, maybe I couldn't take it. And *goddamn* Hank, anyway.

"Katy?"

"Yeah."

"You okay?"

"No."

"Look—"

"What does Hank say?"

"He denies it. Of course."

"Well, *of course* of course, it's not true!" Speaking of denial.

"He says he was trying to help her find her sister who was missing and who fits our Stalker's victim profile. That he has no personal involvement with this woman and no personal motive for an involvement with her."

"And?"

"She says, 'What sister? I haven't got a sister.' "

I let my breath out slowly. Okay. Amber was a bitch. This was fact now, not just my prejudices. "Davis, you knew about Belle, about the sister."

"Katy, I don't know anything directly. I only know what I got from Hank or you."

"Amber called the station all the time. You were the one who told me that."

"She doesn't deny it. She says she called to beg him to leave her alone."

Total bitch. I thought it through more dispassionately and didn't like it one bit.

"She says she's got witnesses at the bar where she works who can identify Hank and can testify that she was upset and crying on occasions when he went there."

"Does she?"

"Yeah. She does. *They* say she was upset. *She* says it was about the harassment. *He* says it was about her sister." He. Hank was *he* now. "You call it, Katy. It's one person's word against another's."

A woman's word against a man's.

"She's got witnesses that put him at her apartment too. Different times of day and night."

"People who were with them?"

"No. Individuals who saw him but didn't hear any conversation or even pay much attention to what went on between them."

So—same thing, a woman's word against a man's. And here's what's ironic: In a situation like this, I'd ordinarily be inclined to believe the woman.

"How bad is it?"

"It's bad, Katy."

"Hank still working?"

"Yes." *For now* were the unspoken words.

"How's he doing?"

"He won't talk." Translation: *Not good.*

"Katy?"

"I'm leaving today."

"Good." There was relief in his voice.

"I'm going to Bakersfield."

"What?"

"Then I'm coming to Vegas."

"Katy—"

"See you soon." I hung up, packed, called my neighborhood kid—again—to take care of the animals, pick up the mail and newspapers. Forty-seven minutes and I was on the road. Fifty-nine and I was gassed up. Sixty-six and I was doing sixty-five. No, the Bronco was doing sixty-five. I was doing more like two-ten and headed for warp speed.

I couldn't bear the thought of Hank crashing. It was more than enough to make me drop everything, even my follow-up plans on Ezra and Chad. I was as mad as I've ever been at Hank, too. That irrational kind of mad and hate and fear you feel when someone you love is in big trouble partly because of a situation that couldn't be helped, and partly because they fucked up.

My stomach growled. I never did get breakfast and now it was going on lunch.

It made me mad, too, that just as I was getting someplace with Courtney's death, I had to drop it. When that happens, you lose steam. Big-time. I had put on enough heat to get someone nervous, and nervous people do stupid things. I love stupid things— every investigator does.

I stopped in Stockton to get a soda and to call Davis from a pay phone. "You don't think he did it, do you?" See? Nervous people act stupid.

"No." Was there a moment of hesitation? "But he hasn't handled this well or covered his ass and that's sure as hell going to come out."

"Okay—" A flock of eighteen-wheelers rumbled by and I stopped talking. I couldn't compete and I knew it. Just think how quiet the world must have been before the Industrial Revolution.

"Where the hell are you?" Davis asked when the rumbling died down.

"Gas station. Stockton." I was starting to sound like Davis.

He grunted.

"What is Amber up to? What's her angle? What can she possibly get out of this? It doesn't make sense, Davis."

Davis laughed, a mean, hard bark of a laugh. "Kat, the woman leads an irregular lifestyle, drinks, maybe does drugs—"

I thought of the empty refrigerator, the moderate lifestyle—except of course for her underwear habit. "Maybe. Wouldn't Hank notice?"

"Depends."

I thought that one over.

"She puts the moves on Hank," Davis said. "He turns her down. I'm guessing she didn't like that much. So maybe this is her idea of payback. Or fun. Katy, a lot of the people we deal with are a couple of sandwiches short of a picnic. We can't figure out why they do what they do. Hell, maybe they can't, either."

Three lowriders packed to the dash with young male Hispanics pulled into the gas station. All the engines were roaring, all the mufflers blasting, all the kids swaggering. I bet they didn't know why they were doing what they were doing, either.

Davis was still talking, I think, but I couldn't hear a word. "Call you later," I hollered into the phone, and hung up. I walked over to the minimart and got a diet Dr Pepper and a Hershey with almonds. Three food groups: caffeine, empty carbos, and protein. The kids made way for me. They didn't speak or jostle me around but their eyes were hostile. At the last minute someone muttered something in Spanish and they all laughed.

Did anyone know why they were doing what they were doing? Ask a sociologist. Did Amber know what she was doing? I thought so. The trick now was to prove it.

I'm pretty good at that trick.

Traffic was heavy in Stockton but south of town it eased up. It's a straight shot from there to Bakersfield, a north/south hypnotically boring line of freeway with an occasional rest stop but no towns.

Only tumbleweed and dust and desert, and sometimes the blue glint of the California Aqueduct or the green haze of irrigated crops. Truckers often take Highway 99, which runs parallel to the east but is broken up by towns. That way they are less likely to fall asleep. I always take I-5—where 65 mph is the legal speed limit, which meant we were all doing 75. Minimum.

The other thing that had me riled, pissed off, and jumpy was all this bouncing around. Not just geographically but emotionally too. I like simple linear progression. I like to pick things up at the beginning and then tidily march along to the end. I like this, even though it hardly ever happens that way. Never, actually. Usually I get things somewhere in the middle, in the messy part, and then I try to figure out the beginning and piece together the end. Sometimes I get them at the end and then it's even harder. And messier. And always there are side trips, detours, and road blocks. Like the one I was on.

California's Central Valley drifted past me—wide, flat, endless. It was green but not for long. Rains were over now until October or November. In another month or so everything not irrigated would be shades of dust or dead. It used not to be so. The indigenous grasses of California stayed green all summer, had adapted to summer drought. They were all gone now, displaced and replaced as early settlers introduced European grasses dependent on water. It wasn't just the grasses, either. Gone were the wildflowers, the wide, meandering rivers and vernal pools and the flocks of birds so thick they blocked out the sun for minutes on end when they passed. And fish and game in the same abundance. Gone.

A Camaro and a Mustang—local wildlife—blasted by doing at least 90. Asphalt, automobiles, and assholes—that's what we had now. Bad trade. Another car blasted by going even faster than the first two. Black and white and flashing red and blue. CHP. I smiled. Sometimes the good guys do score.

I'm not usually this cranky and negative, I know, but Hank was in trouble and it was getting to me.

A couple of miles down the freeway I spotted the speeders and the cop neatly aligned on the side of the road. The patrolman looked up and I waved a Way-to-go! wave and grinned as I passed. He gave me a small wave in return.

A bad guy fucks up; a good guy nails him. That's the way it's supposed to happen.

Monday, May 16

Bakersfield

Thirty-four

Neon Fish
and Dead Dreams

Bakersfield is oil and cotton. In 1851 gold was discovered in the bed of the Kern River; in 1865, oil, black gold. And the soil is rich and fertile. The race was on. This is redneck country, pickup country, gun-rack country. It took me five hours on I-5 to get to 58 East, which I followed into Bakersfield through orchards and cotton fields—acres of cotton fields and power lines—and oil pumps kerchunking and thunking away like huge rooted grasshoppers intent on endless, mindless repetition. I had a country-music station on the radio; Bakersfield is country music too. Garth Brooks was singing a song about how he had friends in low places.

Yeah. Don't we all.

It was almost three-thirty by the time I hit the outskirts of town. Too late for the first thing I had in mind, too early for the second. I pulled into the parking lot of the Red Lion at the junction of Highways 58 and 99, checked in, then immediately headed for the restaurant in the hotel. I needed to eat before I caved in, slumped over, and collapsed in a heap.

The restaurant was slow, the waitresses in their midforties with hair and makeup running a decade behind. It's like this in some small towns. Bakersfield is not that small a town, but I guess it was like that here too. Those are the towns where the young people, the ones with hopes and dreams and determination, leave. The ones who stay get caught immediately in spouses and kids and mortgages and the dreams of youth that cling tenaciously like cobwebs.

Luanne brought me a smile and a glass of water. Her name tag not only told me her name but that she was the waitress of the month. And I was wrong, way off the mark. She was nowhere near forty, was in her twenties somewhere still. And trapped. A wedding ring, a charm bracelet with children's silhouettes, sensible shoes, shut-down eyes, and enough hairspray to keep her in place at a shuttle launching.

"Hi. What can I get you?"

So far today I was short a major food group. Grease. "Double cheeseburger, hold the onions"—I love onions but investigating was offensive enough without onion breath—extra-large fries, and a diet cola."

By the time she returned with my Pepsi I had Amber's picture out and a story all made up. "I'm looking for this woman," I said as she put the glass down.

"Oh *my,*" Luanne said with a little gasp.

"Her name is Joanne Marie Larkin. She also went by JoJo. She grew up here in Bakersfield, left after high school. She is now in her midtwenties. She didn't look like this back then."

"No," she agreed, looking at Amber, who wore a smile, a G-string, and pasties. "Why do you want her?"

"Her mother is ill, perhaps dying, and the family doesn't know where she is. The last word they had, she was a dancer in Las Vegas."

"Oh. I don't know her."

Luanne said it in the tone of voice that thanked God for that blessing, affirmed that she didn't want to know Joanne Marie Larkin, and *especially* that she didn't want her husband to know her.

"Sure?"

She twisted her wedding ring. "I don't really, uh, know people like that." Translation: *sluts.*

"I think when she lived here, she was pretty everyday." Translation: *Normal, like you and me.* "Maybe she worked in a bar or club. She wasn't necessarily a professional dancer then."

"Oh. Well, there are a lot of bars in town. I think. I don't go to them, of course." Translation: *I'm not a slut.*

"Any suggestions?"

She shrugged. "I don't know. There are a lot of bars out on South Union, the kind that maybe she would go to. I don't know." She twisted her wedding ring again.

"Luanne," a disembodied voice called, "order up."

"Oh. Your burger." She trotted off.

It had been a shot in the dark. And cruising bars alone in Bakersfield wasn't exactly going to be a hayride. I sighed. Couldn't do it until evening either, since I needed to catch the night shift of bartenders and drinkers. I sighed again. There is always a big turnover in bar employees. Bartenders and cocktail waitresses are a mobile bunch. And the photo. Sheesh. Guys would glue themselves to it. Damn. Real long shot. Hank was the only person on earth I'd do this for.

Luanne returned. "Here you go. Would you like anything else?" She rushed on. "I'd like to help you, you seem real nice and all, and anyway—no matter what that girl looks like—well, if her mother is dying and all—"

I waited expectantly. My stomach growled. Loudly. I didn't even glance at my burger. Control.

"Would you like me to show the picture around to the other girls? Not," she hastened to add, "that any of them have worked at those kinds of places, but maybe they'd recognize her, I don't know." She twisted her apron in her hands.

"Thank you, that would be great." My stomach growled again. The cheeseburger called my name, the fries sang my song, even the pickle whistled. I kept my eyes averted from the plate and handed her the photograph. She had to force herself to reach out and take it.

The minute—ha, the second—her back was to me I fell on my lunch. I tried to chew slowly and make it last but then I figured, what the hell, just inhale it. I'd have dessert if I was still hungry. I was licking my finger to pick up the last crumb when Luanne returned.

"No luck." She was holding Amber's photo by the corner with just the tips of her thumb and fingers, presumably to reduce the possibility of contamination. "Will you be here for breakfast tomorrow? Ellie's working then and she might know." She placed the photo carefully on the table. "Can I get you anything else?"

I shook my head. "Thanks for your help, Luanne."

"Sure. I'm sorry I can't do more. I hope you find her in time."

I blanked and then remembered the sick mom, got over a quick twinge of guilt, and smiled. "Yes. Me, too. Are you working breakfast tomorrow?" She nodded. "Maybe I'll see you then."

"Hope so. Good luck." She smiled and scooped up my plate. I left her a five and paid the bill, then went to my room where I didn't bother seriously unpacking. I hadn't brought that much stuff, and with any luck I'd be out of here tomorrow.

Always a tricky thing, hitching your hopes to luck.

I pulled out the yellow pages and looked under "Lounges." Luanne was right, there were a lot of them. Over three hundred churches and twenty-eight libraries, but no telling how many bars; it's not the kind of thing they call to your attention in the tourist hype and yellow pages. I spread out my Bakersfield map and made notes.

Here's how I had it figured: There were two ways to get Hank out of trouble. One, and this was the best, was just to walk in and prove he was innocent: Repeat my conversations with Amber, report on what I had seen and overheard, testify to Hank's good character and exemplary Boy Scout record. The problem with that was it would be Amber's word against mine—well, Candy's— and I was Hank's girlfriend. *I* knew I was being professional and impartial, but Internal Affairs at the LVPD couldn't really be expected to buy right in on it.

So on to Plan B. Sling shit.

I was taking my cue here from Amber. She was making it up as she went along, and it was working just fine for her. It would work just fine for me too, only I wasn't planning to make anything up. I was planning to walk in with facts. Facts I could play two ways. The simplest was to go to Amber, face her down, get her to back off, even leave town. I couldn't do it that way; it didn't clear Hank. So I would take it to the same people she had. Public presentation, exposure, humiliation (okay, I *was* still sore about the Victoria's Secret stuff), recantation, and apology. That should do it, all right.

Only one thing missing—the facts I was going to nail Amber with. Details. I yawned and stretched and looked at the clock, then climbed onto the bed for a half-hour nap in preparation for hours of bar crawling. As I drifted off, my last thought was that when this was over Hank was going to owe me. Big-time.

I slid into a dream where I was in a bar showing Amber's

picture and asking questions. The bartender was Jack Nicholson and his face kept changing as he laughed that laugh of his and then Amber's face started changing too. Everything did as I reached frantically to grasp things and hold them in place.

A three-ring circus chameleon nightmare.

I woke up at five twenty-nine, got up and washed my face. I stayed in my jeans but changed to navy-blue flats, a cream blouse, and a navy blazer. You know, the low-key but professional PI look.

I stopped at a minimart, picked up a six-pack of diet Dr Pepper, a bag of pretzels, a small tablet of construction paper and tape. So much for that twenty-dollar bill. I hate minimarts.

Almost six and the night shift would be on. Me too.

I made a folder for Amber's photo with a cutout that just showed her face. Then I taped the photo in and the folder closed. I couldn't face a whole evening of guys getting hormonal surges.

There are millions of bars in the world and they are not alike. They have a character, a flavor, distinction. London, Paris, Boston, L.A., it's all different.

But dives are all the same. Dives are dives, honky-tonk bars with surroundings, decor, and customers that could be dropped into Anywhere, U.S.A. Probably the rest of the world too, but I don't know that from experience. Dives are dark and dingy and smell of smoke and stale beer and Lysol when you get close to the bathrooms. They have lighted beer signs, cardboard cutouts advertising alcohol, and sometimes a flash of neon. The bar stools and booths are covered in vinyl, cracked and worn, often ripped. The drinks are cheap and the bartender smokes. If it's a woman, she'll be either too heavy or too skinny. Hair spray and red nail polish are optional but usual, and the jukebox is playing more often than not.

There are not usually a lot of customers at places like this. Traffic will be steady without being heavy. The customers are regulars and have their favorite spots at the bar staked out. Everybody knows everybody else and their stories. You could skip town for five years, walk in, sit down, and folks would say—*Hey, where you been? Haven't seen you in a while.* And the bartender would pour your drink—would remember, not ask—and set it in front of you, maybe even buy the first one because it had been a while.

You see? Bar after bar like that and things started to blur. I kept track of the bars, names, and addresses; I kept a tight grip on the photo. I wasn't drinking but I stank of smoke and divey bar and male lust.

Maybe it wouldn't work. Most people can't see beyond the obvious. It wasn't a sure thing picking out and recognizing a small-town girl in this glossy showbiz photo. Today's almost naked and tarted up Amber probably didn't look much like yesterday's JoJo. A lot of people go incognito with a couple of small physical changes, never mind something dramatic like this.

There were working girls on South Union. And Johns. Pimps too, probably, though I didn't spot them. By eleven I was moving on grit and determination alone. The low-life hopelessness of the bars was getting to me.

The Sportsman's Club had neon fish. It was a nice change of pace, although every town I've ever been in has had a bar called the Sportsman. Inside, it was just like all the others. I almost walked. Almost. It was the bartender. She was young and pretty and about Amber's age. I climbed on a stool and ordered a non-alcoholic beer, showed her my photograph.

"Well, I'll be damned." She popped her gum. "JoJo made it after all. I figured it was all just talk."

Thirty-five

Shaking
the Dust Off

I changed my story just like that. No more dying mom. As it turned out, I didn't need much of a story.

"Is she in trouble?" The bartender's eyes were unconcerned but curious.

I laughed; I couldn't help it. It was the first interested question I'd had all night; it also sounded like she knew JoJo reasonably well. She laughed with me.

"Isn't that an odd thing to say?"

"Huh-uh." She shook her head with vehemence. "No way. Not if you knew JoJo. Do you?"

I nodded. "But not well."

"She has a good heart, a good head, and good plans, but somehow she always messes up. Then instead of cleaning up her act, figuring it out and starting over, she digs herself in deeper until finally the girl has dirt in her eyebrows. She means well but she sure can't pull it off.

"Oh hey—" She caught herself. "That's not fair, is it? It's been—what?—three years, I guess, since I've seen or heard anything of her. Maybe she's changed."

"Did she leave soon after high school?"

"Not right after. JoJo was around town for a couple of years. She got a fake ID and started working in clubs as a cocktail waitress. She had the kind of looks that could pass for older—especially with the right clothes and makeup. JoJo always wanted to be older, to be doing what the older kids or crowd was doing. She was never satisfied with where she was. Never. And she always thought her lucky break was just around the corner."

"Was she nice?"

"Oh yeah, would always help out, lend you money, clothes, whatever."

"Honest?"

She shrugged. "We-ell. Hey, I gotta make a coupla drinks." She scooted off and I thought about the hesitation in her last answer. So Amber was and wasn't honest.

A guy walked in and hollered, "Hey, Sue Ellen, what *do* you know?"

"More 'n you," Sue Ellen answered good-naturedly, and got him a beer. Eventually she worked her way back to me.

"Did you know JoJo's sister?" I asked.

"Huh? JoJo doesn't have a sister. She had an older brother but he went into the army years ago and, as far as I know, no one has heard from him since."

"Are her parents still in town?"

A head shake. "Her mom died some years ago, lung cancer I heard, and that's when JoJo left. Her dad ran off—aw shit—we were in junior high, I think."

Was it any wonder that JoJo was up to her eyebrows in dirt? I thought sadly.

"Hey, I been talking a lot and you never answered my question. Is JoJo in trouble?"

"May I ask you one more question first?"

She shrugged.

"Did JoJo ever get into trouble over blackmail?"

"Huh? Blackmail?"

"Getting money or a favor to keep quiet about something she knew, something someone didn't want known. Probably involved a guy." Technically that's extortion, but we weren't being technical here.

"She's in trouble." Her voice went flat.

"Yes, probably. And like you said, she doesn't know when to get out. I'm trying to blow the whistle on her, keep her from getting in any deeper. Over her eyebrows."

"When she left town—" Sue Ellen began.

"Sue Ellen—hey!"

"Keep your shorts on," she called without looking. "She was making dates with guys, married guys, then getting them to give her money or presents, clothes and stuff, new tires for her car once, all so she wouldn't tell their wives on them. Then she went too far and one of the guys went to the cops."

"Did it go to trial?"

"Nope. She skipped town."

"Hey, Sue Ellen, this a bar or a fuckin' waiting room? I ain't here for my health."

Sue Ellen shrugged her shoulders but didn't move.

"Do you know any of the guys' names?"

"No. Maybe I could find out, though. This is to help JoJo, right?"

"Right," I said with a firm voice and a relatively clear conscience.

"Sue Ellen!"

"He's got his shorts in a snap. I'll be back."

I nursed my non-beer and waited. As I waited, I tried not to count my chickens. Some of the eggs would be rotten, I knew. And, considering it was JoJo/Amber, that statistical probability was higher than normal. It was hard holding myself back, though. I wanted to run with it. Bad.

Sue Ellen leaned on the bar. "Is JoJo still doing that? What about this picture? I mean, it's professional and all. Isn't that the kind dancers get? Aw shit, I wanted her to make it. I wanted *someone* from Bakersfield to make it."

Someone dropped a bunch of quarters in the jukebox and started punching buttons. George Jones singing a sad song. Figured.

"Well?" The bartender put her hands on her hips and glared at me. Mad at JoJo but I was handier.

"She's not in trouble yet, not really. But my guess is if someone doesn't stop her, she will be. You think you could get a name or names for me?"

"This is really to help JoJo, right? It *really* is?"

"Yes."

"Hold on, then. Lemme make a call."

After George, Tammy Wynette came on the juke singing her heart out about how a gal should stand by her man. Wasn't she the one who sang "D-I-V-O-R-C-E" too? A gal could only stand by her man for so long and so much, I guess. Made perfect sense to me. If Hank—

"Here." Sue Ellen pushed a cocktail napkin, bar stationery, across the bar to me. There was a name, Doug Jeffers, and a local phone number scribbled on it. She pointed to the number. "That's work, he sells real estate. Hey, I don't even know your name."

"Kat," I said. "Kat Colorado."

"Will you let me know how this turns out?"

"All right."

"And tell JoJo I'd like to see her. I'd help out too if she needed. Don't tell her that, though, it'd just put up her back."

"I'll give her your message."

She turned the napkin over and wrote. "My home phone," she explained, pushing it toward me.

"What high school did you and JoJo go to?"

"Bakersfield High."

"Sue Ellen, howsabout a Bud down here?"

"I've got to go," I said.

"Don't forget."

"No." I left a ten under my non-beer bottle.

The Crickets were singing "That'll Be the Day" as I walked out. So far this was my day for sure. And it was almost over. A hot shower and bed, that was what was left.

I woke up with a cigarette smoke / divey bar hangover. It had to be that because I hadn't been drinking. Nine o'clock and I had Doug Jeffers on the phone. He was cordial and sounded thrilled to hear from me. Of course, that was before the subject turned from real estate to extortion.

"I'm hoping you can help me, Mr. Jeffers."

"Sure. What are you in the market for?"

"I'm a private investigator. I'm looking for information, not a house."

Silence, the kind I'm used to hearing after the words "private investigator."

"I'm working a case that looks like extortion. The victim is male and the blackmailer is a young woman from Bakersfield."

More silence. Jeffers wasn't going to help me out here.

"JoJo Larkin," I said.

"Yeah." He sighed. "I figured we were coming to that. Look, I can't talk about that right now."

I could hear voices in the background. "Pick a house," I said. "I'll meet you there."

"Huh?"

"Let's go see a house."

"Oh. All right." He gave me an address on Elm Street and told me he was driving a blue Skylark. "Fifteen minutes."

I beat him. I was leaning against the Bronco with spring sunshine in my face when the Skylark drove up. He cut the engine and motioned to the passenger door. I climbed in. There were two child seats in back.

"You don't look like a PI."

"My Hawaiian shirt's at the cleaners and my three fifty-seven Magnum is in my other purse."

He laughed. He didn't particularly look real estate either, more like a big, good-looking jock only slightly out of shape. He was tan with muscles and gentle brown eyes.

"So JoJo's at it again?"

"I don't know what she was up to before, so I can't answer that."

He drummed his fingers on the steering wheel, then stopped abruptly. "You know, I could never figure it. She was—hell, undoubtedly still is—a beautiful girl. No dummy, either. There was no reason she couldn't make money in a legitimate way. I never could figure the blackmail angle. When you think of blackmailers, you think of a piece of shit, at least I do, and not some young, pretty girl."

"Mr. Jeffers, would you mind if I taped our conversation?"

An eyelid flicked rapidly three or four times in a nervous twitch. "What's the deal?"

"I would rather not explain before hearing your story. With your permission I'll tape our conversation. After hearing me out, you decide whether I keep the tape or you do."

He thought it over. "Fair enough."

I turned on the recorder, stated the date and place, identified myself, asked him to identify himself, and then stated we would be discussing Joanne Larkin, aka JoJo Larkin.

I started off. "Please tell me about any encounter or encounters you had with Joanne Larkin."

"She called me one morning at the office—"

"You were in real estate at the time?"

"Yes."

"When was this?"

"Three years ago. Same time of year, spring. She called and said she wanted to look at a listing I had and would I please meet her there and show her the house. I agreed. We spent some time in the house. She asked a lot of questions, seemed real interested. At the end she kept looking at her watch like she was rushed, so I suggested she think it over and get back to me. She said no, but she had a proposition for me."

"Proposition?"

"Yeah. At the time I thought it was an odd word to use." He laughed sourly. "Turned out that's exactly what it was. She looked me in the eye and said five hundred dollars would make her forget that I'd come on to her, tried to kiss and fondle her. I said what the hell you talking about, nothing like that happened.

"She roughed up her hair, smeared her lipstick, then pulled her clothes around and said, 'That'd be your word against mine, wouldn't it, and I'm a good actor.' Damned if she didn't start crying to prove it. And then she said she really didn't think my business could stand that kind of publicity. Said it was just five hundred and then she'd leave town and that would be that."

The tic was back; he rubbed his eye.

"I told her to give me a little time and we settled on meeting at the house again the next morning. Then I went to the cops. She got wind of it somehow, I guess, because the next day she was a no-show. Word got around town somehow too. Over the next coupla months three guys told me she'd pulled the same stunt on them."

"They paid?"

"Yeah. They did. Not as much. Two, three hundred. She was getting greedier, I guess."

"Who were they?"

"I don't feel right giving you names. I went to the cops with it but these guys paid to keep it quiet. All three were decent guys with families and jobs and good reputations. One was a high-school teacher, another a dentist, the third had been her supervisor on a summer job. She gave 'em all the same line she gave me."

"Nothing happened between them and JoJo?"

"No. That's what they said and I believed them."

"The police—"

"She skipped town before they caught up with her."

"Anything else?"

"She was a real pretty girl. She looked so sweet and innocent. Hell, if it hadn't happened to me, I'da probably believed her and not the guy. She was that good. She looked like butter wouldn't think of melting in her mouth."

"Have you seen or heard of her since?"

"No."

"Do you know her by any other name?"

"No."

I pulled out the photo of Amber and identified it for the tape recorder.

Jeffers whistled. "She's left the sweetness and innocence behind, I guess."

"Can you identify this woman as JoJo?"

"Yes."

I snapped off the recorder. "She went to an off-duty police detective in Vegas and asked for help in finding her missing sister. The cop is a nice guy and tried to help. Then she turned around and accused him of harassment, of using his badge to pressure her into sex."

Jeffers pushed the tape recorder across the seat toward me. "Tape's all yours. I hope you nail her. You need it, I'll try and get the others to talk."

"Thanks, Mr.—"

"But not if you mister me again." He grinned at me.

"Thanks, Doug." I gave him my card. "You ever need a northern-California favor, it's yours."

He nodded. "Let me know if you get her. I can't tell you what that kind of an accusation does to a guy. Me, I'm a nice guy. There's no excuse for a man ever to lean on a woman. Ever. There's no excuse for this, either."

I reached across the seat to shake hands with him. "I'll let you know." I started to slide out of the car, then remembered. "Which way to Bakersfield High?"

He pointed me in the right direction, waved as he drove off. I stood in the sunshine and laughed, happier than I'd been in a while. I clambered in the Bronco, cranked the windows down and the radio up, hollered.

Bakersfield is a Valley city, no question. I drove around a little. Downtown was full of square, beige, uninteresting buildings, wide, straight streets, not a lot of trees, not a lot to keep a body awake and alert. I could see why JoJo had gotten restless. In the older part of town I passed a plastic cowboy who was twice life-size, a statue of an early padre. Then I drove under a large sign stretching across the road: BAKERSFIELD. The old highway had undoubtedly gone through there at one time.

Palm trees, oil derricks, fast food, mobile homes. Kids who should have been in school climbing on a metal fence and swinging on a gate. Fast food, bars, small businesses, pickups with farm dogs in the back. Lots of Fords and Chevys, but I didn't see a single BMW, Volvo, or Lexus.

It was a working town and a family town. It was also, I knew, a town a hungry young woman might yearn to leave. Shake the dust off, pick up her feet, and head for the glitz and glitter, fame and fortune and bright lights of Vegas.

I couldn't wait.

Right after Bakersfield High.

Thirty-six

A Beautiful Body,
a White Horse,
and Extortion

I called Davis from the hotel.

"Where the hell are you, Kat?" Testy.

"Still having fun in Bakersfield."

He snorted. Mean. Bad. Snarly.

"Did you run an NCIC check on Amber?" NCIC stands for National Crime Information Center.

"Naw, Kat, I consulted my Ouija board."

"Nothing?"

"Nothing."

"Try Joanne Marie Larkin, aka JoJo Larkin."

"Hang on." Forget testy. He was interested now. I could hear the computer clicking in the background, then Davis whistled.

"Outstanding warrant for her arrest?"

"You got it."

"What?"

"Dunno. I don't know the California codes offhand."

"I think it's an extortion charge. Call the Bakersfield PD. Get them to send you her picture too, DMV photo probably, and anything else they have, okay?"

Silence. Then: "Sorry I snapped at you, Katy."

I felt a rush of emotion. What would I do without friends like this? I couldn't stand to think about it. "It doesn't matter. Keep this quiet for now. We'll put together a package. I've got one more thing to do here and I'm on my way. A couple of things to do in Vegas and then it's party time. Our party: We call the shots, we invite Amber. Tell Hank not to worry. Tell him I love him. I'll see you tomorrow.''

''Riding in on a goddamned white horse?''

I thought about it. ''Yeah.'' A white Bronco was close enough.

The high school was a typical California one-story public-building structure in the beige-concrete-block mode. No one had taken home an architectural prize for designing it. A few hardy bushes and the ubiquitous palm trees were scattered about. I sat in the parking lot and contemplated asphalt and plausible stories.

A pleasant-looking slightly red-faced middle-aged woman greeted me as I walked into the office. ''May I help you?''

''I hope so. I'm a private investigator''—I pulled out my license—''looking for a missing person. Her name is Joanne Larkin and she was a student here five or six years ago. Her family has been out of touch with her and her mother is dying.''

The secretary's face crumpled in sympathy and compassion. The dying-mom story gets everyone.

''I'm backtracking on the off chance that I can find someone or something to lead me to her. In time,'' I added on a solemn note.

''All our records are confidential.''

''I see.''

''Dying?''

I nodded. ''Her heart just plumb gave out. She's a widow trying to raise four children and—''

''What was the name again?''

''Joanne Larkin. Her nickname was JoJo.''

The secretary walked into a back room, then reappeared with a file which she placed on the counter between us. I followed along, wishing for the one millionth and third time that I could read upside down.

''She seems to have been an average student. Hmmm. Sometimes below average. Intelligent but not academically motivated, wasn't involved in clubs or sports. In her senior year she skipped a lot of classes and ran a bit wild. She almost didn't graduate.''

''Are any of her friends mentioned by name?''

She browsed. I got a crick in my neck trying to do the same.

"Apparently she was kind of a loner. Oh, and she ran with an older crowd, not kids here at the school."

"Did she have any problems with other students or teachers?"

"No-o-oo, I don't see anything." Her voice filled up with doubt. "Now, you know, this *is* odd. In senior English she was transferred out of Joe Reed's class, into Jim McDonald's and then to Ann Sheldon's. I wonder why. Well, I guess that's about it. Gosh, I can't let you see this but I've got to go to the back room for a minute." She winked broadly at me.

Everyone watches too much TV.

I pounced on the folder the minute she turned her back. First the home address. I couldn't very well ask for that since dying mom would know. Then the picture. Bingo. Our Amber Echo looked younger and slightly more innocent but the eyes were bold and brassy. The copier was in the corner. Took me forty-five seconds, tops. I was on the visitor side of the counter when the secretary came back. The folder was neatly closed.

"Is there any chance of my catching Mr. Reed or Mr. McDonald?"

She walked over to a schedule. "Joe Reed is free right now. Prep period. He might be in the faculty lounge if you want to try. Here, let me issue you a visitor's pass."

She did, then pointed me in the direction of the faculty lounge. I opened the door on two women who sat in the corner talking and a man who sat at one end of a long table correcting papers. I walked over.

"Joe Reed?"

He was about my age and good-looking. I guess JoJo liked the lookers. He glanced up immediately and focused in on me with interest. I introduced myself, flashed my license, and changed my story.

"Do you have a minute?"

"Sure." He leaned back and looked me over. "Sit down."

"Do you recall a student by the name of Joanne, or JoJo Larkin?"

His expression didn't change but his eyes became guarded. He nodded.

"Anything in particular stand out about her?"

"What are you getting at?"

I bit the bullet and told the truth. "I'm investigating a possible extortion attempt. She's accused a man of sexual harassment. He claims he's innocent. Sound familiar?'' It did. I didn't have to wait for the answer; I could tell by the look on his face.

Reed cleared his throat, then nodded slowly. ''JoJo stayed after school one day, supposedly to talk about an assignment. She propositioned me. She was very physical about it.'' He wiped his forehead as though the thought of it still made him sweat. ''I marched her right down to the principal's office, explained the situation, demanded that she be transferred out of my class immediately, and suggested counseling.''

''Good for you.''

''I love my job, Kate—''

''Kat.''

''Sorry. I love teaching. Bakersfield isn't exactly an intellectual hotbed but we've got some smart and determined kids here, kids who don't want to work cotton and oil like their folks did. I got a wife I love. We just adopted our first baby. No way I was going to let this screwed-up girl mess up my life.''

''Tell me about Joanne.''

''Someone taught her real early that what she had and what was going to get her somewhere was her body. End of story. It's too bad, because she was bright and capable.''

I took out the photo of Amber and handed it over.

''Yeah,'' he said. ''Beautiful body, beautiful girl. That's not all there is, not by a long shot, but that's all she knew.'' He handed the picture back.

''Is your baby a boy or girl?''

''Daughter.'' That smile again. ''She's beautiful too. I want her always to know that she's beautiful on the inside as well as on the outside. I don't think anyone told JoJo that.''

I didn't either.

I pointed to the picture. ''She goes by the name Amber Echo now.''

''I'm not surprised. I've got to leave for my next class. Anything else?''

''Could you show me the library, maybe introduce me to the librarian so she won't mind if I look around?''

''Sure.''

''Mind if I use your story as background defense for the man she's accusing?'' I asked as we walked down the hall.

"Be my guest." Joe Reed pushed open the library door and leaned in. "Marie, this is Kat. She wants to look around a bit, okay?" We shook hands, I thanked him and he was gone.

Marie smiled at me. "May I help?"

"I'd like to look through the yearbooks."

"Surely. We keep them in a back room, otherwise they would walk off. Let me show you."

It was a small room with a table, chairs, and a number of books in special collections or on reserve. Marie showed me around, then left me on my own.

I started with the year JoJo graduated and pulled out that and the five previous years' worth of yearbooks. JoJo first. I found her, but the girl who smiled out, somewhat shyly, was the girl Amber had framed in silver and called Belle.

It took me a long time to look through the rest of the yearbooks. I did it slowly and methodically because I didn't want to miss it. People change a lot in the years after high school. I found it in the yearbook that was four years earlier than JoJo's. No sister, Sue Ellen had said, but she had an older brother. I recognized the boy immediately.

It wasn't a coincidence. It also wasn't connected. Not yet.

Marie made copies for me, of JoJo and of the boy. And no, she hadn't known either of them, was there anything else? No, thank you, I said. Not here, anyway.

One more stop: JoJo's old address. I looked it up on the map and drove out to a run-down neighborhood. You know the kind, more cars than houses, more weeds than the two put together, lots of cars on blocks or partly torn down, an occasional beer can and hubcap. I knocked on seven doors before I found someone who remembered. He was an old codger, late seventies maybe, and dressed in a frayed bathrobe and a frown.

"The Larkins? Yeah, I remember the Larkins. Trailer trash." He slammed the door in my face.

I phoned Davis again. Got him again. Amazing. Sometimes Ma Bell is on your team; sometimes not.

"Nice work, Katy."

"Extortion?"

"Yes."

A kid with a boom box walked by sharing his choice of rap

music with all of us in a quarter-mile range. Thoughtful. I paused for a moment. Naturally. Like I had a choice.

"Doug Jeffers?"

"Yeah." He was surprised.

"Good. I've got more too. See you soon."

I had enough on JoJo/Amber now. I thought about Amber and underwear and cleavage.

Almost enough.

Like JoJo I shook off the dust of Bakersfield and headed out for Vegas. But not for glitz and glitter and fame and fortune.

For the truth.

Tuesday, May 17

Las Vegas

Thirty-seven

Mean as a Rattlesnake

It was early evening by the time I got to Vegas. Nowhere near too late to think about making trouble in the city that was open for trouble twenty-four hours a day.

I went to Maggie and Davis's to stay, not to Hank's—which was an odd feeling, and not a good one. I crossed my fingers like a superstitious kid hoping it was temporary. It was just Maggie and me; Davis was working late. I was rumpled and crumpled and cranky from the drive, so I had a shower and changed. Maggie made us a snack.

Then I was ready. Ready to go out looking for trouble, ready to cause trouble, ready to play dirty just like the rest of the gang.

I called Amber at home, hoping she would be there and looking to do something. That was first-choice and best-case scenario.

"Hello."

I could hear loud music in the background. I didn't recognize it because it was the kind of music I never listen to.

"Hey, Amber, it's Candy."

"Candy, what's up? I thought we were supposed to have lunch."

"We were and I'm sorry. I got caught up in a bunch of stuff." I heaved a sigh. "And then things got kind of messy. *Guys,* my God. They're *clueless!*"

She laughed and I laughed. We were laughing at different things, but so what?

"What are you doing now?"

"Nothing much."

"Okay. Let's get into trouble, then."

We laughed again. Same deal.

"I'll swing by your place, shall I?"

"Sure. It's too early to go out but—"

"But not too early to drink."

"Damn right."

Good. I'd guessed right on that one. "I'll bring something. What do you like?"

"Oh, anything. Screwdrivers, maybe."

Screwdrivers it was. On the way over I picked up vodka, orange juice, tonic water, and lime. The headline on the paper at the store screamed

SERIAL KILLER KILLING LAS VEGAS BUSINESS

I didn't bother to read the article.

Amber answered the door with a drink in her hands. When it's time to drink, it's time to drink.

"Hey, Candy, c'mon in. I started without you. Here, lemme take that." She reached for my paper bag and headed for the kitchen. I followed her. She was barefoot and wearing white shorts and a T-shirt that asked WHY WAIT? Why, indeed? Amber got a glass out of the cupboard and ice from the freezer. The TV blared at us, a sitcom with low-budget canned laughter. *Ha ha ha. Heh heh heh.* "Make yourself something while I turn that damn thing off, okay?"

I opened the vodka, poured a healthy shot down the sink, and then filled my glass with tonic. By the time I'd found a paring knife to cut the lime with, she was back to refuel. She grabbed a bag of potato chips, then headed for the front room.

"Tell me your story," Amber said as she sprawled into an armchair and tossed her long tanned legs over one of the arms. "What's with the clueless guy?"

Uh-oh. I should have spent more time on lies before I got here. Amber reached for a handful of chips. Once again I wondered how her body stayed so gorgeous on the diet she offered it.

"I met him six months ago and, I'm not kidding, he was a basket case. *Basket.* His wife had left him. She didn't say a word or explain. Nothing. He just came home to an empty apartment one day."

"Everything?"

"She left a card table. It was set up with a plate, a knife and fork, a napkin, and a glass. There was a picture of a TV dinner on the plate. There was a dead flower in the glass, a white rose, like he always brought her on their anniversary."

"That was it?"

"That was it."

Amber grinned. "Well, shit, it's mean as a rattlesnake but it's kind of funny too. I'll have to remember that one. What else?" She looked eager.

"She cut the crotches out of his jockeys, the toes off his socks, and the sleeves off his long-sleeved shirts."

"Shit, Candy, she *was* mad. Or crazy."

"No kidding. He said that she did it for nothing and that he was a great guy, but I don't know."

"Yeah." Amber nodded. "That's mad. It makes you wonder, all right."

"He was pretty upset, needed a drink bad."

"Sure, who wouldn't? Crotches, toes, and cuffs. Shit. Wonder what Freud woulda made of that?" Amber giggled.

"She left a six-pack of beer in the refrigerator."

"Hey, that was nice. Or maybe she just forgot it."

"No. She'd twisted off the tops, poured every one of those suckers down the sink, and then twisted the tops back on."

Amber slapped her thigh and cracked up. Me, too, minus the thigh slapping. I cracked up only on the outside, though. On the inside I am thinking: What in God's name is with me? Why can't I tell a simple lie like everyone else? I used to be able to do it. When had that stopped? Maybe after Alma had started telling me the good parts from her soap operas.

"There's more." I was a helpless pawn in the grip of my lie. It had a life of its own now, though obviously I didn't.

"Yeah? Shit, what's left?"

Good question, I thought. "The bathroom."

"The bathroom?"

"Same thing. She poured out his shampoo and aftershave, then put the tops back on. The deodorant was rolled out, the toothpaste squeezed, and the toilet paper down to the cardboard roll. Even the aspirin bottle was empty.''

Amber laughed. ''And you know this guy now needs aspirin as bad as he needs alcohol.''

''No kidding. So, anyway, I meet him three months after all this and he's pretty okay. He can even laugh about it. Well . . .'' I frowned. ''Not *laugh* laugh, chuckle maybe.''

Oh God, I thought, despair in my heart and mind. Why didn't I just sell my house, quit my job, and move to Hollywood? It was clear that I was a one-in-a-million natural for writing soap operas.

''So we had a real good time together, *real* good. And next week his divorce is final.'' Tammy Wynette and ''D-I-V-O-R-C-E'' played briefly in my mind. ''So guess what?''

''No-o-o-o. God*damn*, men are such bastards. And fools.'' She didn't have to guess, she'd seen it coming. Not a woman over eighteen—no, make that fourteen—who hasn't heard of or experienced this.

''Yeah. So they're back together again. He bought her a ring with diamonds, emeralds, and sapphires and took it to her along with six-dozen white roses and a magnum of champagne.''

''Goddamn!''

Amber walked over, sat down next to me on the couch, and gave me a big hug. I was crying. I mean, I am a *born* storyteller.

''You *poor* kid. Shit. You got his house key? Crotches and toes and sleeves, here we come.'' She giggled.

Me, too, through the tears. I almost said *yes* too, caught myself just in time again.

''So that's why I've been such a jerk. I was out of it, just couldn't cope for a while there.'' I played out *cope* nicely, something between a whine, a whimper, and a wail.

Amber gave me another hug. ''It doesn't matter one bit. I understand. Too well.'' She grimaced. ''I've been there too. C'mon, time for another drink. Bottoms up.''

I bottoms-upped my tonic and followed her to the kitchen, watched while she poured two drinks, mine stiff, hers killer—or at least comatose. As she poured, I admired the method in my madness. It was, I thought, perfect. I'd spilled my guts about a guy. Now she would too. That's how it works.

''Hey, I'm tired of sad stories, Amber.'' I sniffed as I caught my breath and let my voice wobble a little. ''Tell me your story. Last I spoke to you the plan was getting together with the cop. What happened?''

"What happened?'' Amber echoed me.

"With Hank? You know, that good-looking cop you wanted.''

"Oh,'' she said.

"Remember, we saw him on TV that night with the Strip Stalker's victim and then he came by the day I was here because you'd called him all worried about your sister.''

"Sister?'' she said.

"Are you okay?'' I asked.

She pulled herself together. Then spoke: "He *was* cute, wasn't he? And nice. I don't know how many times I tried to get him into bed. He was too serious, always thinking about work. Nothing like your guy, well, ex-guy. I gave up finally, though I hated to. I mean, *man*, what a body, and I loved the way he filled out his pants in front.''

Once this would have bothered me, but not today. "Who knows? Maybe he'll call still. Are you interested?''

"Yeah, yeah I am. I'm mad, too. Shit, Candy, I like to get what I want. That's important to me.''

"It's not over until the fat lady sings.''

She laughed. "I don't think she'll be singing my song.''

Not a fat lady, no, but somebody. And soon.

"Hey—'' I was going to say I was sorry that things hadn't worked for her and Hank but that was one lie even I couldn't manage. "What about your sister?'' is what I finished that "hey'' with. "Any news?''

Amber started to cry.

If I were a nice person who didn't know Amber's story, I would have felt sorry for her. I would have walked over there and given her a hug like the one she had given me. I am a nice person. I also knew her story, so instead of feeling sorry, I egged her on.

"Amber, what about Belle? Where's her picture?'' I looked around the room. "I don't see it. Did that cop, Hank, help? I know you said you met him because you thought he could. And he tried too, right?''

"Yeah. He was real nice about it. Shit, he was more interested in finding her than in balling me, that's for sure. Aw hell, Candy, I don't want to talk about it, it'll just make me sad. Maybe I'll forget about it all, pretend I never had a sister, pretend she never got lost and I never got worried.''

That was the truth so it shouldn't be hard. We weren't at the truth yet, though.

"Oh." I acted startled. "You can't do *that.*"

"Yeah," she said. "I think I can, I really do. I gotta go blow my nose."

I picked up the drinks and walked into the kitchen, dumped my almost untouched vodka tonic and Amber's ice into the sink. Then I made new ones, mine tonic, hers vodka, splash OJ. When I got back to the living room, Amber stood in front of the window, staring out.

"You ever done something you're ashamed of, Candy?"

"Like what?"

"Like make trouble for a decent person just for the hell of it or for business or something?"

"Big trouble?"

"Yeah. Big trouble."

"What?"

"Oh, you know," she said evasively, although I didn't; wouldn't, either, with clues like this.

"If you're ashamed of it, don't do it. Make it right instead."

"I can't. It's gone too far and I'm in too deep. Never mind." She shrugged her shoulders as though she could throw off the burden of guilt.

Impossible, I could have told her, *because I've tried it before and it can't be done.* I didn't, though. I didn't say a thing.

Amber shook herself. "Hand me that drink. Hey, bottoms up!"

We bottoms-upped and I marveled at Amber. If I were drinking the way she was I'd be on my knees, or throwing up, or both.

"I'll get us another." She slurred her words slightly.

"Orange juice for me. I gotta slow down," I said. We walked into the kitchen. She bounced off the door ever so slightly.

She poured juice for me and vodka with a squeeze of lime for herself, gulped half of it, filled it up again.

"I want to be a dancer, Candy, I want that more than anything. I'd do anything to make it happen."

"Anything?"

"Yeah," she sighed. "Anything." She sipped her drink and ate potato chips.

I thought that professional dancers probably didn't eat and drink like this but I didn't say anything.

"Did you have your audition yet?"

"I didn't make it." Tears in her eyes. "Shit, I don't want to be an exotic dancer and—well, whatever. That was just supposed to get me through." She shrugged. "You know, I don't feel much like going out now, maybe another time? Can we take a rain check?"

"Yes, sure. It'll be okay, don't worry. Your sister will turn up. Forget that cop, too. You're a great-looking girl and there're a lot of guys who'll want you, so who cares about him?"

"Yeah," she said dully. "Yeah, who cares about him?"

As I left, she was fixing another drink. If I were a really good person, I would have felt warm and compassionate and sorry for her. But I didn't; I was saving all that for someone who deserved it. I'm not *that* good a person. I climbed in the Bronco, locked the door, reached up under the bulky sweatshirt I wore. It took me a minute, a few obscenities, and a little pain to scramble out from under the tape holding the microcassette recorder in place.

The good thing was not that Amber had admitted everything —the good thing was that I had it on tape.

Even so, Amen.

Thirty-eight

Angelic
Beyond Belief

Davis set it up.

I was due at the Las Vegas Police Department at eleven. Hank and Davis would be there. Their lieutenant, Steve Thompson, the one to whom Amber had addressed her complaint, would be there. As would Amber. It was, as far as she knew, the next step in pursuing her complaint of sexual harassment against Hank. As far as Hank knew too. The lieutenant knew a little more, but not much.

Davis and I were the only ones who were clued in, so we were the only ones looking forward to this meeting. I was dressed for the occasion: black suit, pantyhose, and shoes, pale-pink blouse, and briefcase. Official, you bet. I could have passed for a lawyer.

Davis and I walked in on a silent trio in Thompson's office, Hank staring at a wall looking serious, the lieutenant a combination of serious and bored, and Amber looking angelic beyond belief and not hung over at all, which was amazing to me.

She, too, was dressed for the part. Her skirt was navy and so were her high-heeled pumps. Her white blouse was buttoned to the neck and pinned with a gold circle brooch. The conservative Sunday-school-teacher look. There were pearls in her ears, and a navy ribbon held her hair back at the nape of her neck. No makeup other than a smudge of pale pink blush and lipstick. Her legs were crossed at the ankles, her hands were folded demurely in her lap—I could just see the flash of red nail polish—her eyes were modestly cast down. Hot damn, she was something.

Mentally I applauded and handed that Oscar right over. No, not yet, her main performance was still to come. I took it back.

I preceded Davis into the office and greeted everyone with a cheery "Good morning!"

"Katy!"

"Candy?"

"Hello."

Hank, Amber, and the lieutenant, in that order. Hank looked at me hard but said nothing further. Amber looked at me hard too. She didn't know what was going on yet but the idea had probably occurred to her that she wasn't going to like it.

Davis got the ball rolling. "This is Kat Colorado, a private investigator from Sacramento, California. She is a friend of Hank's, a friend of mine as well."

Amber's jaw dropped—I am not making this up—and hung there slackly.

"While in Vegas recently, Ms. Colorado has also used the name Candy."

"Man, I can't *fucking* believe this."

Amber stopped and blushed as the obscenity bounced around and mocked her angelic appearance. Had Ezra Dillard been here, it would have rated an *Even so, Amen.* Had Tammy been here, it would have earned me a verse or two of "Stand by Your Man."

I was on my own. I snapped open my briefcase.

"I would like to present information regarding the charge Ms. Larkin has made against Sergeant Parker," I said formally.

The corner of Hank's mouth twitched the way it does when he's starting to enjoy himself. He knew that I had something, that I would never fake it in a situation like this.

I addressed the lieutenant. "I have two tape recordings here, along with printed transcripts of the taped conversations." Maggie, Davis, and I had been up half the night transcribing, printing, and collating. "If I may, I will describe what is on the tapes, then leave it to you to decide how to proceed."

"Go on." Thompson nodded curtly, pushing around a stack of papers under a paperweight on his desk.

"The first is a conversation I had with Doug Jeffers—"

"Fuck!"

We all looked at Amber. She cleared her throat and dropped her eyes.

"The second is a conversation I had yesterday evening, as Candy, with Ms. Larkin."

Amber shifted in her seat.

I hit the high points of the tapes. "I have other information that is not on tape but can be corroborated." I told them Joe Reed's blackmail story, then included the three men who had come to Doug Jeffers with similar stories. Amber looked like hell.

"Davis?" I tossed the ball to him.

"I ran an NCIC check on Amber Larkin."

Amber looked blank.

"National Crime Information Center," I said helpfully. "It maintains information, including criminal records."

"I don't *have* a criminal record," Amber said, outraged. I liked the outrage part. Nice touch.

"Nothing," Davis continued. "Then, on Ms. Colorado's suggestion, I ran the name Joanne Marie or JoJo Larkin."

"A California DMV photo and a high-school graduation photo establish that Amber Echo Larkin and JoJo Larkin are the same person," I chimed in.

"The second NCIC check showed a warrant out for the arrest of Joanne Marie Larkin on an extortion charge."

Amber moaned.

"Ms. Larkin?" Thompson spoke.

"Okay, I withdraw my charges against him," she said in a shaky voice, staring at Hank.

"Was there any truth to your allegations against Sergeant Parker?" the lieutenant asked.

"No," she whispered.

"Speak up, please, Ms. Larkin."

"No," she said loudly. "Look, I've gotta go—I— See ya." She stood.

So did Davis. "It's not that simple, JoJo."

Her eyes swung around the room. "Okay, *okay,* I'm sorry. Now I gotta go."

"You're under arrest, JoJo."

"Huh? I said I was sorry."

Boy, talk about unclear on the concept.

"There's a warrant out for your arrest in California. I'm arresting you."

"You can't do that."

"Yeah, I can, that's my job description. You break the law, I arrest you."

"Goddamn motherfucking asshole pig cops—" Amber lunged for the paperweight on the lieutenant's desk. "Goddamn bitch Candy!"

I ducked. Good thing—the paperweight sailed over my head and made a big dent in the wall behind me, though I didn't notice that until later. At the time I was focused on Amber as she lunged at me. She'd yanked a shoe off her foot and was swinging the spiked heel at me like a weapon. I saw the flash of red fingernails as I backed up hastily, then fell over a chair.

"Bitch! Slut!"

The spike slashed through the air as I tumbled and rolled. What the hell was going on here? Why was I in a catfight when I was in a room with three cops? There was something *really* wrong with this picture.

"I trusted you, how could you?" she screeched. "How— *Goddammit*, leggo, you're hurting me. Goddamn fucking pigs, *leggo*, I said. Leggo!"

Well, *finally*. Davis and Hank had her. I scrambled to my feet.

"I *hate* cops and I hate you, Candy! Or whatever your fucking name is."

She lunged at me but didn't go anywhere. Her hands were cuffed behind her back and she was unsuccessfully trying to drag along the large cop that was hooked onto each elbow. Froth foamed in the corners of her mouth. She'd blown the angelic angle for sure.

"How *could* you?" she panted at me. "Really, how could you? I *trusted* you."

I thought that one over. "Explain to me, JoJo, how a career blackmailer can get so upset about the betrayal of a trust."

She snarled. I guess words failed her.

"You broke pattern on this one, though, didn't you?" I continued. "How come you didn't ask Hank for money to drop the charge? Or was that coming after you fucked with him a little more and really had him sweating?"

"I don't have to tell you shit," she said sullenly. And she

didn't, that was true, but we were all giving her the opportunity. Nobody read Amber her rights but it didn't matter because I was the one asking and I'm not a cop.

"I don't think that was the point, though, was it, JoJo?"

She snarled again.

"This time the payoff was something else."

Her eyes flickered. Bingo.

"Aw, fuck you." She sounded tired now, defeated. She wasn't Oscar material anymore as she stood there in handcuffs and stocking feet. "There wasn't any guy, was there, Candy? No cut-off crotches and sleeves? You just made it up, didn't you, to get me?"

"Yes."

"And that bit about you hating cops and stuff the day you hid in the bathtub. That was a lie too, right?"

"Yes."

"He's your boyfriend?" She jerked her head in Hank's direction.

I nodded.

"I wish someone loved me like that, enough to get me out of trouble, to help me." She sounded sad and wistful.

I'm a sucker, but I decided not to fall for it.

"Let's go, JoJo." That was Davis.

"Lemme get my shoes," she said on another pathetic and plaintive note.

"Sure, JoJo." Davis laughed and started to walk her out. Barefoot. She tried to kick me as she passed. Missed. She tried to spit on me too. Missed.

"Get her out of here." Thompson sounded irritated.

I looked at the dent in his wall and the glob of spit on his carpet. Who could blame him? When I finally looked at Hank, he was smiling at me. Boy, about time. Way overdue, actually. I kicked one of Amber's shoes aside and started toward him.

"Candy?" he asked, still smiling.

"Parker, I want to talk to you." The lieutenant wasn't smiling. So I left.

After all that, it was a comedown. For sure. Then I thought of Amber Echo Joanne JoJo Marie in the slammer with new silk underwear and no shoes.

That made up for it.

Thirty-nine

The Snake Charmer
and the Hot Shot

The plan was Mexican food and margaritas. It was only one of the many plans that the Strip Stalker destroyed that day.

Maggie and I sat in her front room balancing plates on our knees, the pizza box on the table in front of us, the TV on.

Her name was Ginny Neuman and she was from New Jersey. She had two sisters and a brother and parents, and all of their plans were changed now and forever. They stared into the TV camera and wept openly as they spoke of their plans and dreams.

They had wanted to see the volcano and tigers at the Mirage, to walk between the paws of the huge MGM lion into the vast Land of Oz, to see the Sphinx at the Luxor and the Pirate Battles and Treasure Island. Ginny longed to drive to the Hoover Dam because she had studied about it in history class. She was a teenager, a good student and a good sister and daughter, someone who had lived and laughed and loved her way through yesterday and today.

And now there were no plans and no tomorrows. Ginny was cold, bloody, and lifeless in a Las Vegas alley.

"I don't know what we'll do." Ginny's mother wept into the camera as though it were a friend. "We don't know, we don't know," the children echoed.

"She wanted to walk down the yellow-brick road and see the Secrets of the Pyramid," her father said, and he, too, wept.

They showed her picture, a pretty, dark-haired fifteen-year-old with a shy smile and eyes that looked up at you through full lashes. A voice-over discussed the leads the police had. None. And the tips and information the police had. None. And the special Crime Alert number if anyone did have any information. And the voice spoke of how women could protect themselves— sensible suggestions, good suggestions, even though no one is ever really protected. One way or another, we are all vulnerable.

"When will it stop?" Maggie asked.

"Why is there even one pretty dark-haired young woman in Vegas? Why aren't they on a bus, a plane, a train, or a skateboard out of here? One-way ticket."

Which was missing the point completely, but Maggie was too kind to point that out. Things like innocence and vulnerability and death are not places you can put on a map and then leave behind you somewhere. We can't outrun death or sorrow.

Davis got home at eleven. He looked beat-up, physically and emotionally, kissed his wife, held her for a long time. Life and happiness are fragile and precious.

Davis washed up and then sat down with us, a beer in one hand and cold pizza in the other. In unspoken agreement we avoided the subject of the Strip Stalker.

"Hank?" I asked him.

"He went back to the office to check on something." Davis smiled at me. "This morning seems a long time ago, Katy. You did a real good job."

"Amber helped."

"Yeah, she did. She wouldn't have blown it if you hadn't nailed her, though."

"What will happen to her now?"

"We'll hold her. If Bakersfield wants her bad enough, they'll come and get her. If not, we'll turn her loose."

"And Hank? It's over? He's cleared?"

"Of the allegations Amber brought against him, yes."

I didn't like the sound of that. There was a *but* in there.

"He didn't handle it well, Katy. He shouldn't have gotten in-volved on a personal level like this. He didn't follow procedure, report it to Missing Persons. If he had, none of this would have happened. The lieutenant will chew him out, I don't know what else. Hank's a good cop. Everybody makes mistakes." Davis rubbed his forehead, then stood as the phone rang. I could tell by the way he spoke that it was Hank.

"For you, Katy."

"I'm home," Hank told me.

"I'm on my way," I answered.

"All right." He sounded tired and defeated.

It took me twenty minutes to get there. He was on the couch, staring at the fireplace. No fire, so that was a bad sign. He didn't get up to greet me and that was another bad sign. Neither did Mars, but at least he wagged his tail. There were three empty beer bottles on the coffee table in front of Hank. He put the one in his hand down. Okay, four. Drinking beer and getting stupid. Bad sign number three.

"Maggie and I had pizza. We got enough for you too. You want it hot or cold?"

"I don't—"

"Warm? Fine," I said with an I-could-get-dangerous tone in my voice.

He smiled at me. "Thanks, Katy." And stood and kissed me. Finally. "That Candy, she's something."

"Yeah." I smiled back. "She is, huh?"

"What was that about crotches and toes and—?"

"Sleeves. I'll tell you sometime. I'm a little worried about that, actually. I used to be able to tell neat, simple little lies. No more. Like that one—it was a three-ring-circus lie," I added glumly.

Hank laughed and hugged me to him as we headed for the kitchen. "Let's go warm up that pizza and I need another beer. A glass of wine for you?"

"Sure." I tossed the pizza into the toaster oven as Hank got us drinks.

"I'm not making light of it, Katy."

"What, Hank?"

"What you did, you and Candy. What took you fifteen minutes to run this morning was hours of investigation and effort at a time when you had other things on your mind, and I've been— I'm not doing a good job of this, Katy. If this hadn't gotten straightened out, it could have cost me a lot. It has cost me."

I looked at his face, lined with fatigue and pain, and decided that was a conversation for another day.

"You're welcome, Hank. I'll tell Candy too."

He kissed the top of my head and reached over to pull the pizza out of the oven. "Smells good."

"Did you eat today?"

He thought it over. "I don't think so."

We still had a way to go to get back to normal. I was thinking of eating and talking and everyday things, but there was more. A lot more.

No way I had thought of it.

No way I was prepared.

Davis called the next morning. "Katy."

"Hi, you're too late. Hank's gone."

"I want to talk to you."

"Oh." I sounded puzzled. I was puzzled.

"It's JoJo."

"Yes?"

"She wants to talk to you."

"Why?"

"She wouldn't tell me. I told her I'd give you the message. I didn't tell her I'd tell you to ignore it, which I am."

I thought about the pictures in the Bakersfield High yearbook. "What's this about, Davis?"

"What could it be about, Katy? My guess is she's mad. So what?"

"Is she getting out on bail?"

"Unlikely, not with a fugitive warrant."

"I'd like to see her, Davis. Can you set it up?"

Davis gave that a lot of silence. Finally: "Remember all the conversations we had about Hank getting personally involved and how that's a bad idea?"

"Look, Davis—"

"Remember, Katy?"

"I remember."

"Good. See any parallels here?"

"Please, Davis."

"Okay. I'm not telling you what to do, just offering you advice. Be here at ten, all right?"

"Yes."

"Ask for me."

Good thing I hadn't packed my bag yet.

▫ ▫ ▫ ▫

Davis was silent.

Me, too.

It was, on his part, disapproving what-the-hell-you-doing? silence. I followed him in this silence down a long corridor and around a few corners. He ushered me into a drab room. Amber was already there. Amber? JoJo? I didn't quite know what to call her.

"You want me to stay, Kat?"

"No," said Amber.

"That's all right, Davis," I said.

Davis nodded, then looked over at Amber. "You sit in your chair and you talk, that's it. Nothing else. Nothing fucking like last time. You want to get in trouble, big-time trouble, you pull a stunt like you did yesterday. Understand me?"

Amber nodded, sullen and resentful. Of course, the jail garb—shapeless, overwashed clothes—was enough to explain that. Even Amber's figure didn't have a chance. I was sure it was the kind of thing that lowered her spirits; it would have lowered mine.

Amber waited for the door to close behind Davis, then spat: "You think you're a fucking hot shit, don't you?"

"Good opener, Amber, especially since I'm doing you a favor being here."

"You're doing *yourself* a fucking favor."

"Really? Well, I'm not going to be doing myself this favor much longer."

She stared at her hands and I stared at the ceiling. "Remember when I said I wished I had someone who loved me enough to come and bail me out of trouble?"

"I remember." I remembered the foam in the corners of her mouth, the dent in the wall and the spit on the floor, too.

"I said Hank was harassing me, trying to make me sleep with him. You didn't believe it."

"Nobody believes it, Amber."

"Yeah. Well, you're right. I lied about that."

Speaking of lies, I thought, and then spoke. "The night the Stalker killed a girl, the night I drove you home?"

Amber didn't react.

"Why so upset? Why the big act? You don't have a sister. There never was a Belle. You made her up."

"It wasn't an act."

My turn to stare in silence.

"I told it so many times, I got so I almost believed it. I wanted that, a family, like I wanted someone who would care and watch out for me the way you and—" Amber ran her fingers over the surface of the scarred wooden table next to her chair, over names and obscenities carved in a small, sad effort to be heard and remembered.

"Anyway, it wasn't an act. For a while I was someone—someone nice who cared about her sister and did good stuff and I had someone nice who cared about me and thought— Aw fuck, what the hell do you care, anyway?"

I said nothing. She was right. I cared, but not about her.

Her fingers traced out letters on the table: LIFE SUCKS.

"You got a lot of things right, Candy, but you know what? You got the reasons all wrong. You think you're so smart. Like you think I did this just to make Hank give me money."

"No. As a matter of fact, I don't. I think it has to do with a crime in—"

"And it probably never occurred to you that I could just be interested in Hank for who he was."

It had occurred to me that she was interested in Hank. She was obvious enough that it would have occurred to a box of rocks. Interested in him for who he was? No, that hadn't occurred to me. Maybe it was because what Amber said she found most appealing was the way Hank filled out his pants.

"Or that Hank could be interested in me."

No, that hadn't occurred to me. Well, it had and it hadn't. I remembered their two silhouettes becoming one and the silence while I eavesdropped in the bathroom and—I stopped. I knew better than to do this.

"You were so sure he wouldn't have anything to do with me because of his job. And because of you. Weren't you?"

I was silent. I could see the gloating in her eyes, though I couldn't see what was coming.

"And you were right. Sort of. He said he wouldn't compromise his job and I believed him. He never said that about you, you know."

Don't believe her, my mind shouted with passion and conviction.

This is a woman you put in the slammer. She's trying to get you, to hurt you.

And it's working.

"You know what he said about me, you know what he liked about me?"

Besides the obvious? I thought. Nothing. There was nothing about this woman that would appeal to him, that would hit him in his mind and heart. Amber had the sex-and-beauty angle covered, but that was it.

She laughed. "He liked it that I needed him, that I leaned on him and relied on him. That I got scared and unhappy and had trouble with stuff. That I needed and wanted his help. He liked that, he liked that a lot."

I willed my face not to move, not a blink, a flicker, a twitch. Nothing.

"I needed him, unlike you, Ms. Total Independence, Ms. I-Can-Do-It-On-My-Own. And that's how I could have—maybe would have—gotten him. Later, after the Stalker, after—" She broke off and thought for a moment.

"You know what he would do? He'd call me to see if I was feeling okay, not too depressed. Once he sent me flowers and he gave me this." She put her thumb under a gold chain, lifted it away from her neck. It was a gold locket with some kind of pattern on it. I didn't lean forward to see.

"Isn't it pretty? It has a *B* on it. He said that it was to remind me that Belle was out there and that she would be back. Wasn't that sweet? Hank did lots of things like that for me. Once he brought by food because he was afraid I wasn't eating enough."

Don't believe her, the voice in my head said, but it wasn't as strong now. *He was doing all this for Amber and was too busy to answer my calls, go out to dinner with me, or to— No, that was too painful. Anyway, she's lying. She's saying this to hurt me.*

"Remember the night you were there and he called because he was worried about me and hoped I was all right? That was *so* typical of him, so sweet and thoughtful, don't you think?"

Davis was right: I shouldn't have come here.

I should get out of here. Fast.

Jail was not the only place with bars.

She threw back her head and laughed. "You know what's really funny? He wanted *you* to need him, but then *he* needed you. He got into trouble. You got him out. How do you think that makes him feel?"

I thought of last night, of bed after he finished the pizza. Bed and sleep with an acre of cold sheets between us.

"How do you think that made him feel?" she taunted me.

Listen, but don't believe. Consider the source. Check it out. Talk to Hank. I said all the right things to myself and they didn't help.

I took the photocopy of the yearbook page out of my purse and passed it to Amber. She looked carefully at the photograph I had outlined with a red felt-tip pen.

"You know him. Not just know him, you were in business with him." A statement, not a question.

"Oh, well—" She smiled. "You're the hotshot private investigator. You figure it out. Me? I just wanted you to see that maybe I could have taken your boyfriend away and you never would have had a clue, Ms. Hotshot. Funny, isn't it, that all those good things about you might be the reason someone leaves? You put me in jail." She smiled again. "I just wanted to rub your nose in this."

Amber got up, walked to the door and pounded on it. A uniform opened up. "Interview's over." She turned and looked at me. "Not so damn smart, after all, are you?" She left.

I left too. Davis caught up with me on the way out. "Well?"

"Davis, I'm not as smart as I thought."

"Who is, Katy?" He said it gently.

I walked out without even saying good-bye. That's how upset I was. I'm not as polite as I thought, either.

Thursday, May 19

On the Road:
Las Vegas, Bakersfield

Forty

A Fistful
of Rattlesnakes

I went back to Hank's—I didn't think of it as home anymore—
and paged him. He called back in twenty minutes.

"I need to speak to you. It's important."

"I can't, Katy. Not with this latest killing. I'll be home as soon
as I can. For dinner, I promise, even if I have to go out again
later."

Once I would have accepted that—the job, the words, the tone
of voice—I would have taken it all into consideration. Not now.
Was Hank taking into consideration that I wouldn't make a request like this unless it was urgent?

"I didn't say everything in the office yesterday, Hank. I didn't
use it because I didn't need it and it didn't reflect well on you. I
said nothing about the evening you dropped by, on work time,
and spoke with Amber on her terrace. Nothing about the time
you called her after the killing before this one. Or the afternoon
you dropped by. I was a witness to all of this."

"No," he said, denying I don't know what.

"You found a lot of time for Amber even when you were busy.
This can't wait or"—I thought it over—"or it can wait a long
time." I hung up.

Then I packed. I'd give him an hour. In my present mood that
was generous. Phooey. I made it forty-five minutes; that was reasonable. He made it in just under twenty.

His face was closed and stormy. No hello. Nothing but anger. "Well?"

I sat at the kitchen table. "Did you want to sit down or shall I stand up?"

He went to the refrigerator, got a Coke, and sat down. Everything about him was hostile, his eyes, the set of his shoulders, the way he moved.

"This morning Davis said Amber wanted to see me. I went, though Davis told me not to, said that she probably only wanted to get at me. He was right. She said things that would hurt me a lot if they were true." *And I'm already hurt,* I thought.

"What is it, Katy?" He sounded like a cop, an impatient cop. He looked at his watch.

"She said that you called often to see if she was all right, that you brought her food and flowers, a heart-shaped locket," I said. "And other things."

Silence.

"Did you?"

More silence. God, I hate conversations like these. I hate it when the good guy / bad guy roles get scrambled and what's okay or even marginally acceptable and what's not get tossed around like a Scrabble game that someone was careless about and knocked over.

"Do you have to make it into a big deal, Katy?"

"I don't have to make it into a big deal," I said.

"Good." He drained the Coke and put the can on the table with a click.

"It already is a big deal. These are not the kinds of things that happen between a man in a relationship and another woman. Especially a man like you."

And someone like me.

"Katy, do we have to talk about this now?"

I recognized and accepted defeat. Amber was in jail but she had won.

"No," I said.

"Good."

We both stood.

"I'm leaving today, this afternoon."

He nodded, leaned down to kiss me on the cheek. "Have a

safe trip." His hands were on my shoulders and then he was gone.

I said good-bye to Mars, then I was gone too.

It's an eleven-hour drive from Vegas to home, and that's seriously speeding, which is okay. I seriously speed all the time. I didn't try to do it, though. It was late, almost one before I left Vegas, but that wasn't the reason. I wasn't being sensible—I just didn't have the heart or the energy for it.

I haven't said Hank's last line to me, either. You try to forget, or deny, or hold the pain in. Sometimes it works and sometimes it doesn't. He walked to the front door and turned, his hand on the knob, and said: "I let a woman get me into trouble; I let a woman get me out. I've got a lot to be proud of, don't I?"

"It would be different if I had been a man?"

"Yes."

"I shouldn't have gotten you out of trouble?"

"I'm grateful you did." Which didn't answer the question, of course. "It also changes things."

Well, *goddamn*, I thought. It should. It should make him thankful.

"How?" I asked.

He looked at me as though I should know the answer and left.

By the time I got to Bakersfield, six hours later, I still didn't have the answer, though I thought it had to do with gender stereotypes, with guy thinking, with traps I never thought Hank and I would fall into. I decided to spend the night in Bakersfield. I had dues to pay and I was dragging-my-tail-in-the-dirt tired. I stayed at the same hotel. Déjà vu. I checked into my room and called.

A child answered the phone at the Jeffers residence and said hi like a two-year-old. I asked to speak to his daddy and he thunked the phone down. I waited three, maybe four minutes.

"Hello?"

"Doug? Kat Colorado, the investigator from Sacramento. We spoke the other day." I rubbed my temple. Was it only the other day? What day was it and how long had it been? I couldn't sort everything out. Bad news. Not enough sleep and too much turmoil.

"I remember. What happened?"

"The Las Vegas police arrested her."

"Good, I'm glad to hear it. I'd like to see her stand trial."

"Your story and those of the other potential witnesses went a long way toward exonerating the officer she accused. Everyone but JoJo appreciated that."

He laughed softly. "Good. No one should have to go through that. What happens now?"

"First of all, Bakersfield has to want her badly enough to come after her. That means sending an officer to get her. Assuming she waives extradition, of course. If she doesn't, there will be extradition proceedings as well. Sometimes they decide it's not worth it."

"Not *worth* it? JoJo might walk?"

"She might."

"Well, sh—shoot." He remembered his two-year-old just in time. "Is there anything I can do? How about I call?"

"I think that's a good idea. Mention the other cases you know about. There's a teacher at Bakersfield High who might help out too."

"Call the cops here?"

"And the DA. Keep calling and talking until you find someone who's interested. The point is JoJo did not just make one bad move. She made a habit, a career, of bad moves."

"I'll do that. Thanks, Kat."

"You're welcome. You've got my card. Call me if I can help."

"Daddeeee," a little voice said in the background, "Mommy said it's dinnertime."

Doug thanked me again before we broke the connection. It's nice when it works out this way, when the exchange is even and the satisfaction is on both sides.

I wasn't so sanguine about the next call.

Someone at the Sportsman's Club told me in a surly I-don't-give-a-shit tone that this was Sue Ellen's night off. I tried her home number then. Bingo. And she was as happy to hear from me as Jeffers had been. This was a welcome change from Vegas, where I was definitely the last-to-be-picked-for-the-team kind of kid. I hoped it would last.

"You asked me to let you know about JoJo," I said. "She's in jail. There was an outstanding warrant for her arrest in Bakersfield on an extortion charge. And she left the state, so that made her a fugitive."

"JoJo's in jail because of what I told you?" There was anger and regret in her voice.

"No." I *hate* this kind of thinking. "JoJo's in jail because she committed a felony and got caught."

"But if I hadn't said anything?"

"She could have been stopped by a traffic cop for a busted taillight and gone to jail, Sue Ellen. She chose to be a black-mailer, then to run away. It doesn't have anything to do with you. Her name's not JoJo anymore, either. She goes by Amber Echo now."

"She's a different person then, Kat?"

"I don't know." That was too big a question for me.

"Do you think she'll want me to be her friend?"

Another thing I didn't know. "I guess that's something you'll have to find out, to work out with her."

Myself, I'd just as soon clutch a fistful of rattlesnakes to my naked breast while swallowing rusty razor blades, tap-dancing, and whistling "Dixie."

"Thanks for calling, Kat. I guess."

"You're welcome."

"Blackmail is a hateful crime, isn't it?"

"Yes. It is."

We said good-bye.

I went to bed then with murder, blackmail, and a cheating boyfriend on my mind. *Sweet dreams.*

Friday, May 20

Sacramento

Forty-one

On Everyone's Shit List

I came home to a welcoming committee. Well, maybe "welcome" is the wrong word. "Committee" is, too, as that implies organization. I came home to a small and surly band—that was closer to the truth. They had several things in common. Even though they hadn't killed her, they had all wanted Courtney out of the way, and they didn't want me to know that. They wanted me to think that they were nice folks. And they were afraid I didn't.

They were so right.

Robert Corwin was the first to find me. Walked right in and started berating me without so much as a *howdy*, a *how you doing?* I used to think Miss Manners was overly picky about etiquette details. Not anymore. First the manners go, and the next thing you know it's fires and fiddlers and a downward progression that is not promising.

"I've been trying to reach you for several days!" Corwin stormed at me.

"Good morning," I said formally, and smiled my formal smile, the one that doesn't light up my eyes or show my dimples or laugh lines. "Fine, thanks. How are you?" I looked up at him briefly from the mail I was sorting. How could I have bills? I'd just paid a whole slew of them. On time too. "Won't you be seated? Care for a cup of coffee?" Oops, that was rude—offering a Mormon forbidden caffeine. "Or herbal tea?"

Corwin made a guttural muttering sound. "Listen here, you."

"Kat," I said genially. "But do call me Ms. Colorado. And do sit down. Or leave. I don't care which." I thought that one over. *Wrong.* I preferred that he leave.

"You threatened me."

"Threatened you? Nonsense."

"Threatened to go to my Church and expose . . . expose . . ."

"Oh, *that.* That wasn't a threat. Not at all. I see myself as a concerned citizen doing my civic duty." Mmmm. Good line. I'd have to remember that. "Not just civic," I amended, "but a higher duty as well. 'Do unto others,' you know. It doesn't seem to me that a man who attempted rape, violated his religious vows, and threatened a defenseless woman with the loss of her reputation, Church, and community should go unnoticed. These are, after all," I stated blandly, "quite noteworthy things. When we add to that the possibility of your being involved in a murder—"

"Shut up, woman!" he roared.

I raised my eyebrows slightly. *Tsk Tsk.*

"This is nonsense, absolute total nonsense!"

"Then you have no cause for concern."

"True. Nevertheless, I would not care to discuss such matters as these with—"

"You're right," I said, and nodded. "So many of us believe that there is no smoke without a fire."

"I insist you drop this immediately."

I laughed in his face. "We covered this before, Corwin. You are in no position to insist on anything and I am the last person that you can push around."

"You don't understand, do you? I'm not asking you, I'm telling you."

I sighed. God, I get tired of male posturing. "Who's threatening whom?" I asked politely.

His face darkened. "Just so you understand. I'm not kidding about this, about any of it."

He loomed over me in the guy mode that is supposed to scare the wits out of women. It is the sort of thing that works better on Medora or Lauren than on me. He turned on his heel and walked, stopping at the door.

"It's not a good idea to push someone too far," he told me.

I thought that one over in the silence he left behind him. He was right: It wasn't a good idea; it wasn't safe either. Corwin was a man who threatened women, who used physical violence—or the possibility of it—to intimidate and get his way. Maybe even the kind of man who enjoyed the feeling of power and control such dominance gave him. How far had he gone? Would he go?

Courtney lying smashed on the freeway, her skirt hiked up, her chest crushed, her foot torn off. Blood everywhere. Cinderella's dream dead.

Accident? Vengeance? Atonement?

There was a light knock on the door. I looked up into Chad's smiling face. Hey, how did everyone suddenly figure out that I was home? How was this choreographed?

"Hi, Kat, I was just in the neighborhood and thought I'd pop in."

My enthusiastic greeting wasn't entirely feigned. I liked him better than Robert, found him a lot more interesting too.

He perched on the arm of the visitor's chair and handed me a bag. "Have one of these. Sweeten up your smile."

"What are they?"

"Scones. From New Helvetia."

Yum. I started to reach for one. "They're not poisoned, are they?" I asked, making my voice suspicious and heavy.

"Just with calories," he said, laughing. "Why?"

I got out a diet soda to drink with my scone—how's that for logic?—and offered one to Chad. We munched and sipped and I explained that I was on everyone's Shit List.

"Why?"

"Too long to get into. I get exhausted just thinking about it." Too long, too complicated, too bloody, but I didn't want to get into that, either. "What happened in the child-kidnap case?"

"God, Kat, I hate that kind of stuff. It's two parents who love their kid and will never see eye-to-eye. Look, how's it going with your investigation into Courtney's death?" His voice was calm but body language gave him away. The stakes were high here too, but in a different way. "Any leads? Are you still convinced that it's . . . that it wasn't an accident?"

"Yes and yes. But no answers. Give me a while. Better yet, let me get back to you."

"Sure." He smiled. "I know you're doing your best. It's just that I can't imagine—"

"Yes. I understand. It's hard."

Blood and betrayal. Very hard.

The rest of the afternoon was peaceful and boring. I enjoyed it, found it a welcome contrast. In the middle of the afternoon I called Medora and, when her whispered assurances told me the coast was clear, asked my questions.

"Please don't be offended by this. I know every mother thinks—"

"It's all right. You may ask what you wish."

I took a deep breath. "Medora—was Courtney an honest person?"

"Mothers see as clearly as anyone else," she said matter-of-factly. "It's hard sometimes to admit or condemn, but we see. Yes, my daughter was honest, the most honest and trustworthy of all my children. I say this not because she did what was right or what was expected of her, but because truthfulness was as important to her as life itself.

"She could not bear lies, not even half truths. And she could not bear to be around people who did these things. It was not enough to shun such practice, she felt an obligation to speak out." Medora chuckled. "I remember when she was a small child, not more than four or five, she saw a person at the market eating grapes out of the bin. 'Mommy, that's stealing, isn't it?' she asked me. I was embarrassed but how could I reprimand her? The child was right."

Yes. Of course, that is precisely the kind of right that lands you on people's shit lists, as I knew to my sorrow.

"Medora, where would Courtney have hidden something?"

"Hidden something?"

"Yes."

"Hidden something?"

"Yes."

I tried to be patient, even though we were both speaking English and it was not a difficult sentence.

"She wouldn't. She had nothing to hide. She was a very open person."

Everyone has something to hide. I didn't say this, I just said good-bye. And I thought I knew what Courtney had hidden. Naturally I didn't say this, either.

Courtney's roommate, Janie, wasn't home. I left a message asking if I could come by that afternoon or evening to look for something. The something that a person who has nothing to hide would hide.

The phone rang on three occasions—I pounced on it each time—before Janie called.

"Sure, Kat, come over. Can you come now? I have to go out soon. Not that that matters. You can stay as long as you like."

"I'm on my way."

She answered the door, smiling, young, and pretty. My heart closed up again at the waste and loss in Courtney's death.

"Come on in, Kat. Do you want to look in Courtney's room or everywhere? Whatever, it's okay."

"I'll start with her room."

"Sure."

"Any more break-ins or trouble of any kind?"

"No, thank goodness. I've been here a lot though, studying for tests and stuff. They wouldn't come when I was here, would they?"

"I don't think so." I hoped not. One death was enough, was too much.

"Make yourself at home. Or maybe I should say at work?"

I smiled and did just that.

I sat in Courtney's silent room, the faint memory of a living woman there still, lingering, almost gone now like the whisper of perfume in the air. Medora said her daughter had nothing to hide. No secrets. That she was an honest and open person. I thought something was hidden here. Not her secrets, but some-one else's. I had hoped for, and not found, anything in Court-ney's records, schoolwork, or mementos. It was a given that Courtney would have been an amateur at concealment. Where would she have put it?

I went through the room again, looked under drawers, behind furniture and pictures. Nothing taped there. It would be a simple hiding place, I thought. Nothing complex. I went through the pockets and linings of Courtney's clothing.

"Kat, I'm going now." Janie stuck her head in the door. "Lock up on the way out, okay?"

"Yes, thanks, Janie."

"Anything I can do. Anything and anytime."

I poked around in the freezer, stuck a spoon in the flour canister. *Simple,* I thought. *Think simple.* Peeled the rugs back, looked between the bottom layers of towels, behind the washer/dryer. Simple. Obvious. So obvious I hadn't noticed?

Had it been the car, after all? I thought back. No. The only place I hadn't checked had been the spare tire and that wasn't simple. You had to let the air out, pry the tire away from the rim and cram something in. It took strength, agility, and time.

I went back to Courtney's room and sat at her desk chair, then on her bed, then leaned against the corner wall trying to see things in a new way and with new eyes, trying to see the clear and simple.

I got up and walked to the closet, picked up the umbrella that hung from the hook next to Courtney's raincoat. It was a fold-up umbrella tucked into a slim case. I slipped the case off, flopped the umbrella open and stared at the paper tightly coiled around the umbrella shaft. Hot damn. Sixteen photocopied sheets. *Hot damn.*

I unrolled the coiled pages and read.

I would get Courtney's killer now.

I made two sets of copies, put Courtney's copy in the office safe, mailed one to Charity for safekeeping, and sat down to look over the second. I called a friend to clarify some of the fine points, but the overall picture was starkly clear.

Chalk outlines of human figures, the kind the police draw on the ground around a homicide victim, danced in my mind like demented hollow gingerbread men. Then they filled up with blood, overflowed, blurred, became a carmine river that splashed bloody drops. I put my head down on my arms and willed the pictures away, concentrated on thoughts of the killer.

And tomorrow? Tomorrow, I thought drearily, I had to return to Las Vegas. One more time. One more loose end to tie up.

Something thudded in the hall. Hadn't I locked the outside door? *Careless.* Heavy, running footsteps, a slam. *Ominous.* I pushed my door open slowly, feeling the resistance push back, stepped out.

Not much resistance. I looked down at the tumbled corpse of the bunny. A small one, a young one. Its throat had been cut. Slashed from ear to ear. Bright drops of blood glistened on the pristine white fur. I touched it gently. Still warm.

Later—after I'd looked for the perpetrator I'd waited too long to catch, after I'd disposed of the dead animal, after I'd locked up and after I'd stopped shaking—I called.

It was after hours but I thought Manny lived above the gun shop, thought most likely he would answer the phone.

"Hello."

He spoke and dragged on a cigarette. I identified myself, my voice sounding mean and angry. I hadn't been able to scrub up all the blood. He dragged on his cigarette again.

"Who did you tell about me?"

He exhaled. "Huh? I don't know what you're talking about."

"Yeah, you do. And if you make me drive out there to get it out of you, I will."

Dragging, exhaling. A cough this time.

"What makes you think I—"

"I don't think, I know. This is as patient as I'm going to be. Spit it out."

"Well, I might've mentioned it. I guess," he said casually. Way too casually.

"Yeah," I said. "Might have mentioned it to who?" As if I didn't know. As if I cared about grammar.

"Might have mentioned it to Ezra Dillard."

"Yeah," I said, and hung up, hatred a live and ugly thing within me.

More blood, more death.

Saturday, May 21

Las Vegas

Forty-two

The Oldest Line
in the Book

Las Vegas was beautiful, the way spring in the desert is. Hard blue skies, clean, clear crystal light, and cactus, tumbleweeds, and palm trees. There was no room in me for anything but thoughts of murder and hatred. And determination. I parked on the street, headed for Amber's apartment. Dead-bolt lock. Damn. So much for on-the-spot physical ingenuity.

On to Plan B: lies.

I knocked on the manager's door.

Potbelly, T-shirt with grease and egg stains, three-day growth, and an attitude. Swell.

"Help you."

He said it but he wasn't sincere. Okay, I could get behind that, I was in that mode too.

"Hi, my name is Laura." Lie number one. I do kind of look like a Laura, though. "I'm a friend of Amber's." Stretching it a bit. "She's kind of in a jam now, so she asked me to stop by and pick up some of her clothes and things." Lie number three.

"I know. Heard she's in jail. I'm going to get my rent, ain't I?" He sounded aggrieved.

"She told me to tell you to let me in and to give you this for your trouble." I flashed a twenty as I uttered lie number four. "She said to tell you that everything was going to be okay." Five.

He held his hand out for the twenty. Like I was born yesterday.

"After you let me in," I said.

"Yeah. Well, lemme get my keys."

He let me in. I let him leave. He didn't want to.

"Amber would be embarrassed if you saw me packing her underwear and stuff."

He didn't look convinced. Who could blame him? But he left. I shot the dead bolt behind him and looked around. I knew exactly what I was looking for this time.

I found it in a kitchen drawer, a jumble of bills, receipts, notes, personal records. I pulled out the drawer and headed for the dining-room table where I dumped it. Then I went back and punched the message-retrieval button on the phone machine. Two messages. One was Brandi, the friend of Amber's I'd met at the bar; the other a familiar male voice. I reset the machine, then lifted the tape.

I started through the drawer. Fortunately Amber was a black-mailing stripper—a job category in which she excelled—and not a bookkeeper—a job category for which she showed no talent or aptitude whatsoever.

I pulled out her three latest phone bills. The number I was looking for appeared numerous times on the most recent bill. I set all three aside. Found a note scribbled on the back of an envelope. 2 for 2.

Nothing else of interest in the drawer. Nor on the kitchen or bathroom counters or in the living room. I found it in the bedroom on top of a pile of—clean? dirty?—underwear and next to perfume and a tipped-over bottle of nail polish. Tiger Princess and Jungle Red. It fit her, no question.

The envelope had been crudely ripped open. No note, just the check, two thousand dollars' worth. And the signature I was expecting. 3 for 3.

I had it nailed down.

I was out of here.

The key turned in the dead bolt as I finished tucking the tape, phone bills, note, and check in my purse. No way I could make it to the bathtub this time and no place else to hide. Talk about bad timing. I smacked an innocent look on my face.

He didn't look surprised to see me. Why not? I was surprised to see him. A little. "Well, Kat, what an unanticipated pleasure."

"Hello, Chad." I took the car keys out of my purse, zipped it, swung the bag on my shoulder. The bag wasn't heavy enough to be a weapon; the keys would have to do. They can take out an eyeball or pierce a windpipe. Wouldn't that make me a favored customer at the rental-car company?

"Don't be in a rush, Kat. You're just the person I want to talk to."

"Really? Let's do lunch, then. I'm starving." I started for the door, the one he had shut behind him and now body-blocked. Might as well make my move now; it wasn't going to get any better.

Chad reached into the pocket of his windbreaker and pulled out a gun.

I thought wistfully of all the things it could have been—a handkerchief, a box of Cracker Jacks, a pair of movie passes, a winning lottery ticket—but no, it was a nine-millimeter.

"Sit down, Kat." He waved the gun at the dining-room chair where I'd been sitting.

I sat. A gun is the kind of thing I notice, the kind of argument I find persuasive, compelling even. "I had no idea you'd get so cranky just because I turned down a job. Jeez, Wharton, get a grip."

"How much do you know, Kat?" He sat opposite me. How cozy. Like Mom and Dad at the dinner table.

"Very little." I was in Lying Mode, remember. Also Survival Mode.

He shook his head. "I might have believed that yesterday; I don't now. Yesterday I came to your office hoping you hadn't come up with anything, needing to know, to check it out. You were open, friendly, unsuspecting. You treated me as you always have, and I fell for it. I should have remembered Aunt Sophie and how easily you dissemble, how well you play a part."

"I wasn't playing a part. How I acted yesterday was and is exactly how I feel," I said, dissembling and playing a part. Chad didn't know how much I knew and I sure as hell wasn't admitting to anything. I watch cops do this all the time—say they know what went down when they don't know jack shit, and then sit back and wait for incriminating statements. It's surprising how often it works. Today was not going to be one of those times, though.

"Whatever is on your mind, you are certainly overreacting." The gun lay on the table near his hand. I shrugged, wishing I had a gun to overreact with. "We can talk about whatever you want, Chad, but let's do it without guns and over lunch."

"Like I said, I left your office yesterday thinking you didn't know anything, thinking everything was okay. Then I got Amber's call. The dumb shit is in jail and she calls me, that's how smart she is. I told her I'd get her a lawyer and I told her to shut up. I found out through the lawyer that you'd put it together. Amber said you had a copy of an old yearbook, that you'd circled my picture and figured Amber and I knew each other."

I'd figured it, yes. I'd come down here to be sure. Now I was, for all the good it was doing me. "You were a friend of her brother's, weren't you?"

"JoJo and I go way back. There's always been something between us. We've always stayed in touch." He laughed. "So then I knew you knew; I just didn't know how much."

"The second one goes down easier, doesn't it?"

"The second what?"

"Peanut. Beer. Killing."

His eyes narrowed. "So you do know."

I nodded. I was talking now. It was out now.

"How did you figure it?"

"Your mother told me."

"My *mother*? No way. No way she— What the hell are you talking about, Kat?"

I shrugged.

"Tell me or don't tell me. Either way, you're dead."

Yeah, I figured that's what the stakes were in the game we were playing. I figured it, but I hoped I was wrong. I wondered if the manager would come back to check on me. Not the kind of thing to pin a hope on. Maybe the expression "You're dead" was just colorful colloquial use on Chad's part. I looked at his eyes. Maybe not.

"I know most of it. I've guessed pretty close on the rest of it. What you need to know is that this is all very carefully documented and recorded. I mailed a copy of it to my lawyer this morning before leaving town."

He smiled thinly. "That's the oldest line in the book, Kat."

I thought it over. "Nah. Third, maybe. After 'The check's in the mail' and 'I love you for your mind.' And sometimes it's not a line, it's the truth. Like this time."

"Suppose I call your bluff?"

"Then you go down for two murders instead of one. You walk away from this now, plead temporary insanity in a lover's quarrel, you're out in a few years." *Ha. Over my dead body.* A shiver ran through me. Wrong expression.

"How much do you know?"

I answered. Talking was better than some of the other alternatives. "I knew it was murder early on from physical evidence on the scene."

He cocked an eyebrow.

"The tire. The force of a blowout would have blasted all the tire fibers out. Instead I found a tear with an attempt to pull the fibers out. Other things too."

He whistled. "I underestimated you."

"I was looking at several possibilities."

"Suspects?" he asked wryly.

"Suspects," I agreed, thinking of Robert and Ezra, who were still highly suspect and guilty, by God, of a bunch of things— though not murder—things I still planned to nail them on. "Your mother pointed me in the right direction when she spoke of a conversation that she overheard between the two of you the night you had dinner there. She said that you were fighting and that Courtney was upset because she was an outsider and you all were insiders. Your mother's interpretation didn't make sense to me; it didn't sound like what I knew of Courtney." I pushed my chair back and ran my fingers through my hair. "You were the one who broke into Courtney and Janie's house."

"Yes."

"Only you didn't find it."

"And you did."

We were on the same wavelength now. Too bad we weren't Trivial Pursuit partners and I wasn't having more fun.

"Yes. As Courtney had. You were a busy boy, Wharton."

His eyes were dark and unreadable. His hands fooled around with the gun.

"I thought about what your mother had overheard and discarded her interpretation, came up with—not insiders and outsiders in the family or in a social sense—but the possibility of insider trading. That made a whole lot more sense.

"The papers I found at Courtney's documented that and

more: insider trading through a complicated chain of friends and associates—unauthorized trading that would, I'm sure, have been a big shock to your clients; money laundering. There were a sizable number of cash buys in amounts under ten thousand, an amount that goes unreported to the federal government, then quick rollovers, again into cash. Drug money?''

Wharton ignored that. ''Some women could have enjoyed the extra money, looked the other way and not asked questions.''

''Not Courtney.''

''No.'' He said it bitterly. ''She was so goddamned fucking honest.''

''She broke off your engagement—'' I slid back my chair again and tested the distance with my legs. Perfect. ''—but even that wasn't enough.''

''She was going to turn me in. I would have lost my license, my partnership—''

You would have gone to jail, pal. Silent words in my head. *You still are.* I was committed to it, not just for Courtney's sake. For mine, too.

''I would have lost everything.''

''So you killed her.''

''Yes.''

''You fought first at your parents' house and then again later when you walked her to the car.''

''I loved her, you know. I really did. I didn't want to do it. I hated to do it.''

''Your parents live in a secluded area. I imagine you killed her there. Or disabled her.'' I made Courtney a rag-doll figure in my mind instead of a human being so I could bear it, so I could keep going. ''How?''

''I didn't want a lot of blood.''

Premeditated. I added on more prison time.

''I said something looked wrong with her tire and opened my trunk to get a tool. I hit her in the chest with the tire iron, then wrapped her in a blanket and put her in the trunk of her car. The rest you know. I parked on the side of the freeway in a dark stretch, did the tire, waited for an open spot in traffic, and dumped her body.''

Her body. ''Was she dead, Chad?''

''I—I think so.''

I could tell by his eyes that she wasn't. Had she known, felt the rough asphalt on her cheek, heard the engine sounds, the singing of tires and then—

The phone rang, jerked Chad's attention away from me. My feet were braced on the legs of the heavy wooden table. I pushed hard, slamming it into Chad. He took it in the chest. Like Courtney.

I bolted for the door.

Forty-three

The Killer
and the Dame

I almost made it. Almost counts in horseshoes but not in Death Tag.

He pushed the table back and lunged for me as I ran for the door. Hand hitting my shoulder hard, groping at my hip. I kneed him in the groin, giving it everything I had. He doubled up and went down. The problem was I was under him. He held on, groaning. My legs were pinned but I went for the eyes, for the throat.

Another good shot but it wasn't a fair match. I was outweighed and outpowered. Chad held me down. Then, a hand gripping my wrist, he grabbed my hair, bounced my skull off the floor.

No words. We both lay there and recovered. He was positioned on me almost as though we were lovers exhausted after loving. Except that your lover isn't deadweight on you. Or trying to kill you.

By the time Wharton moved, I was fighting for breath. My head was still on its merry-go-round and I sure didn't have the brass ring.

"I'm getting up, Kat. You move and I make you look like Courtney. Understand?"

I stared at the ceiling. I wasn't through fighting but this wasn't the best position to go into ATTACK mode. And right now on a scale of 1 to 10, I was beat-up. Kinda bad too.

"Understand?"

His pressure everywhere on my body increased. I nodded.

"Okay. Don't fucking move."

Where was the gun? I wondered. Wharton struggled to his feet, looked around. The gun was on his mind too. He found it and stuck it in his belt with a grunt of satisfaction.

"I've got to go to the bathroom," I announced.

"Too fucking bad."

"No," I said. "I've got to."

"Shut up. Just shut the fuck up!"

I stopped whining and started moaning.

"Get up."

He kicked me in the ribs, the son of a bitch. I rolled over, then staggered upright, using the wall as support, trying to look as feeble and beat-up as possible. Not that hard, actually.

"Go on," he said.

I started for the bathroom and he followed me. I turned and stared at him. "You'll have to leave. I can't go with you in here."

He snarled.

"Check it out but then let me close the door."

He herded me in. The bathroom window was small, only opened six inches. The medicine cabinet had aspirin, bandages, and cough syrup. No guns, no machetes, no cellular phones. Nothing useful at all. He growled but he left. I shut the door.

First I pulled the shower curtain around the tub. Slow and silent. I walked to the window, smashed it down, then up, then hopped into the tub behind the shower curtain and scrunched down. The bathroom door flew open, bouncing off the wall, and Wharton headed for the window. I was out of that tub like a racehorse out of the gate, slammed the door shut behind me and flew for the front door. *Out!* Yes!

Blam! Once again I was tangled up with a man. I could smell sweat and beer and cigarettes. I pushed him off and struggled for balance. Something large and hard smashed into me and bounced me off the concrete.

"Help! Police! Call the cops someone!" I hollered. "This man's trying to kill me. He-e-e-lp!"

Hands—four of them—dragged me back inside. The door closed. Wharton and the manager stood side by side looking at me.

"Call the police," I said to the manager. "Now! This man's a killer."

"Damn, officer," the manager said, shaking his head. "I can see it now, but I never would of figured her for a hooker. Feisty, ain't she?"

Officer? Hooker? That lying sack of shit! I took a deep breath. "I'm not a hooker and he's not a cop."

"Yeah." The manager laughed. "He said you'd say that when we talked outside. He said you'd talked your way out of a lot. A real sweet-talker, yeah, that's what he said."

"Just call nine-one-one." I made myself speak calmly. "Let them figure it out."

The two men looked at each other and smiled. Complacent. Conspiratorial. Smug.

I was had.

Wharton knew it. I knew it. The manager was a dummy who believed what he was first told, or believed Wharton because he was a guy—who knows? Maybe Wharton had paid him off.

"Thanks, pal," Wharton said to the manager. "The department won't forget this."

"If you're a cop," I yelled, "let's see your fucking badge!"

The guys laughed as I yelled "Let's see your fucking badge" over and over. Then the manager left. It was just us again, the killer and the dame. Well, *shit.* So I didn't take that thought any further. Bad for morale.

"Here's the deal," Wharton said. "And this is sweet, real sweet. You're going to be the next victim of the Strip Stalker. Your head all smashed in like all those other girls."

"Like Courtney," I said.

He smiled. *Smiled.*

"I don't fit the victim profile," I said. "It won't work."

"So it's a copycat killer then. Either way you're just as dead; I'm just as out of it. But that's not the best part."

I didn't ask, I wouldn't give him the satisfaction. Also, I didn't want to know.

"The best part is that your cop boyfriend is on the case. They'll call him to the scene. Amber told me all about his involvement. I wonder if he'll recognize you right away. He won't have a face to go on, remember."

He grinned. It was the all-American wholesome-boy grin of an all-American wholesome boy gone bad.

Real bad.

I was scared.

Real scared.

Forty-four

The Taste of Blood

Wharton was pissed. It was a bad-guy dilemma, all right, but he wasn't getting any sympathy from me. Transportation to my murder site was going to be a problem. He couldn't very well stuff a sock in my face and load me into the trunk. A. Cops don't do that. B. It's just the kind of thing your average citizen calls to the attention of the police.

He sure as hell didn't want me rattling around in the car, combination loose cannon, loudmouth, and bottle rocket. And he couldn't find anything to tie me up with. He made me look into drawers and closets, following me around and waving the gun. Nothing: no rope, no duct tape, strapping tape, adhesive tape, no electrical cords. Nothing.

"Tsk." I shook my head. "Should have picked up some handcuffs when you picked out your badge."

"Shut the fuck up. I don't want to hear another fucking word out of you." Okay. Always agreeable, I started whistling. "Take Me Out to the Ball Game."

"Shut up."

Jeez. I thought everyone liked that song. What kind of an American was he, anyway? Wharton finally found a bungee cord on a box in the bedroom closet.

Five minutes and we were out the door, me with my hands bungee-corded behind me, him hanging on to my arm and trying to look like a cop. Yeah. Right. The manager gave us a little wave. Otherwise I saw no one so I didn't waste my breath holler-ing. Wharton belted me into the front passenger seat, then buck-led himself in, started the car, released the hand brake.

"You hired Amber?"

"Hired her? No. We're friends, Kat. I told you we go way back, back to high school, back to growing up together. We've always kept in touch and I go to Vegas a couple of times a year to gamble, to play."

"With Amber?" With built-like-a-brick-shit-house Amber?

"With Amber, yeah." He laughed. "We helped each other out. Always did. So, no, I didn't hire her. I gave her money, yeah, but that's Amber."

I tried to figure where we were; I thought we were headed out of town. To the desert. To a nice quiet Killing Zone.

"Then you gave me your cop's name in Vegas."

I winced. I thought I was being clever with that, remember?

"Amber knew a showgirl who knew a cop in Vice. That's how she found out about Parker. She did a good job."

She did, yes, though I didn't feel much like discussing it. "You were trying to pull me away from the investigation into Court-ney's death with this, with the kidnapped child?"

"Yeah. I figured getting your boyfriend into trouble was a good start. I didn't figure he'd be such a hard sell."

Not that hard, I thought. Not hard enough.

"I hadn't figured you to be so stubborn. Or smart." He said it grudgingly.

Not that smart. Tied up and on a one-way trip to the desert? Not that smart at all.

It was almost dark.

I knew what that meant.

Wharton was nervous and jumpy. Me, too. I kept my eyes peeled, especially for police cars. He stayed on the back streets. It got darker. There were few cars on the roads we traveled. No pedestrians. We were as far away from the neon as you can get and still be in Vegas.

Wharton slowed at a yield sign. A young woman with a bag of groceries climbed out of a station wagon parked parallel to us.

"Help!" I hollered at her. "Police. Call the police!" Her eyes went wide and stunned. Vegas, after all, was a city terrorized by the Strip Stalker.

Wharton swore and smacked me in the mouth, then floored it. Tires squealed. I hoped that she was the good-citizen type who would dash to the phone. The good-citizen type with a memory for license-plate numbers and the make and model of this car. I tasted blood on my lip. Wharton was swearing. We came up on a street that was more crowded, a strip mall on the corner. There were cars, traffic lights, pedestrians.

I waited until we hit the intersection, then tromped down hard on Wharton's accelerator foot. The car went flying into oncoming traffic. Wharton pulled it out, but barely, then overcorrected and we sideswiped a parked car. His fingers clawed into my leg. Horns blared. Wharton slammed me in the belly and I doubled over, freeing his accelerator foot. *Goddamn.* Struggling for air.

I heard a siren. It sounded far away but maybe it was just the blood and jostled brains plugging up my ears. I gasped for air, sucked in a breath, then another. The sirens were louder. I blinked the tears out of my eyes. The sirens were on top of us; red-and-blue revolving lights spilling over the car.

I could hardly breathe and I could taste blood but I was smiling.

Wharton wasn't. He was snarling and swearing. And speeding. *Shit!* Maybe I started smiling too soon. I hate high-speed chases, hate feeling out of control. I mean, we are talking about someone who won't ride roller coasters and closes her eyes in movie chase scenes. We careened around a corner. The sirens followed.

"Fuck! Goddamn motherfucking—" Wharton hit the brakes, rode up over a curb, then back onto the pavement. Something huge loomed up in front of us. We hit it. Metal crunched against metal. The impact threw my body against the seat belt. The car bounced around and then stopped.

Lights and sirens surrounded us. There was water on the windshield from a busted radiator.

"Driver, open your door. I want to see your hands. Now. Driver, let me see your hands now!"

Cops. PA system. I leaned back awkwardly against my bungee-corded hands and the seat. Almost over. Through the water on the windshield I could see a delivery truck. The driver stood beside it, scratching his head. Pampers. We had hit a Pampers truck. I started to laugh.

"Driver, get out of your vehicle *now.* Keep your hands up."

I was still laughing when they helped me out of the car and untied my hands.

"You okay, miss?" The uniformed officer sounded dubious. *Dubious,* I thought. *What a goofy word,* and that set me off again.

The officer tipped my chin up with a thumb and knuckle. "Let me see your eyes," he said nicely, but firmly.

"I'm okay," I said. "That guy—the driver—tried to kill me. He killed someone else. Please call Davis Merkovitz—he's a sergeant in Homicide. Tell him it's Kat."

"Cat?"

"Please. Just tell him."

It took Davis thirty minutes to get there. They let me sit in the front seat of one of the patrol cars. Wharton was in the backseat of another one. Someone offered me a coffee. It had cream and sugar but I drank it anyway.

"Where is she?"

I heard Davis's voice and stumbled out of the car. Davis caught me in a hug. "Katy, what the hell happened?"

It took a long time to tell. There were a lot of stories, after all: Courtney's, Wharton's, mine, Amber and Wharton's.

"What?" Davis asked when I got to that one.

"They're old friends. Davis, Wharton was using Amber to get to Hank so it would get to me so I would lay off the investigation of Courtney's death. Did I say that in English?"

"Sort of."

"I can prove it. It's all in my purse which is back at Amber's. The reason Hank got into trouble was my involvement in Courtney's death. Wharton was trying to get to me through Hank."

"The reason Hank got into trouble," Davis said darkly, "is that he was acting like a dumb shit."

Yeah, okay, I thought wearily. *That, too.*

I didn't notice when they hauled Wharton off to jail which was a big disappointment. I wanted to thumb my nose, make rude noises, and laugh in his face. Maybe holler *Sayonara* or *See you in court, asshole.*

I rode in Davis's car over to Amber's to pick up my purse. A patrol car followed us. For the manager's story, I guess, and the evidence I had in my purse and— *God,* I was tired.

"I want you to get that dumb fuck, Davis."

"Which dumb fuck, Katy?" Davis asked gently, patiently.

"The manager. Me a hooker and Wharton a cop. Jeez!"

"On what? There's no law against stupidity."

"Well, *goddamn!*" I rubbed my temple, licked the cut on my lips. "How about you scare the shit out of him, then?"

"We can do that," Davis said agreeably.

I smiled. First time in a while.

"Hi."

I was leaning against the doorjamb of the manager's place and smiling at him with a crooked smile and a busted lip.

"Remember me?"

He did, no problem. His eyes widened as he took in me, Davis, and the two uniforms standing behind us.

"And these guys are cops. Real cops."

"Uh-oh," he said.

Boy, did he have that right.

Maggie helped me pull my clothes off, then stuck me into a hot bath with Epsom salts. After that I had tomato soup and grilled cheese, and then I went to bed. Maggie tucked me in and turned out the light and never asked questions. I was grateful that everything was turning out happily ever after.

Everything except Hank and me.

It took me a long time to fall asleep. Then I slept until ten the next morning and I was still tired. In the movies the good guy gets in a fight, wins, saunters home to toss off a gourmet meal, drinks lots of booze, makes love all night, and in the morning starts it all over again. Real life is nothing like the movies.

Believe it.

I was on the afternoon plane home, the taste of blood in my mouth still.

Sunday, May 22

Sacramento

Forty-five

Rhinestone Presents and Presumption

The party was at five-thirty. It had started out as a family event and grown from there. I came early to help Alma with the food and preparations.

"Alma, I invited some people."

"That's nice, dear." I had about half her attention, maybe a quarter. "Who? Not a man? I don't care if you and Hank are quarreling, I don't think that you should—"

"Not another man. Well, Bill Henley but—"

"Oh, good, I like Bill. Who else dear?"

"Face it, Melinda, he's not coming."

Alma stalked out of the kitchen and I followed her.

"He knows who you are now, he knows everything about you—that your husband died young from taking the wrong medications under your care, that you put your beautiful baby up for adoption just because he interfered with your social life, that you lied and stole from your mother as she lay suffering and in unbearable pain on her death bed."

Alma put her hands on her hips and spoke to the TV. "My God, if that doesn't beat the band. She is a lying, sneaking, treacherous little schemer. And that's her *good* side. Ha!"

Compared to Melinda, I thought, Hank wasn't all that bad. Of course—compared to Melinda—who was?

"Look at you—all dressed up and nowhere to go in your thousand-dollar wedding dress with its pearls and sequins and rosebuds. But there

is no one to take your hand and say I Do because he doesn't. Hahahahahaha!"

"Serves her right," declared Alma, marching back to the kitchen. "And on top of all that she chews with her mouth open. I just have no use for that girl, none at all. Could you finish flouring that chicken, dear, and we'll get it in the fryer?"

I dredged chicken through seasoned flour and tossed it into the fryer. Low fat / low cholesterol cooking was not one of Alma's strong suits.

"Alma, I invited Medora Dillard and Lauren too, and when they get here—"

"Mmmmm."

"Don't swear, don't be wild and rowdy and please don't drink shooters."

She sighed loudly, pathetically. "Now, Katy, can you honestly say I've ever embarrassed you?"

"Yes. Remember the time you stood on the dining-room table with a lampshade on your head and acted out your favorite parts in *Gone with the Wind*?"

She brightened. "That *was* fun."

"And then sat down in a bowl of stuffing."

"That was an accident, dear."

"Alma!"

The doorbell rang. She gave me a hug. "Don't worry so, Katy."

Okay, she was right. I dredged some more chicken through the flour and heaved it into hot grease.

"Hey, Katy." Bill Henley walked in the kitchen followed by a twittering Alma, who walked right back out again.

"Hi, Bill, I'm glad you could come. Beer's in the refrigerator." I waved my floury hands at him.

"Ohmigod, you won't believe this." Alma stalked back into the kitchen. "Mac went to the airport to pick up Chrissy, only who should get off the plane but his long-lost twin sister. Everyone thought she died years ago but she didn't, she had plastic surgery instead. Then Darren, that stinkbug, had a horrible fight with Julieanne and he made her get out of the car in the middle of a ghastly blizzard. Somebody ought to pin his ears back!"

"Huh?"

Poor Bill. "Soaps," I explained. "Alma tapes them to watch

later." I finished the chicken and washed my hands. "Let's go out on the porch, Bill."

We walked out and pulled up porch chairs.

"Lindy a senior and going to the prom." He shook his head. "It's something, Kat."

Like me, he remembered the Lindy I pulled off the streets, a sullen, hostile teenage runaway and hooker. He'd been around to lend a fatherly helping hand over the years too.

"Hey, Bill, if I do your job, can I have your paycheck?"

"Hell, yes. Got a stack of cases you can have too."

"Want another one?"

"The one you told me about?"

I nodded and told him the rest.

He whistled. "Nice work, Katy. Yeah, I'll follow up on that. Glad to."

"There's more." God, I *love* dropping dimes on bad guys. It's definitely one of the perks of my job. I told him about Ezra. "Do you think we could get narcotics to check out his place?"

"We could," he agreed.

I'd already called the IRS and Child Welfare on Ezra Dillard. The pregnant teenager haunted me. Ezra was lost, but she wasn't. Lindy had been about that age when I'd found her.

"Hey, you two lumps. Get off that log and come help me. We need to slice up eggs and potatoes for the potato salad. Cucumbers and tomatoes, too."

Bill and I meekly followed Alma into the kitchen and into soap opera.

"Del had a fight with Delia. That made her suicidal so she stopped taking her medication and then took a goshdarned turn for the worse. Went out like a porch light, to be exact. Lordy, a two-week-old kitten has more sense."

Bill and I chopped and sliced and shook our heads in sympathetic horror. The doorbell rang and Alma let Edna in.

"*Nice* T-shirt, Edna." I introduced her to Bill and got them both a beer. Her T-shirt said: I MAY BE OLD BUT I'M FORMIDABLE!

The doorbell rang again. I got it; I was tired of slicing hardboiled eggs. Lauren and Medora came in. Well, sidled in nervously was more like it. Lauren looked terrified, Medora looked uneasy. I had begged Medora to do whatever she had to to bring Lauren. I hugged them both.

"Come in. I want you to meet my family and our friends. Edna's here, too."

We squeezed into the kitchen.

"This is Courtney's mother, Medora, and Courtney's best friend, Lauren. It's because of their bravery that we got Wharton."

"Yours, too, Kat." Medora tugged on my elbow. "And I have good news." She spoke shyly but her eyes shone as she waited for my response. My encouragement?

"Please tell me."

"Courtney has been rebaptized."

Didn't you need a person for a baptism? I must have looked as puzzled as I felt.

Medora responded: "In our Church, you may be baptized after death. Because Courtney was excommunicated, she was condemned to hell. Now she can be called home to God!" The words tumbled out.

"Knowing as we do that she was innocent—that, though she had strayed from the path and left the Church, she had tried to do the right thing—knowing that . . . Oh, Kat, *thank* you. Orson, her father, could never come here, could never say these things, but I know he, too, feels them in his heart.

"Our Daisy has been called home!" There were tears in Medora's eyes.

"You're welcome," I said, at a loss for more than that simple response. *Called home.* There was comfort in that, indeed.

She hugged me. "This is for you, Kat."

I looked at the check. We hadn't discussed money recently and this investigation hadn't been cheap. Medora had underestimated it by quite some, but I knew the amount on the check was a lot for her. And the investigation hadn't just been about Courtney and her death, but about Hank and me and our lives. So I accepted it.

"Please come meet the police officer who will help us."

I left Medora with Bill and looked around for Lauren. She was drinking lemonade and looking lost. I sat down next to her.

"This is presumptuous of me, I know, but I wanted you to meet my family. I wanted you to know that there are many definitions of family and community. Alma, my grandmother, and I are not related. She adopted me informally. Lindy, whom you'll meet soon, calls me her cousin. We're not related, either. She was a discarded child, a teenage runaway and prostitute when I found her and hauled her off the streets."

Lauren listened without expression.

"Alma adopted her too. Now Lindy is graduating with honors. Lauren, it's never too late to change, and nothing is too awful to leave behind. I wanted to say that to you."

She stared at me wordlessly. The doorbell rang again. Janie. I introduced her to everyone, and she and Lauren and Medora hugged and cried and all spoke at once.

"Where *is* that child?" Alma said as she stomped by. "She should be here by now."

The door blew open and Lindy walked in.

My heart stopped. We gaped at Lindy. Her skin was pale and creamy against the shimmery ebony of her short, tight beautiful dress. Charity's borrowed diamonds sparkled in her ears and around her neck.

"Hi, everybody! *Oh,* this is so wonderful. What a great party! This is Jeff, my friend," she announced proudly as she towed him into the limelight.

The silence disintegrated into laughter and chatter.

Lindy could hardly eat, she was so excited. "Do you like him, Katy?" she whispered to me.

"Yes. Jeff seems very nice *and* very handsome."

"He is, huh?" She grinned, then looked at me closely. This kid can read minds, I swear. "Don't be sad because of Courtney, Katy. She was a brave and happy person. And you have to be happy for what you have, not what you don't have. Remember? That's what you always tell me." She gave me a quick hug and went off to reclaim Jeff.

Charity arrived late, just before Lindy and Jeff left. Lauren and Medora started to leave after Jeff and Lindy. For the first time since I'd met her, there was a light in Lauren's eyes. "I had fun. Thank you."

That's when I remembered the rhinestone clips in my pocket. I had meant to give them back to Lindy for her shoes and had forgotten. Now I had two presents for Lauren, though I wasn't sure she would recognize either one as a gift.

"I blew the whistle on Corwin," I said.

"What?" She looked as though she was holding her breath.

"I wrote a letter detailing what happened in the visit Robert made to Daisy when he was a missionary—the threats and rape attempt. I said that he was, for a time, under investigation for attempted murder. I recounted his threats to me, including the fact that he hired someone to follow me." The guy in the Thunderbird. I'd wormed enough out of Corwin's secretary in fifteen minutes and five or six lies to put it all together. She was as gullible and trusting as she was perky.

"I said that he had also threatened friends of Daisy's. I didn't use your name. And I said that when the threats didn't work on me, he'd tried to buy my silence."

"Did he?"

"Yes." Not only was Corwin dumb enough to try to buy me, he was dumb enough to put it in writing. "I sent a copy of the letter I wrote to every official in the Mormon Church from here to Salt Lake City."

"Oh my." She covered her mouth with her hand. "But this— oh *my.*"

"This is all of his own making, Lauren. He is not a good man. And he, like the rest of us, must live by the choices he has made, the actions he has taken." Uh-oh, that was a little preachy.

"Ye-e-es." Her voice was hesitant.

It would take a while, I thought.

I pulled the rhinestone clips out of my pocket. "These are for you. I hope you will wear them to a party like this someday."

Cinderella shoes, I thought. *Shoes made for hope.* Lauren gazed at me, confusion and doubt in her eyes, but she took them.

Later I stood alone in the kitchen looking at the stacks of dirty dishes.

"That danged Lena," Alma burst into the kitchen fuming. "She and Clyde ran off to the circus. The *circus!* What does she think life is, anyway?"

But that wasn't life, it was soap opera.

I had a glass of wine with Alma. Then I went home to my life, an empty, cold house.

Thursday, June 2

Sacramento

Forty-six

Roadblocks, Neon Lights, and Miracles

Kitty and I were stretched out on the couch, Ranger on the floor beside us, when someone knocked on the door. Ten-thirty. So it wasn't exactly a social call. Ranger barked. I didn't answer the door.

"Katy!"

Ranger recognized the voice and whined eagerly. I recognized it too. I didn't move. The knocking and banging stopped at ten thirty-five. At ten forty-seven the phone rang. The machine picked it up in silence, adding—I assumed—another message to the five that were there when I got home. I hadn't listened to them, either. At ten fifty-three the knocking started again.

An angry voice. "Open the door, Katy, or I kick it in."

I got up off the couch, opened the door. "You're too fucking late," I told Hank.

Ranger, the traitor, danced around licking Hank's hand and whining happily.

I got a glass of wine but didn't offer Hank anything. This is perfectly okay behavior when someone threatens to kick your door in. Miss Manners, Abby, and Ann would all agree.

I climbed back on the couch, wrapped my arms around my knees, and listened to Hank help himself to a beer from my refrigerator. One more thing to add to the list of things I was furious at him about.

"I miss you, Katy." He stood in front of me. "I love you."

"Sorry," I said. "You've confused me with someone who gives a shit."

"It's over, Katy."

Yes. Speed bumps and roadblocks surrounded us and love was looking like roadkill on the highway. It would take a miracle now.

"We got him."

I looked up. I wasn't following this—I was on roadkill. "What?"

"We got the Stalker."

I stared, spoke finally. "How?"

"A combination of good police work and luck but mostly luck."

On the prowl, I thought. *Incessant, obsessed prowl. Unmarked police car with a psychologically marked policeman in it.*

"I saw a guy pull over his car, stop, talk to a young, dark-haired woman. She got in the car with him after a few moments of conversation."

I started to tremble. "Is she all right? Is she? *Tell me.*"

"Yes."

I relaxed. A little.

"I followed for a while. When he started out into the desert, I pulled him over."

"Over?" I asked numbly.

"Doing fifty in a forty-five-mile-per-hour zone. Can't have that," Hank said with a smile. "The girl was unconscious in the front seat and there was an open bottle of vodka on the seat next to her. I got him out of the car, radioed for backup and an ambulance."

I realized I was holding my breath; I let it out slowly.

"We found a tire iron, blankets, and plastic sheeting in the trunk. Bloodstains."

I started trembling again. "The girl, did she—" I couldn't finish.

"She fit the victim profile. Exactly." Hank answered my unfinished question.

"Did he admit it?"

"Yes. Bragged about it," he stated quietly. "Said there were others we didn't know about yet."

"But you got him? It's over?"

"Yes. Forensics will nail it down but we've got him."

I put my head in my hands. *No more dead girls,* I prayed.

"Katy, let's start over. Please."

The Strip Stalker was in jail and Hank had time now for the rest of his life. For me.

"I can't, Hank," I said at last. "Too much is wrong and we can't make it right just like that." *Too much harm. Too much betrayal.*

"I brought this for you."

He opened a small box and I looked at the gold bracelet set with gemstones.

"The stones all mean something," Hank said. "Love, faith, remembrance, hope, happiness."

"Things we don't have anymore," I said. "Except maybe for remembrance. Do you want to know what I remember?"

"Yes."

"You had an affair. You lied to me and you cheated on me. Now you bring me a present. Is that supposed to make it okay? You don't say you're sorry and you want to go on like nothing much has happened."

"I didn't—"

"Don't start," I said, and I was as dangerous as I sounded. "Don't tell me that because you never had sex with her it wasn't an affair. You were emotionally involved. And it was physical, sexual. I saw you together. You gave her gifts and time and attention. You gave her *you* when you wouldn't give *me* the time of day. And you lied to me about all of it."

"Katy, I—"

"Lying, cheating bastard! I'm the good guy here, the one who pulled your ass out of the fire, and Amber's the bad guy. So who did you get mad at? *Me.* "

"Katy—"

"Amber said that you liked it that she needed you, was dependent on you."

"It's nice to be needed. Sure. There's nothing wrong with that."

"That kind of needing is not sharing and loving, it's *using.* When I needed you, when I wanted your help and understanding and support, you weren't there."

"I'm sorry. About all of this. It wasn't just that you didn't lean on me. You saw me at my worst, you bailed me out. And that's hard for me. I'm used to being in control, on top of things and not needing help. Katy, I love you. I used Amber just as she used me, used her to hide from tough questions. There's no excuse for that. I won't make one and I won't do it again, either.

"Please, Katy, I want us to try to work things out."

The stones in the bracelet sparkled in the light. Was it a beginning? Love and happiness and the other things the gems stood for?

Or just glitz and glitter?

Like the neon lights in Vegas.